Spinning Sun
Grinning Moon

Max Evans

SPINNING SUN
GRINNING MOON

Novellas

MAX EVANS

FOREWORD BY ROBERT J. CONLEY

R·E·D
CRANE
BOOKS

First Edition

Manufactured in the United States of America

Design by R. Suzanne Vilmain

Jacket and text paintings by Gregory Truett Smith

Library of Congress Cataloging-in-Publication Data

Evans, Max.
    Spinning sun, grinning moon: novellas / Max Evans;
    foreword by Robert J. Conley. — 1st ed.
        p.   cm.
    Contents: Xavier's folly — The mountain of gold — My pardner —
    One-eyed sky — Candles in the bottom of the pool — Old bum —
    Shadow of thunder.
    ISBN 1-878610-52-X
    1. Southwest, New—Social life and customs—Fiction. I. Title.
PS3555.V23S67   1995
    813'.54—dc20   94-37531
                                    CIP

Red Crane Books

2008 Rosina St., Suite B

Santa Fe, New Mexico 87505

⁘ CONTENTS

THE PLEASURE AND ENLIGHTENMENT OF BEING KICKED BY A MULE

I first met Max Evans in Sheridan, Wyoming, at a writers' convention. I was on the program, and I had just made my presentation, complete with question and answer period. Someone had asked me a question from the floor which I could not answer. I had said, "I don't know."

When the session was over, I was wandering the halls of the motel, and I stepped into the bar to look around and see who I could see. Just inside the door a man and woman were seated at a small table. The man stuck his hand out in front of me. I hoped he was friendly because he sure did look tough.

"I'm ole Max Evans," he said, shaking my hand, and then he added something like, "I just wanted to shake hands with a man who has guts enough to say 'I don't know' when someone asks him a stupid question."

That seemingly insignificant moment proved to be the beginning of a long and close relationship between me and ole Max and my wife Evelyn and Max's wife Pat. The lady with him at the table, by the way, was Pat. I'm proud to be able to call Max my good friend, and I'm deeply honored and more than a bit overawed at the prospect of writing this introduction.

The publication of this book, *Spinning Sun, Grinning Moon*, a collection of seven of Max Evans's greatest novellas, is a major publishing event. I fear, though, that it will not be recognized as such by the literati, the admen, or the general reading, book-buying public. Such a lack of well-deserved recognition is an old story with Max.

In 1977, for example, *The White Shadow*, a beautiful and powerful allegorical novel, was brought out by Joyce Press in a handsome hardcover edition which unfortunately and inexcusably read like a set of uncorrected galleys. The book vanished almost as quickly as it had appeared.

Max's *Shadow of Thunder* (published by Swallow Press in 1969 and reprinted in this collection) was retitled *Satan in Paradise* for a planned major motion picture with Universal Studios. Somewhere between $2 and $3 million was spent on producers and screenwriters, including Rod Serling, and the project was announced all over the world. Then it was shelved and forgotten.

Rounders 3, which pulled *The Rounders, The Great Wedding,* and *Orange County Cowboys*, the three stories of Dusty Jones and Wrangler Lewis, together in one volume for the first time was issued by Bantam-Doubleday-Dell in April 1990 in a Doubleday hardcover edition and then in December of that same year as a Bantam paperback. Although I hailed that book as a major publishing event, no one else seems to have agreed with me.

Bluefeather Fellini, Max's long-awaited, monumental epic novel of the Southwest, published by the University Press of Colorado in 1993, has met with a better reception, selling extremely well for a university press book and receiving several excellent reviews from respectable sources. Even so, it has not gotten the attention it so richly deserves—recognition that will come perhaps when the sequel *Bluefeather Fellini in the Sacred*

Realm is published this year.

I was privileged to read the manuscript for both these books at the time the two books were one—a mammoth eleven hundred pages from that master of the short story and novella, Max Evans. I read for two days straight, stopping only to eat and to engage in other activities vital to survival. I remember thinking, "The big boys in New York will be stabbing each other in the back to get their hands on this one." But they didn't. It wound up at a university press, where editors have not yet learned that *literature* is a dirty word.

The book astounded everyone initially, simply because of its length, something Max responded to by saying simply: "*Bluefeather Fellini* is the world's longest novella." As usual, he's right. Its prose is as tightly packed and as compact as any Max ever wrote. It should be on all the bestseller lists, and it should have been given every literary prize ever offered, but it isn't and it hasn't.

Not only has Max had more than any one man's personal share of experience with this kind of supreme irony, he has written about it over and over again. Dusty and Wrangler with their grand schemes smell riches just around the corner more than once, through three novellas, only to have their hopes dashed at the last minute. It's a recurrent theme in Max's work, explored sometimes comically, sometimes tragically. But that's just scratching the surface. With Max's work there's always more—much more. As that grand old man of southwestern letters, the late C. L. (Doc) Sonnichsen, once said of *One-Eyed Sky*, "Max told the whole world in a sandy arroyo."

I know of no other writer who can dish out such stark realism, raucous slapstick comedy, heart-tearing tragedy, and surreal mysticism equally well and sometimes all in one bowl. This has caused more than one editor in more than one major publishing house to shy away from a Max Evans manuscript with horror and dread, knowing that said manuscript is doubtless a work of great stature, but having no idea how to approach it.

This synthesis of realism and surreal mysticism in Max's writing has also led some critics to label his work "magic realism," claiming that he has fallen under the influence of those writers for whom the expression was coined. But if Max's work is indeed "magic realism," then I know for a fact that he has been writing "magic realism" since the 1950s.

And I don't really know if "magic realism" is the proper designation. (I'm always either greatly annoyed or mildly amused with the crying need of critics and publishers to pigeonhole writers and their books. They call to mind the categories of drama delineated to Hamlet by Polonius: "Tragedy, comedy, history, pastoral, pastoral-comical, historical-pastoral, tragical-historical, tragical-comical . . .")

However, Max has been labeled before. He's been called a "western writer." That's a confusing term. Although it could be a regional designation—"western" as opposed to "southern"—unfortunately, to most folks it means a writer of "westerns," the old-fashioned, shoot-'em-up stories of writers like Zane Grey, Max Brand, Luke Short, and, more recently, Louis L' Amour. Now, although I'm not putting down such stories— I've read a bunch of them myself and even written a few—I'm here to tell you that Max has never written that type of book. Perhaps that's the reason he's remained such an enigma to so many publishers. What does one do with a "western writer" who doesn't write "westerns"?

I do know that if Max Evans owes a literary debt to anyone or anything, it is to experience, to the works of Balzac, and to a long and close association with Woody Crumbo, famous

Potawatomi Indian artist, miner, mystic, and a man whom I have heard Max refer to, more than once, as "my mentor."

Born in Ropes, Texas, in 1924, Max was a working cowboy in New Mexico by the time he was twelve years old. Employed by several ranches—the Coleman Ranch, the Rafter EY, the San Cristobal, the Lower Pankey—he continued in that back-breaking profession until the early 1940s when he bought his own ranch. Then at the beginning of World War II, Max enlisted in the army.

As a combat infantryman, he landed at Omaha beach on D-1. "Shortly after the Saint Lo breakthrough," he has written, "I was blown into the basement of a bombed-out building by an artillery shell at Vire, France, and survived for several more months of combat all the way into Germany—by way of the Battle of Brest—then, back to northeast New Mexico to start painting pictures (introduction to *Rounders 3*)."

Following his service in World War II, Max sold his ranch and went to Taos to live the life of an artist. It was there that he met his wife Pat, also an artist, and it was there that his association with Woody Crumbo began. Max did paint, and he did sell paintings, but he and Woody came up with a scheme to get rich quicker. "We climbed mountains over several western states," he writes, "prospecting. We opened up scores of old tunnels, some that had been caved in for nearly a hundred years. We promoted mills and mines all over. We got rich. Then in one hundred and twenty days the price of copper dropped from forty-eight cents to twenty-four cents. We were broke (introduction to *Rounders 3*)."

Then Max came up with what most professional writers would call the dumbest idea yet. He decided to write a book in order to make some money. He wrote *The Rounders*, and of all things, his idea worked. The book was a tremendous success, and it was made into an equally successful film, directed by Burt Kennedy and starring Henry Fonda, Glenn Ford, and Chill Wills. There was even a short-lived television series based on the novel, still seen occasionally in reruns.

The success of *The Rounders* led Max into a long association with Hollywood and filmmaking, mostly fixing up existing scripts written by other people, for no credit and money under the table. During these years he drank, brawled, and worked with the likes of Sam Peckinpah, Lee Marvin, Morgan Woodward, Slim Pickens, Warren Oates, and Brian Keith.

All of this raw experience is reflected in the tough and often brutally realistic prose of Max's tales. When Max writes about something, you know he's been there, he's seen it, felt it, and experienced it with profound understanding.

But raw experience alone does not make an artist; Max's life started to take shape early, even though the sense of it seems to have escaped him for a while. His mother taught him to read before he started school, and the twelve-year-old working cowboy was also reading Balzac. All his life Max has been a voracious reader; a conversation with him about writing and writers will be filled with references to Balzac, Shakespeare, Gogol, Chekhov, Maugham, Faulkner, Joyce Cary, Walter Van Tilburg Clark, Collette, and others.

And finally there's that added element that has caused some to call Max a magic realist, that mysticism that is almost always there, sometimes just under the surface, often looming before us like a heavy cloud, obvious but puzzling, inviting but elusive, lovely but frightening.

Just who, for example, is Duvall in *Shadow of Thunder?* To the ranchers in the story, he's the devil. To the farmers' and the ranchers' wives, he's something else—but what? To critics and other readers, he will probably remain a total enigma, as richly ambiguous and puzzling as Melville's Moby Dick or his relentless pursuer Captain Ahab.

Will we ever quite know what to make of Joshua Stone III in *Candles in the Bottom of the Pool,* of the visions he sees in the walls of his ancient adobe house, of his "gathering," his mysterious murders, or his "candles in the bottom of the pool"? I doubt it. If we read the story over enough times and puzzle over it long and hard, we might come close, but I don't think we'll ever quite get the man pinned down—and I don't think we should.

The desperate and dogged pursuit of an elusive dream is magnificently portrayed in *The Mountain of Gold,* a story enriched by Max's firsthand knowledge of miners and mining. As syndicated columnist John Sinor wrote in his introduction to the University of New Mexico edition, it's a story that is "simple, funny, sad, and touching . . . full of love and courage."

In *Xavier's Folly* the dream pursued takes on a surprising new form. Xavier Del Campo, Mexican plumber with the soul of an artist, wants nothing more out of life than to sponsor a local performance of "Tamara, the great Russian ballet star." Xavier does come close to achieving his dream; in fact, we might say he is one of the few characters Max has given us who does achieve his dream. It's just not quite on the scale he had imagined it to be.

My Pardner brings us back to earth with the story of a boy learning a hard lesson in life from a crusty old cowhand. It's a fictionalized account of a real life experience, and, though fictionalized, I'll bet every word is true.

Old Bum was originally published (like seven other of Max's stories, according to John Milton, editor) in the *South Dakota Review* (Spring 1993). That's a real puzzler for the label-makers—a cowboy writer appearing in a respected literary journal. I'm not even going to try to say anything about *Old Bum* except that it's a hell of a story.

Because all Max's writing is exceptional, it's extremely difficult to pick only one title that's my favorite. But if I were backed up in a corner and threatened, I'd have to name *One-Eyed Sky* as being at least way up toward the top of the list. About that tale, Max told me, "I always try to tell both sides of a story, but in *One-Eyed Sky* I told three sides." He did, and he told them beautifully and believably, and I can almost guarantee that reading this story will forever change your thinking about a lot of things.

Sitting here thinking about why I quit being a professor of literature to start struggling with the realities of being a full-time writer, it occurs to me that a large part of it is because some things are just too great to talk about or write about, to try to analyze to discover the secrets of how and why they work so effectively. When I've just read *One-Eyed Sky* or *Shadow of Thunder* or *The Hi-Lo Country*—just about anything ole Max ever wrote—I get a feeling that reminds me of having just been kicked in the solar plexus by a mule. That's the power of the emotional impact, and most of the time I feel like that's where we ought to leave it and forget the analysis.

This volume is a treasure. It gives you some of Max Evans's very best writing, some of which was previously difficult to lay hands on. Read it. Read it and enjoy it. Read it over and over again. I have, and there's always something new and wonderfully surprising. It's rich writing from a master, Max Evans, one of the great literary figures of our time.

Robert J. Conley
Cherokee author, *Mountain Windsong* and *Nickajack*
Tahlequah, Oklahoma
June 1994

IN LIEU OF A BAG OF GOLD

With much love and appreciation to our twin daughters, Charlotte and Sheryl, who shared both the rough times and the smooth with equal good humor while we built page by page this little house of books.

Many thanks to the great New Mexico bookman Dwight Myers for starting the meeting-of-minds with Red Crane Books over this special volume.

Our everlasting friendship, admiration, and thanks to John Milton, whose *South Dakota Review* is in the front ranks of American literary journals.

Large respect and affection for Dale Walker, who kept the belief in *Bluefeather Fellini* all the way and writes wondrous nonfiction on unlimited subjects. A true giver . . . rare as a Rembrandt.

Multiple wild yells to our friend Rusty Rutledge, who out-walked me and our mutual amigo, Slim Pickens, in the Chama mountains. He did, however, come in a distant second in our marathons between Caravan East and The Embers.

Highest regards for Billy Marchiondo and family all the way back to Raton, New Mexico, and far, far beyond.

Love to our dear pals Luther and Judy Wilson of the University Press of Colorado, with precious memories of fishing streams, many warm visits, and the Great Baca Expedition.

XAVIER'S FOLLY

he creature moved across the hill, struggling through the thick black grass with determination. Xavier Del Campo opened his eyes a little more and watched the bug straining through the jungle of hair on his heavy arm. The sun formed tiny prisms of light here and there. He imagined they were shining on a vast stage, and he could see Tamara, the great Russian ballet star, pirouetting under their golden glow. He could hear the music, especially the strings, and then she finished. The applause shook rocks loose in the earth. She was beckoning him to come and share her glory on the stage. Imagine!

Xavier lifted his head from his arms and slowly sat up, rubbing the heavy, curled hair on his head. He stared off at the blue hump of the Rocky Mountains rising like prehistoric monsters out of the earth. His eyes looked above them into the sky. He liked to look at a cloudless sky, since he discovered that

it was full of holes. He was entranced by the firmament. The holes pulsated with greens, pinks, and purples. He felt sorry for people who just saw the sky as a blue curtain. They were missing so much. All they had to do was really look. That's all.

His wife was one of those who missed. Shortly after they were married, he was pursuing his hobby of "sky staring" when she stepped out of the house to hang out the wash. She asked, as she walked past him, "An eagle?" When he didn't answer, she asked, "A hawk?"

"Look at the sky," he said, "it's full of pretty holes."

She cast a suspicious eye upon him. Seeing he was serious, she snorted. "It's your brain that's full of holes."

Their relationship had deteriorated after that. His great Mexican eyes dropped back down to the sage-covered foothills of the mountains. He could see their little house and sheds there. Lonely. Aloof. He tried not to think of her, but it was no use. Tonight he had to tell her of his great plan. A feeling of dread caressed his short, muscled body. He stood up and looked at the ditch in front of him. Manuel usually dug the ditches while Xavier tended to the fitting of pipes. He didn't mind digging, but it took up valuable time. As a plumber, Xavier was an artist. All metal fit perfectly and was sealed the same. He was immensely proud that his pipes never leaked. Never. Now, however, he must dig. Yesterday he paid Manuel, so it was reasonable to figure that today he was drunk. Xavier might have joined him, but he had to save money. It would take a lot of cash to fulfill his plan. He already had thirty-seven hundred dollars hidden in a bucket behind the outdoor privy.

He lifted the pick from the loose dirt and stepped into the ditch to dig. The steel point pierced the earth and bit away chunks as he swung up and down in powerful rhythms. The spring air was not hot, but sweat soon darkened the underarms

of his shirt. When had he promised his clients to have the plumbing installed? They came every day from town to check on his progress. They were anxious to move into their new adobe. It was expensive living in a hotel, they informed him.

Xavier swung faster and harder at these thoughts. Today, though, they failed to come, and he dug straight till dark, almost finishing the ditch. He dug it over three feet deep, so the harsh winters could never freeze the pipes. All his customers complained at his seeming slowness, but later they commented on the perfection of his skill and recommended him to others. He was never without work.

When he could no longer see clearly what he was doing, he dropped the pick, got in his faded old red truck, and headed home. It had to be tonight. Yes, he had to tell her now. He took a shortcut around the town of Taos, chugging into the foothills towards the light in the window that glowed deceivingly warm. A coyote loped across the winding road in front of him, glancing sideways, and vanished in the sage and darkness.

The two old cur dogs moved off the porch and barked a halfhearted welcome. As he got out of the truck, the dogs smelled his legs and waved their tails so slightly it was only a suggestion. He thought that somehow they had adopted a certain attitude of their mistress.

As he opened the door, he wondered why he didn't feel the contentment that men were supposed to feel on the return to the hearth. Where was the surging pride in a hard day's work to share with his lady?

She and her two daughters were just finishing the evening meal. One girl was fourteen, the other sixteen—Suzanne and Suzette. They had the same gray eyes of their mother, watery, dull, and somehow appearing a bit out of focus. They moved these orbs slightly upward in greeting. Both

had buckteeth, and when they smiled their lips pulled back and a wad of flesh wrinkled up over the gums. It had come to Xavier on occasion that their mouths reminded him of a mule's behind when he strained to pull a deep plow through dry earth. He had long been curious as to what their real father looked like. But he would never know, for the man had died years before, from the bellyache. Xavier would soon understand more about his demise.

Marion looked up, saying between chews of spaghetti, "You're late. We went ahead and ate."

"Aw, that's all right. I'm not very hungry anyway." He washed his face and hands in a tin pan of cold water and sat down. The girls got up and went to their room. He watched them go, shaking their rounded tails far more than the dogs. He reached for the bowl and took the little bit of spaghetti left. As he buttered a cold biscuit, she poured him a cup of warm black coffee. He ate. She sat.

He knew exactly what she'd say when she did speak.

"When are you gonna finish the Bently job?"

"Next week if Manuel gets over his cold."

"Cold? He's too full a wine to catch anythin'. You said you'd put in our plumbin' when the Bently job is done."

He took a long drink of coffee and tried very hard to see out through the old adobe wall. In fact, he tried to *be* outside. It didn't work.

"You been sayin' you was gonna put in our plumbin' after every job for a year now. It's gettin' embarrassin' to explain to folks. The girls are ashamed to bring company home. How can they explain to their friends that they have to go outside to the toilet? Some plumber you are."

Xavier never knew why he said it. The statement was against his nature and made his important announcement much more difficult.

"It's cleaner to crap outside."

He knew he'd stepped over the bounds with her. When she was mad, she pulled at her stringy, mouse-colored hair and squinted her eyes. She was pulling and squinting right now.

"You tryin' to get funny with me or sumpthin'?"

"Marion, I got something important to tell you."

"You tryin' to get funny, huh?"

"Marion, I . . ."

She got up from the table and started gathering the dirty dishes. She took his coffee before he was half through and made a lot of noises doing all this.

"You smell."

"Smell what?" he asked.

"You. You, that's what. You smell like a boar hog. If you'd put a bath in, at least you could take a shower before settin' down at the table with us."

"I'll take a tub bath tonight," he placated, "but first I want to tell . . ."

"Imagine havin' to bathe in that old tin washtub. A plumber's wife. Jist imagine," she said.

"Now, Marion, I promise. I'll even promise on a Bible." He walked over and got the book out of a dresser drawer to show faith. "Now see here, I got my hand on this Bible."

She stopped washing dishes and glared at him. "Well?" she said, waiting, almost believing him now.

"All right now. I promise on the word of the Lord that as soon as I put on my ballet presentation I'll put in the plumbing."

"Your what?" she shrieked.

"The great Tamara. I'm going to bring her to Taos. I'm going to present her."

Marion just stood and squinted till he couldn't even see her eyes, only a tiny, thin line where they had been. She was

almost pulling her stringy, mouse-colored hair out by the shallow roots. What poor Xavier didn't know was that Marion had married him to get her plumbing installed. She had always intended to kick him out just as soon as that was accomplished.

Finally, she said in a deadly flat tone, "I always knew you was crazy. I knew it from the first time you was tryin' to find holes in the sky. Ballet? Ballet? My God! I ought to have you locked up!"

"But . . . but ballet is beautiful."

"My God! There ain't nobody in Taos that even knows how to spell the word. Beautiful my wild ass."

Xavier rubbed at his curly hair and twisted around on his feet, still holding the Bible as if God himself might just materialize from the pages and smite him dead. His stomach hurt. How was he going to make her understand?

"Just because folks don't know is no reason that they can't learn to like beautiful things."

She hurled the dishtowel across the room and sat down on the battered-up divan. "Beautiful. Beautiful, he says. All I ever want in the world to make it beautiful is a bathroom, and now you tell me that I have to wait while you bring a bunch of idiots here to dance around on their toes. I'm tellin' you, you even bring it up and the people of Taos'll laugh you plumb into Texas. My God! Toe dancing! People never was meant to dance on their toes. They might as well try swingin' from their tails like monkeys."

She got up and went in to talk to her daughters. He could hear sounds from the room, but he couldn't make out the words. For this he was thankful. He got himself a cup of cold coffee and sat down trying to think.

She came out slamming the door with a victorious air

about her sagging breasts. She stopped in the middle of the floor, her feet spread apart like a boxer's, and said, "You know what we're gonna do?"

He looked up at her, knowing that whatever they were going to do would not be to his benefit.

"We're going into town first thing in the mornin', and we're gonna draw ever dime out of the bank." She smiled now like a coyote with a rabbit by the hindquarters. "And we're gonna hire Ben Gonzales to put in our plumbin'. There won't be no cockeyed ballet, no nothin'." She paused, relishing the sad look on Xavier's face, and then threw the coup de grâce at him. "Now won't the folks of Taos get one hell of a laugh outa the fact your competitor is puttin' in *our* plumbin'? Huh?"

Things didn't get any better that night. Xavier had his choice of sleeping on the divan, which had springs that punched one's body, or sleeping out back in a shed with the goats. He wrapped up in an old rag rug and said to the goats, "Don't worry, it's just for tonight."

Marion lay in bed and exulted over her move. Not only would she make a laughingstock out of Xavier, but she'd run him off as soon as the plumbing was installed. She had recently learned that the useless-looking sagebrush land her first husband had left her could be turned into a housing development. At least that marriage had paid off. The land ran all the way into the timber on the mountains. The realtors told her she would make a fortune, but it would take time. In the meanwhile, she'd get her bathroom and then run Xavier off before he could share the benefits from any real estate profits. Marion was a lady who made plans.

Out back with the goats, Xavier thought of himself as a coward. He just couldn't muster up the guts to tell her there was only four dollars and thirteen cents in the bank. But with

all his immediate troubles, and the fact he'd been demoted to the animal shelter for the night, he dreamed big dreams.

Xavier's mother and father drowned in a flash flood when he was ten years old. He was sent to live with an uncle and aunt in Los Angeles. His uncle was a plumber, and Xavier was apprenticed. He learned how to cut and thread pipe; how to measure and fit; how to melt the lead and permanently seal the joints. He learned fast. The first two years he went to public school, but then he had to quit because he became too valuable to his uncle to be wasted on reading and writing.

They lived upstairs in a very crowded section of old houses. At night, after helping his aunt do the supper dishes, he'd sit out on the walk-up porch, look at the city, and conjure up visions of all the things the millions of people were doing at that moment.

Across an alley was an empty-looking old building. One night a light beamed from the big window, and there, for the first time, he saw ballet. A lady had opened a dance academy.

At first, Xavier thought their actions very strange and foolish, but each night he was drawn back to watch. Gradually he began to feel the grace and dignity, and finally he had the courage to slip down to the window for a closer look. He was entranced.

There was one longhaired girl who looked to be of his own blood—Mexican. She seemed to float when she leaped. He kept hoping that she would truly learn to fly with a hawk. Each time she danced, his muscles twitched in his short frame with her and for her. He fell in love with her; he fell in love with the dance. A thirst was upon him. Oh, he didn't deceive himself that *he* would ever dance. Not with his build. He would simply look like a fat rubber ball bouncing about. No, he participated with his soul.

Finally, a night came when all the parents arrived to see the results of their money and their children's dedication. Xavier had saved pennies for weeks so he could attend. His uncle laughed, but his aunt smiled, somehow knowing.

When the lights came on and the longhaired girl was spotlighted, he thought he'd faint it was so lovely. As she danced in the dark with the light following, it became a glorious, sensuous thing to Xavier. He felt that he himself was the light and that he completely enveloped her while she moved with the grace of a Maltese cat.

He waited outside that night as the people left chattering with their children and friends. When she came out (he never remembered her name), he touched her on the arm and said, "You . . . you are beautiful."

She stunned him with a smile that radiated right straight through his heart. Then he ran.

Xavier was grown now. He was a master plumber. He had returned to his own beloved Southwest and started a business in Taos. Then one day a movie called *Red Shoes* came to town. It was an old and timeless film. Never, not even in Los Angeles, had he seen anything so hypnotic. The dark, flame-lit red hair of Moira Shearer floated with her like thousands of tiny writhing snakes. Her white face and body were from other planes; they were from heaven. When she had thrown herself from a window in front of the train, he'd died with her! And when the camera had shown the red satin shoes and the pink tights with the blood coming through, he'd died a thousand times more. But even so . . . what a film! What a lady! What a dance! Finally, he knew what the word *magic* really meant. It meant ballet.

Later he saw a photographic study of Tamara in a national magazine. He looked at it until the pages were worn and shredded. He knew now what he must do. He knew what he was born for—his whole purpose. He would die to accomplish it. He would bring the great Tamara here to Taos and present her. He could see it now: XAVIER PRESENTS.

He had already started saving his money for this dream when he met Marion. She had seemed so sweet when she invited him up for supper. He'd even been treated with a smattering of kindness from her daughters. The food had seemed all right, too, for her flattery had numbed his tastebuds. And in the dark that night she had felt good.

As always, though, the light finally comes. The woman was as obsessed with indoor plumbing as he was with ballet. He could not afford to do the work on her home. That would take time and money away from his presentation. If only he could have told her sooner, but until tonight he always got a knot in his throat and could never say the words. Now he had a knot in his stomach as well.

The goats kept him awake most of the night trying to eat the rag rug right off his body, and so when the first rooster crowed, Xavier, stiff and sore, arose. He had dug in the earth all the day before and bedded on it all night.

It took the sun awhile to climb the other side of the mountains. They seemed flat and black against the rising oranges and yellows, but once the mighty globe shoved its brilliant sabers of light between the peaks, the mountains took form, and suddenly the valleys were violet and the hogbacks golden and green.

The chickens scratched around and started visiting. A bird talked somewhere out in the sagebrush. A trailer-truck groaned over a rise on the highway below. A thin blue haze

hung over Taos from early morning piñon fires. The two curs moved over against the adobe wall where its reflection would give them a double warmth.

Xavier took his morning relief behind the privy, staring at the spot where the money was buried. He had an urge to dig it up but knew that Marion and the daughters would be awake. He was hungry. He headed for his truck, not looking at the house. He walked in an arc to the conveyance as if a pressure exuding from the house had pushed him off a true course.

The old motor choked and spit. Xavier pumped the gas pedal with some hint of desperation, glancing at the house, expecting Marion to crash right through the thick walls and devour him. Finally, the motor, gas, and sparks all coordinated, and Xavier raced the truck backwards, bumping up on top of a huge clump of sage. He then gunned it in a circle, hit the road hurtling back and forth across it, settled down, and rolled on to town.

He had breakfast at a truck stop and went to work. Manuel was there. He was hanging on the pick where it appeared to be stuck in the bottom of the ditch. He had swung at the earth with admirable intent, but the earth had jumped up, meeting his move halfway and jarring his whole body, as sometimes happens when one steps from a curb that is not supposed to be there. For the moment, he was taking no chances on any kind of movement.

Manuel was about three times as long and not a great deal bigger around than the pick. He had spent so many years digging that the instrument was simply an extension of his arms. No matter what his physical discomfort, the visual aspects suggested a very long-armed man leaning comfortably on the world. Xavier's closer inspection of Manuel's face, however, gave the truth away. Sweat was protruding all over

his forehead, and his Adam's apple chugged up and down in his throat, necessitating as many swallows to keep the wine down as it had taken to get it there in the first place.

Xavier asked a silly and unnecessary question, as most people seem to do at moments like this, "How you feeling?"

Manuel allowed the question to reverberate through his head a moment until it had time to settle down. "I feel *lack* I been *shoot* at and *mees, sheet* at and *heet.*"

Xavier felt he needed no further description of his associate's condition, and he entered the house and went to work. In spite of the various forms of turmoil within him, he worked harder, faster, and more efficiently than ever. When the Bentlys arrived that afternoon and posed their perpetual question, he could honestly tell them they could move in three days from the present one.

By late afternoon Xavier was so delighted with the fine day's work that he decided to help Manuel in his recovery. They stopped in at the Chico Bar for medicinal purposes only. As the wine was repeatedly served, there was a distinct change in Manuel. There was no doubt that he now felt as good or maybe even better than he had the night before. Not only did he do a Mexican hat dance without a hat, but by midnight he was singing "Guadalajara" and envisioning himself as the Caruso for the entire Spanish world. How the rest of the patrons saw him remains private with them, for all had learned long ago that Manuel's skinny muscles were like those of an eagle. You don't mess around close up with eagles.

Occasionally, certainly not on purpose, Xavier's thoughts drifted to Marion's home on the hill. He knew she'd be waiting for him. However, these thoughts were fleeting indeed, for Chico's place exuded warmth, companionship, and safety.

By one o'clock he knew that Manuel was in as good condition as it was possible to attain in that length of time, and so he pondered on his own pleasures, and there by the music box he conjured up the great Tamara. My, what a talent! She could even dance to "Guadalajara." She whirled and turned and leaped and flew, and smiled at him, then vanished behind the multicolored music-maker.

The two o'clock closing time came. This did not deter Manuel. He took several bottles of wine and his boss home with him. They sat on the porch out of courtesy to Manuel's wife and seven children. Xavier insisted they must not enter and disturb their sleep. He had not considered that they would probably wake up the entire neighborhood.

They talked of many truths, and spilled a few lies. Xavier told Manuel about the ballet. But Manuel thought it was some kind of Indian corn dance and said many toasts to his Indian brothers.

". . . and to you, Xavier, my boss, one man who helps makes piss on this earth. Marries gringo womans, and dance with Indians."

Manuel went to sleep on the porch. Xavier took a bottle of wine, crawled sleepily into his truck, and headed home. He drove up just as the sun knocked the shadows out of the sky. He'd been gone exactly twenty-four hours. He was no longer afraid. He knew what he must do, and that was it. He'd tell Marion and make her understand. Xavier took another drink of wine just to be sure he wouldn't forget.

The new sun had slightly blinded him, and it was a moment before his eyes adjusted to the room. It didn't matter that much for the voice was everywhere. It ricocheted from wall to wall, spun in circles, and danced up and down. It whizzed around in his head, kicking his stomach from the inside. A

Neanderthal instinct caused him to move around so that the table was between himself and the strongest point of emission. It was fortunate that Marion had no training in baseball, or Xavier would already be dead. Things, heavy things, were zapping through the room along with the voice. It's possible that her aim became faulty because of her movement around the table to get nearer her target. Xavier, himself, moved to get farther away from the catapult. Fortunately, she was just no good on moving objects.

"Where is the money? The money? You . . . you . . ." She stopped, sputtering, desperately trying to find words that would express her deepest feelings and a weapon that would kill.

Xavier had never been able to say the right things to his wife. In their moments of forced communication, such as now, he was a total flop. As she hesitated in her fury, he stuck the bottle of very cheap wine out in front of him and politely suggested, "Would you like a little nip?"

Before she could answer, he took a large swallow, watching her around the edge of the bottle. This was no time to get careless.

Marion found words again, "Son of a bitch! Son of a bitch! Son of a bitch!"

The daughters were bravely yelling encouragement to their mother, while at the same time wisely staying behind a bolted door.

Xavier, like most honest people, was a poor liar. It comes from a lack of practice. He ventured, "I . . . I lost the money gambling."

"Liar! Liar! You lying bastard!"

He realized that she'd caught on. He had no time to dwell upon it, though, for she now expressed many of those

deep feelings she'd been searching for. "I'll have you jailed. I'll sue for the money. I'll sue, you hear?"

Xavier said, "Now, honey . . ." How he came up with that sweet word he could not comprehend.

She went on: "All my life I've had to go outside to the toilet, in blizzards and blazin' sun! It ain't right! You . . . you worthless little pig! You think fixin' a place up is paintin' the toilet door! That's all you've done since we've been married! You didn't even bother to fix the cracks. The wind freezes my ass off in the winter and melts it off in the summer."

Xavier now realized that it was either indoor plumbing or Tamara. No compromise was to be reached. His decision took no struggle at all. He set the bottle down on the table, toward her side. She glared at it, breathing so hard that her drooping breasts actually pushed out momentarily. Her eyes were squinted so that Xavier doubted if she'd ever be able to get them fully open again. There was no use concerning himself about the anger or the disarray of her hair.

She said with meaning, "You son of a bitch."

As always, Xavier spoke the improper words to her, even though he did so with restraint and a certain touch of politeness, "I wish you'd quit calling me by your family name."

That certainly did it. She went right over the table, grabbing the wine bottle on the way. Xavier turned and ran for the door. But now the odds were finally fulfilled. She hurled the bottle, and it went straight to its mark, thudding against the back of Xavier's skull just as he was trying to escape through the screen door. He was propelled out and off the porch, face down, in the dirt. The cur dogs were both barking and nipping at him as he stumbled to his feet. The world tipped and rocked, trying to flatten him against its bosom. He could hear the screams behind him and feel the breath of the dogs on his legs.

He stayed upright. It wasn't easy either. He managed to fumble his way into the truck and release the brake just as Marion reached out to claw his eyes. But the truck was moving, and as he jerked the door shut it knocked her down. He gave the motor a turn, and the saints were kind—it started. He rolled swiftly down the hill and didn't even glance in the rearview mirror.

It took nine stitches to sew his head up and the knot throbbed for a week, but he and Manuel worked and worked and worked.

Xavier went to see the attorney, Mr. Granger. He smiled at the little plumber, and said, "Yes, I was in show business for a while. It's possible that I could use some of my old connections to find Tamara for you." He made it seem like a very difficult task before he was through. The truth was, Xavier had barely left the office when Granger called a performers' guild in New York and acquired the address of Tamara's agent.

The agent said there was a possibility that in late summer Tamara might have time for a night in Taos. It would all be up to the cash offered, availability of proper music, etc., etc. Granger let Xavier wait three weeks before telling him about the ten minutes of calls.

In the meanwhile, Xavier rented a very small room in an alley, barely big enough for a cot and all his tools. He ate all his meals right from the cans and had no luxuries. He now worked at night when the houses were new and empty, and by sleeping little and worrying much was accumulating more money all the time. The cache behind Marion's house still had to be recovered, but he simply couldn't bring himself to invade her domain as yet. The new scar on his head still itched.

Marion had told around town that he had attacked her in a drunken rage, and she'd fought for her life. She had the law arrest him, but it was only a formality. They quickly observed that she didn't have a scratch on her, and Xavier had a nine-stitch hole in his head.

Granger finally received word from Tamara that she could stop over, enroute from Chicago to Los Angeles, the twenty-first day of August, for one night. The cost, Granger said, would be thirty-five hundred and expenses. Actually it was twenty-five, but Granger had to live, like anyone else.

He explained to Xavier that at the Met and other large theatres, Tamara worked with a sixty-piece orchestra, and he was having some difficulty convincing them that even though they could only deliver thirty pieces, it would be very satisfactory. For a moment this shocked the ecstasy out of Xavier's body, but Granger told him not to worry because he had to make a business trip to Denver soon, and he would take care of all the arrangements.

"Strings," exulted Xavier. "Get lots of strings."

Now the word was around town about Xavier's madness, and he was greeted with, "How's the impresario today?" "Give my regards to Broadway," and such like.

He rented a small lot in the desert on the opposite side of town from Marion. About thirty yards back from the highway, he started building his stage. Local jokesters called it the "poor man's Met." At first the verbal cuts had hurt, but now he just worked, and dreamed. He tied on to the power line, and when he wasn't plumbing at night he sawed, measured, and gradually nailed his stage together. It would be an outdoor stage with the whole vast Southwest as a background. He built a railing for the orchestra. He did Tamara's stage with fine wood, solid and smooth. He put up poles on the corners and in the middle and

strung small ropes crisscrossed over it. On these he hung scores of tiny colored flags.

When the last piece of red cloth was draped, he walked excitedly out into the desert, not looking back till he was on a promontory a good half-mile distant. Then he turned; the beauty almost overwhelmed him. It was like a carnival, so gay and joyous. It was alive and breathing. It was his . . . his and Tamara's. The local populace drove by and laughed; strangers stared in wonder at the apparition, but Xavier loved it.

Then Granger called him in for a meeting. It was decided that the cost of attendance would be a flat five dollars. It was now time to have the show cards printed. Xavier had already worked out the design and color. When he took his idea to the newspaper for printing, he never dreamed they would do a story on him.

In a few days, he got the eighteen by twenty-four-inch cards. They were grand—red and yellow with black letters and a photo of Tamara. His name was right next to hers. They read:

XAVIER PRESENTS

The

GREAT TAMARA

Ballerina Supreme

They gave the date, hour, and price of admission, as well as the location (as if everyone in the whole of Taos County wasn't aware of that). He proudly drove around town, putting the cards in every saloon, gas station, and shop. He even put them up in the courthouse and the county jail. This activity turned almost every individual in town into a comic. Oh, the wise remarks that exist in doubting souls.

Xavier went about building the benches and stringing the lights. He had to import an electrician from the Little Theatre in Albuquerque to install the moving spots. These were covered with pink gel to soften the glow. He kept the man two extra nights just to be sure they were of a proper quality for his Tamara. Yes, she was *his* right now, and forever, no matter what. The electrician would return, for a price, the night of the big DO.

Then the local paper came out with these large letters on the front page: LOCAL PLUMBER TO BE IMPRESARIO???? and the story followed. In spite of the question marks, the local comments of ridicule slowly subsided. They gave glances of fear now, barely smiling. Hadn't the paper actually said the ballerina was coming? What if he really pulled it off? From some of those who had teased the most, he now got an occasional, hesitant pat on the back. They were having third and fourth doubts. Everyone fears a winner, except other winners.

Marion had received an advance on the land development and had Ben Gonzales up at the house putting in her plumbing. She was so excited about this that she only had time to curse Xavier about one hour out of three. She got a lot of extra work out of Ben by flattering him and stating that he was lucky. Xavier would be broken and shamed out of the county, and Ben would have the plumbing business all to himself. At this thought, she started working on him in other ways as she had once done to the little ballet producer. The lady was determined to have her own personal plumber.

Manuel didn't really know what was going on, but with a sense of destiny he dug deeper, faster, and longer than any man in the history of Taos. It was a busy time for plumbers.

As mid-August came, the town of Taos filled up with tourists. Each day hundreds passed through on their way to Colorado, but many stayed. The motels were 90 percent full, and the plaza was overflowing with visitors, in varying percentages, from all the states. The chamber of commerce and one drugstore handled Xavier's tickets. To everyone's amazement except Xavier's, they were sold out by the sixteenth. There were requests for standing room. Many had agreed to bring their own seats and sit in the desert itself.

On the morning of the twentieth, Xavier handed over the needed funds to Granger. The attorney, knowing Xavier's fine earning record, had given checks for the orchestra, etc. Xavier had taken care of all construction, printing, and the like.

Granger raised pencil from paper and said, "Now, that takes care of everything but Tamara and the hotel bill."

Xavier was thanking Granger, "Mr. Granger, I don't know how to . . ."

"Now, now, Xavier. It's all in my duties. Nothing to it. Just glad I could be of help. We're proud of you here in Taos." He took on his courtroom voice now, rubbed his prosperous stomach, and continued, "Very proud indeed." And then as an afterthought, "It looks like you're going to have a financial success on your hands as well." And he smiled at Xavier like Santa Claus's great-grandfather.

Xavier had several hundred dollars left, but he could avoid it no longer, he had to go to Marion's and get his buried money. In the adventure, the glow of creating a classic presentation, he'd kept delaying his duty on the hillside until he'd hidden it so far within himself, it had actually been forgotten. Well, the dark of night was well suited for digging up money

buried ten steps behind the wooden outhouse with a painted door. Even the wise old coyote knew things like this. Xavier had always believed in following nature whenever possible.

Now he would go out and make his last inspection, because tomorrow he would be too busy. The day was warm, the blue-gray foothills rolled up, merging with the base of the mountains. An aura hung over it all . . . an unseen mist that caused the rays of the sun to break into infinitesimal sundrops exploding in the air with billions of tiny sparkles. The soft sound of a dove cooing caressed the bright air. The bobcat and the coyote rested in the first jumble of rocks, digesting food from last night's hunt, waiting for the moon again. The gophers and the rats were in their dens hiding from the sun. Some of them would not escape the night hunters. Some would. Bugs and lizards crawled under small rocks. The snakes waited in the shade of the sage and cactus and watched their movements. Higher up in the aspen and pine, deer fed, becoming lazy and fat. But at the first explosion of the fall hunter's gun, they would quiver, run, and hide, trying to survive. Some wouldn't. But all the movement Xavier could see in this expanse was a hawk circling and the slight stirring of the flags as they made love to a fluctuating breeze. Behind the mountains the clouds rose, shoving up like sails being raised on giant sky ships. Their heaviness turned their bottoms dark with shadow.

The mood of the day, of the time in Xavier's existence, had caught him up in a reverie of dreams, of glory. Then the first heavy drop of rain hit his shoulder. He looked up. Two more splashed against his face. Then it came down hard, fast, clean, and pure. The curtain of moisture moved on over his kingdom and down the hills to the west, wetting a path perhaps two-thirds of a mile wide.

The freshness of everything was almost more than Xavier could take. What luck! The dust would be perfectly settled for the crowd tomorrow night.

Xavier checked out the ticket sales and the hotel reservations. He called on Granger again to be sure about the orchestra. All was in order. His universe was complete, or would be, after a little trip to the *casa* in the foothills.

At dusk he bought a box of dog biscuits. Then he went to his crowded room and fed himself a can of Vienna sausage, some crackers, and an apple. He lay down on the cot to wait. The alarm was set for two o'clock. That would get him at Marion's about three, when she would be sleeping the soundest. The girls didn't concern him. They were too lazy to wake up. Sleep avoided Xavier that night. There was too much to think about on the morrow, not counting the risk of facing Marion tonight. He rubbed the scar on his head. The alarm rang, and he quivered all over from shock at the sound.

The moon was almost full. It shoved the blue lights out over the sage and made Xavier wish for total darkness. He thought that the earth's second biggest spotlight was not needed this night. He pulled from the highway, turning off his lights before he did, drove up a little draw, and hid the truck. He put on his jacket and emptied the dog biscuits in one large pocket.

He used the country road for a while, trying to walk softly. He felt that every step was surely jarring the foundations of the house and rattling dishes in the cupboard. He envisioned Marion sitting, cocking the hammers on a brand-new shotgun. If she hadn't hated the outdoor privy so, he was sure she'd be waiting there to blow him in half, cursing the undone plumbing while he kicked his last.

Sure enough, when he was within a couple of hundred yards of the house, the two dogs ran around barking like never before. Xavier knew they sensed his fear. He jumped off the road behind some sagebrush and held his breath. Xavier *tried* not to *be*—to exist—but he *was*. He was right here cowering while the money resided up there in an unfeeling bucket, not caring whether he recovered it or not.

Inside, Marion pushed at Ben Gonzales's sleeping back until he awoke. "There's somethin' out there, Ben."

Now Mr. Gonzales had labored day and night getting her plumbing all in order and had finally finished the task that very evening. He was tired. "Ish jiss a coyote," he mumbled, and went back to sleep.

Xavier moved up to meet the dogs and whatever other demons lurked there for him. He knew now what courage it took for a foot soldier to attack hidden machine guns and cannon. As he neared the dogs, or vice versa, he tried whistling to them with friendship. He really didn't know if he was making a sound or not. Dogs are supposed to feel vibrations beyond the capability of the human ear, and he was not about to exude enough air for Marion's ears.

Now the dogs faced him, and they had a combination of irritated barks and disgusted snarls for their former half-master. He pitched some biscuits in front of them, whispering love songs as hard as he could.

"Oh, you beautiful dogs. You kindhearted dogs. You wise and thoughtful dogs. You hungry dogs. Dogs are my friends. Hello, my friends."

It worked somewhat. They did grab up the biscuits greedily. And then stood back with bristles up, growling softly to see what kind of trick or treat was next. Xavier was busy. He made a wide circle to come in behind the outhouse, all the

time dropping biscuits to the growling dogs and trying to watch the door to Marion's house. He listened hard, too.

The dogs had decided to adopt the ancient attitude of let's wait and see. They had a growl bottled up just at the end of their tongues ready for instant action if the biscuits were stopped permanently. The jacket pocket was only half full now. Xavier would have to work fast.

And then he saw! The outhouse was gone, and all the ground around had been graded smooth! There was Gonzales's work truck. No doubt Gonzales also occupied his late unlamented bed. To save his life, his soul, his presentation, he could not divine the spot where the small structure of relief had stood.

Christ! If he'd just had enough sense to bring along his electronic pipe locator, there would be no problem. In a small, hysterical moment he thought about borrowing his fellow worker's. It was probably in the back of the truck. However, the truck's proximity to the doorway of Marion's house forbade that.

The dogs were circling now, feeling his anxiety and letting little portions of growls escape. Any moment they might go the whole route. He pitched them two more biscuits, buying time. He thought. Not an easy thing to do either. Watching the door and the dogs, he spotted a stick in a pile of wood that had once been the privy. If he remembered correctly, the contents of that little building had been somewhat above the level of the earth. That would mean it would be mixed with the soil that covered it.

He made a wild guess as to its location and an even wilder decision. He must become a dog. He threw the rest of the biscuits out around him and dropped down on his hands and knees, punching at the earth, looking for a soft spot, and sniffing back and forth from side to side like a thoroughbred

trail hound. At this unusual action, the dogs even forgot the biscuits. They growled and let out two rather confused barks.

Marion was not going to accept the coyote theory. This time she kneed Gonzales in the kidneys and forced him up. He stumbled around, trying to find the bedroom door.

Suddenly Xavier plunged the stick into soft soil, and he got the scent all right. There was no doubt at all. Now he moved back and forth trying to define the edges of the covered hole, sniffing, dropping his head right to the ground to better pin down the outer edges correctly.

Gonzales finally found the door and sort of wobbled through the kitchen and looked out. He tried to rub the sleep from his eyes, and then he saw through the blur that there were three dogs in the dimming moonlight. He disgustedly made his way back to the bed and said, "Jish another dog."

Xavier drew the line in the soil and stood up, putting his heels on it, and took ten steps straight toward a prominent sagebrush. He knelt and scooped the few inches of dirt from his beloved bucket, pulled it out, stood up, looked at the house, then at the dogs. They were doing their growling trick louder now, for they realized they had a real thief in their backyard.

Xavier started his circle away from the house, again whispering loving words to the dogs as he went. His steps got faster as they got louder. Then he broke into a run. Now, dogs have a great attraction to anything that runs from them, whether it be rabbits, cats, cars, or plumbers. They pursued. Loudly. They nipped and circled, making all kinds of exciting noise. Xavier was fending them off fairly well with the bucket. Since he was going downhill and also nearing his means of escape, his speed increased. So did that of the dogs.

Marion sat straight up in bed and suddenly reached over and hit Gonzales on the side of his snoring head. He never did

know how he got the sore spot nor why he'd awakened so suddenly.

Xavier made his truck, opened the door, and as he jumped in one of the dogs latched onto his coattail and the other to his leg. But nothing could stop him now. He kicked them loose, and the truck responded to his desire by starting right off, and he drove like hell for town as the greatest day of his life announced itself beyond the mountains in the perpetual sky.

Granger had volunteered to take his private plane and pick up Tamara and her three associates at the Albuquerque airport. The orchestra was coming in on a chartered bus from Denver. The stage was as ready as it would ever be. Manuel was given the day off, and all work stopped. Xavier went to J.C. Penney's and bought a new suit, tie, shirt, socks, and even underwear. None of it quite fit, but then creative people are sometimes shoddy in their dress.

The local newspaper carried a half page on the activities and said that representatives of two major TV networks would cover the show out of Albuquerque. Everywhere Xavier went, he found friends. New friends, old friends, and friends of friends. He just wandered around accepting the attention with smiles and thanks, but his mind was on the night. Tonight, yes tonight, he would actually cast his eyes on the moving, living, lovely flesh of Tamara. Had any man in all time ever been so blessed? He said a quiet prayer of thanks. He was so happy and full of wonder that he failed to notice a twenty-mile-long column of white clouds peeking constantly higher over the Rocky Mountains.

He checked at the chamber and the drugstore. All tickets were sold. They had even sold out of standing room. The town was full of people, and a crowd was gathering in front of the Taos Inn. Everyone wanted a glimpse, a touch, a part of the great Tamara.

He worked his way through the crowd to the lobby, where he was welcomed by the mayor, the chief of police, the hotel manager, and newspaper and TV reporters. He was frightened. He was numb. He was in agonized ecstasy. The clicking cameras, flashing lights, and pointed questions whirled around Xavier in a blurred vortex.

Then he heard the noise, and all the flesh moved to the door. He just stood in the lobby and waited. He could not push to see her. It had been too long. It was a long wait of only a minute. His hands perspired, and he rubbed them over and over against his coat. He didn't want his right hand wet when he finally touched hers. His feet had melted to the floor. He felt that if he took a step, part of the hotel rug would pull up and go along with him.

Then he saw Granger smiling, gregariously efficient, leading . . . leading . . . yes, it was Tamara. The lovely Tamara! He saw her dark eyes floating ghostlike through space up to him, and he took her hand in both of his and kissed it. That's all he remembered until someone handed him a cup of tea in her suite.

Her wardrobe mistress was busy unpacking. The ballet master and manager was on the phone long distance, already planning the next show in another city. One helper held two elegant Afghan hounds on a joined leash and constantly answered the door. With haughty politeness he refused to allow anyone to enter. Granger and the mayor were the only local people present.

Tamara was giving orders on clothing and food for after the show like a true and crowned queen. Xavier was amazed that she was only five feet one and ninety pounds. In her photos she looked six feet tall. In fact, she appeared that now.

Suddenly she turned full on Xavier, asking, "Mr. Del Campo, could we order you drinks, food, anything? I do neither until after the performance."

He shook his head no, and choked that he would wait too. Then he took a swallow of the tea he had forgotten all about. He couldn't believe he was actually talking with her. They were saying words to each other across the room. They had shared eyes while doing so. She was far more beautiful and graceful than could be imagined. Every move was a poem . . . no, a symphony! Xavier dared not even blink his eyes for fear he'd miss a priceless gesture.

The low, distant growl of thunder came to him subconsciously, but he ignored its existence. Granger walked and looked out the window towards the mountains. He didn't comment, but gave Xavier a quick glance.

The next hour was a fog to Xavier. He did remember later that she'd commented on the beauty of the land and how refreshing it was to perform out of a big city in such clean air.

Outside, and above, the clouds humped over the mountains and spread across the foothills and the valleys. They were dark and solemn like dynamite just before the spark touches. They boiled now and moved together, and the lightning burst out of them, crescendoing sound across the land and shaking the windows of the hotel.

Then there was a pause. A stillness. Tamara, busying herself with her wardrobe, glanced at the window and then at Xavier. Xavier stared into the bottom of his teacup. He was afraid to feel—to know. Then it came, great gushes of water

splashing against the panes with its brother wind, running off the walls and joining the little rivulets on the ground. The thunder and lightning became the same sound now, the same entity. So did the beating of Xavier's heart. No one talked for a while, then Granger and the mayor said they'd call the airport for a weather report and left.

Tamara made light chatter and smiled at Xavier many times. He just sat smiling, with his face. A small smile to be sure, but there, just the same. The storm seemed to talk louder and pound harder.

Suddenly Tamara sent her entourage away. She brought him another cup of tea, and as she bent over he saw the ocean of her eyes. The waves splashed against and over his whole being.

She was at the phone talking. He did not hear. Then the waiter was there, and they sat across a table from each other. There was food he didn't taste, champagne he didn't savor, and talk he didn't hear. But he felt. Had any man *ever* felt all the things he had in the last few seconds, minutes, hours, eternities?

She left him and went to her bedroom, motioning him to wait. Then she came into the room in the dress of the dying swan. She danced. The entire orchestra was down in the bar drinking, but Xavier heard them playing, playing, playing. She floated and flew. Xavier swore to Manuel later that there were whole minutes when she didn't even touch the floor. And then she died. Just for him. Fluttering the life from flesh that had become that of the most graceful of all the world's creatures—the white swan. The bird lay there dead, but the lady slowly rose and bowed to him. He clapped so hard his head jarred, and just as his dreams had predicted she came to him, taking his hands, saying, "Thank you, Señor Del Campo, thank you from the bottom of my soul."

She led him to the door and whispered that it was late. Then she bent slightly and kissed him on the mouth, holding his head in her hands with infinite tenderness. Her eyes spread around him and went with him into the hall, keeping him warm and glowing. It was midnight. He could not go out the front and see anyone. He could not share this moment. It was his alone. He moved to the end of the hall and stepped out onto a fire escape. He walked down it into the wetness of the same alley he lived on. The rain was over. The eaves still dripped a little. The clouds were spreading apart, making holes for the light of the moon. One beam hit a puddle in front of him. He splashed into the blue mirror.

It was never known if anyone drove along the highway at sunup the next morning, but if so, they would have seen the open-air stage where the little colored flags hung limp, wet, and heavy. A closer examination would have shown a short, chunky man standing there looking at his muddy feet. He took two timid steps forward, raised one leg, and whirled almost all the way around on the wet wood. And then he smiled.

THE MOUNTAIN
OF GOLD

The young man swung the axe expertly and with much force into the spruce. It bit clean and white, first under then over. The V widened, and the chips, smooth and fresh, scattered about upon the ground. The muscles under the red-brown skin of Benito Anaya moved in graceful ripples. Strength and youth and health glowed about him like the holy aureola of the saints.

The spruce toppled to the ground, slowly at first then faster as it gathered momentum in its death plunge. Quickly Benito trimmed the branches and chopped off the small end. He stepped back to where his shirt hung from a bush and pushed his wavy black hair from his brow. After a moment of cooing in the mountain breeze, he put on his shirt and the old felt hat. This would make a good corral pole. Six others lay nearby, neatly trimmed as this last.

Benito leaned back and took a breath of the forest with all its scents of pine and spruce and cedar and undergrowth and the myriad of wild things that came from it then returned. With his eyes closed, he smelled his Little Princess Eloisa above all this. What a wedding! What a *baile*—the music, the friends, the wine. And then his Princessita, the Little Princess, alone with him at Casa Mia . . . my house, her house, our house. Casa Mia. She was there now, waiting, straining her dark misty eyes upwards towards the massive sides of Black Mountain for her beloved's return.

Suddenly Benito decided six poles would be enough for this trip. But his work had only started, for nothing came easy from Black Mountain's sides, and she gave her timber with reluctance. Now he must toss the poles from a steep rock bluff, then circle perhaps half a mile to reach them. He would toss the poles again and then once again before they would be near enough to drag to his cart where the young, white work mare stood tied.

Benito started the drop. The first two logs plunged over, down, and away from the bluff, kicking up a cloud of dust and vegetation as they landed in the soft overburden far below. He hoisted the third up to his right hipbone, leaving one end to drag in the dirt. With the downhill pull, it tracked along behind him without much strain. Then, something turned from under his foot, and he came down hard. The log rolled over him and on past.

Benito sat up, wiping the pine needles from himself, staring numbly for a moment at the white quartz rock that tripped him. Looking closer, he noticed wirelike strings of something running through it. He leaned over on his knees and one hand to pick it up. For a moment the hand hesitated then plunged about the rock. He drew it closer to his widening

eyes. Now, with shaking hands, he pulled a knife from his pocket and jerked the blade open. Swiftly he scratched at the metal in the glassy white rock. The knife blade cut into it easily, and there before him was the unbelievably dull yellow of pure gold.

He turned it over and over in his hands, feeling the weight, estimating the percentage of gold to quartz, which he guessed as close to 50 percent. It must be a large vein, judging from the size and weight of the float rock. His blood was singing the song of discovery as it pushed on through his body faster and faster. He scratched wildly about in the dirt, knowing there should be much more where this came from. But he found only one small rock with a nugget plastered to its side. It had probably broken from the larger one. How big the rock must have been when it broke away from the mother vein!

Benito leaped to his feet and ran to his axe. Placing the gold quartz on a large granite boulder so that it would be in plain sight, he took the axe in hand and swung it deep into a mighty pine. Three notches perhaps six inches deep he cut. There! That would mark it well and from now on, for no one would dare attempt to remove a tree of such magnitude from Black Mountain.

Now he must get off this mountain and to his Little Princess. There were many plans to lay, for how many had such a fortune in their grasp? Ha! How many indeed! He almost snorted through his fine nostrils as he slid recklessly down the sides of the old Black Mountain with the gold clasped in one large hand, filling the hand, and just beginning to make its weight felt.

There was no holding him back now. Benito leaped from ledges that would frighten a mountain mule. He slid, he fell, he rolled, but his young body absorbed the shocks as nothing.

Down he plunged to the waiting mare. She threw her head up, nostrils wide, ears pitched forward, straining against the lines, feeling the excitement racing towards her. But she did not bolt.

"Ah, old Blanca," cried Benito, "I'll fill your stall with hay and oats, and you'll live in a horse's heaven all your days on this earth. We're *muy rico*, four-legged *compadre!* Do you hear, pure white one? Listen to Benito, the rich one!"

From the spot on Black Mountain where the pine stood with three notches slashed through her bark to Casa Mia out in the desert was perhaps twelve downhill, winding miles. To the white mare it must have seemed a hundred, from the speed the demon behind her demanded, yelling wild things at her and urging her on with the ends of the lines. Her nostrils flared wider now as if they would peel back from her muzzle. Her heaving sides were gray where first the sweat had soaked her and then the dampness had gathered dust and turned brown, but on she went. The cart tipped as it skidded on the turns, but somehow all stayed upright and moved on out across the desert. They finally reached the stream, the tiny, life-giving, life-taking trickle of water with its banks stained green with willows and chamisa in bloom. Down along its winding way, staying parallel in the dim trail, they flew. The Arroyo Hondo would lead him straight to Casa Mia. The sustenance of its waters was the reason they could live so far from the village of Sano.

The logs had been forgotten. All had been forgotten. One purpose only remained—to get to the Little Princess Eloisa with his message. And what a message to share with her this first week of their marriage!

He saw her standing in the trail in front of the adobe house where she had run to meet him. A yell moved up into his throat and out of his mouth. It pierced the late afternoon

air, making the dog bark and turn sideways and the magpies rise chattering from the banks of the Arroyo Hondo. A coyote sleeping on the hillside three-quarters of a mile away raised his head and sniffed into the wind. The Little Princess Eloisa knew not what made this crazy man of hers act so, but her heart fluttered excitedly and tiny particles of coldness ran out of the pores on the back of her neck. The stallion in the pasture ran to the pole fence with his black, glistening head high. The sheep and goats stood heads jerked up, chewing rapidly. The chickens listened for a second and went back to their scratching in the yard around the house. The mare came to a slow halt, her muscles quivering. She stood head down, legs apart, her lungs pushing her ribs in and out like large bellows.

Benito leaped into the waiting arms of his bride.

"What is it, my darling, my darling?" she asked him between kisses. "Tell me what has driven you to this state."

Benito stepped back. "Look at your fine figure of a husband. Notice closely the bearing he now possesses. The elegance of his stance. For you, Princessita, are looking at a man of substance and great wealth. Look!" he said, thrusting the heavy gold rock before her staring eyes. "Look! Gaze upon the wealth of the ancients, and it's your *hombre* alone, my Princessita, who has discovered this treasure."

"What is it?" she asked.

"What *is* it?" he screamed. "You are looking at the most precious of all metals. It is . . . gold!" he said, his breath struggling around the word.

Eloisa stared more and longer. "Is that all?" she said.

"Is that all?" he wailed, holding his hand to his head. "Is that all?" he repeated. "How many brides of one week have been presented with such a gift? Why, we could live a year off this one rock alone, but we shall keep it as a memento forever.

And for sure, there are thousands more like it."

"Have you found them?" she asked, dark eyes widening a little.

"No, but I shall. Yes, I'll find them before the sunset tomorrow. Ah, come, I'm thirsty for water and for your love. Come, let's go to the cool shade and lay our plans."

They sat on the old bench in the shade of the porch and talked. She listened silently while he stroked her long, thick hair.

"My little one," he said softly, "I'll buy you the smoothest silks to wrap about your lovely brown body. We'll sail the world around on a great ship, and I'll cover your fingers with jewels and enclose your feet with shoes made from the very gold of the Black Mountain. We'll hire many men and dig many wells of water, and we shall have horses by the hundreds and cattle and sheep by the thousands, and we'll have beautiful, brilliant children by the dozen."

"Ah, my amour," he went on, as he nuzzled her behind the ear, "for you, we'll build an adobe castle with walls so thick the summer sun will go mad before it touches your tender skin. The winter winds shall cry and wail like lost goats and never touch one shiny hair of your head. You'll have a room larger than a *cantina* with one wall a *grande* mirror to sit before, and all the perfumes and powders and fancies of the world will be yours for the reaching. And your kitchen, Princessita, will burst with chile and beans, meats and mangoes from Mexico, fruits and vegetables ripe and tasty from our own rich gardens! And many señoritas will move quietly about, on sandaled feet, bringing to our table the delicious steaming foods. Can you not see it now?"

"Yes," she whispered to him. "Yes, my man. I see it through your eyes, and I smell the perfumes and taste the

food, but above all, my darling, I know you'll be with me, and that's what matters most."

"Of course, I'll be at your side," said Benito, and he held his wife close, "until we're taken away to the heavens by the great saints because of all the good deeds we'll do with our money."

They were both silent.

The sun moved out to the right of Black Mountain and behind the desert hills to the west. The dark shadows lay in the canyons and crevices of her sides, but on her western edge, for a moment the red-orange of the sun stroked her shoulders then disappeared, and all her rocky mass joined the black of night.

The morning sun was still hiding in the east when Benito crawled from beside the warm, young body of his wife. He stepped softly through the curtain door into the kitchen and lit the wax candle on the table. The little flame flared up and then settled into a small soft glow. Lifting the lid from the iron stove with an iron handle, he swiftly and deftly built a fire from the short piñon sticks. Its roar added a warmth to the room even before the iron was hot.

Benito moved the candle over to the table above which hung a picture of San Ramon, the Saint of Childbirth. But Benito's young mind was not on the San Ramon this morning. It was on the rock lying there, looking richer now, in the light of the candle. He sat on the rough handmade bench and looked. He turned it this way and that, smiling, breathing harder as he caressed the strings of yellow. In a few hours now, he would have enough of this rock to last for years. In a week, enough to do a careful man for a lifetime. In a year . . .? Why, it was beyond comprehension.

A rooster crowed, and then a coyote made his last yapping yowl of the night. The sheep and lambs moved about in the still, cold air and nibbled at the fresh green grass between Casa Mia and the creek. A great night owl left the bank of the Arroyo Hondo, his wings brushing in ghostly sound against the receding night air. He flew south to the shallow, crevice-lined canyon before the day could catch his wide night eyes. The day moved up with the sun and spread out across the sage, sparkling golden as the metal in Benito's hands. It shoved the purple of dawn away and brought the birds out to sing of its perpetual warming wonder. But Benito did not notice. He sat murmuring softly to himself and did not even hear the bare feet of his wife until he heard the coffeepot clink on the now steadily burning kitchen stove.

"I'm sorry I awakened you," he said, "but my mind would not rest and my body craves to move toward Black Mountain."

"It's all right," she said, looking at him with a smile.

"At what would you guess its value, Princessita?"

"I do not know," she said. "A great deal, I should think."

"It must have thirty ounces of gold in it! Viva the mother mountain! Thirty ounces in a rock the size of my fist! It would be a wise wager to place that it's worth two or three hundred pesos. Maybe even more. Men have given their lives for lesser treasures. No?"

Eloisa set the steaming hot coffee before her husband, prepared his eggs, and warmed the tortillas. Benito thrust down the food hurriedly. He ate only to fill the emptiness of his belly, for he had no time for tasting. Finished, he arose from the table and said, "I'll get the black stallion. The white mare will be too stiff from the hard run of yesterday."

He walked out into his pasture toward the black stallion.

He held the *morral* out and gave the oats inside a tempting shake. The stallion stood as if to run, ears forward, head high, but the smell of the oats made him stand. Benito slipped the rope smoothly around his outstretched neck.

"Now, my black beauty, this is a great day for you. Never before has a horse had the opportunity to share in such a discovery. Why, a queen of Spain would be glad to carry a saddle on her back this fine day, if she could but share your honors!"

Benito saddled the stallion and led him to the back porch of Casa Mia. "Come, Chiquita," he called. "Hurry, I must be on my way."

She stepped from the kitchen onto the porch.

"I must go now," he said, pulling her to him. "I'll return by nightfall. If it takes a little longer, don't worry, for what's the sense of returning when another hour will surely reveal the source of our great wealth?"

"My Benito, if you don't find it the first day, stay another." She spoke with a swelling in her throat and with tears misting her dark eyes. "Go, now, my love, and return when you must."

She stood at the door for a long time watching the black stallion grow smaller in the dust, and she looked at the mountain as a jealous woman does a rival.

"Why, he's taken nothing to eat!" She started to run after him, but now the stallion was only a small dot almost lost in the vastness of the desert.

The sun arched up, and the sweat began to stain the stallion's neck. Dust powdered under his hoofs and kicked up small clouds that coated the sage and sparse grass alongside the

trail. The mountain loomed larger. As they moved nearer, glimpses of deep canyons and sharp-edged bluffs appeared through the pine and piñon.

White lather foamed at the black's mouth now, and Benito could feel the sweat on his own body as it rubbed against the hard leather of the saddle. His eyes squinted narrower from the glare of the overhead sun as he rode into the scattered cedar and dwarf piñon of the lower foothills. The stallion was blowing from the steepening grade, but on and upward they moved.

A doe leaped across the trail, then a buck followed. His antlers reached up in treelike majesty. They stopped on a rise and looked back, curious yet alert. Benito thought of how easy it would be to swing the sights of his rifle up to the buck's shoulder and down him with one shot—he had brought no food. Now his stomach felt drawn and empty from his hard ride. Oh well, no matter, he would fill the bags before sundown. But just the same, he should have brought his rifle in case it took an extra day.

At last he could ride no farther. He untied his rope and staked the stallion next to a small spring in a little glade. Quickly he removed the canvas bags from his saddle and started the climb.

His heart beat hard at his rib cage as he strained upward on the steep grade. Pulling himself with his free hand, now by grasping a limb, a bush, a projecting rock, he moved up, never stopping except to survey the terrain ahead. He struggled around massive granite boulders, through bush that pulled and scratched at his body. Salty sweat ran into his eyes and down into the corners of his mouth. His strong, young heart pumped red, rich blood faster and faster through his veins. The old mountain gave nothing easy, even to the young and strong.

Each rise appeared to be the last, but always another was there, hard, steep, cruel, uttering silent disbelief that this one of flesh could conquer its ageless sides.

Benito could still see the golden-laced rock, lying back at Casa Mia under the care of its mistress. Yes, he would bring it company tonight.

At last he was there. He stood staring at the fresh cuts in the mighty pine. Now he forgot the climb. He even forgot his Little Princess at Casa Mia. He looked hard into the earth, as if, by staring with enough force, he could make her unveil her secret.

He walked and he walked. Up and down, around, under, over the mountain. He knelt, he scratched. He prayed and begged to the mountain. But he did not find the vein. *Well now,* he thought, *I must go back to the pine and start over. I was too anxious. I worked too fast. I must have muy patience.*

Benito had wandered much farther from the pine than he realized, and by the time he returned he noticed the sun was beginning to brighten the sky in the west as the world dulled to the east. Desperately, he started over. He scratched until his hands rubbed raw and bleeding in the overburden. Then suddenly it was dark. He was through for this day. The mountain had won the first encounter.

He had been foolish to leave without food and water. There was water below where the black stallion was staked. The stallion would be all right until tomorrow, but Benito's throat constricted and his tongue seemed to be swelled and stuck dry to the roof of his mouth. Yes, he was a fool.

He waited for the moon to rise. Even then he knew it would be risky to attempt the descent of the mountain, but he must have water. In the early morn he could gather some wild berries, or perhaps kill a rabbit with a rock. He leaned back

against the pine. His body told him how tired it was—bone marrow tired, muscle fiber tired. But his mind raced on.

The moon came up and shot blue-gray light into the heavens, but it would be an hour or more before the mountain would permit the mother moon to shine her heralded beacon across the flank wherein lay Benito Anaya, gold seeker.

The way down was faster than the way up, but in the supernatural glow of the moon, casting dark shadows across his path, were many loose rocks and sharp benches that cut and tore at his legs and hands. Down . . . down . . . sliding, falling, he felt no pain now, only his thirst and a powerful desire to rest. Just to lie in the grass and rest.

The stallion snorted as the white mare had done the day before. Ah, water. He drank deep and felt the dryness vanish and dampness return to his throat. He took his saddle blanket and rolled up in it. The night was cold, but the day had been long. His mind stopped now, giving in to the exhaustion of his body. He slept.

In the coldness of daybreak he awakened. At first he lay in the blanket, feeling the stiffness of his body and shivering at the bite of the early morning dew. He felt light-headed from hunger. The cuts and bone-deep bruises on his legs would barely allow him to rise. His hands were so tender it took all his courage to place their rawness against the piñon sticks he gathered for a fire. But, as he held their soreness out to the blaze, the force and hope of youth returned and downed the pain.

Food. He must now have food, for a terrible climb awaited him before he could hold the treasure in his grasp. He found a few wild berries—bitter, tasteless, but food. Then he spotted a rat's nest. He dug into it with a pointed stick and

prodded up several piñon nuts. Swiftly now and with jagged hands he dug. The pile of nuts increased before his eyes into a bonanza. He filled all his pockets and covered the rest back up so the birds and other small game would not find them.

Well, there was no time to cast away. He had a much longer day ahead than the one just past. After he had restaked the horse, he soaked the canvas bags in the water. Then he dipped some water in one side, and tied it firmly in a knot so the precious fluid could not escape.

Up the mountain he went, eating the nuts without tossing the shells away. He was somewhat slower than the day before, but even more determined and certain of his success.

He began again at the notched pine and worked carefully. He looked in a hundred draws and mounted a hundred rises. Time after time he spotted the broken white quartz. Each time a coldness swept across his heated body, and he would leap upon the rock, grasping it and pulling it close to his face. But none of these crystal-pure specimens contained any gold that the naked eye could see. Endlessly he moved, head down, stiff joints grinding together, kinked muscles pulling, stretching, aching.

Late in the afternoon, his energy began to fail. His steps slowed, and a dullness came over his eyes. The piñon nuts and a few berries had been consumed long ago. Now his body moved on the food of his own flesh and was rapidly weakening.

Slowly he made his descent back to the black stallion. Leadenly he walked to the animal and untied the stake rope. He unwound the four strands, then with a purpose about his hunger-numb body, he sought out three dim game trails leading up to the water hole. He tied a noose in each strand from the rope and carefully set a snare trap. He must have food by

morning, or he would barely have the strength to mount and ride to Casa Mia.

Casa Mia. Ah, the thought, so tempting, came again and again. The chile beans, the tortillas, the hot coffee that lifted the spirits, and the warm, soft wedding bed. The tender gaze and loving touch of Little Princess could all be his in but a three- or four-hour ride.

But no, he could not return. He had said so much to Little Princess. Far too much. He must keep his promise of silks and spices if it took all this week. Yes indeed, if it consumed an entire month.

That night he dined on dry piñon hulls and spring water. The throbbing of his hands and the wound of his legs overcame his exhaustion. He slept little, moaning and rolling about. Before morning, pains had started in his stomach. He had moved his blanket back away from the spring and the game trails so as not to frighten any living food from his traps.

At the first blue, cold rays of the coming day, Benito forced himself to a sitting position, then to his knees, then to one foot, then upright. It was difficult at first, but the growling hunger pains of his stomach forced him into movement.

The first snare had been tripped by a porcupine. The quills were stuck in the hemp, and a few were scattered on the ground. The second snare had not been disturbed. In the third there hung a mountain hare, fat, ready for skinning.

He did not use his pocketknife, but pulled the tender skin from the juicy flesh with his bare hands, giving thanks all the while to every saint in the heavens. Another day was now his on the sides of the reluctant Black Mountain.

But the mountain did not give in that day nor the next. And indeed, her sides seemed to swell and steepen and the

rock to harden under his feet. But now he fought back.

Acquiring tree limbs as near the same length as possible, he built a lean-to up near the pine tree. There was plenty of grass in the glen, so he only had to go down every other day to water the black. He set his snares every night. Sometimes he went a day or so with the pangs of hunger whipping at his insides. But he stayed.

He learned to take the entrails of the rabbits and toss them out to the large, gray camp robbers. The fearless and foolish birds would dart from nearby trees for the meal so easily won. With a short strand from one of the snares, Benito tied his pocketknife to a long, lean pole, then just as the bird reached for the bait, he would deftly spear it with the knife. Thus did he live each day. Even though it took a great portion of his time and energy to avoid starvation, he ceaselessly pursued the main goal—the mother vein of quartz with the snake-like strands of gold.

Night after night, when his fire had died, Benito would lie back and look out the lean-to opening, which he had faced toward Casa Mia. At times his heart faltered as he wondered if the Little Princess had gone, leaving Casa Mia for the desert winds to inhabit. Maybe she thought him dead and had returned to the village to live with her parents. Maybe she had tired of all the hard work, the drying of squash, corn, and chile, the caring for the livestock and all the rest. Maybe. Was it too much to ask of her to wait all this time? Was it? He would fall asleep in the blanket on the hard ground, wondering with all his being.

As the summer passed, so did his carefully hoarded matches. For a while he kept the fire going by putting on logs just green enough to burn slowly. Finally, though, the rains

came, loosing their torrents upon the side of Black Mountain to the echo of thunderous flashes of stabbing lightning. Benito was soaked, and his fire was out. He now must eat what little meat he could gather raw like a savage. The cold rain dripped down into the lean-to where he slept, and for days at a time he slipped and fell and searched on, with the water squirting out of his shoes at each step.

When the rains finally stopped, the mountain appeared fresh and clean, but beneath the deceptive surface, Benito knew her heart was as black as her shadows. He had hoped that the waters, coursing down her sides, would uncover his treasure, but such was not the case. He hunted on.

Day ran into day, into night, into dawn, into day and into night again. Benito's bones showed nearer the surface of his skin. His hair was tangled and twisted and dirt brown. His eyes were dark, circled, and sunken. He searched even harder. And, just when his body was beginning to fail him and his entire system lose its strength, the first blast of winter wind charged through the brush and timber. And the mountain seemed to say, "Get off my sides, or I will cover you with a blanket of white and starve you and freeze you and bury your corpse under the ice of my winter raiment."

With slumped shoulders, drawn face, and skull-tight skin, he rode the stallion from the Black Mountain, off her great swelling breasts and the valleys of her belly, out into the desert toward Casa Mia. He spoke to his mount, "Oh, Horse, faithful Horse, will she be waiting for me? In our little home I deserted the first week of our lives together—will she, Horse? This starved, threadbare figure of a man? What have I to offer

her now? Riches? No, not even one small rock to keep the other one company in the long winter so near upon us. But maybe she'll love Benito Anaya yet." And then he looked up and felt surely he had left his sanity on the bitter slopes of Black Mountain, for there she was, coming down the road at full speed on the white mare. He stopped and waited. When she was near, he leaned to her, speechless, arms seeking, but his strength gave way and he fell to the ground.

"Ah, my love, my love."

It was too good to be true. It could be no other arms encircling his neck and no other tears spilling from those dark unreal eyes onto his cheeks. He was too happy to talk. He just lay there and held her. Then they arose, and she helped him onto the black stallion.

Now he spoke, "Thank you, my wife, thank you so much."

After he had eaten and drunk pots of steaming coffee and loved and eaten again, she took him by the hand, leading him slowly to their pastures.

She had gotten help from the village for the shearing, and several bales of rich wool were safely stored in the barn. The lambs were fat. Strings of corn and red chile were dried and hung. The wild delicious plums were cured, and a pig was fat and ready to butcher. Oh, she had done it all and so well. It would be a long winter to sit by the fireplace and grow fat and lay his plans for his next attack on the brutal Black Mountain. It would commence when the snow was first gone.

"You see, my darling," he said, "anything as great as this treasure must take some effort. The saints only tested our wills this one summer. Now that they know our courage and faithfulness, we'll be rewarded before the birds have nested next spring."

And so it was, the hearts of Casa Mia beat strong and waited for the springtime . . . and another spring and another.

For nine springs Benito packed his supplies on his horse's back, kissed Little Princess and his three growing children goodbye, and rode away to continue his fight with the Black Mountain, and the mountain always met him with unforeseen challenges.

Such was the time when the mountain sent a big black bear with cubs to Benito's lean-to. When he returned, unarmed, from a long walk, the bears had eaten up his corn and were starting on the venison. The mama bear heard him coming. She came charging downhill growling, with great white teeth bared ready to tear Benito to bits. Maybe having the cubs made her so mean, or maybe the mountain had poisoned her heart. Benito could almost hear the old mountain cheering the monster on.

The bear had such speed, and was so heavy, that Benito quickly sidestepped, and she went on past him down the mountain. Before she could stop and turn, Benito raced to the lean-to and grabbed his rifle. Kneeling on one knee, his heart cold as he saw her roaring up at him, he fired between her legs. She stumbled, but kept coming. He fired again. This time she fell but rose swiftly, and before he could shoot again she was on top of Benito and had his arm in her jaws. Then she died. She died just before she could take his arm off.

After the bear incident, the mountain pulled another trick. The old mountain had a great overburden where the logs and leaves and brush and the insects and the animals had all returned to her sides, making millions of tons of rich earth. Benito knew she had hidden her treasures somewhere underneath, and that someday a puff of wind sent by the saints or a

wild animal digging for food might uncover them.

This time, a great cloud, as big and black as the old mountain herself, with mighty tongues of fire and a growl like ten thousand bears, raced over the mountain. Then this cloud opened up like a funnel and dropped water by the lakeful. Rivers ran down Black Mountain's sides. Benito was certain the vein would be washed clear and clean for his hungry eyes to see. The cloud moved away and on into the heavens.

After all was still, and the birds flew out from under branches to sing, Benito came out of the lean-to expecting to make his discovery. He walked along, seeing where the mountain had been washed clean to the bone. He knew that somewhere near, maybe up this very draw, he'd see the white and golden rock shining as bright as an angel's halo. But this was not to be.

The old Black Mountain knew how close he was to her vast treasure, and she hunched and shook her huge shoulders, and a million tons of rocks and dirt came tumbling from her top side down into the draw.

Benito felt her move. He looked up to see tall pines splitting and tossing about like feathers in the desert wind. He leaped under an overhanging ledge of granite just in a second of time as these same tall pines and boulders weighing many tons crashed down, over, and around him. The mud, then the dust underneath, filled the air until he could hardly see or breathe at all. The noise was so great that it was days before his ears quit ringing.

Oh, it was a terrible thing this mountain tried to do to Benito, but he was too quick for her this time. Imagine her anger and disappointment when he stepped from under the ledge in safety.

Then one night Benito had a strange prophetic dream in

which he heard a voice from the sky saying, "Oh, yes, the devil. Well, it isn't altogether the devil. Deep down under old Black Mountain, the devil has his home, you see. Of this I am sure, Benito Anaya. The devil is very worried, for he knows that you'll use this treasure to bring happiness into the world. He can't stand that. It makes him angry, and he pulls his horns and bites his tail and runs around in a circle like your old red dog used to do when he had worms."

The voice hushed as the devil came up out of his pit, still smoking and smelling like burned manure. And he said to the mountain, "Old Black Mountain, I've a proposition for you. One I'm sure you'll relish in the very foulest part of your wicked heart."

"Speak, oh Evil One," said the mountain, "Let me hear this proposition."

"Tomorrow a little black cloud will pass over. It'll be so small that a certain creature on your sides won't notice. I'll charge this cloud with the fires from my hottest pits."

"Might this creature be Benito Anaya, this one who has tormented me for nine years, oh Evil One?"

"None other," said the devil, beginning to cough more and more and getting worried that he might get consumption in all this fresh air.

"What will you do with this inferno you plot to install in the tiny little cloud?" asked the mountain.

"Ah ha," said the devil, "it will descend in the form of lightning and strike this Benito Anaya dead. Dead. Dead!"

"A deal!" shouted the mountain, and all the vegetation on her sides stirred in the great breeze created by her excitement, and Benito was frightened even in his dream.

Then the devil leaped back into the black pit.

"Go on, Voice, tell more to the ears of this *hombre*," Benito demanded.

"The devil leaped into the pit," said the voice.

"Yes, yes," said Benito. But the voice vanished and so did the dream.

The next day Benito didn't even notice the little cloud come over until he felt a few drops of rain. And although he knew one should never get under a tree in a storm, because the tallest tree is where the lightning is most likely to strike, Benito did just that. When the thunderous stroke of lightning shot from the sky, the pine shuddered and many of its limbs were scorched, but she stayed fast. Only a small part of the lightning managed to get through her. For neither the mountain nor the devil of his dream realized that this tree was marked with his sign and was his friend, his guide, and his companion. However, the bolt was enough to knock Benito unconscious and singe and blacken parts of his body. The tree had remained true and faithful. Benito Anaya lived to return.

Benito Anaya rode the white mare across the snowbanks from Casa Mia with his head down. He hunted now, not for gold, but for meat. The buck's tracks were hard to see between the drifts on the frozen ground, but in the banks of snow, where he had broken through the crust, the widespread signs were plainly visible.

The buck had stopped to eat at a clump of oak brush. The limbs were torn fresh. Something had frightened him a short distance on, for he had made a great leap to the side, scattering the snow apart. Then Benito saw where the tracks of the coyote had followed for a time, then turned off, knowing this game was too big for his kill.

Looking up at the Black Mountain, standing shimmering under the deep blanket of snow, Benito forgot the deer for a moment.

"Old Mountain," he said, waving his fist in the air, "this buck is heading for your sides, but I shall cheat you as you've cheated me these many years. I'll place a bullet in his heart, and I will use his flesh for the power to conquer you. What do you say to that, Old Mountain? I feel you laugh at me now, but I laugh back at you, because I know that under your garment of white your heart's black and jealous. You're very much afraid. For these many, many moons in time you've hoarded this gold, and now you refuse to release it to one the saints have chosen. Ah, Old Mountain, you've caused me much pain and long hardship, but you've not won."

Benito dropped the clenched fist and moved on out after the buck. The tracks were fresher now with each stride of the mare. He could tell by the spray of undersnow, where it had not yet frozen hard. Then he found where the buck had made water so fresh it was still foamy and steamed slightly.

Rapidly he dismounted, taking the rifle from the saddle scabbard in the same motion. He tied the mare to a small bush and crawled on his belly across the snow. He edged up near the crest of the rise. He was almost there now, and the excitement of the hunt coursed through his body. Slowly he raised himself to look, and there he was. What a buck! Standing as if he owned the entire world, head high, nostrils quivering, eyes searching, a great rack above his head.

The front bead settled down into the back V of the rifle barrel and centered on the shoulder of the buck. He eased the shot off, feeling the bullet spin out of the steel barrel, plunge across the draw and strike the shoulder blade, burn through the flesh, and split the heart apart. The buck reared up, swung

around, and fell, sliding down the side of the rise, streaking it with red and coming to a stop so still it was almost a noise.

Swiftly Benito raced across, and taking his knife he cut through the bristles of the neck and severed the main artery. He dragged the buck around so that his head was down for better bleeding. Then he walked back to the mare and led her up to the buck, which he loaded onto her now aging back.

Benito gutted the buck and removed the scent glands. Struggling, he balanced it across the saddle and with a leather thong tied the front feet to one stirrup, the back feet to the other. Then he tied the stirrups together under the horse's belly. It was secure now, and he mounted behind the saddle, reining down across the desert toward Casa Mia and his family.

Now the Little Princess Eloisa would not need to butcher one of her lambs for his summer trip. The lambs were sold in the fall for what little extra money the Anaya family had.

As he neared Casa Mia, Benito looked back at the mountain and smiled at her. Under his breath he said, "I've robbed you of one of your own, Old Mountain. Soon now, the sun'll melt the whiteness from your sides and I'll return to duel you. Have your weapons ready, stingy one."

"Papa, Papa," came screaming the voices of Manuel and Roberto and little Maria. All ran out to meet him. "Papa, is he a big one?" "Did you get him with one shot, Papa?" "Can we have some for supper?"

"Now, my precious ones," said Benito, laughing, "calm yourselves and talk one at a time. Yes, I got him with one shot. Yes, we'll eat the heart and liver fresh from his body. The rest we must save for the summer."

"To take to the mountain, huh?" said Roberto.

"Of course," said Manuel, "what else?"

Little Maria held on to her father's leg as he hoisted the deer up with a rope and tied him to a tree limb with hind legs spread apart for butchering.

Eloisa walked across the yard smiling, bringing the knife and the saw. "Oh, he's a very nice one," she said.

"Yes, Princessita, and he'll be tender and good, too."

Benito began to peel the hide back from the flesh, keeping the knife cutting and moving swiftly just where the hide parted from the meat.

"Dos Maria, stand back, so the blood won't soil your pretty face," he said. She smiled and looked up at him—the same look in her eyes, the beauty and kindness, of his faithful wife. The look that had captured his heart and would hold it forever. That was why he called her Dos Maria, Little Princess Number Two.

The deer was sawed in half and cut into strips for jerky. Eloisa took the heart and liver and prepared them for supper. What a feast! The rich, ripe meat hot from the skillet, with a sauce of her own making, *frijoles*, great round, hot tortillas, and then the wild sweet plums made into a quivering pudding.

Benito leaned back in his chair away from the table, took a last drink at his coffee, and shaped a cigarette.

"Papa, tell us about the old mountain. Tell us how she put the bear after you."

"All right, my children, be quiet and I'll tell you about the mean old mountain." He'd told these stories of the mountain so many times he could recite them by heart, but they were always new to the children.

"First, I wish to say, my pets, the old mountain's afraid of your papa because she knows that very soon now I'll take her

heart from her. That's why she fights me so hard. Do you understand?"

"Yes, Papa," they said in unison, eyes wide, ears straining in anticipation.

"Now, before I tell you about the bear, remember this, never forget the treasure I hunt is there. *Comprende?*"

"Of course, Papa!"

So, he told them of the bear and how it almost destroyed his arm. At the end of the story Benito said, "One second more and your papa would be going around like this." Benito pulled his arm up out of his sleeve, dropping it inside his shirt. The sleeve hung limp and empty. The children laughed loud and shrill as he pranced around with the sleeve flapping like fresh wash on the clothesline.

He told them how the mountain had tried to bury him and many other things. Eloisa listened quietly, smiling with warmth and pride, but with fear and dread in her heart, for soon it would be time for her loved one to leave her once more. Nine times he had gone. Nine times he had returned, but the fear held in her heart all during the summer labors that he might not return this time. Although her whole being ached for him the summer long, she gave thanks for the winters and prayed the cold winds would come early on the mountain and send her man to her side. The same love that made her wait and slave and pray for his safe return told her that it was the way of life for women like herself. That a man had things happen to him if he were a man at all. She must, then, give of herself to his cause—to his obsession. There must be something good waiting for him when he returned from the mountain. How many times she had wished she could make a motion with her small hand and the mountain would vanish. It

was hard to keep hate from her heart for this great bulging mass that had taken her love from her so often. Many long nights in the still of summer she would lie alone in her bed and talk to the mountain.

"Please, take care of him. Give him what he wants and he will leave you alone. Beautiful Mountain, your heart must be full of kindness. I beg of you, lovely Black Mountain, return him, my love, to my side."

At the end of the stories Eloisa spoke, "Look, it's snowing again." She was much affected by snow. For at the threat thereof did he return and at the melting thereof did he depart.

"Papa," said Manuel, "let me go back with you and help whip this old Black Mountain. Together we can do it easy."

"No, my son, this is a personal thing between us. Only I, Benito Anaya, can settle it. Yet we all fight this battle together. As you grow up, you make it easier for Mama. Without her thoughts and love, I could not have endured that first summer, and without her faith and labor and love, I couldn't think of returning. Now, we have lots of hay to put up. Our stock will winter well. There's more food for everybody. You do your part, here at Casa Mia. Don't worry, my son, you are with me all the time up there. Although we're apart, we are always together. That's what makes a family, and a family is a world. Remember that well. Anyway, I'll conquer her this summer for sure. Then I'll buy you a pony and a new saddle and a horse and buggy for Manuel and a pretty red ribbon for Dos Maria."

"Come, my children," Eloisa said, "it's time for bed."

Benito and Eloisa lay side by side in their warm feather bed and felt the soft snow dropping against the adobe house. Together they were one in a world of many.

The muscles in Benito Anaya's legs were like those of a mountain lion. So many miles of up and down were worked into them that he could walk and climb the whole day long without stopping except to take a quick breath into his strong, leathery lungs. The mountain had forged this strength in him. So now he walked with his shaggy, graying hair eternally bent forward, and with that hump that comes in the prospector's shoulders from the ageless bending—pressing forward, and with the leanness and mobility of muscled legs and thighs— and the set, stabbing stare of eyes fronting for a dream. The hundreds of miles behind had no meaning. All that mattered was the next step. Each time Benito made another track, he felt sure his eyes would fall upon the white quartz rock, pregnant with the glistening strands of purest gold.

Benito worked with a system today as he had done so many days before. He notched the trees ahead, and upon coming to a certain point, he would notch again, turn square away, and notch again and again, until he had formed a square of marked trees. In this square he walked until he knew every pebble, twig, and animal inhabitant. Then he would tell himself to move on. It was not to be found there. The next notched square would reveal it.

All over the mountain, where canyon lay in canyon and brush sometimes clung as thick and painful as a porcupine's quills, he walked and cut. Walked and cut some more. In some squares, the corners had been notched many times, where he had returned, certain that one foot of the ground had gone unobserved. Then he worked in ever-narrowing, cautious circles, one within the other, growing smaller to a point. Then he moved out, enlarging the circle, until the ragged fangs of

the granite bluffs or the tentacles of the thick brush threw him off his course. Sometimes, in the dry heat of summer, before the evening coolness, the mountain looked much greater than one man's lifetime. Then he would tell himself it was not so; he would find it. Yes, praise to the saints who had promised him this treasure; he would find it. It was only a matter of time. He stopped and gave solemn battle to the mountain, casting his own stones at her black, uneven sides.

"Your solitude is yours, Old Mountain. You have every right to it, for you're but an outcast. Ah, yes, I know you for what you are. You belong to no range or chain of mountains. You are forever doomed to stand alone, rising black and dry, cold and mean, out of the warm desert reaches. You're infected with evil. I've known your treachery these many summers. The milk has long soured in your breasts. You're poisoned with hate and jealousy. That's why you resent me so, why you deny me my right of discovery. Ah, *sí*, *sí*, I know you. It's fear I feel running through your insides, Old Mountain. Look, I stomp on you with both my feet. I stand, solid and strong. And I'll take from you yet that which you hoard so close to your vile old heart."

Benito looked through an opening in the trees, across the miles of sage, so far below. His eyes noticed the deep, soft, luxurious purple, spreading out across the blue-green sage like the shadow of a giant bird, and on to the soft blue of the far distant ranges beyond Casa Mia. A moment later, a burst of golden yellows and orange-reds washed the bodice of the mountain in a glorious blaze of light. Cartwheels of color shone in eternal rays through the castle-high clouds above—flaming, screaming color, reaching high into the sunburned sky, proclaiming to Benito the glory of the universe, as the earth-wide brush strokes of sunset faded into soft pink and violet. The

saints had spoken to him, renewing his courage and strengthening his faith in their promise. It was a good omen.

The day died, patiently and with dignity, giving its life over to the night for a spell entwined in eternal time. The things of night moved about now—cautious, sniffing the wind for foe or prey. Then moving on out for the hunt to sustain the beating blood. Some moved out to die, thereby extending life in others.

Benito heard the rush of the wings of the night owl as it flew into the rocks with a kangaroo rat held in its claws. An old bitch coyote stopped and scented the air. She was lean, and patches of ragged summer fur hung around her. The four half-grown pups by her side waited, watching the old one. Again, she stopped and turned her head to the night sky with a high wail. The pups joined in, and the sound shot out across the surface of the mountain, down the canyons, and out into the desert. Away off across the mountain another answered, another out in the desert, and another on beyond. She moved down towards the foothills and food and life.

The buzzards, the sweepers of the earth, now filled with the hide, the guts, and the stringy meat of a dead deer, roosted together in a clump of piñon, their bellies tight. The branches of the piñon were spotted with their black-and-white droppings. The old mother coyote walked around the buzzards' roost, sniffing the air stealthily. With her pups following, she ran to the carcass of the dead deer, tearing, pulling, stripping at the thin, tough hide, peeling it back to get at the lean meat beneath. They ate silently, ravenously, their bellies swelling bigger and bigger. Their sharp white fangs gnawed down to the bone.

Then the lion that had killed the deer the night before

leaped at them with a spitting growl, scattering the pack and claiming his own.

Up above in some rocks, a mountain hare sat just at the mouth of a crevice. Its nose twitched, scenting for danger. Then it hopped down into the little glade where a few sprigs of grass offered its tempting green. It had not moved unnoticed. A bobcat lay watching with its sharp night eyes. Slowly, softly, gracefully, he stepped across the rocks. Soundless, he moved just above the rabbit. Motionless. He heard the nibbling noise below. The hare raised its head, eyes big. The bobcat dropped upon it. The claws clamped through the tender skin and into the meat. The head dropped, and fangs crushed the neck bones and stopped the half-finished squeal of death. All the wild things of the mountain heard and understood. And so did Benito Anaya.

Benito prepared and finished his meal. He lay, belly full, letting the strained muscles relax, as a drowsiness came over him. He heard, and even more, he felt this life-and-death struggle pulsing, bursting out around him. Even the mountain moved in silent rhythm beneath his body. The pine needles wafted their scent into his nostrils, as they returned by infinitesimal degrees to the mountain's soul. And the stars spotted the sky, defying him to look beyond their light. The wind, cool and teasing, whispered of all it knew to the tall pine with the three aged notches and the lightning-burnt sides.

Benito arose and walked to the clearing, as he had done every night for these many summers. He looked through the darkness, his heart seeking out the tiny mud house so unrevealed on top the moving earth.

"Ah, my wife, I know you listen. I send you a kiss across the desert darkness. It is a kiss of great devotion. I send you a

thousand more of love and gratitude. I can feel your warm body close to mine and smell your hair and see the sweet moisture of your eyes. Ah, *vida mia*, you're here with me. I hear you saying all is well, and you'll be waiting. Good night my loved one. Dream of heaven and of me, my love."

But this night, as Benito lay in his bedroll, a loneliness came upon him. He was restless and could not sleep. He arose and put on his clothes and walked down the steep, winding trail toward the water hole. He could see the mare grazing in the slow-rising moonlight. She raised her head.

"Hello, old ghost of a mare. I've come to visit you, for I'm lonesome for my Princessita and the little ones. I can see that you ask me to mount and ride to her, and I say to you, Blanca, it would be fine and beautiful. The Old Mountain puts such tempting thoughts into my head, showing me the easy, sweet way to defeat. No, I must put down such thoughts. Look at me, Blanca," Benito said, "stop eating a moment. Raise your head and listen to me. See, I'm ragged and wild-looking as the old bitch coyote that roams the mountain. I'm turning as wild as these animals so I may survive. . . . Haaaa!" he shouted, throwing a small stick at the mare. She bolted sideways and then went back to grazing. Benito followed along beside her, talking. "All right, go on with your eating then, greedy one, but you'll hear me out all the same.

"So, you think I should toss the saddle across your broad back and race like the wind to Casa Mia? Well, let me tell you, Old Blanca, my entire body aches to do this thing. I'd love to hear the laughter and tears of my little Dos Maria and see my sons growing strong like cedar posts. The mountain is making us feel this way. Ah, the feather bed, the tacos, the *frijoles*, the hot coffee, the *niños*, and my sweet little Princess pull at my heart like a magnet. But don't you see, Old Blanca, don't you see?

Look up and listen, old mare. Didn't I work six days, building the pole fence across the glade so you'd not have to be tied with a stake rope and could roam and eat at will? What small appreciation you show to one who has done you such favors. Raise your head!" he shouted again, louder.

The mare did indeed raise her head and turn her dark solemn eyes to him.

"There you go again with that look. No, I won't do it. I must stay until the winter winds drive us home. To leave now would break the rhythm of the mountain, and she would have gained on me by perhaps a whole year. Do you think a regiment colonel would win many battles if he went home to a feather bed right in the middle of an attack? Why, old mare, you profane the name of Benito Anaya with such thoughts! It can't be. I must win and walk up like a good husband and father and say, 'My loved ones, victory is mine. Look, I have here enough gold to take us around the world ten times.' As we will surely do very soon, now. Why, old mare, while you're grazing and getting fat on the grasses of Casa Mia, we'll be in Spain at the great fiestas, and we'll watch the matadors and see the big parades. Ah yes, and we'll have a castle like the rocks above and all the fine things the world gives to those who deserve her bounty."

The white mare raised her head, tossing one ear forward for a moment. "All right, Old Blanca, I'll leave you now. Eat until your belly is so big and your flesh so fat that your legs bend from the strain of holding you upright. The next time I see you I'll have a hundred pounds of gold for your back, and then you'll not be quite so eager to race away to Casa Mia. Good night, old mare, and good grazing to you, gluttonous one." And thereupon, Benito turned and started the steep climb upward to his bedroll.

The morning came all too swiftly. Benito arose with a renewed purpose about him. This day and the next and for many more he drove his legs harder, longer, faster. He strained, his eyes searching until they became red and sunken in his head.

The aspen leaves had begun to turn the color of the metal he sought. The nights were sharper, and it was mid-morning, now, before the fall sun warmed the mountainside. Benito walked on, head down, hour upon hour and day upon grinding day. Then the winds came cold and gave their brief warning. He walked even harder, looked even longer.

"Now, it will be now," he muttered under his breath a thousand times each day. "Now, the very next step will reveal it forever."

The storm struck about an hour before sunset. The gray, rolling clouds moved down from the north like icy phantoms. A gust of tremendous force pulled at Benito. As he raised his head, he felt the cold grayness close about the mountain, hiding him as if he were never there at all. He knew he would be fortunate to get off this mountain before the darkness moved in with the clouds.

Then the snow started, big wet flakes at first, mixed with stinging drives of sleet. There was one consolation. Down below in the desert at Casa Mia the snow would melt as fast as it hit the ground at this time of year. The only question, the one he feared to answer, was could he get off the mountain in time? For in the black of night, it would freeze near to zero.

He had no time to pack his remaining food, nor bother with his bedroll. He grabbed his old leather jacket, pulling it down, and stepped out of the lean-to into the tusks of the storm.

Visibility was now only a few feet ahead. He must hurry. The cold flakes stung at his face and eyes, and the wind whistled around his ears and down under his collar. The snow was beginning to whiten the ground, and the trail was becoming increasingly hard to follow. Hurry, hurry. The Old Mountain was trying to cover her wrinkles before he could find his way to the mare. Hurry . . . go . . . go.

The wind howled at him now and lashed out in cries like mourning devils. His hands and face were numb. His exertion drew the freezing air into his lungs. The snow was thick, and he stumbled, grabbing out at the brush along the trail. Sometimes he fell and rolled over. He struggled to his feet and on, to fall again and again.

The mountain had lured him into her trap and enlisted the aid of this devil weather. He could hear her chuckles as he fell against the snow, and he could hear her screaming laughter along with the ghostlike whistling of the wind.

The wind shrieked at him in the voice of the mountain.

"Hurry, fool, hurry to your grave and freeze in my bosom the winter long, and when the snows melt from my sides in the spring, ah, what a feast for the buzzards, and your bones will decay and turn to dust and help cover that which is mine. Hurry, fool, hurry."

And he did, into a wall of moving white. And then the mountain shoved a sharp object into his path and he fell, crashing into the snow. One leg crossed over the sharp fang of rock. He leaped up, but the leg collapsed and bent under him. Once more he tried. No use. The mountain had broken his leg, just below the knee. There was no pain, it just felt gone. He sat a moment hunched up, feeling at the swelling knot where the bone had splintered apart.

The old mountain had him in her powerful arms at last,

and now she would crush him in the powdery white coldness and take away the breath of his life. Coldness far more than the snow struck at him then. He turned and felt the first pain. It raised him up and back, gritting his teeth, with hard-closed eyes. He began to draw himself along, trying to forget the hot pain below his knee that chewed at his nerves and shot black blankets of fear behind his eyes. He crawled until his hands were almost frozen. Then he sat and slid. Then he dragged himself on the side of his good leg, and where the snow smoothed out, he slid on his belly.

He no longer knew if he was on the trail or not. He only knew that he was going down. Once he rolled off into a hole between two rocks, and when he tried to crawl out, the rocks gave way and he crashed into a twisted heap. His head seemed to spin round and round on his body and twist in a redness of jabbing pain. Then he tried again and fell all the harder. He sat, breathing hard, for a time to gather his senses. He could not make his thoughts center. The mountain had caught him napping and attacked with swiftness and ferocity. Every advantage was hers. With this thought, Benito's mind cleared, even though the pain from his leg throbbed on.

First, he must get out of the hole. Oh, how tempting to lie there. It seemed almost warm in comparison with the moaning winds just above. He crawled over and grabbed a piñon limb. With his good leg, and bracing his hands against the sides of the hole, he managed to stand upright. His head began whirling in the red-black void again. He waited for a moment, then with all his strength and more, he managed to get astraddle of the limb. He tried to ignore the leg. It was there—broken. There was nothing he could do about it. The rest of his body was bruised and almost frozen but still whole. Now, he braced a hand across the crevice, balancing one leg

atop the limb. He weaved and slipped, but held on. His searching hands found the upper edge of the rock and, inch by inch, he pulled himself up and out, over the top into the inferno of white.

Now the mountain talked again through the wind. "Hurry," she laughed. "Hurry now, you fool! Ha, ha!" the laughter roared and went away and returned again.

But down the mountain Benito moved. He felt the coldness far more than the hot pain now, and he knew he must never stop moving or he was done. The tiny blood veins of his outer skin would turn to ice first, then the larger veins, and then the life-giving arteries would slow. The heart would stop, and all would soon be ice. All would be over, and the mountain would have won. No, if he must die, he would die at the bottom of the mountain, where they could find him early and maybe the buzzards would be later than his Princessita.

"Ah, Princessita, I cannot leave you now. I have so many promises—unfulfilled promises. Yes, Old Mountain, I will hurry like a fool, for my Little Princess waits for me. And a fire and my children and the old mare wait below. The mare will starve and die if I fail."

Down into the universe of frozen white, down into the numbness and the no-longer-knowing, he moved. It was as he had told the old mare . . . he was like one of the wild things of that mountain. He needed no trail. It was a sense. He had been on the mountain so long now that he was one of them, and that animal sense kept him going and sent him to the mare through the anguished screams of the mountain and wind and the frozen air.

He pulled himself up onto the mare by holding her ankle, her knee, and then her mane. He struggled to her back, keeping in mind that he was really there. He was mounted. Now, if

he could open the pole gate still keeping the mare between his legs he would make it. He leaned over, almost fainting, and pulled at the top pole. It slipped out of the slot. He leaned over further, holding to the mare's mane with one numb hand. He slipped the other pole loose. He knew nothing now but to hold on, as something moved under him. All was solid black and then white. Was he riding a snowbank or the mare?

After civilizations of white time had passed, he felt no movement. He saw no snow on the ground. It was in the air, though, falling softly and melting fast. There was a house—or was it? Yes, a house—Casa Mia. The mare stopped at the yard gate. Benito could make no sound. The mare nickered at her black two-year-old gelding in the pasture, and he answered.

Benito called now, in a weak voice. The old red dog came out from under the porch, shook himself stiffly and let a small bark from his throat, then came wagging his tail.

Benito's voice rose again, stronger.

He awakened, and there were Eloisa, Manuel, Roberto, and Dos Maria. The smallest one yelled, "Papa, Papa, they cut your leg off. Doctor Garcia cut your leg off."

And he fainted away into the deep warmth of Casa Mia.

It had taken all winter for the leg to heal and with the coming of spring, Eloisa Anaya's heart was heavy, for the pain and the loss had been hers, too.

"Don't you think you should grant the leg more time?" she asked.

"But Chiquita, it's healed," Benito answered, "and the mountain waits for no one. Her life is a million years—and

what is mine? No, I must go now. Besides, the leg I've whittled works like a *bruja's* charm, and with the padding you made for it I can hardly tell the difference. I'll do a little walking now. I shall stab the mountain with the powder and steel you acquired for me. I'll return her injuries pain for pain, flesh for flesh, and you'll hear her cries all the way to Casa Mia." And so it was decided.

So strong was his desire to return to the mountain that the tenderness of the leg was forgotten. The first trip in was not so bad. He rode the white mare and led the two burros, their pack saddles heavy with the drill steel Eloisa had bought from the sale of six of her fattest lambs. This he piled at the foot of the steep, zigzagged, upward trail and returned for more. Each trip required three days, but finally all the supplies were delivered to the foot of the mountain, and on the last trip, he took the jerky, *frijoles*, dried chile, and other foodstuffs.

There it was, a massive pile of steel, wood, and food. Hundreds of feet up the sheer sides of the mountain was the pine tree, and just above it the spot where he would drive the giant hollow eye into the face of the mountain.

Leading, begging, beating the burros, digging the end of his wooden leg into the ground one step after the other, Benito lessened the pile at the bottom and increased the one at the top. At nights, before he slept from exhaustion, he soaked the stub in alum water to help toughen it, but by the next night it was raw and bleeding again.

"I must forget the leg," he told himself. "I must put the pain from me and think only of the mountain."

So, he ground his teeth in the agony of the climb and wiped the cold sweat from his face and, finally, everything was there. Then he took the burros back down and put them in the enclosed glade with the mare. His climbing was not through,

though, for every third day he must return for water.

First he cut poles and enlarged the lean-to so he could keep his tools from the weather. He dug into the mountain four or five feet and covered the hole with logs and put up a door with leather hinges. Around this he shoveled several feet of dirt. This was his powder box. He *must* keep the precious powder dry.

The day came. He arose, ate, gathered his pick and shovel, and walked over to the chosen spot. First he knelt and prayed to the saints.

"For many years now, O Saintly Ones, I've prayed you to give me strength to conquer this evil black mass before me with my own power. But now, heavenly saints, if it's your will to withhold this treasure from me, I pray you to at least grant me the power to rip this evil mountain to bits."

He arose and struck the pick hard into her sides with the wooden leg sticking out from under him like a piece of fire-wood.

"I hear your mirth, Old Mountain, but you laugh in vain. In those boxes buried over there I have a thousand times the power of a mere human leg. You'll feel the force that will shake your eye teeth and rattle your insides like a baby's toy."

He drove the pick over and over again. With his shovel he pitched the dirt back from the face of the mountain, but the more he dug the more she sloughed her sides, and it was two weeks before he reached the solid rock. With his axe, then, he cut timbers for bracing the inside walls.

"I don't trust you, Old Mountain. You'll drop one of your huge rocks upon my frail body and crush me to nothing, so I put these timbers under you as I placed them under the bridge across the Arroyo Hondo. The bridge still stands, and so will you until you practice your deceit on me again. And if

you do, I promise I'll fill your insides with all the powder my Little Princess's lambs will buy, and I'll blast such a cavern in you that you'll fall into it, and there will be nothing left but a thin hull, like a rotten piñon nut. I've given my warning. Now, I strike!"

With the steel, half again as long as a coyote's tail, in his left hand and the heavy-headed hammer in the right, he hurled himself at the mountain. The mountain moved and humped under the powder of the explosions.

"Haaaaa!" Benito shouted at her, waving the hammer. "You know some of my pain now, Old Mountain. I'm inside you out of the blazing sun. Your rock is hard, but your nerves are becoming raw and tender as the stub of my leg. As I pound this steel into you and tamp the powder into the hole, I sense your cry of pain. And when the powder goes, I feel you shake the timbers so that you wake all the wild things clinging to your sides. And, as I push this wheelbarrow full of broken rock to the tunnel mouth, I feel your grief at your loss. Then I dump it upon your face, and you are defiled with your own insides!"

The dark socket moved in, and the front of the tunnel stared back, blank, unseeing, like the face of a mummy. It grew ever dimmer. The light of the portal grew smaller as gradually the tunnel deepened. The steel rods wore. The hammerhead flattened. Benito's leg became a throbbing, searing nerve. But the tunnel moved inward.

The long wondering wait of the night was worse than the day, for each rumbling, rock-breaking blast left another three feet inside Black Mountain laid bare. The unbearable waiting and wondering—wondering if upon entering the tunnel he would see the gleaming gold revealed to his starving eyes. It was always the next round that would count. Who

could say what it would reveal? Only the mountain could tell.

Now it took Benito a long while to walk from the face of the tunnel to the lighted hole opening out into the world. He was so deep that he had to use carbide lamps to light the inside of the tunnel.

The winter, white and long, passed and then the spring, and again the walk out was lengthened. There was always the new, clean face of rock, as yet undrilled, undisturbed for numberless centuries. Virgin rock. The next round. The next round may be it. It will be! It must be!

Benito cut the fuses and made ready to blast. He tamped the powder, and all was ready. The rocks belched forth from the mouth of the tunnel, and the Black Mountain shook and quivered and gave up a tiny part of herself to Benito's shovel. Benito walked through the portal into the damp coolness of the tunnel. He followed the beacon of the carbide lamp. He hobbled on, step after wooden step, toward the pile of muck. As he neared it, he felt his pulse swell, his breath come fast. It could be now. He raised the carbide lamp, staring, half-praying, half-disbelieving, but with hope. Was it? Could it be now? He was almost afraid to look. As his chest heaved in wonder, he looked at the newborn face of rock. No, it was the same blue-gray rock as always.

Well, the next round would do it. He started shoveling the muck. In the pile of shattered rock was a fuse that had burnt to a broken spot. The flame had died, but nestled snugly at its end was the explosive primer in the stick of powder—unexploded.

Three wheelbarrows were filled and methodically pushed to the end of the tunnel and dumped. When he plunged the shovel into the crumbled pile of rocks, the powder burst out in

terrible force. The mountain leaped at Benito, and he was driven back, back, back, into utter darkness.

After many hours, when the sun had vanished and the moon had come and almost gone, Benito stirred. He did not remember how or when he crawled from the tunnel, but on the morning of the third day, he looked through a tiny purple slit and saw a streak of blue. He moved his head and saw the tree with the notches. He saw the lean-to. He looked on around the mountain. Yes, there was the tunnel entrance. Now, with great effort, he raised his hand to the massive swelling of his face and felt for the eye that was gone. He sat up then, leaned over, and crawled to the lean-to. With all his strength he tipped the canvas bag and drained the water into his scorched throat. Now that his reasoning had returned, he tried to eat. He managed to get down one bit of jerky and then another. It was an hour later before the third and fourth bites had been swallowed. A small web of strength returned to his bruised and shaken body. He mixed some alum with water and carefully splashed it against his face.

It was a week before he could travel the distance from the water hole back to his camp, in the same day. A week filled with the devilish laughter of the mountain ringing in his one uninjured ear.

Rocks were scattered the full length of the tunnel. He picked them up one by one. He could not return to Casa Mia until the tunnel was cleared of muck and the face bare and clean for the next round of drilling. When he was younger he might have left, but not now. It took hours and hours of dizzy stooping before all was clean and ready for the next drill steel.

"I tell you, Evil Mountain," he said, "You've done your job well. You've turned my own power against me. But I tell you this, if I escape from your sides and back to my Little

Princess, and if she and the saints see fit to heal my wounds, I'll return. And I'll strike you even harder with more powder and more steel. They'll make up in strength what I've lost to your treachery."

Eloisa Anaya smoothed the iron across the worn shirt sleeve. It will never last another winter, she thought. The next trip to Black Mountain would see the cloth part and shred beyond repair. Her heart had felt this same shredding the lonely nights she had lain abed and felt her body age, her hair grow whiter, and the skin of her face draw closer to the bone.

She looked across at her husband. She now called him Papa as the children did. He sat, his head turned slightly for better hearing, with the wooden leg propped out in front, stiff and unfeeling. A cedar cane lay across his lap. The black patch over the sightless socket contrasted sharply with the long, wild, white hair.

"Papa, where are the kids?" she asked. "See about the kids."

"They're all right," he said. "They're playing by the creek."

They spoke of the grandchildren as if they were their own. Roberto was married, lived in the village, and worked in the mercantile of Ysidora Sandoval. The two children at Casa Mia were his. Manuel lived at Cerrillos and worked in the mines. He had five children, the oldest almost grown.

Benito stared at the photograph of Dos Maria hanging on the mud wall. In his mind his Princessita still looked like this.

"Just think," he said, "Dos Maria working in a theatre. What does she do there?"

"She sells tickets, Papa."

"Why does she not marry?"

"I think perhaps she will soon, but she is having too much fun."

"That's good. The young must have fun. When I return, with our treasure, we'll go to visit her in the city. She'll want to see us before we go to Spain. Won't the children be proud when they hear we had an audience with the queen of Spain?"

"Yes, Papa."

"I'm sure, when she learns of our great wealth, she'll want to know us. Don't you think?"

"Yes, Papa. I'm sure she will."

He sat now and stared across at the blue-gray bag lying on an old bureau. It was the only gift he had ever given her. His sixth summer of driving into the mountain he had spent long evenings plaiting a rawhide quirt for Roberto to sell.

"When you get the money, buy my Princessita a bag. A handbag. So she will have a place to carry her perfumes when we go to Spain."

"What color, Papa?"

"Blue, my son. Blue like the skies above Casa Mia."

The children, Tina and Alex, burst in from outside.

"Grandpapa, Grandpapa, look! I have a toad!"

"Let's see, my son."

"Here, look," Alex said, wide-eyed and breathless. "It's a horned toad."

Benito took the toad. Tina stood and twisted about on one foot. "Watch," said Benito. He scratched the toad's belly, and it closed its eyes and remained motionless. Carefully, he placed it on the floor.

"Is he asleep, Grandpapa?"

"Yes, he sleeps."

"Will he wake up if I make a lot of noise?"

"Not for a while."

When the subject of the toad was exhausted, Alex stuck his hands deep into his pockets and said, "Tell us about the mountain, Grandpapa. Tell us about the devil and the bear."

And Benito told them all as he had told his own children so long ago. He told of the landslide, the storms, the lightning, the blizzard, the loss of the leg, the eye, the ear. But the things he would like to have told them about the mountain he could not. For among many, many things she had instilled in Benito was a gift so precious that only the great men have it. The mountain had honored Benito with PURPOSE.

"Did it hurt?" Tina asked.

"What's that, my child?"

"When you lost your leg."

"Of course not, little Tina. Look." And Benito rose stiffly and walked about the floor with his cane and wooden leg making a clicking sound. "See, I'm better off than anyone. I have three legs."

The children laughed and felt the wooden leg.

"Does it get cold, Grandpapa?"

"No, my boy. That's another advantage I have over others. I can only get half as cold and half as tired as the ones with two legs."

"What happened to your eye?"

"It is on the mountain. But I don't want it, for I see twice as much as anyone. You see, I only blink half as much."

The children laughed, and then, with a look of great seriousness, Alex asked, "Grandpapa, when I grow up can I have a wooden leg like yours?"

"And a black patch?" added Tina.

"I doubt it, my children. Few men are as fortunate as I, and they must be chosen by the saints."

"Grandpapa, can I ride the old black horse?"

"Yes, but hold on tight. The bridle is in the shed," he added.

The children raced out the door, eager for the next moment of life.

"Princessita, when do you think Manuel will bring me the new single jack? My others are old and flattened, and I'm anxious to get back to the mountain."

"Any day now, I expect," she said, hoping it would be a long time.

"I wonder if Manuel saves his money from the mines."

"I don't know, Papa. A little, I imagine. He has many mouths to feed, and prices are high these days."

"I'm going to buy him a nice rancho near here," said Benito. "So we can see more of them. And anyway, we'll need someone to look after Casa Mia while we travel around the world. On the other hand, they might wish to go with us. Maybe we could all go. We could hire a private boat. Do you think they would like that, Princessita?"

"I'm sure they would, Papa. It would be a great pleasure to us all."

"The children would probably get seasick. But we might take Doctor Garcia along with us to look after them. He hasn't left the people of the village for thirty years. It would do him good to get away for a while."

"Yes, Papa."

And then the children rode the black horse out in the front yard, yelling, "Someone has come! It's two wagons. It's Manuel and Lucy and Mama and Papa. Come, Grandpapa, and look. Here they come!"

Benito and Eloisa moved anxiously to the porch and watched the wagons roll in the dust behind the horses to the front of Casa Mia. They were all there, even Dos Maria.

She ran first and hugged Benito tight and said, "Papa, you look so good. My, how young and handsome you look!"

"You have learned flattery in the city, Chiquita, but it's the song of the angels themselves in an old man's ears."

They all embraced. All talked at once. The children raced around the old black stallion, all wanting to ride at the same time. The grownups entered the house.

Presently Manuel said, "Papa, get your precious stone, laden with gold."

"Why, my son?"

"Never mind, just get it."

"Here," said Eloisa, taking it from the mantel below the print of San Ramon.

Manuel opened an oblong box slowly. All smiled. "Now, look through this," he said, as he held the large magnifying glass over the golden rock.

"What beauty!" he said. "Look Princessita, just look!"

And she looked and saw the gold enlarge and leap up near the eye in a radiant, kingly color. "It is truly a thing of beauty, Papa."

"Thank you, my children. Thank you from the bottom of this old man's heart." A tear coursed down his lined, scarred cheek.

It was a big night at Casa Mia. A lamb was butchered, and there was much else to feast upon; and the women talked of women's things, and the men talked of horses and ranching and mining. The children listened to Grandpapa's tales until, one by one, they became sleepy. Then Manuel said, "We must go now, for the ride is long."

"Must you go so soon?" asked his mother.

"Yes, for our jobs depend upon it."

"Did you bring my single jacks, my son?"

"Oh, yes, Papa, I almost forgot. New ones from the company store."

"You see, Manuel, I'm anxious to get back to the mountain. I'm far into her now, and I can be only a short distance from the vein. I'm certain one or two rounds will release it from her grip."

"I'm sure of that, Papa," said Manuel. "Did you know that I'm up to be made foreman on the night shift now?"

"No. That's good to hear, my son. Mining is a hard life, but it's a good life."

"Yes, it's a good life. It takes good men to mine far under the world, Papa. I have good men who'll work for me."

"Remember, son, always watch your timbers. If the timbers are good, the tunnel is good."

"I'll remember, Papa."

They were all gone. A profound silence enveloped Casa Mia.

"I miss having children around," said Benito.

"Yes, it's awfully lonesome when they're gone."

They retired to their bed. Eloisa lay silent and still, for tomorrow her man would leave her again.

She awakened and felt for Benito. He was gone! She leaped from the bed, her heart racing. But he had not left. There he sat in the kitchen, as he had done another time so many years before. He held the rock and studied it under the glass.

"Ah, Linda, I didn't mean to waken you."

How like the words he had uttered in their very youth!

Was it all a fantasy? Were they just starting their lives together? No. Her breasts sagged where once they had been proud and full. Her hands were hardened and trembly where once they had been soft and sure. Her step was stiff and unsteady that had once been light and certain as the mountain doe. No. It was real. Only the time had changed.

"There is so much in this rock I couldn't see with my naked eye," Benito was muttering, "so many little flecks I'd have missed. I'm so proud of my children for thinking of me. I'll wrap the glass good in oilcloth and take it to the mountain with me, so I can study the face of ore and see when I near my treasure."

They had their breakfast and their coffee. Benito puffed at an old pipe.

"Come," said Eloisa, "let's look at the stock. Some of the sheep don't seem to be feeling well. I'm sure they need your attention."

"Why, Princessita, only yesterday you mentioned how good they were doing."

"Oh, did I? Well, I must have meant last year."

Benito walked with her around the pastures, hobbling along on his cane, and they looked at the sheep, the goats, the pigs, the chickens, and all.

"Don't you think the chickens may be getting the croup? See, their combs are pale—a sure sign all is not well. And the milk cow, her bag seems to have fever."

"Only because it's full and needs milking," he said.

"Casa Mia has a leak in the roof, Papa. It will ruin our walls."

"I fixed it last week, Princessita. Remember?"

And then she knew it was no use. There was nothing more to say now. She held onto his arm a moment on the way

back to Casa Mia. "Get your horse and powder ready, Papa. I'll pack your clothes and food." She dropped his arm and walked determinedly on her aging legs toward the house.

Benito dismounted the black gelding and turned it loose in the glade as he had its mother and father for so many years. "Eat and get fat, Black One," he said fondly.

Using only one burro, for there was still powder in the powder house and over half the summer was gone, he started the climb. He moved slowly, stopping to breathe and rest his good leg at each switchback of the trail. His heart beat much harder against his chest than in the years before.

"Old Mountain," he said, "I'm getting old and you make this climb very difficult, but when I get inside you again you'll think I am a three-year-old stallion."

It took a long time to reach the top. He unloaded the pack saddle and started back down with the burro. It was dark when he finally made the climb again, and he was very tired. The lean-to and the bedroll overcame his desire to take the carbide lamp and his glass to examine the face of the tunnel. But at the first sting of gray-green daybreak, in advance of the violets and yellows of sunrise, he entered the tunnel. Back he walked into the silent mountain.

"Why are you so still, Old Mountain? Answer Benito Anaya. Is your breath taken from you at my return from your last onslaught? Is that it? It's almost farther than I can walk without resting. I know I'm very near to my long sought treasure. And you know this too, Silent One, for surely your last efforts were made in desperation."

The glow of the carbide lamp glanced across the face of

the tunnel. Holding the light just right, Benito peered hard through the glass and studied the rock long and carefully. What was that? He backed the glass up and readjusted the distance, both from his eye and from the rock, until it was focused exactly. *Wait!* The shine was different from the bare blue-gray county rock. He strained his eye long at this labor, the excitement rising and dying over and over again.

"I believe it is. *I'm sure it is.* Ha, Old Mountain, now I know your reason for this silence. It's because I've touched the first tiny veinlet of your precious hidden heart! I'll drive my steel into you, and this next round I shall put twice as many holes and twice as much powder, and I'll drain your life's blood from you like that of a stuck pig!"

Hobbling swiftly, swinging the wooden leg in a short arc around and out in front, he hurried towards the tiny sky-covered portal. As he neared the light, he noticed with alarm that the timbers were beginning to rot.

"Now, I see through the treacherous haze of your scheme. Black Evil One. The rottenness of your heart has crept into the timbers. If I hadn't first noticed and fired the powder, you would have dropped your skin down over this wound, and sealed it from me forever. I'm on to you, Old Mountain. There'll be no blasting this day."

Nor was there the next, nor the next, nor two days after, for Benito spent his time cutting new, fresh, strong timbers to replace the old, rotting ones inside.

"Now," he said, as he reached down into the brush to drag the last timber free from trimming. "Now, I've spoiled your scheme. When the fresh timbers are set and my powder blasts your heart, you are done. I'll then hear your last dying groans."

Benito felt a sharp pain strike twice in his fingers. He

pulled his hand back and heard the dry rattle. Grabbing his axe he scrambled forward and parted the brush. There, coiled, black tongue darting, head back, beady eyes gleaming, was a mountain rattlesnake. Viciously, Benito swung the axe over and over until he had severed the snake many times.

Only then did he look at his hand. The little finger and the one adjoining showed the two purple marks where the fangs had pierced. There was no time to think. Benito laid his fingers against a pine tree, curled the other fingers out of the way, and swung the axe in a short, swift arc. The axe stuck in the tree. The ends of the two fingers dropped from one side of the blade to the mountain soil. He dropped the axe and stumbled, pale and sick, to the lean-to.

It was several days before the sickness left him, but gradually the hand healed. "Ah, Princessita," he said one night, "as her last hope, the Old Mountain called upon the serpent from the devil's own garden. Though the pain is leaving, it's been a hard thing to bear. The magic glass has told me that I am only inches from our treasure. All your waiting will not have been in vain. Oh, hear me, my beloved Little Princess, hear what I tell you, for victory is ours."

He paused a moment and gazed across the desert darkness. Again, he could see the large, tender eyes, so dark and filled with kindness. He could see the long, black hair and feel its heavy shining texture. And he could feel her heart beating against his breast.

"Oh, my darling, I miss you so much this night." He turned and crippled slowly back to bed, as he had done countless nights before.

On the morn he started the retimbering, easing the old timbers out with the prize bar and slipping the new ones in

quickly. The tunnel was silent. His movements echoed into the cavern and back at him again. On the sixth set, some thirty feet in, he began to have trouble. The ground gave slightly, and a few gravels dropped onto the floor of the tunnel. On the seventh set, as he put the cap in place, a rock slipped and he managed to get the notches only about one-quarter locked. A few more bits of gravel peppered down, and he could feel the weight pushing against the timbers. If he could but make it hold a second more and prize the rock enough to get the notch locked, he would have it.

He strained against the prize bar. The sore finger stubs hindered his efforts. More small rocks began to drop in an almost steady rhythm. Then he felt the voice of the mountain. It was a deep, dull rumble. The timbers moved toward him slowly.

Benito glanced at the blue, air-filled sky of the tunnel entrance. He could turn loose and leap for it. Now the rumble came deeper. The air began to fill with rocks and dust. If he leaped to safety, he would never be able to open the mountain again. Time had decided that. Choking in the dust, he looked out the portal once more. He thought he saw a hawk circling lazily in the blue, blue sky. . . .

MY PARDNER

After twenty-odd years, the image of Boggs is just as clear as the day he came walking towards me with his head leading his body a few inches. His skinny legs were bowed like a bronc rider's, but he wore the bib overalls of a farmer and a dirty old brown hat that flopped all over. Both boots were run over in the same direction, so he leaned a little to the left all the time. His nose was big and flat, and his mouth so wide it turned the corners of his face.

As he moved closer, I could see that there was only one crystal in his thin-rimmed glasses. A funny thing though—he had one eye gone and the crystal was on that side, leaving a single blue eye beaming from the empty gold rim.

He swung the heavy canvas bag from his back to the ground and stuck out a hand, saying, "Reckon you're my pardner, Dan. Well, it's shore good to meet you. I'm Boggs."

"Howdy, Boggs," I said.

"Why hell's fire, boy, you're purty near a grown man. Your pa didn't tell me that. How old are you, boy?"

"Twelve goin' on thirteen."

"Hell's fire, I was punchin' cows with the top hands when I was your age. By the time I was fifteen I was out in Arizona mining gold."

Suddenly I felt real small. Course I didn't weigh but ninety some-odd pounds. But I'd felt pretty big awhile ago when Papa had handed me the map and the three dollars and said, "It's up to you, son. I'm dependin' on you and Boggs gettin' those horses to Guyman, Oklahoma, by ten o'clock July nineteenth." He had gone on to explain that we'd be out on the trail nearly sixty days because every other day he wanted the horses to rest and feed so's they'd get in looking good and ready for the big sale. That was the key thing to remember: balance the moving and the stopping so the horses would pick up weight.

I looked over at the corral and counted five mules and sixteen starved, ragged-looking horses of every color. Well, Papa had more confidence than I did, but I couldn't help swelling up a little when he shook hands and said, "I ain't worried a peck." But then Papa had lots of guts. Here we were on the edge of Starvation, Texas, living in a shack that was held up by hope, on land that the drought had singled out to make an example of. Half farm, half grassland, and only half enough of either one.

At heart Papa was more of a trader than a land man. He'd traded for a hotel once in Starvation, but when the drought came a few years back, everybody left Starvation except the pensioners, the postmaster, and a few others too broke to go. Then he traded the hotel for a herd of goats, and the goats for some dried-up milk cows, and the cows for a truck, and the truck for a car. Somehow or other I liked the old Ford better than the hotel. Anyway, in between he kept something to eat on the table, and Ma made it taste good.

Well, lately Papa had done some more figgering. The drought of the thirties had broken, and people were putting a lot more virgin land into wheat and cotton. They'd need lots of horses to plow with. Most folks still hadn't gotten used to the idea it could be done cheaper and better with a tractor. The way Papa looked at it was this: by July nineteenth all the wheat farmers would have their wheat in, and by then the grass would be made for the stock to finish fattening on. People would feel like buying horses for the next plowing. That is if it rained in early July. The spring rains had already been good. So, Papa had started trading for livestock, and finally come up with this ugly bunch. He and Uncle Jock would head up north about a week before we were due and get the sale handbills out and so on. Uncle Jock was an auctioneer, so it wouldn't take much money to pull it off. If everything worked right, we might be able to pay the mortgage, buy some seed, and put in a crop of our own the next spring.

Boggs said, "Let's git goin', boy."

My horse was already saddled, and I'd thrown the rotten old pack on the gentlest of the mules. I had two blankets, a jacket, a stake rope, and a sack of dried apricots tied on it. That was all. Papa had said we could find *plenty* to eat along the way. He hadn't explained exactly how.

Boggs hung his canvas bag on the pack and fished out an old bridle. Then it dawned on me he didn't have a saddle.

I said, "Ain't you got a saddle?"

He grunted, caught a bay out of the bunch, grabbed his mane, and swung up bareback. We turned them out and started

across the mesquite-, shinnery-, and grass-covered pastures to Oklahoma.

Boggs rode out front and led the string. They weren't hard to lead, because they were in such poor shape, but riding the drag was something else. They just wanted to stop and eat all the time. I was riding back and forth every minute yelling them on. All the same I felt great again—sorta like a man must feel on his first ocean voyage.

Along about noon I could feel my belly complaining. We rode up to a windmill and watered the horses. After my horse had finished I got down and took a drink. Then I reached in the pack and got a double handful of apricots, and handed some to Boggs. He spit out his chew of tobacco, wiped his mouth, and threw in the whole batch and went to chewing.

When he finished, he said, "Boy, get up on that horse. I want to show you something." It took me kind of by surprise, but I crawled up. "Now look here," he said. "Look at your knees. See how they kind of bend when you put 'em in the stirrups. Now look here," he said, walking off. "See them poor old bowlegs of mine? Why you could run a grizzly through there without him even knowin' it. Now ain't that a disgrace?" he said.

"I don't see as it is," I said, having always felt bowlegs to be some sort of badge of honor.

"Well, by jingos!" he said. "You don't see, boy? You don't see? Do you realize that I'm a highly educated man—havin' traveled far and wide and knowin' all about the isns and ain'ts of the world? Young feller, I'll have you know that at one time I was made a bona fide preacher. Yessir, a man of the Lord dwellin' in his own house, spreadin' the true and shinin' light. But what happened?" And he jumped around in his runover boots waving his long arms in the air. "What happened?" he

shouted, putting that sky-blue eye on me. "Here's what happened," he said as he squatted down and pulled off his boots and overalls and waded out into the dirt tank. "Look," he said, "look at them legs. By jingos and hell's fire, boy, how would you like to be baptized by a preacher with a pair of legs like that?"

I burst out laughing, even though I was half scared I'd made him mad.

"There you are," he shouted, running out of the water. "That's another thing that happened . . . peals, barrels, tubs full of laughter burstin' across the land. You see, Dan"—he suddenly lowered his voice and it was like dragging satin over satin—"a young boy like you with his bones still growin' and shapin' should never ride a saddle. Otherwise, your legs will get bent like mine. A long trip like this will doom the young sapling. Let me have that saddle, son, and save you this terrible disgrace. Grow up straight and tall like Abe Lincoln. And besides"—he leaned at me with his hand in the air signaling for silence—"besides, when our duty is done I'll buy you the fanciest present this side of the pearly gate."

Well that was fancy enough for me. I just crawled down, unfastened the cinches, and handed him my saddle. He threw it on his bay horse, then went over to the pack and took out a half-gallon crock jug.

"Cider," he said, tossing it over his arm and taking a long pull. "Ain't good for young'uns," he said, corking the jug. "Cures the earache. Always got an earache." He rubbed one ear and put the jug back inside the bag. Then he took out a long plug of tobacco and really bit him off a chew. "Let's git goin'," he said, and we struck out.

About five hours later the horses quit. There wasn't any way to keep them all moving at once. Well, I had an inkling why. My belly was just plain gone. It had lost confidence in ever being fed again and had just shriveled up to nothing.

Boggs rode back and said, "We'll pitch camp right over there." He pointed to a dry lake bed with a heavy growth of mesquite most of the way around its edges. Off to the northeast I could see a clump of trees sitting like a motionless prairie ship in a green-grass sea. I knew there was a ranch house there with beans and bacon and good black coffee, but it would be late the next day before we'd make it. Tonight we'd dine on apricots. Dried.

He unsaddled his horse. I took my rope and staked out one for a night horse. I wasn't worried about the others running off. They were too hungry. Besides, they would be easy to hem up in a fence corner about a quarter of a mile off.

I spread my blanket out, and Boggs reached in his canvas bag. He had another pull of ear medicine. He fished around in the bag and came up with a coffeepot and a little dutch oven. Then he said, "Gather some wood, boy. I'll be back in a minute." He struck out in that rocking-chair walk of his, leaning to the west.

I started picking up dead mesquite limbs, watching every now and then to see what Boggs was doing. I could see him twisting some loose wire on the corner post. I didn't know what he was up to, but if a rancher caught him we'd sure be in trouble.

He came back carrying a six-foot strand of barbed wire and said, "Come on, let's git goin'."

I followed. We walked out through the mesquite. All of a sudden he yelled, "After him! After him!"

I saw a cottontail rabbit shoot out between us. I took after him, feeling like a damn fool. The fastest man on earth can't catch a rabbit. Well, that cottontail wasn't taking any chances on it. He ran and jumped in a hole. I stopped, breathing hard, but Boggs just ran on past me, right to the rabbit hole. He squatted down, took one end of the wire, and spread the strands about two-thirds of an inch apart. Then he bent about ten inches of the other end out at forty-five degrees. He put the forked end into the hole and started twisting the wire. To my surprise the wire went right on down, and even passed the spot where the hole turned back. Then I could see him feeling his way. His eye was bugged out in concentration. His face was red and sweating. Then he gave another couple of twists and said, "Got 'em, boy. Now the secret is *not* to bring 'em up too fast or you'll pull the hide out and they're gone. If you bring 'em up too slow, then they'll get a toehold and the same thing will happen."

He backed up now, and I could see the rabbit.

"Grab 'im!"

I did.

"By jingos, he's a fat one. A regular feast," he said, and he wasn't joking.

We built a nice fire, and Boggs scraped the fat off the rabbit hide, then we cooked him in his own juice. I'm telling you that rabbit woke my stomach up and really put it back to work. We finished it off with a cup or two of black coffee and half a dozen apricots. The world was all of a sudden a mighty fine place.

I leaned back on my elbow and watched the flat rim of the prairie turn to bright orange. High above, some lace clouds got so red, for a minute I thought they would just drop down and burn a man up. Then the cool violets and purples moved in and took over. Bullbats came and dived in the sky in great swift arcs, scooping the flying insects into their throats. The crickets hummed like a Fordson tractor, and away off the coyotes started their singing and talking howl.

Then Boggs said, "Boy, you ever been to Arizona?"

"No."

"Course you ain't. But you will. That's a great country, boy. That desert and all that gold just waitin' to be dug." He went on a little while, and I looked at the sky full of stars and my eyes got heavy just trying to see past the first bunch. Then his voice came again, "I'll tell you all about Arizona one of these nights, boy, but right now my ass is too tired."

I could hear the horses grazing nearby, snorting now and then, slowly in contentment. The fire was a small red glow teasing the night goodbye. I slept.

"Let's git goin', boy."

I sat up in my blankets.

"Here." He handed me a cup of hot coffee and kicked dirt over the fire.

It was just breaking day. I swallered the scalding stuff and tried to stand up. This took some doing. I was sore and stiff in every joint, but that wasn't what bothered the most; it was my hind end. The rawboned back of the saddle horse had rubbed my rump like grating cheese. I had to walk with my legs spread apart. It was not a good condition for horseback riding.

The sun got hotter. My setter got rawer. Every little bit I'd slide off and walk, but the insides of my legs were galled so bad I couldn't keep up with the slowest of our horse herd. There was nothing to do but get on and go.

By eleven o'clock I was hurting so bad, and the sun was so hot, I got somewhat ill-tempered. I was cussing Boggs, not altogether under my breath. "You old liar and conniver. You old nutwut. You old . . ." It eased my pain.

By two that afternoon we pulled up to the trees. There was a water tank about fifty yards long and a windmill pumping at each end. But the ranch house had long been unoccupied. It looked like now it was occasionally used as a temporary camp for cowboys. It was a disappointment. While not thinking about my sore bottom, and when not cussing Boggs, I thought about the beans and bacon, hot gravy and biscuits we'd have had at the rancher's table. I just got down and lay in the shade and listened to my belly growl.

After the horses watered, we turned them all loose in a little horse trap where the grass was coming good.

"Reckon there's any rabbits around here?" I asked Boggs, chewing on an apricot.

"Might be," he said, looking in the tank.

"There ain't no rabbits taking a swim in that tank," I said.

"You're right, boy, but I'm tellin' you there's some catfish in there."

"Catfish?" I said, bolting up out of the shade.

"Yessirree Bob."

Then I settled back down. "Well, we ain't got no way to catch 'em. Guess we better get to lookin' for a rabbit."

"Now look here, boy, you're givin' in too easy. We're goin' to have an ample amount of rabbit before this trip is over anyway, so let's try doing a little thinkin'. It's all right to go through life just plain feelin', that's fine, but when your old gut is cryin' 'hungry' to your soul, it's time to think. You hear? think!"

Well, we walked around the yard. If you could call his bowlegged and my wide-spraddled motions walking. We went into the ranch house: nothing but an empty table, cupboard, and four chairs. Out in a shed, we found some tools, old and rusty, a can of axle grease, and a stack of empty feed sacks tied in a bundle.

Boggs said, "Look here, the great gods above done smiled down on us poor sinners. By jingos, boy, we're in for a treat." He gathered up the sacks, and out we went.

After untying and splitting the sacks, he spread them out on the ground and began sewing them together in one big sheet. Then he tied some rocks along the bottom, put sticks on each end for handles, and we had us a dandy good seine.

Boggs went back in the shed for a minute. "Here, boy," he said, handing me a can of axle grease.

"What's that for?"

"Rub it on your hind end."

I just stood there holding it in my hand.

"Well, go on," he said, "we ain't got much time."

I rubbed it on. It was sticky and left me a little embarrassed when I walked, but it did ease the pain.

"Pick you out a couple of them sacks to ride on tomorrow."

I did.

"Now, come on, boy. We're wastin' time."

Boggs told me to go to the deep end and start throwing rocks into the tank and yelling. He said this would booger the fish into the shallow water so we'd have a chance at them.

About middle ways down, we shucked our clothes and waded in. I sure was glad I had applied the axle grease in the right place. That water would have really finished chapping me. I pretty nearly choked to keep from laughing at Boggs's bowlegs until he got them under water. The seine was spread, and he told me to keep the bottom just a little ahead of the top so the fish couldn't get underneath.

"Now, boy, move in steady to the corner, and when I yell, come out with the bottom first and hold tight. Then give a big heave out on the bank."

We moved along.

"Haawwww!"

Up we heaved. Sure enough there were seven or eight nice cats, three perch, and a goldfish. I didn't heave quite enough, and two of mine fell back, but the next trip through we got another good catch and Boggs said, "Hell, that's all we can eat, so let's go swimming." He put the fish in a wet gunnysack, and we took a cooling swim.

When we crawled out, the sun felt good for a change. Just when I thought I was going to faint from hunger and the extra exercise, Boggs said, "Boy, get out there and get a bunch of wood."

I went after it. When I got back with the first load, he had dug a hole about a foot deep and a yard long. He built a fire in this hole, and I kept packing wood for it. After the fish were cleaned and wrapped in some pieces of brown paper sacks we'd found in the shed, he mixed up a batch of mud and rolled them in it. When all the wood had burned down to glowing coals, he buried the fish in them.

We waited and we waited.

"Don't you think they're done, Boggs?" I asked, feeling the saliva run into my mouth.

"Not yet."

"Lord, I'm starving. Looks like to me those coals have done gone out."

"Not yet."

Finally, he took one out and broke it over a rock. The baked mud fell away, and there it was, the juicy, white meat of the catfish. Everything was soon gone but a pile of bones cleaned as slick as crochet needles.

All the next day we let the horses rest, water, and eat. We did the same. Then, on the move again. The wide, green tablecloth of a prairie soon turned to shinnery bushes and sand where the sun was meaner and the earth drier. We ate rabbits and apricots until the apricots were gone, and that left *just* rabbit.

Then we could see the little clumps of trees increasing in the distance, and we knew we were finally on the edge of the farm country.

We checked our map. If we were lucky, we could make it to a Mr. Street's farm before night. He was supposed to be a friend of Papa's. Papa said Mr. Street was a pure farmer and wouldn't have any pasture grass for our horses, but he would have plenty of cane bundles to give us. It was here I was to buy two hundred pounds of oats out of the three dollars and start graining our herd.

As I followed the old white horse into Mr. Street's road, I finally figured out why he was behind the others all the time—one ankle was twisted just enough to make him slower. He was a stayer though. I was getting to feel friendly toward him and wouldn't have liked any of the other horses back with me.

I went up to the front of Street's house, leaving Boggs out in the road with the horses where they grazed along the bar ditch. It was a neat, white house with a paling fence around it, and a few elm trees scattered about the place. I could see a big barn, several corrals, and feed stacks. Down below the house was a shack for the Negro hired hands. Mr. Street was rich. I could sure tell that.

I tied my horse at the yard gate, went up to the door, and knocked. It didn't feel as if anyone was home. I couldn't hear a sound. Then I knocked again and waited. Just as I raised my hand, the door opened.

"What'd you want?"

I looked up and up and sideways and all around. That door was full of woman. I felt like I was standing at the bottom of a mountain.

"Well, what'd you want?"

"Is Mr. Street in?"

"What'd you want?"

"My papa . . ."

"Your papa? What about your papa. Come on, boy, speak your piece."

"Well, uh, my papa is a friend of Mr. Street's."

"Who *is* your papa?"

"Ellis Thorpe."

"You know any Ellis Thorpe, Nate?" she said back over her shoulder.

"Yeah, used to," he said. "Ain't seen him in years."

I never saw such a woman—little bitty ankles with massive muscular legs above to hold up the rolls and rolls of blubber that ran right up under her ears and spread over her cheekbones so it made her eyes look little and mean. Sure enough they were.

"Well, what *do* you want?" she asked again.

"Papa said you might put us up and feed our horses for a day."

She went in and talked to Nate in low tones. Then she filled the door again.

"Nate says times have been hard what with overcoming the drought and all, but he says you can bunk down at the shack with the help and you can have all the bundles you want at a nickel apiece."

"I, uh . . ."

She started to shut the door.

"Just a minute," I said, and pulled out the three dollars. "I guess we'll take two bundles apiece for the horses. How much'll that be?"

"How many head you got?"

"Sixteen horses and five mules."

"Forty-two bundles at five cents." She counted on her little short fingers . . . "Two dollars and ten . . . er . . . twenty cents."

I handed her the three, and she brought me eighty cents change. She slammed the door.

I felt sick. There went the grain money. I'd already started letting Papa down.

We took the horses to the corrals and started pitching them the bundles. Then Nate came out and counted them. He was a little man with a quick, jerking motion to everything he did. When he was satisfied we hadn't cheated him, he said, "Tell your pa hello for me," and walked off.

Over on the other side of the corral stood four big, fat Percheron workhorses. They made ours look like runts, and I began to wonder if Papa had a good idea or not.

It was almost night when we walked down to the workers' shack. Three little Negro kids grinned at us from the steps. Boggs spoke to them, and a man came to the open door.

"Howdy. What can I do for ya?" he asked.

"Well, Mr. Street said we could bunk with you tonight."

"Sho, sho, come in," he said. "I'm Jake."

He introduced us to his wife, Telly. She was almost as big as Mrs. Street, but somehow in a different way. There was something warm about the place.

Boggs sent me to get our blankets and his cider jug off the pack saddle. Telly sat out three cups, and they all had a drink.

"Sho fine," said Jake.

"Better'n fine," Telly said.

"Best cider in Texas," said Boggs, winking at them, and they all busted out laughing.

Then Telly fixed us a big stack of hotcakes, and set a pitcher of black, homemade molasses on the table. I smeared a big dip of churn butter between about six of them and let the molasses melt all over. I forked three strips of sowbelly onto my plate and really took me on a bait of home cooking. Then two tin cups of steaming coffee finished it off.

A while after the eating was over the three grownups went back to that cider jug.

Every little bit Boggs would say to Jake, "Ain't you got a bad earache, Jake?"

"Sho nuff, Mr. Boggs, I do. I ain't never knowed a ear to hurt like this'n."

Telly said, "Well, you ain't sufferin' a-tall. Both my ears done about to fall off."

The only earache I'd ever had hurt like seventy-five. I never could figger out how these people were getting such a kick out of pain. I spread my blankets on the floor and lay down to get away from all this grownup foolishness.

It was soon dawn again, and it was Boggs again.

"Let's git goin', boy. Leave the eighty cents on the table for Jake."

I was too sleepy to argue.

We moved the horses out fast. Then I said, "Boggs, where's the pack mule? We forgot the pack mule."

"Shhhh," he said. "Shut up and come on."

In a little while, maybe three-quarters of a mile from Street's, I saw the pack mule tied to a fence. On each side of the pack saddle hung a hundred-pound sack of oats.

"Where'd you get 'em?" I asked, bristling up.

"From Street."

"That's stealin'!"

"No, it ain't, son. I've done him a real favor."

"How's that?" I said smartly.

"Why, boy, you ain't thinkin' again. This way him and your pa will remain friends."

I studied on it all day, but I was a full-grown man before I figured it out.

"Well, anyway that's too much for that mule to carry," I said.

"That shows how little you've been around the world, boy. That mule is plumb *underloaded*. When I was mining out in Arizona, we packed four hundred pounds of ore out of the mountains. *Mountains*, you hear. This mule is at least a hundred pounds underloaded."

"Oh," I said, and we moved out with me staring that old white horse square in the rump.

After a while we stopped at a little grassy spot along the road and poured out some oats. Those old horses were really surprised.

"You know something, boy?" Boggs said, filtering a handful of dirt. "This here's sand land. Watermelon land. They come on early in this soil. Fact, just about this time of June."

He raised his head, kind of sniffing the air as if he could smell them. Then he got up and ambled off through a corn patch that was up just past knee-high. I sat and watched the horses eat the oats, thinking what a damn fool Boggs was for figuring he could just walk off across a strange country and come up with a watermelon. I'd stolen watermelons myself, and I knew better than that.

The ponies finished their oats and started picking around at the grass and weeds in the lane. I began to get uneasy. Maybe somebody had picked Boggs up for trespassing. Then I heard singing. I listened hard. It was coming through the corn. I heard loud and clear, "When the saints . . . Oh, when the saints go marching off. Oh, when the saints . . ." closer and closer till I could see the long stringy figure of Boggs, and the watermelon he had under each arm.

"Had a little trouble finding two ripe ones. Most of 'em's still green."

I didn't say a word.

He took out his long-bladed barlow and stuck her in a melon. It went *riiiiip* as it split wide apart like a morning rose opening up. I knew it was a ripe one. He cut the heart out with his knife and handed it to me. I took it in both hands and buried my head plumb to my nose in it. Good. Wet. Sweet. Whooooee.

I ate every bit of that watermelon except the seeds and rind, and my belly stuck out like I'd swallered a football. Boggs didn't waste much of his either. It was a mighty fine lunch.

When we stood up to mount our horses, I said, "Boggs, sure enough how'd you know them watermelons was over there?"

"Look right there in them weeds under the fence."

All I could see was a bunch of flies buzzing around. I walked over. Sure enough there was a half-ripe watermelon that somebody had busted open the day before.

"I just figgered nobody could carry one any further than that without seein' if it was ripe. Knew they had to be close by."

"Oh."

We got our horses and rode. We soon came to the main highway to Brownfield, Texas. According to Papa's map, we'd be riding along this bar ditch for a long spell now. It was late afternoon, and that watermelon belly had disappeared and the usual holler place was making itself known.

We looked around and finally found an old fallen-down homestead out in a cotton patch. It was vacant, and there was a lot of weeds and stuff growing around the barns and old corrals for the horses to feed on. But we still had to water them. The windmill was cut off, and if we turned it on in the daylight somebody might see it and maybe have us arrested for trespassing. We had to wait for dark.

Boggs said, "Let's see if we can find a rabbit."

We'd already lowered the rabbit population of West Texas a whole lot, but I was willing to thin it out some more. We rode along the fencerows, all around the old place, but there wasn't a cockeyed rabbit to be found. About half a mile from the homestead, we looked out over a weed-covered fence. There was a farmhouse with chickens, milk cows, chickens, some white ducks in a little pond, chickens, and dogs.

"By jingos, boy, how'd you like to have some roasted chicken tonight?"

"Sure would, Boggs, but we ain't got any money."

"Money? Why only a sinner against mankind would pay money for a chicken."

"What do you mean?" I asked, feeling fingers made out of icicles grabbing my little, skinny heart.

"I mean we'll procure them chickens. Now you know the lady of that house is overworked. She's probably got six kids to look after besides her old man. All them ducks to feed, and the churnin' to do after milkin' those cows. Now it's just too much to ask of her to take care of *that* many chickens and gather *that* many eggs, ain't it?"

I started to say it was stealing, but my belly set up those growling noises again, and I felt my legs trembling from hunger weakness.

"What about the dogs?" I asked.

"No bother a-tall. I'll take care of the dogs while you steal the chickens."

"Me?"

"You."

"Now listen . . ."

"Now you listen close, and I'm going to tell you how to get the job done. Why hell's fire, boy, you're just the right size for such an operation."

I wondered how in the world it could make any difference to a chicken whether I weighed ninety pounds or two hundred.

"Now about them dogs. I'm goin' to go off to the right of the house and howl like a coyote. The dogs will come out barkin' and raisin' cain at me. It'll throw everybody's attention in my direction. Get it?"

I swallered.

"Now the minute you hear me holler and the dogs start barkin', get to that henhouse. Here's the secret of chicken stealin': first, a chicken sleeps pretty sound. About the only thing that will wake 'em is one of their own taking on. *That* you have to avoid. Be as quiet as you can gettin' into the henhouse. When you're used to the dark so you can see a chicken, grab her right by the throat and clamp down hard so's she can't make any noise. Then just stick her head under her wing. A chicken's so dumb, it won't make a sound. Now, as soon as this is done, carry her outside and do 'er 'round and around in the air," he said, and made a circular motion with his arms held out. "Like this. She'll be so dizzy, it'll take 'er ten minutes to stand up again and that much longer to get her head out from under her wing. You can steal a whole henhouseful in twenty minutes."

"Do we want 'em all?"

"Hell's fire no, boy. Just one apiece."

Darkness came, and the lights went on in the farmhouse. Every once in a while the dogs would bark. I think they heard us.

Boggs said, "Let's git goin'."

He circled off to the right of the house, and I eased along to the left behind the henhouse. When the dogs started barking, I stopped. They quit for a minute, and I heard that coyote Boggs hollering his head off. I dashed up to the henhouse with my breath coming in quick gasps and cold prickles just breaking out all over. I was scared but at the same time thrilled. I slipped around to the door and fumbled for the latch. The noise pierced the night like a runaway wagon. It was too late to back out now. Besides, I was too durned hungry.

I heard the chickens stir and talk a little as I went in. I stood still just a minute. My heart thumped louder than the chickens. I could make out a dark mass over on the roost. I moved as quietly as I could with my hands outstretched. The dogs were really raising the dickens over on the other side of the house. I wondered if maybe they had Boggs down chewing on him.

Then my hand touched a chicken neck. I squeezed tight, and holding her with one hand I stuck her head under her wing with the other. Outside I went. Whirl that chicken I did. I plunked her down, and she just sat there like Boggs had said. This gave me confidence. In a half a minute I had another one outside on the ground all dizzy and still. Then I relatched the door. That Boggs had started me thinking tonight. I grabbed up a chicken under each arm, and sailed out of there.

Boggs got back about twenty minutes after I did.

"What took you so long?" I asked, feeling kind of important.

This seemed to rock him back for a minute, then he said, "A funny thing, boy. Just as I raised my head to let out that coyote yell, a sure-enough live one beat me to it. I just hung around a few extra minutes to see what'd happen."

The cooking took place.

The eating took place.

The sleeping with a full belly took place.

And I dreamed.

We went through Brownfield before sunup, right into the heart of cotton country. It stood up straight and green everywhere. In a few more weeks the hard, round boles would form. Then, in the fall, they would burst open into the white white of ripe cotton. The fields would fill with bent-over pickers dragging long canvas bags behind them and their hands snaking cotton from the vine to the sack. Wagons by the hundreds would pull it to the gins, and the gins would hum day and night for a brief spell, cleaning and baling the cotton for shipping and sale all over the world. Now, it was still, and hot, and green.

The people in the autos traveling parallel to us all waved. I guessed it had been a long time since they had seen a remuda of horses on the move. All the horses, except the old gray, were beginning to pick up flesh. Just the same, I couldn't help worrying some. In the first place, if that thieving Boggs got us in jail, our time schedule would be thrown off, and one-half day late would be just the same as a month. I couldn't figger Boggs out. One minute he'd be preaching, and the next he was stealing. Sometimes his speech was like a school professor's, and then like an uneducated dunce. On the other hand, I would have starved nearly to death without his help. We were hungry most of the time anyway. Besides worrying about letting Papa down, all I could think about was getting enough in my belly to last a whole day.

We moved on through Meadow, Texas, and then out to the edge of Ropesville. We had a two-day holdup here if we wanted it. There was a patch of heavy grass by the road where a sinkhole had held back some extra moisture from the spring rains. We decided to take a chance on the horses grazing alone on the road while we did a little exploring. This was risky because if someone took a notion to impound our horses, we were done. It'd cost five dollars a head to get them out. That would be impossible to raise in time to make the sale, but Boggs had said, "Our luck's holdin', son. You can't beat luck— even with thinkin'. The odds are that no one'll think but what the owner is keepin' his eye right on 'em. You got to be willin' to take chances. The way to survive this world is knowin' when to duck. That time generally comes when a man has made a mistake while takin' a chance. Now you take my whole durn family. Ma, for instance. She died having me 'cause she didn't reckon she needed a doctor. Now, my brother got killed robbin' a bank. He walked in when two plainclothesmen were making a deposit. He should have watched *everybody* instead of just the guard. That sister of mine jumped in the Rio Grande to save a drowning boy. The boy caught hold of a limb and swam out—she sank. Pa didn't do so bad. I don't reckon you can hold it against a man for gettin' choked on a piece of bear meat. By jingos, boy, you can't hold that against a man, especially since he killed that bear with his own hands wingin' an axe."

"No," I said, "you cain't."

"You're right, boy."

We cut across a pasture looking for a place to hide the horses for a couple of days. The nearest house was about a half-mile away, and we had to get out of its sight.

"Looky there!"

"What?" I said.

"A rat's den!"

It was a whopper—three feet high and six or eight feet in width and length—made up of broken mesquite limbs, thorns, bear-grass leaves, and cow chips, with numerous holes woven in and out.

"Rats!" he screamed into the air, throwing his long arms up as if seeking the help of the Almighty. "Rats! Rats! Rats! Oh gracious and powerful Lord give me the strength to wage battle against these vilest of creatures. Pass on to me a small portion of your power so that I may stand strong and brave through the conflict about to come upon us. Lend me some of your skill and eternal magic while I slay the carnal beasts. Guide and protect this innocent young man as he follows forth the bugle's glorious call."

I was getting boogered and looked all around to see what might be fixing to tear us in pieces when he jumped from his horse and handed me the reins.

"Here, boy, this is your duty. I Iold the mounts that we may yet escape to wage war another day."

He raced to the large pile of trash and put a match to it. A lazy rope of smoke rose, then burst into flames. Boggs had secured a long, heavy mesquite limb, and he had it drawn back in a violent gesture.

"Ah, you four-legged offspring of the devil, I have turned your own fire and brimstone against you. Seek ye now the world of the righteous."

Well, they started seeking it. Rats were fleeing the burn-

ing nest in every direction. Boggs was screaming and striking with fury. Dead rats soon covered the ground.

"There, pestilence!" he shouted as he bashed one to a pulp. "Die, evil creature of the deep. Return to your ancestors' wicked bones. Bring the Black Death into the world will you? Destroyer of man, his food, of his life. Die, rats, die!"

When he could find nothing else to strike at, he turned to me breathing heavily, still waving the stick.

"Rats have killed more people than all the wars combined. Did you know that, boy?"

I shook my head "no," trying to quiet the nervous horses.

"Well, they have. They are man's one mortal enemy. They live off man's labor, off his love for other things. They can't survive without man. It's a battle to the great and final death. People shouldn't fight people, they should fight rats. Here, give me my horse."

He dropped his stick on the dying fire and mounted.

"We better get out of here," I said. "That smoke will draw some attention."

"Just the opposite, if it's gone unnoticed till now, we'll be safe in pasturing our horses here. Let's git goin'."

I was in such shape after the last few minutes of action that I just rode obediently along and helped gather our horses. It was almost night, and that same old weakness of all day without food was upon me. It never seemed to bother Boggs, or at least it didn't show. He rammed a plug of tobacco in his mouth and chewed on it awhile. He seemed to be studying hard.

Turning to me all of a sudden, he spoke. "Boy, I'm takin' you out for a steak dinner."

"We ain't got any money."

"That's right, boy."

"Well?"

"Don't ask so many questions. Would you like a steak dinner? It's too late to catch a rabbit."

"Yeees," I said meekly.

Ropesville, Texas, had two tin cotton gins standing huge and sightless like blind elephants. The cotton lint from the ginning last fall still hung in dirty brown wads from the phone and light wires and in the weeds and grass around the town. It was a small place, maybe a thousand or twelve hundred people in and around the town. But it was a big town to me this night.

We tied our horses in a vacant lot off the main street. I was scared plumb silly. I had no idea how Boggs was going to get us a steak dinner without stealing it. And I just couldn't figger any way to steal it without a gun.

We marched right around to the first restaurant we came to, stepped in, and got us a table.

A woman came over smiling like she meant it and said, "Good evening."

"Evenin', ma'am," said Boggs.

"A menu?"

"It's not necessary. My pardner and I desire one of your finest chicken-fried steaks."

There wasn't any use ordering any other kind of steak in the backwoods of West Texas in those days. They all served the one kind.

"Would you kindly put a little dab of mayonnaise on our salad? And pie? What kind of pie you want, boy?"

"Apple?"

"Apple for me, too, ma'am."

"Coffee?"

"Coffee for me and orange soda pop for the young'un."

"All right." And she went away writing.

In a little bit there was a whole table load of stuff. I stuck my fork in the steak and sawed my knife back and forth. I put a great big bite into my mouth. Whoooeee! Was it ever good. Before I hardly got it swallowed, I took a big bite of the mashed potatoes on the plate and another of salad. Then when I got my mouth so full I could hardly chew, I'd wash it down with a big pull of orange pop. Great goin'! For a minute I quit worrying about how we'd pay for it.

The time came to face up to it. Boggs was finished, and so was I. The lady came over and asked if there'd be anything else.

Boggs said, "Another soda pop, coffee, and the check please."

Well, I drank on that soda and watched Boggs. I'd been scared plenty on this trip already, but he was really headed for the deep end now. Every once in a while he'd grab out in the air like he was crazy. Then I saw him put his hand over his coffee cup like he was dropping sugar in it. But the sugar was in a bowl.

All of a sudden he straightened up and said seriously, "Lady. Lady, come here."

The lady walked over smiling. Boggs pointed silently into his coffee cup. She looked. The smile crept off her face.

"I . . . I . . . I'll get you another cup."

"Lady," Boggs said under his breath, "I don't want any more coffee—that ecstasy has been denied me now and probably forever. One of the true pleasures of life will now raise only a ghastly memory to my mind at every thought. I feel I should bring suit against this café." Boggs rose now and so did his voice.

The other customers had stopped eating, and the woman

ran to a man behind the counter. He looked up, listened, and walked over to our table.

"Please, please," he said. "Just quiet down and leave. I'll take care of the check."

Boggs stood a minute with his gleaming blue eye on the man. "Very well," he said, standing there with his head thrown back, "but you haven't heard the last of this yet. Boy, let's git goin'."

As I walked around the table, I leaned over just a minute and looked in the coffee cup. There were two big, fat flies in there, and only one had drowned.

Boggs woke me up, praying. I'd slept late for once; it was nearly noon. All we had to do this day was feed and water ourselves. It didn't sound like much, but it could turn into quite a chore. Anyway, I heard this voice talking on. I raised up in the blankets and tried to rub my eyes open.

"Lord, now listen to me close. We're goin' to be in the land of plows and man-planted things for over eighty miles now. It's goin' to get harder and harder to live off the land. We made a promise, me and Dan, to deliver these fine horses on time and in good shape. We got to keep that promise one way or the other, Lord. All I ask of you is to help me think. And listen, Lord, if I mess up, which being one of those so-called human bein's I'm liable to do, I want you to know I ain't blamin' it on you. Amen, Lord." Then looking over his shoulder at me he said, "Mornin', boy. It's a great day. Care for a cup of coffee?"

"Uh-huh." I looked at it to see if there were any flies in it.

Then he said, "When you finish, let's go to town."

I swallered. We went.

We were riding along the highway when he spotted a big piece of cardboard leaning against the fence. He got down and cut out a couple of eight-inch squares. Then, with a stubby pencil he wrote on one: I'M DEAF AND DUMB. This one he hung around my neck. On the other he wrote: I'M BLIND. This one was his. I didn't need any explanations this time to figure out what *we* were fixing to pull.

He took off his glasses and put on a pair of dark ones he had in his canvas bag. He put his floppy old hat in the bib of his overalls, pulled his yellow hair down over his forehead, and rubbed some dust on his right eyelid. When he closed it, it looked sunken like his blind one.

We tied our horses in the same alley and started down the street carrying a large tomato can he got from the bar ditch.

"Now, boy, if anybody tries to talk to you just shake your head and make Indian sign language."

"I don't know any Indian sign language."

"They ain't nobody goin' to know the difference. Here, boy, hold my hand. Cain't you see I'm blind?"

I took his hand and walked into the lobby of the town's only hotel. I held the tomato can out in front. An old lady put down the newspaper she was reading, reached in her purse, and dropped fifteen cents in the can. She rubbed me on the head, saying, "What a pity."

I blinked my eyes real hard for her.

The man at the desk gave me a dime, and on our way out a man and his wife stopped and watched us. The man fetched a nickel out of his pocket, but his wife glared and gouged him in the ribs with her elbow. He came up with fifty cents this time.

The drugstore was next. We left there with nearly two dollars. Boggs dragged his feet along, not only looking blind, but acting like it. The grocery store was good for eighty-five cents. Then a garage for forty. A little girl with a nickel in her hand kept following us around from place to place, running out in front once in a while to stare at us. All of a sudden she ran up and dropped the nickel in the can and gave me a kiss. If my knees had been trembling before, they were going in circles now. Boy, I sure wished I had time to get to know a girl who would give up a bar of candy and a kiss for a dumb boy—and a stranger at that.

We made it on down to a red brick building at the end of the street. There was a bank and a dry goods store. The bank was closed, but the dry goods was worth ninety-five cents. By the time we'd covered the entire north side of the street, we had fourteen dollars and sixty-three cents. We went into the alley to count it.

"By jingos, we're rich," I said. "I ain't *never* seen so much money."

Boggs smiled clean around his face. "I used to make this much in a day when I was panning gold in Arizona."

"How come you left?"

"The gold was gone."

"*All* gone?"

"Hell's fire, no, boy, not all of it, just all of it in this one spot. I'm goin' back someday. Besides, I decided to try to find my gold already coined in the form of buried treasure. So I left Arizona and went treasure huntin' up at Taos, New Mexico. You ever been up there, boy? Course you ain't. I keep forgettin' you ain't been out of West Texas. Well, Taos is one of them adobe towns full of Mexicans, Indians, gringos, and nutty artists. A feller had sold me this treasure map and told me to look up a *bruja*. You know what that is? Course you don't. Well, it's sort of fortuneteller and witch combined."

He gave that tomato can full of money a good rattle and went on, "Well, I found her. Yessir, by jingos, I found her all right, and she said the map was true and the treasure was buried there, but a lady had built a house over it. So we went to this lady, and she said she could tell by the map her bedroom was right smack over the treasure, and if we'd split we could tear up the floor and dig it up. Well, I tore up the floor. The *bruja* said, 'Dig there,' and I dug. I had dirt piled all over the place. Pretty soon the *bruja* said, 'The devils are at work, and they have caused us to dig in the wrong place.' Well, sir, she grabbed a poker hanging by the fireplace and rammed it about three inches into the dry, hard ground and said, 'There! There it is!' Hell's fire, I stood right there and pulled on that poker, trying to get it out of the way so I could dig. And the harder I pulled, the deeper in the ground it went. When it went out of sight, I naturally couldn't hold on any longer. Now, I ain't the kind of feller to scare easy, but I broke into a run, and I ain't been back to that insane town since. Ain't hunted much treasure either."

"What about the floor?" I asked.

"I never did write to find out."

He would have gone on for two hours telling me yarns, but I suddenly remembered how hungry I was so I said, "Let's go over to the café and buy us a big dinner. I'm starvin'.'."

"Now there you go, not thinkin' again. We just can't go in there like this. If they catch us faking this blind act, to jail we go. Come here," he said, and ducked my head under a water faucet and washed me off. Then he pulled out a dirty comb and slicked my hair back. "Take off your shirt and turn it wrong side out. Now," he said, "you can go over to the store and get us some grub. Hell's fire, you look just like the mayor's son. I don't hardly know you myself."

He handed me a list, and I walked over to the store. I got cheese and crackers, a loaf of bread, and four cans of sardines for tonight. Then I got us another big bag of those dried apricots and a slab of cured bacon. We could take these along with us, and they wouldn't spoil. Besides, we had lots of money left. I went all the way and bought Boggs two new plugs of tobacco and me a Hershey bar.

We rode out to our camp that night with Boggs singing "When the Saints Go Marching Off," just chewing and spitting between notes.

The next day we just loafed around and watched the horses graze. It was the first time we'd been sure of eating for over one day at a time.

Boggs said, "Boy, you ain't wrote a line to your mother since we've been gone."

"She don't expect me to."

"That's right, boy, she don't. But that ain't keepin' her from hopin'. Now is it?"

"I reckon not," I said, getting scared again.

Boggs tore a piece of brown sack up and handed it to me along with a stub of pencil.

"I ain't never wrote a letter home," I said.

"Might as well start now," he said. "It ain't much work, and it'll do your ma a lot of good. It'll even make *you* feel better. You can drop it in the mail when we ride through Ropesville."

Well, I was out of arguments with this man Boggs, so I wrote my first letter home.

Dear Ma,

I'm sending this letter just to you 'cause I expect Pa is gone off somewhere on a deal. He generally is. How is old Blue and her pups? I sure hope we can keep the brindle one. He's going to make a real keen rabbit dog. I can tell because the roof of his mouth is black. That there is a sure sign.

Did the old red hen hatch her chicks yet? I hope she saves all of them so we'll have fried chicken this August.

Me and Boggs are making it just fine. Ever time he talks it's about something different. He kind of puzzles me.

Is the cow giving lots of milk? I bet her calf is fat. Are you going to try and can everything in the garden like you did last year? Don't work too hard on the garden or the canning either.

This man Boggs is a funny feller. Sometimes I think he's the smartest man in the world, and sometimes I think he's the dumbest. Are you getting any sewing done? Don't worry about patching my overalls for school. I just plain know we're going to get into Oklahoma with all these horses and make us rich. The horses are looking better.

Love,
Your son Dan

There was no question now, the horses were putting on good solid meat. I could tell by looking, and I could tell by my sore hind end.

Ropesville had been good to us. We fed regular—regular for us, and the horses had done the same. Besides, we had some money in Boggs's pocket and some sowbelly and pork and beans in that pack. Things looked better all the time. That's what I was thinking about five miles out of Ropesville when I noticed the old gray horse throw his head back and stop. The horse in front of him had also stopped and was holding up one foot.

"Boggs," I yelled, "come here. Something's wrong with this bay horse."

Boggs reined back, and we both dismounted. He picked up the forefoot and examined it. I could see it was a bad cut.

"He stepped on a piece of glass, looks like to me," Boggs said.

I walked back a few steps, and sure enough there was a broken bottle.

"What do we do?" I asked, fearing what he'd tell me.

"There ain't a thing to do, boy. With the best of care this horse is going to be lame for a month or more. The frog is cut deep. We'll just have to leave him. I'll go up here to this farm and see what we can work out."

He was gone maybe ten minutes before he returned with a man. They both looked at the foot again.

Boggs said, "He's yours if you'll doctor him."

"I'll give it a try," the man said, looking worried.

"Now listen," Boggs said, "soon as you ease him up to the barn, throw some diluted kerosene on it. It might burn him a little, but it'll take a lot of soreness out quick. Then make a poultice out of wagon grease and churn butter. The grease will keep the flies from getting to it, and the butter will take out the fever."

"I'll give it a try," the man said again.

I wanted to say that my hind end could still use some of that butter, but I felt too bad about the horse. Now we were

falling short on delivering the goods, and we had a long way to go yet.

"Let's git goin', boy."

I rode along now feeling blue and upset. After a while I thought I might as well try to cheer myself up, so I started trying to guess what the fanciest present this side of the pearly gates would be. Maybe Boggs would get me a new hat. Or even better, a new pair of boots. I'd never had a new pair of boots—just old brogan shoes. It was a disgrace. Why, I'd be thirteen my next birthday. And that birthday was tomorrow, according to the calendar in the Ropesville café.

All of a sudden Boggs rode back. "Look there, boy, there's Lubbock."

"I was there once," I said, blowing up a mite. But I was really too little to remember. The tall buildings stuck up out of the plains so's you could see them for miles around. "Man that must be a big town."

"Naw, it ain't nothin', boy. You should see Denver, or San Francisco, or Mexico City."

"You been all them places?"

"Hell's fire, yes, and a lot more besides."

I still wasn't going to give up on Lubbock. "How many people you reckon lives there?"

"Oh, maybe twenty-five thousand."

I whistled.

"See that building? The tallest one?"

"Yeah."

"Well, that's a hotel. I still got a suitcase in there. One time I was driftin' through here and went broke as a pullet bone. I figgered and figgered how to get out of that hotel without paying."

"You was thinkin'," I volunteered.

"By jingos, you're right, I sure was. Well I took a shirt and put all my other clothes, all my shaving equipment, and some crooked dice I happened to have with me, in this shirt. Then I tied it up in a bundle so's it would look like a bundle of dirty laundry. As I stepped out into the hall, one end of that shirt came open, and dice and razors and all sorts of stuff fell right out on the floor. A porter and two maids just stood there and stared while I gathered it all up and tied it back tight. That was where they let the hotel down. Before they could get to a service elevator to squeal on me, I was already down three flights of stairs and asking the desk man where the nearest laundry was. Well now, once ole Boggs got outside I was gone. That little Ford car just purred me right out of town."

"Ain't that cheatin', Boggs?"

"Why, Lord, no. What's the matter with you, boy? That's what you call tradin'. I left them a sure-enough good, empty two-dollar suitcase for a week's rent and feed."

The closer we got to Lubbock, the more my eyes bugged. It sure was a whopper. We skirted around the east side of town next to the Texas Tech campus. Boggs pulled up.

"Here's a nice little pasture to hole up in. I've got to get on into town and do a little shoppin'. You'll have to stay here with the horses, boy. Part of my shoppin' you wouldn't understand anyway."

Well, just as we were unloading the pack mule, we heard a truck coming. There were two men in it, and one of them said, "What the hell you think you're doin' turnin' a whole herd of horses in my pasture? I've a notion to impound 'em."

Well, my little, skinny heart was tearing my ribs out. That was all we needed to fail Papa completely.

"Why, my good sir," said Boggs, "let it be my pleasure to inform you kind gentlemen that we have merely paused a

fleeting moment in our travels to relieve for an instant the burden of this fine pack mule. I am a preacher of the gospel. Myself and my young apprentice are heading north—our eventual destiny to be deepest Alaska. There we intend to bring about a revival of the Eskimos that will shake the northern world. Our horses we shall trade for reindeer upon our arrival. There are some things a reindeer can do that are beyond the capabilities of the American horse. Suffice it to say that with another moment's kind indulgence we shall wend our way over the great horizon to far distant shores."

One of the men just stared puzzled, the other one said, "Well, I don't know about that."

"And what, my beloved fellow inhabitant of this celestial globe, can I inform you of?"

"Jist git out, that's all, jist git out." They drove away mumbling under their breaths.

"Well, we shall skirt on around town, my boy. There's a canyon full of grass to the north of town. Yellow House Canyon by name. We shall perhaps find a better sanctuary there."

I was wishing he would shut up that silly talk and quit practicing on me. Hell's fire, I was ole Dan.

It took us another hour to skirt town, and sure enough there was a nice little canyon with lots of grass. We pulled up and pitched camp.

Boggs said, "Now get a good rest. There's plenty of grub for a change. I'll see you afterwhile." He rode off on a black, leading the pack mule. I had me a nice meal. Worried awhile about losing the horse and finally fell to sleep.

It was getting somewhere close to ten o'clock the next morning when I heard a heck of a yell. I looked up, and there came Boggs down the other side of the canyon. He kept yelling and singing. And that mule was having a hard time keeping up with him. There was stuff hanging all over the pack.

"Happy birthday, dear Dan'l, happy birthday to you." He was really singing it out and swaying in the saddle till I was certain he'd fall off. He jumped off his horse and shook me by the hand so hard I thought he was going to unsocket my arm. He lifted the jug from the pack and said, "Here's to you, Dan'l, and a happy birthday it's goin' to be. I got no more earaches, Dan'l. Whooooppeee! Happy birthday to you!" He ran over to the pack and grabbed a secondhand No. 3 washtub. "Gather the wood, boy."

I knew better than to do anything else. But since the mesquite was thin here, I had a devil of a time keeping him supplied.

He dumped a ten-pound sack of flour in the tub. A five-pound sack of sugar followed. Then he threw in a can of baking powder, and I don't know what else. He wouldn't let me stay to watch. Said it was going to be a surprise. I watched for a minute from off a ways. He ran down to a little muddy spring with a rusty bucket and got some water. Then he stirred it all up with a mesquite limb.

Well, when I got back with my next load of wood, the fire was blazing under this tub, and he said, "Here's your surprise, boy. It's a chocolate cake. Now what boy on this earth ever had a chocolate birthday cake like that?"

I had to admit that I doubted if there had ever been such an event take place before. Well, I kept carrying the wood. And he threw it on the fire and stirred. After a while, the cake started rising. He kept shushing me to walk quiet.

"Hawww, boy, watch your step, you'll make this cake drop."

Well, I figger that nine hundred buffalos could have

stampeded right past and that cake would not have dropped. In fact, it rose up in the air about eighteen inches above the rim of that tub and just ran out in all directions. Boggs had taken his earache medicine and bedded down.

For a while I thought I needed his help when it looked as if the cake would fill the canyon, but when it finally cooled and I took a bite I was real glad he was asleep. I choked for thirty minutes. After I got finished choking, I hauled most of it off and fed it to the magpies. I didn't want to hurt his feelings. I should have had some consideration, though, for the magpies, but in those days I was just a growing boy.

We worked our way north of Lubbock through country spotted with cotton fields, sorghum—thick and heavy leafed— and here and there the brown stubble rectangle of an oat patch already cut and stored. On past Plainview we got into some grassland again, and that's where something happened.

We were moving out of a small draw through some cutbanks when the old, gray horse pulled out of line reaching for a special clump of grass. I reined over to the edge of the sharply sloping cutbank and yelled "Haaarr" at him. Just as I did, my horse bolted to the side and I went down hard against the ground. I was sort of off balance laying on the slope of the cutbank. I reached up to get hold of a thick clump of grass to raise myself, when I heard the rattle. The snake lay coiled on a level patch. That's what had boogered my horse.

We looked each other right in the eye. I strained my left arm where I held the grass clump. The snake struck out right at my head, but he was short an inch or two. Now, I *was* in a fix. I could tell the grass roots would give way if I put any more weight on them. If they did, I'd slide right on top of the snake.

His little black eyes looked at me over his darting tongue, and suddenly they seemed as big as lightbulbs. And that forked tongue popping in and out was nothing to make me happier. I could feel the sweat all over, and a ringing in my head. For a minute I nearly fainted. Then, for some reason, I thought of Papa and how he was depending on me. If I panicked and got snakebit, the whole thing would be blown up. Everybody's hopes would be done in. But I didn't know what to do. If Boggs just knew, but of course, he couldn't. He couldn't see me. I'd just have to hold on as long as I could, and maybe the snake would go away. It wasn't advancing, but it wasn't backing up either. It just lay there coiled, its head in striking position, shaking those rattlers a hundred miles a minute. I kept feeling like I was sliding right into those fangs. I couldn't move, but just the same I pressured my belly into the dirt hoping to hold.

Then I heard the voice coming, easy and sure. "Don't move, Dan boy. Boy, you hear me, don't you? Well, keep still now. Just a little longer, boy."

I didn't even twitch an eyeball. I saw him crawl into my range of vision. He had a stick held out in front of him, and he was kind of humming the same note over and over and twisting the end of the stick in a slow circle. Closer, closer, hum, hum. The stick circled near the snake's arched neck. Nothing but the tongue and the rattlers moved now. Then the head shot out, and Boggs scooped the snake onto the end of the stick and hurled him way down to the bottom of the draw.

I was paralyzed another moment. Then I leaped up screaming, "Kill him! Kill him, Boggs!"

Boggs sat down beside me, and said, "Now, just calm down, boy. You're fine, and the snake's fine."

"Ain't you goin' to kill him?"

"Lord a Mercy, no, I ain't goin' to kill him. Why, that

poor old snake's in the same war we are."

"War?"

"Sure enough, boy, he's fightin' those pack rats harder'n we are."

I forgot all about the loss of the horse, and when I found out that Amarillo was a bigger town than Lubbock, I even forgot about the rattlesnake for a while.

I did wish I could go uptown and see all the sights, but Boggs said that would come for me soon enough; besides, we had to stay on the march and take care of our horses now.

Between the towns of Amarillo and Dumas, Texas, runs the Canadian River. We drove our horses along the highway until we spotted the long, narrow cement bridge crossing it.

Boggs threw up his hand and stopped the horses. He rode back to talk to me.

"I don't believe we better try to take the horses across the bridge. We're goin' to block too much traffic. And besides, we've got to have a permit, as well as the highway patrol to watch both ends. It's too late to get either now. We only have one choice, boy; that's bend the horses back to a gate and ride east down the river till we find a crossing."

This we proceeded to do.

I could see the storm sweeping toward us from the west and north. It must have been over a hundred miles in width. We had to cross the Canadian before it hit. This river is nothing to play with. It is full of quicksand and bog holes, and when it rains heavily to the west a front of water drops down out of New Mexico and West Texas with great force and speed.

Most of the time, though, the Canadian is a quiet river.

Many places in its bed are as wide as the Mississippi, but during dry spells only a few small, red, muddy streams trickle through its bottom. Cottonwoods break the treeless plain along its banks, and cattle come to water from it for hundreds of miles up and down. Wild turkeys, quail, coyotes, antelopes, and many other kinds of wild game love the Canadian. But to man, it is always treacherous.

For ten or twelve miles on each side are the sand hills— thousands upon thousands of tiny, rough, ever-changing hills of sand—spotted with sage, shinnery, mesquite, and yucca. The yucca was green now, and the pods were soon to open their beautiful, milk-white blooms.

We rode hard, pushing the horses through and around over the sand. The old gray could only be moved so fast, so that I was constantly having to yell and crowd the poor thing. But he did his best for me.

There was no sun as the huge cloud blanket moved on towards us and shadowed the land. The lightning was cracking so fast now that the thunder was a continuous roar, never letting up but varying its sound like rolling waves. Even without the sun it was hot—sure enough hot. The horses were lathered white. And my almost healed-over hind end was sweated to the back of my mount. The Canadian looked fifty miles wide to me but was actually only about three-eighths where Boggs finally chose to cross.

I crowded the old gray down into the clay and sand of the bottom. There were tracks where a cowboy had crossed here. The forefront of the storm clouds was moving up over us now. I kept glancing up the river, fearing that wall of water I knew had to be moving upon us from the west. The wind was intense, and the horses' manes and tails blew out almost parallel with the ground. We struck a few shallow bog holes where our mounts went through to the hard clay underneath.

Way up the river bottom I could see the rain reaching out into the banks, and I knew a head of water was racing right along with the storm. I saw a small tornado drop down out of the sky for the ground and then return like a hand reaching out of a shawl to pick up something. Several writhing snakes of cloud broke loose in torment. I could hear the roar of the rain above the thunder now and its chorus—the river.

I almost panicked and left the old, gray horse. More than anything I wanted to get out of the river bottom and up to the banks above the cottonwoods. Even if there was a tornado there. And there *was* one just beyond. I could see the inverted funnel ripping at the earth. Black. Mad.

Now we were on a huge sandbar that carried all the way to the bank. There was no turning back. There was no detour. Underneath the slight crust of its top was quicksand. Deep and deadly. The sand shook and quivered like Jell-O. The bank was nearer now.

The old gray stumbled, and the extra force against the ground broke the crust. He went in up to his belly. I rode up beside him and pulled at his mane. My horse was sweated and excited and almost jumped out from under me. For a moment I thought the quicksand would get him. The more I pulled, the more the old gray fought, the deeper he sank. I was crying and begging the old horse now. And it wasn't just because it meant another loss to Papa, but it was a loss to me. He was my friend, this old horse.

And then I heard Boggs. He was riding back across the bar. "Git, boy! Look!"

I saw the terrible churning wall of dirty, red water racing at us. He slapped me hard up the side of my head and said, "Ride!"

I rode on by the old gray, and I saw his nostrils almost tearing his face. His eyes rolled back as he sunk to his withers. In his eyes there was an acceptance along with the terror.

We rode up on the bank as the rain hit us harder and the edge of the tornado squalled on by. I got one glimpse of the old gray straining to throw his head above the river's blood, and then he was gone.

It rained for two hours, and then the sun came out. We were very cold and very wet. It didn't even bother me. The river would be up all night. We gathered our horses and moved on across the sand hills. I didn't look back.

I had a numb feeling as we rode along. We were getting into the last stages of our drive, and we were two horses short. It was just plain awful to let Papa down. I was sick thinking about it.

We reached the edge of Dumas, Texas, on a Sunday. We knew that was the day, for the churches were filled with singing and shouting. I watched Boggs up ahead. I could almost see him quiver, he wanted to get in there and go to preaching so bad. He raised his hand and stopped the horses. They milled about and started grazing on somebody's lawn.

He rode back to me. "Boy," he said, "it's takin' all my willpower to stay out of that church. I'd like to go in and talk that reverend into ten minutes with Boggs. There's a lot of sinners in there and they think they're saved, but ten minutes later I'd have 'em lined up and headin' for a baptizin'."

It sounded like he wanted me to say "Go ahead." So I said, "I'll watch the horses, Boggs, if you want to go in."

"That's a magnanimous gesture, boy, but I reckon we've

got to do somethin' about replenishin' this herd of horses. We just cain't let your papa down. And besides, your ma is staying back there worrying herself sick about the mortgages and all that. Now the way I got it figgered is this: these little West Texas towns all have baseball teams. Today is bound to be Sunday. There'll be a ball game around here somewhere."

Well, he was right. We found the baseball grounds out on the edge of town in a big opening. We turned our horses loose on the grass and rode over where a man was dragging the field down with a tractor and scraper.

"Yes, sir, there's going to be a ball game," he said, taking a chew of the tobacco Boggs offered him. "Spearman, Texas, will be here in just a little while. They've got a good team, but we've got a better one."

"Is that so?" Boggs said. "What kind of pitchers you got?"

"One good 'un, and one bad 'un."

"Sounds about right."

I was sure puzzled about Boggs's interest in baseball, but since we were going to graze the horses awhile we might as well have a little fun watching a baseball game.

The crowd began to gather early. They came by truck, car, wagon, and horseback. The teams began to warm up their pitchers, and everybody was getting excited. Seems like this was an old rivalry.

I followed Boggs around till he found the manager of the Spearman team. This man also chewed tobacco, but when Boggs offered him a chew he reared back and looked out over his monstrous corn-fed belly and said, "That ain't my brand."

Boggs said, "How much would it be worth to you to win this game?"

"Well in money, not much. I only got five dollars bet on

it. But in personal satisfaction, my friend, it would be a strain for a millionaire to pay off."

I could tell the way he talked they were going to get along.

"Did you ever hear of Booger Boggs who played for the East Texas League?" Boggs asked.

"Sure. Everybody's heard of Booger Boggs. Why?"

"That's me."

"Ahhh," and he started laughing and laughing. "You're jist a farmhand. Maybe a bronc rider, by the looks of them legs."

Boggs was quiet for once. He let the manager finish out his laugh then he said, "Can you catch a ball?"

"Sure. I *am* the Spearman catcher."

"Well, go get your mitt and get me a glove and ball, my dear associate."

While the unbelieving fat man went after the equipment, Boggs started warming up his arm, swinging it around and around.

"Now, son," he said to me, and I knew he was really going to get serious because of the "son" bit, "this old arm ain't in much shape and it'll never be any good after today, but I just want you to know I'm going to give 'er all I got."

"You goin' to pitch?"

"You just wait and see."

He threw a few soft ones at the manager, and then he let one fly that purty nearly tore the catcher's arm off. I knew he was going to get his chance. He went around and started a few conversations.

"You folks from Dumas don't know when you're beat. I'm goin' to sack you boys out today." As usual, when they looked at Boggs everybody just laughed and laughed. That's what he wanted them to do.

One of the sporting boys said, "If you're goin' to pitch, I'd like to lay a little money on the line. Now, if you ain't just a blowhard, why don't you put your money where your mouth is?"

"Well now, I ain't got no money, my dear compatriots, but I've got something better," and he swept a long arm at our horses grazing off a ways. "I'll bet any four of that fine bunch against any two of yours."

One man got so carried away he said, "I'll bet my good wagon and team with the grain and laying mash that's in it and a box of groceries to boot."

That was the only bet Boggs called. They shook hands and had plenty of witnesses.

The game started. I watched Boggs fan three Dumas men in a row. Then Spearman got a man on base. The next two up for our side struck out, and the Dumas catcher threw our man out trying to steal second. Then Boggs fanned another, and two grounded out to shortstop. And right on into the sixth inning scoreless. Then I could tell Boggs's arm was weakening. A Dumas batter swatted a long, high fly that should have been an easy out in left field. The fielder just plain dropped it. The man scored standing up.

Well, Boggs took off his glasses, pulled out his shirttail, and went to cleaning that lens. He took his time about it. Everybody was wondering what difference it could make if he cleaned a glass that fit over a blind eye. So did I.

The Dumas fans were naturally rawhiding him quite a bit, and the Spearman team was getting uneasy. I watched him closely. He was up to something. I knew that no matter what Boggs was, I'd never see another anywhere like him. Come to think of it, that's a whole bunch to say about any man. He was at *least* three different men and maybe a dozen.

When he got through cleaning his glasses, he slowly put them back on. Then he took off his hat and his glove and held the ball high in the air. And he shouted so that everybody quieted down.

"Lord, up there in the great universe, heed my call. Lord, I'm goin' to ask you to put some devil on this ball. Just let me use him a little. I want a devil curve and a devil drop and a devil fastball, and I'll guarantee you that the end of the game will belong to you, Lord. What I want is victory. Now I know you heard me, Your Honor, Lord. So it's up to me. And if I don't win this game, bring a bolt of lightning down upon my unworthy head and burn me to a cinder. Amen and thanks."

I looked up in the cloudless sky and thought that even the Lord would have to strain to get lightning out of that blue sky.

He pulled his hat back on tight, picked up the glove and ball, squinted out that glassless rim, took a big spit of tobacco, and let fly. No matter what happened to this game, it was quite a sight to see him pitch. Those runover high-heeled boots, bib overalls, and that old, floppy hat sure were different to say just a little.

That ball whistled in there so solid and fast the batter fell down hitting at it. Boggs didn't waste any time now, just wound up once and let fly. The ball broke in a curve, and the batter nearly broke his neck fishing for it. The next one was a drop—breaking sharp and clean. The umpire yelled, "Strike!" and thumbed him out. A great roar went up from the Spearman rooters.

After that, it was a walk-in. Boggs had shot his wad on those three pitches. He was faking his way now. The spirit of the home team was broken. The Spearman players started a seventh-inning rally, and the way they batted I could have been pitching for them and they would have won.

The game wound up nine to one, and we had us a team of horses, one of which was a mare with a colt by her side, a wagon, a lot of feed, plus a big box of groceries.

Boggs was carrying his arm at his side. It was obvious he'd never pitch again, not even for fun.

When we headed out of Dumas the next day, I was sure a happy kid. As soon as Boggs was up ahead where he couldn't see, I just plain let loose and bawled. After that I felt fine.

Now our only problem, if we were lucky, was the time. We were a half-day behind. At the same time, we couldn't push the horses too hard or it would gaunt them and the buyers wouldn't pay enough. I drove our wagon with my saddle horse tied behind. We'd taken the pack off the mule, and so we all moved out pretty good.

Wheat country sprung up all around now. The plowed fields contrasted to the rich green of the sorghum. There was a zillion miles of sky all around. The farms and ranches looked peaceful and prosperous, but every little bit I could see where the drought still showed its fangs—fences buried beneath drifting sand, fields barren, and cut to clay beds. But this new idea of contour plowing, so the land wouldn't wash, was sure enough helping. I didn't like to remember the dust that came and choked and killed and desecrated the land like the earth had suddenly turned to brown sugar. I liked to think about the green, growing things. But I was young, and I know I'd never have appreciated the wet years without the dry ones.

Night and day became almost the same. We didn't sleep or stop much, and when we pulled into Stratford, Texas, in the upper Panhandle, we were dead tired. We camped about four or five miles from town. It was so thinly populated we could see only one farmhouse close by.

We ate, turned the horses loose to graze, all except the one we left tied to the wagon eating grain, and went to sleep.

As usual Boggs was up before the sun. "Go drive the horses over close while I fix breakfast. That way we'll save a few minutes."

I saddled up and rode out through the mesquite. I was surprised the horses weren't nearby because the grass was good everywhere and they like to stay fairly close to the grain. I tracked them a ways and blamed if they hadn't walked right up to this farmhouse. There they all were in a corral. I felt a hurt come in my belly. A hurt of fear. Those horses durn sure hadn't penned themselves, and we were on somebody's private land. I didn't have long to wait before I found out whose.

He sat on a big plow horse holding a shotgun, and spoke in a mean voice, "Thought you'd be around directly. Well now, boy, where's your pa?"

"At Guymon, Oklahoma."

"Guymon, huh? Well now, ain't that interestin'. What's he doin' off up there?"

"Waitin' for me," I said, swallering and feeling the tears start to burn. I choked them back.

"Who's helpin' you with these?" He motioned the shotgun at the horses. He was a short man but broad and big-bellied. He wore a tiny hat that just barely sat on top of his head, and his mouth hung loose around his fat face. I couldn't see his eyes, just holes in the fat where they were.

"I reckon you know you were trespassin'?"

"Yes, sir."

"Well, cain't you read?"

"Yes, sir."

"Well, then how come you didn't heed my 'posted' sign?"

"Didn't see it."

"Well"—he started nearly every sentence with "well"—"I'll tell you one thing, young man, you'll look the next time you come around my place. You got any money?"

"No, sir."

"Well, now ain't that too bad. I'm just going to have to ride into town, get the marshal, and we'll have to have a sale to justify the damage to my land. Five dollars a head, that's the law. If you cain't pay, I take the horses."

"But we ain't got anything else, no way to live . . ."

He interrupted, "Well, you should've been thinkin' about that when you rode on my place and started destroying my grass."

"Please."

"Too late for that, sonny."

I had to stall for time. I said, "Look, mister, I know you're goin' to take my horses, but first, before we go, could I have a drink of water?"

"Ain't no harm in that," he said. "But hurry it up. I ain't got all day."

I went over to the horse trough and drank just as long as I could. I thought I saw something moving out near our camp.

"Hurry it up, sonny. Get on your horse and let's go."

I walked up to my horse and picked his hind foot up. I glanced under his belly and I could see Boggs snaking along from one yucca clump to another, and it sure looked like he was *eating* yucca blooms. The damn fool was going to get himself shot sneaking up this way. My horse heard him and pitched his ears in that direction.

"Here, sonny, what you doin'? That horse ain't lame.

Now get up on there before I give you a load of this here buckshot."

I got up on my horse just as Boggs raised up and broke into a wild, arm-waving, screaming run right for us. The froth was streaming out both sides of his mouth. His one eye gleamed right at us just like a wild man's.

That horse under that man with the shotgun just snorted and jumped right straight up in the air. When his hoofs hit the ground, there wasn't anybody on his back. That feller came down hard, and the shotgun blew both barrels. The horses and mules broke out of the corral and ran back towards our camp, snorting and blowing to beat seventy-five.

I finally got my horse calmed down, and when I did, I saw Boggs sitting on top of the feller who once had a shotgun. He reached over and tapped him up beside the head with a rock. The man slept. Boggs got some rope from the barn and tied him up.

"Go round up the horses," he said, as he stuffed the man's mouth full of shirttail.

I soon had them cornered, and tempting them with a little oats in a bucket, I made them follow me over to the wagon. By then Boggs was back. We caught our team, hooked them up, and got to hell out of the country as fast as we could.

We rode on now through the day and into the night, and then again. We let the horses have twelve hours on grass and a big bait of grain just before we crossed the state line into the Oklahoma Panhandle. The last lap now.

This strip had once belonged to Texas until around 1850, when they sold it to the United States as part of the territory including New Mexico, Colorado, Wyoming, and Kansas. It had been known as the "strip" and "no man's land" until 1890 when the strip was made a part of the Oklahoma Territory.

It was part of the Great Plains we'd just come across. These vast regions shot northward all the way through the Dakotas, Montana, and into Canada. My hind end felt like we had covered our part of it.

Late in the afternoon of the next day we spotted Guymon. We unrolled the map out of the oilcloth wrapper and studied it.

"The sale is tomorrow at noon," Boggs said. "That means we need these horses in there at ten o'clock like your pappy said. The buyers like to look before the biddin' starts."

"We're late," I said, feeling cold and weak.

"No, sir, we turn up here about a mile, and then it's nine more northeast from there. If we ride way in the night, we can make it."

"But the horses'll be gaunted down."

"No, we'll feed them a good bait of grain and give them till eight in the morning to graze. If we find grass where we stop, we'll be all right."

"If we don't?"

"Like I said, son, there's risks in everything. That's where the fun comes in life."

"Let's git goin'," I said.

We pushed the horses on. They didn't like it and kept trying to graze in the bar ditches of the country lanes. We made them move. I left it up to Boggs to lead, hoping hard he was going in the right direction. For a long time we could see the orange light of the farmhouses sprinkled off across the prairie, and once in a while a car light moved in the night. Then all the lights were gone except those of the stars and a half-moon. It was enough. I nearly went to sleep several times, but I'd wake up just before falling off the wagon. It seemed like we'd ridden a hundred years to me. My body was still working, but my mind had long ago gone numb.

Then there was Boggs. "Take a nap, son. There's plenty of grass for the horses right along the road. I'll stay up and watch 'em."

I crawled in the wagon bed, fully intending to sleep an hour or so and then relieve Boggs. It didn't work like that. The sun was up and warm when he woke me.

"Get up, boy, and let's have another look at the map."

I raised up, fumbling sleepily for it.

"Here it is!" he cried. "Here it is! Look, two dry lake beds, then take the first turn to the left for one mile. Look—" He pointed up ahead, and there were two dry lake beds. A tingling came over me. Boggs handed me a cup of coffee and said, "Just a minute and I'll fix you some bacon."

"Don't want any."

"Let's git goin', Dan boy," he said, grinning all over.

It took us awhile to get hooked up and on the move. The colt bounced saucily beside the wagon. The horses were full, and although they weren't fat, they had lots of good, solid meat on them. They were strong, tough, and so was I. I was burned brown as a Comanche warrior, and my hind end had turned to iron.

Papa saw us coming and headed down to meet us in his old Ford. He jumped out and said, "Howdy, fellers. Why look at Dan. Boy, you've growed a whole nickel's worth. Have any trouble, Boggs?"

"No, sir, not a bit."

I didn't tell Papa any different. Besides, he had such faith in us he didn't count the horses. If he had, he'd have found there was one extra.

The sale went over big for us. Uncle Jock really got his best chant going. When it was all over, Papa had cleared over

twenty dollars a head on the horses and nearly thirty on the mules. Ma could rest easy and go ahead and plan her garden for the next spring. Papa gave me three whole dollars to spend just any way I pleased.

Soon as we got home, I went over to Starvation to drink a few orange soda pops and get my present from Boggs. He didn't show up the first day, and he didn't show up for a whole week. I was getting a trifle worried but figured maybe he'd had to go plumb up to Lubbock to find me the new pair of boots. I'd made up my mind that's what he'd give me for using my saddle.

Well, on the eighth day I ran into him coming out of Johnson's Grocery, and said, "Hi, Boggs."

"Well, howdy yourself, Dan. How've you been?"

"Fine," I said. "Did you get me the present you promised?"

"Just a minute, boy," he said, and walked back in the store. He came out with a nickel pecan bar. I took it. He said again, "Just a minute, boy," and went back in the store.

I figured he must be getting my present wrapped up pretty for me, so I hunkered down on the porch and started eating my candy bar. It sure was thoughtful of Boggs to feed me this candy while I was waiting. I'd eaten about half of it before I noticed the funny taste. I took a close look. That candy bar was full of worms. Live ones.

I got up and went in the store. I walked on towards the back, figuring Boggs was behind the meat counter. Then I saw this table that said: ALL CANDY ON THIS TABLE PRICED ONE CENT. There were lots of those wormy pecan bars among them.

He wasn't at the meat counter, and I asked, "Mr. Johnson, do you know where Boggs went?"

He said, "No, I don't. He walked out the back door."

Well it finally glimmered in my little brain what had happened. I got mad. Real mad. I got me a board, and I went all over town looking. I was going to knock his head clean off if I found him. It got dark. I waited at the back of the pool hall, looking through a window for him. I waited till it closed. I waited till the whole town closed. I was in such a rage, I nearly died.

I never found Boggs. In fact, I never saw him again. I don't know where he came from, and I don't know where he drifted to. But by jingos, I sort of miss him. After all, he *was* my pardner.

ONE-EYED SKY

The cow lifted her muzzle from the muddy water of the tank. She must go now. Her time was at hand. She could feel the pressure of the unborn between her bony hips. With the springless clicking tread of an old, old cow, she moved out towards the rolling hills to find a secluded spot for the delivery.

It was late July, and the sun seared in at her about an hour high. The moistureless dust turned golden under her tired hoofs as the sun poured soundless beams at each minute particle of the disturbed earth. The calf was late—very late. But this being her eighth, and last, she was fortunate to have conceived and given birth at all.

The past fall the cowhands had missed her hiding place in the deep brush of the mesas. If found, she would have been shipped as a canner, sold at bottom prices, and ground into

hamburger or Vienna sausage. Not one of the men would have believed she could make the strenuous winter and still produce another good whiteface calf. She had paid the ranch well, this old cow . . . seven calves to her credit. Six of them survived to make the fall market fat and profitable. The coyotes took her first one. But she had learned from that.

She turned from the cow trail and made her way up a little draw. Instinct guided her now as the pressure mounted in her rear body. It was a good place she found with the grass still thick on the draw and some little oak brush for shade the next sweltering day. The hills mounted gradually on three sides, and she would have a down-grade walk the next morning to the water hole. She had not taken her fill of water, feeling the urgency move in her.

She found her spot, and the pain came, and the solid lump dropped from her. It had not taken long. She got up, licked the calf clean, and its eyes came open to see the world just as the sun sank. It would be long hours now before the calf would know other than the night.

It was a fine calf, well boned and strong, with good markings. In just a little while, she had it on its feet. The strokes of her tongue waved the thick red hair all over. With outspread legs, it wobbled a step and fell. She licked some more. Again the calf rose and this time faltered its way to the bag swelled tight with milk.

The initial crisis was over, but as the old cow nudged the calf to a soft spot to bed it down, her head came up and she scented the air. Something was there. As the calf nestled down with its head turned back against its shoulder, the old cow turned, smelling, straining her eyes into the darkness. There was a danger there. Her calf was not yet safe. Nature intended her to eat the afterbirth, but now there would be no chance. She stood deeply tired, turning, watching, waiting.

The coyote howled, and others answered in some far-distant canyon. It was a still night. The air was desert dry. It made hunting difficult. It takes moisture to carry and hold a scent. Her four pups took up the cry, hungry and anxious to prey into the night.

She, too, was old and this, her fourth litter, suffered because of it. She was not able to hunt as wide or as well as in past years. The ribs pushed through the patched hair on all the pups. They moved about, now and then catching the smell of a cold rabbit trail. Two of the pups spotted prairie mice and leaped upon them as they would a fat fowl, swallowing the rodents in one gulp. It helped, but still they all felt the leanness and the growling of their bellies.

The old coyote turned over a cow chip and let one of the pups eat the black bugs underneath. They could survive this way, but their whole bodies ached for meat.

They moved up to the water hole as all living creatures of the vast area did. The old one had circled carefully, hoping to surprise a rabbit drinking. But there was none. They had already worked the water hole many times before with some success, but now its banks were barren. They took the stale water into themselves to temporarily alter the emptiness.

The old one smelled the tracks of the cow, hesitating, sniffing again. Then she raised her head to taste the air with her nostrils. The pups all stood motionless, heads up, waiting. There was a dim scent there. Not quite clear. The distance was too far, but there was a chance for meat. A small one indeed, but in these hard times the mother could not afford to pass any opportunity. With head dropping now and then to delineate the trail of the old cow, the old coyote moved swiftly, silently followed by four hungry pups copying her every motion.

Eight miles to the north a cowboy sixty years old, maybe seventy—he had long ago forgotten—scraped the tin dishes, washed them briefly, and crawled in his bunk against the line camp wall. He was stiff, and he grunted as he pulled the blanket over his thin, eroded body. The night was silent, and he thought.

Outside, a horse stood in the corral. A saddle hung in a small shed. In the saddle scabbard was a .30-30 for killing varmints. If he had a good day and found no sign of strays in the mighty expanse of the south pasture, he could ride on into headquarters the day after next to company of his own kind. It really didn't matter to him so much except the food would be better and the bed a little softer. That was about all he looked forward to now. Tomorrow he, too, would check the water hole for signs. He slept.

She couldn't see them, but they were there. Their movement was felt, and the scent was definite now. She moved about nervously, her stringy muscles taut and every fiber of her being at full strain. When they had come for her firstborn, she had fought them well, killing one with a horn in its belly and crippling two more. But finally, they had won. The calf—weak as all first calves are—had bled its life into the sand of the gully. She had held the pack off for hours, until she knew the calf was dead, and then the call from the blood of those to come had led her away to safety. It had been right. All her other calves, and the one resting beside her now, had been strong, healthy.

The scars showed still where they had tried to tear the ligaments from her hocks in that first battle long ago; she had been sore and crippled for weeks. A cowboy had lifted his gun to relieve her misery. But another had intervened. They roped her and threw her to the ground. They spread oil on her wounds, and she recovered.

She whirled about, nostrils opening wide from the wind of her lungs. Her horns automatically lowered, but she could see nothing. She was very thirsty, and her tongue hung from the side of her mouth. She should have taken on more water, but the enemy would have caught her during the birth and that would have been the end. She would have to be alert now, for her muscles had stiffened with age, and the drive and speed she had in her first battle were almost gone. Then, too, in the past many parts of nature, of man and animal enemy had attacked her.

In her fourth summer, during a cloudburst when the rains came splashing earthward like a lake turned upside down, a sudden bolt of lightning had split the sky, ripping into a tree and bouncing into her body. She had gone down with one horn split and scorched. Three other cows fell dead near her. For days she carried her head slung to one side and forgot to eat. But she lived.

Later she had gotten pinkeye, and the men had poured salt into her eye to burn out the disease.

And she had become angry once while moving with a herd in the fall roundup. She had been tired of these mounted creatures forever crowding her. She kept cutting back to the shelter of the oak brush, and finally she turned back for good, raking the shoulder of the mighty horse. The mounted man cursed and grabbed his rope. She tore downhill, heading for the brush, her third calf close at her side. She heard the

pounding of the hoofs and the whirr of the rope. Deliberately she turned and crashed through a barbed wire fence, ripping a bone-deep cut across her brisket. In that moment, the man roped her calf and dismounted to tie its feet. She heard the bawling, whirled, and charged at the man. She caught him with her horn just above the knee as he tried to dodge. She whirled to make another pass and drive the horns home. Then another man rode at her, and the evil, inescapable snake of a rope sailed from his arm and encircled her neck. Three times he turned off, jerking her up high and then down hard into the earth, tearing her breath from her body until she stood addled and half blind. Then they stretched her out again and turned her loose. She had learned her lesson hard. During the stiff winters and wet spells, she limped where the shoulder muscles had been torn apart.

But the worst winter of all was when the snow fell two feet deep and crusted over, isolating the herd miles from the ranch house. During the dry summer, they had walked twice as far as usual to find the short, shriveled grass. She and the others had gone into the winter weak, and their bellies dragged in the drifts. When they tried to walk on top of the white desert, the crust broke and they went down struggling, breathing snow and cold into their lungs, sapping their small strength. The icy crust cut their feet, and they left red streaks in the whiteness. And the wind came driving through their long hair, coating their eyes and nostrils with ice. They'd wandered blindly, piling into deep drifts, perishing.

Finally, the wagons—pulled by those same horses she had hated so much—broke through the snow. They tailed her up, and braced her, and got some hay into her mouth. Once more, she survived.

The old cow had a past, and it showed in her ragged,

bony, tired, bent, scarred body. And it showed in her ever-weakening neck as the head dropped a fraction lower each time she shook her defiance at the night and the unseen enemy.

The moon came now and caressed the land with pale blueness. It was like a single, headless, phosphorescent eye staring at the earth, seeing all, acknowledging nothing. The moon made shadows and into these she stared, and it would seem to move and then she would ready herself for the attack. But it didn't come. Why did they wait?

The night was long, and the moon seemed to hang for a week, then the sun moved up to the edge of the world, chasing the moon away.

Her tongue was pushed out further now, and her eyes were glazed, but she stood and turned and kept her guard. She saw the old, mangy coyote directly down the draw facing her, sitting up on its haunches panting, grinning, waiting. It took her awhile to see the pups. They were spotted about the hills, surrounding her. But these did not worry her. They would not move until the old one did. Nevertheless, she cast her dimming eyes at them, letting them know she knew—letting them know she was ready.

The calf stirred and raised its head and found the glorious world. First it must feed. She moved swiftly to it, watching the old coyote as she did so. The new one struggled up, finding its way to the teat. The cow saw the muscles tense all over the old coyote. Its head tilted forward as did its pointed ears. Then it moved from side to side, inching closer at each turn. The pups got to their feet, ready for the signal. But it didn't come. The old coyote retreated. It was a war of nerves. And because the coyote fights and dies in silence, when the time arrived there would be no signal visible to the cow, only to the pups.

Now the calf wanted to explore. It wanted to know into

what it had been born. Already the color and the form of plant and rock and sky were things of wonder. There was so much to see and so little time for it. Again the mother bedded down her calf—a heifer it was—and soon the warm air and full stomach comforted it.

By midmorning, the coyote had faked ten charges. And ten times the cow had braced to take the old one first and receive and bear the rear and flanking attacks until she could turn and give contest. She knew from the past they would all hit her at once, diving, feinting, tearing from all sides. But if she could keep the calf from being mortally wounded until she disposed of the old one, they had a chance. With each rise in temperature, with each drying, burning moment of the sun without water, her chances lessened.

By noon, the heat was almost blinding her. She felt the trembling and faltering in her legs. All the old wounds were making themselves known now, and her tongue hung down, parched and beginning to swell. Her breathing came hard and heavy. The nostrils caked from the powdered dirt of her restlessness, and her eyes filled around the edges and watered incessantly. But the coyote waited. And so did the old cow. Life had always been a matter of waiting—waiting for the calf each year, waiting for the greenness of spring, waiting for the wind to die and cold to quit and the snow to melt. But, win or lose, she would never see another spring. They would find her this fall and ship her away to the slaughterhouse. And if they didn't, the winter, the inexorable winter winds, would drive through her old bones and finish her. But now she had a chore, a life-and-death chore for sure. She would do her natural best.

In the middle of the afternoon, she imagined she could smell the water, so near and yet so far away. She bawled out of her nearly closed throat, and the tongue was black, and down

the other side of her mouth thick cottonlike strings of saliva hung and evaporated in the interminable heat. Her legs had gradually spread apart, and she wove from side to side, taking all her strength now just to stand. And right in the pathway to the water sat the laughing coyote beginning to move back and forth again, closer. Closer. As the sun moved lower and lower, so the coyote came nearer, lying down, looking straight at her.

The coyote lay very still, nothing moving but its pink tongue. Yellow eyes watching, glowing like suns. Ten minutes. Twenty minutes. The coyote came from the ground without warning, straight in and fast. The cow knew the others were coming too. She braced herself.

The mother coyote followed the trail into scent range of the old cow. Her nostrils told her of the new one. Cautiously she moved up now, almost like a cat. The young tried mightily to do as well. It was no use. The quick, intense movement of the cow revealed her knowledge of their presence. They would have to wait. Methodically, she went about spotting her young. She ringed the old cow in, giving soundless directions to her pups to stay put.

The scent of birth, the calf, the old cow all brought taste glands into action. The natural impulse was to attack, as their stomachs drew narrow and craving. But the coyote could tell from the alertness of the old cow that an early assault would be sure death to some. The hours would be long, but the cow would weaken. Much of the moisture had been drained from her body in the birth. The sun would be their ally. They could have the early luxurious feast of the tender veal, and the lean meat of the old cow would last for days—even with the vul-

tures and the magpies to contend with. She could fatten and strengthen the pups and make them ready for mating as her mother had done her. Yes, her mother had been a good teacher, and she had learned well. She had been taught to hunt under rotten logs, cow chips, and anthills for insects in case of hard times. The field mouse had often saved her from starvation. The lowly grasshopper had filled her belly many times and given her strength to catch larger, tastier game. She learned to steal into a hen yard, make a quick dash, throttling the fowl and escaping before the rancher could get his guns. All of these things she had taught or was teaching her own. But now must come the ultimate lesson—how to down and kill an animal weighing as much as fifteen of their own kind. Besides, they were desperate in their near-starvation.

The old coyote took the main chance in locating herself in the path of the water hole. This was the weak point, and she must handle it with care, cunning, and courage. She could not fail, for they, too, would weaken in the long vigil.

She carried a .30-30 slug in her belly from the past. She only felt it on cold or hungry nights. Her tail was shortened and ugly at the end. Her ear was split and torn. A scar ran across her back. One foot was minus two toes.

The ear and tail wounds had come at about the same time. She had learned a hard lesson from this action. She was almost grown then, and hunted with the rest of the litter. They had stopped behind a clump of bear grass, watching the pickup truck circle slowly. They had seen these things before, but no danger had threatened. Suddenly, the thing stopped. From its back dropped six large, running hounds. Two teams.

The coyotes moved out too late. Instinct split them in three directions. But the hounds had their speed, and in less than a quarter of a mile each team had downed one of the

brood. She alone escaped. On a little rise she whirled, watching the hounds bear down on her brother and sister, crushing the life away with their awful fanged jaws. She sailed down from the hill and at full speed crashed into the nearest team, knocking them loose and giving her brother a chance to rise. But it didn't work. Two of the hounds flung the wounded one against the earth again. The third gave chase. She strained away in terror, knowing she could not compete with its size and strength. The hound reached for her throat, but missed her and ripped the ear apart instead. They both rolled in a choking spurt of dust. As she rose, the hound clamped her tail. She broke free, leaving a humiliating part of herself in his jaws. The chase was more uphill now, and she learned that hounds slowed on that sort of run, and never again was she caught on the level or going downhill. She escaped. Alive. Wiser. Alone.

She learned to respect the metallic wheeled things for another reason. She had watched one from a safe distance, as far as hounds were concerned, and suddenly a black something stuck from it and then something struck her in the belly, knocking her over and down. It had been close. She bled badly inside, and by the time the bleeding clotted, she was very weak from hunger. All that saved her was the finding of a wounded antelope dragging itself into the tall grass of the prairie to die. But now she could smell a gun from a considerable distance. They would not hurt her again in this manner.

Her first sister had eaten poison and died before her eyes. They would not slay her in this vile way, either.

The scar on her back had come from one of those men who whirl the rope and ride horses. She was looking in a sheep pasture for a lamb to carry to her first litter of pups. She was so intent on her job she did not see the cowboy coming through the gate some half-mile distant. But as he neared, she felt him

even before she cast her glance back over her shoulder. He came on full speed on a fast quarter horse, whirling the rope. She did not know what it was, but she felt its danger as she did that of a gun. He was upon her, and she heard the whirr of the rope mingled with the ground-jarring thump of hoofs. She hit the many-wired sheep fence without slacking speed. She went through, tearing her back on the vicious barbs. Her neck was sore and twisted for many days. But she lived to hunt again.

The worst of all were the steel jaws the men put in the earth. Once, when she had been hungry, the scent of hog cracklings, and also the urine of one of her own, came to her. Bait. This gave her the confidence to inspect, even though the faint scent of man was intermingled. The jaws had grabbed her as she vainly leaped away. She struck the end of the chain where it ran up out of the ground and tightened between the trap and the heavy rock that anchored it. She fought wildly and in great pain for a while, gnawing at her foot until exhaustion stilled her violent action.

She studied the rusty, hard, impersonal steel. It had her. But if she was to die, she would do it on the mesa—her home. Foot by painful foot, yard by wrenching yard, she dragged the rock. The man had intended her to hang the trap in some brush flexible enough to keep from tearing the foot loose. It hung, all right, hundreds of times, but never for long.

It took her two days to get to the edge of the mesa. The foot was swollen almost to the knee joint now, and her yellow eyes were red from suffering. Then the stone hung between a crack in the rocks. She fell off the other side and rolled down the rough boulders. The trap and a part of her foot remained in the rocks.

She lived again, less able than before.

Under the recent rising of the staring moon, the coyote

studied the old cow. It was obvious she was weakening. Soon she would lie down and then . . . but the old cow stood, and at the break of day she suckled her young, looking straight at the coyote and shaking her head in answer to the coyote's slavering jaws. The coyote moved in now, taunting, teasing, draining another ounce of strength from the old cow.

The sun came soon, hot and red, striking the old cow in the side of her head. The pups squatted and waited with hunger pounding at their every nerve.

By midday the old coyote could feel the muscles trembling and jerking with weakness in her forelegs, and the stomach walls seemed glued together, devouring themselves. She badly needed water and food now. At times, the earth diffused into the molten rays of the sun, and it looked as if the cow had dissolved. At other moments, she bunched her muscles, imagining the cow attacking. She sat with her tongue out and an eternal laughing expression in all her face except the eyes. They seared through the sun's rays, hungrily, with a quiet desperation and sureness.

The old cow's head was drooping now. She was slipping fast. But still she stood, and every time the coyote moved in her snake-track advance, the cow raised her head a little and tossed the pointed swords.

There was no backing out now. No changing of plans. The old mother coyote and her brood would soon be so weakened they would surely fall prey to one of their many worldly enemies. Survival now meant the death of the old cow.

The coyote drew in its dry tongue and dropped it again into the dry air and waited. The sun moved on, and the old cow's legs spread a little more. The coyote could see her weaving and straining to stay upright. The tender, living veal of the calf lay folded up beside her.

Now the time was present. She sent her message of alertness to her pups. They stood ready, watching, muscles bunched, hearts pounding above the strain of hunger, thirst, and heat. She moved forward and lay down to deceive the old cow. Motionless, she waited and waited more. All of her being cried to lunge forward, but still she waited. She had decided on the cow's muzzle. She would dart in between the horns, lock her fangs in their breathing softness, and hang on until the aid of her pups downed the old cow. Then? It would be over shortly. A bit torn here and there, and the loss of blood would finish her. Then the feast.

The burning eyes of the old coyote and the old cow were fixed on each other now. They both knew what they must do. The old coyote sent the unseen, unmoving signal to her pups, and she came from the ground at the same instant, aiming straight and swift between the horns of the old cow.

The man arose from the bunk as stiffly as he had crawled into it. It was not quite daybreak. He clothed himself and pulled hard to get his boots on. He built a fire in the squatty iron stove and put the coffeepot on. Then he washed his face and hands in cold water. He placed a skillet on the stove by the coffeepot. Methodically, he sliced thick chunks of bacon from the hog side. He took the last of the sourdough batter, tore small balls from it, placing them in a dutch oven on the stove. This done, he rolled a smoke, coughing after the first puff. Soon he had a large tin cup of scalding coffee. Another cigarette, another cup. Then he ate. He wiped up the syrup on his plate with his bread. He washed the utensils and put them

back on the shelf. He, or someone else, would be here another time. He went out to the corral.

If he was lucky this day and found no strays, he could head for the main ranch house tomorrow morning or, if the moon was good, he might ride on in tonight. He had two horses here. One ran in a small horse trap adjoining the corrals. The other he had kept up for the ride today.

He brushed his horse's back with his hand and under his belly where the cinches would fit, to be sure nothing was lodged in the hair that would cut or stick. He bridled and saddled, put on his chaps and spurs, and led the horse up a few steps before mounting. He rode him around the corral several times to limber him up. Then he dismounted, opened the gate, got back on, and rode south just as the sun was melting the night.

It was eight miles in a beeline to the water hole. If there were a stray in the huge pasture, it would be nearby. He would probably have a twelve-mile ride, what with checking out the sign in the draw and gullies.

The sun was up now, hot for so early in the morning. It was the kind of day that made all living creatures seek shade. Well, he had always wanted a little place with lots of shade trees and water. Especially water. It wouldn't matter how big it was if there was just plenty of water. He would never forget the drought that had sent his family to the final sheriff's sale and moved them from their ranch into a tent on the edge of the little western town to take other folks' laundry, charity, handouts. His pa had already loaned him out to local ranchers. So, he just took a steady job with one of them. At first he worked only for his board and blanket. He gardened, he milked, he shoveled manure out of barns. He patched roofs. He rebuilt corrals. He chopped a whole year's supply of fire-

wood. He ran rabbits in holes and twisted them out with the split end of a barbed wire.

And then the drought was over, and the grass and cattle came back to the land. He was promoted to horse wrangler, which only meant one more chore. He was up before anyone in the morning, riding into the horse pasture, bringing in the day's mounts for the cowboys. But things finally got better. His boss saw him top out a waspy bronc, and he was allowed to ride with the men. He got five dollars a month and felt proud. Mighty proud. He learned the ways of the range and the handling of cattle and horses. And at the age of seventeen, he could draw down twenty dollars a month with room and board. By the time he had worked on ten or twelve different outfits and reached the age of twenty-five, he could demand and get thirty dollars a month. Things weren't all bad.

Then a fellow cowboy with a talent for talk convinced him they were in the wrong business.

"Now look here, Snake" (that was his name at the time from being bitten by a rattlesnake), "we're makin' thirty dollars a month, right?"

"Yeah."

"Well, how much you figure a broke-out saddle horse would bring?"

"Oh, 'round thirty, forty dollars."

"There you are. Now, if a man could ride out say eight or ten a month?"

"I'll have to get a pencil. Besides where you goin' to get that many horses and how much you got to give for them?"

"That's just the deal. Up north in the rough country there's hundreds of wild horses. Now, I had some experience at catching them boogers when I was a kid. We're crazier than hell stayin' around here when we can get rich on our own."

So, he took all he had, two hundred and ten dollars, two head of saddle horses, one saddle, four used ropes, and moved north with the talkin' cowboy. The money went fast. It was used to buy pack mules and supplies.

They pitched camp and started riding the hills and canyons for sign. The horses were there, all right. But a man could ride all day and never actually see anything but tracks. They were wilder than deer by a whole lot. So the two cowboys set to work building brush corral traps in the narrow part of some canyons on the trail to the watering places. Then they built a round pole corral near camp to break the horses out. It took some wild, reckless riding to pen these animals, but pen some of them they did. Then they found the horses fought like bobcats, and it took some doing just to get a rope on one and snub him up. It was impossible to drive them, so they tied a twisted rawhide garter on one leg. The circulation was cut off, and the leg became numb and useless. It wasn't so hard to handle them then.

That was only the beginning of their troubles. When they castrated the studs, half of them died. Most of the rest lost their spirit and became dead-headed and listless.

After a good try, they drifted out of the rough country ahead of the winter snow. They had two half-broken mares. But it beat walking, because without them that's exactly what they would be doing. Well, they went back—at thirty a month—to the cowpunching job they had left.

He started saving again. Finally, a rancher offered him a foreman's job at thirty-five a month, and he could run as many head of his own cattle as he could acquire.

After a few months, when he had some cash to go on, he made his move. He began trading with the Mexicans. A few dollars down, a worn-out saddle, an old rifle, and so on were

his barter goods. In three years he had built his herd up to sixty head of cows, twelve steers, and two bulls. They were a mixed lot and they were his, but the land they ranged on was not. He still couldn't figure why his boss had been so generous. Another thing he couldn't figure out was why the owner and two of his hands did so much riding without him. He didn't ask questions because it looked like a man would be a fool to tinker with good times. They were mighty scarce.

His boss sent him to a roundup over west at a neighboring ranch. His job was to check out any of their strays and deliver them back to the home range. It was a big outfit, and the roundup went on for several days. The last of the work was done right at headquarters. The cowboys ate at the cookhouse. There was a pretty little brown-headed girl doing the cooking. Fine, tasty chuck it was. She was the owner's daughter, Nelda.

Well, he kept eyeballing her, and she kept glancing back. He was pretty good looking at that time . . . in a rough, healed-over way. The aging and scars of the tough life hadn't taken hold yet. On the last day before he started home with his gather he asked her for a date, and he damn near fainted when she accepted.

He borrowed a buggy and picked her up late Saturday afternoon. They went to a dance at the schoolhouse. She was all decked out in a long, flimsy, turquoise dress that hugged her up close around the waist and bosom. Her hair just sparkled like her brown eyes, and that was like a fall sun striking new frost on a golden aspen leaf. He was so scared and so cockeyed proud that he danced every set with her, even though he had a heck of a time fending off the other cowboys.

About four o'clock in the morning, a little before daybreak when the music was slow, he walked outside and leaned her up against the building. While the coyotes howled out in

the prairie he pulled her up hard and said, "I . . . I love you. I sure do."

Although she didn't say anything, she let him know how she felt with her arms and her eyes. Sweet.

They went steady then. His luck just kept running. He got into a poker game with a bunch of mining and timber men and won six thousand dollars. That was more money than he had seen all his life put together. He couldn't wait to get over and tell Nelda.

They rode together in the hills, and he loved her and she loved him. He told her about the money and how it was not only burning a hole in his pocket but was burning right smack through his leg.

"Snake," she said, "you've got a good start on a herd and the Larking place is for sale. We wouldn't owe more than eighteen thousand."

Eighteen thousand dollars! It scared him. It was beyond him. He would never make it. He just couldn't take on a woman like her, the daughter of a big rancher, owing that kind of money.

Well, he got drunk in town and didn't show up for work. The boss fired him and told him to come and get his cows, but at the same time he said there would be no hurry about it. Somehow it didn't make sense.

Snake stayed in town that fall and on into the winter trying to make up his mind what to do. In the meantime, the money was going steadily out for whiskey and gambling.

The winter came, and a blizzard hit. Most of his cattle walked off into deep drifts of snow and froze to death. By the time he sobered up, it was spring and he was broke.

Then the law came and took him. His ex-boss was right there shaking his head and saying he couldn't believe it, after

all he had done for him. They railroaded him, and now he knew that he had been a blind and a coverup for the rancher's thievery. He got a year and a day. After three dreary months inside the prison wall, he planned to kill the man who sent him there, but then they put him out on the prison farm, and he reasoned it wasn't worth it.

He didn't return to the home country for a long time after his release. Nelda married someone else, and he kind of regretted he had been so undecided.

He tried a lot of things after that, plunging hard to come back—prospecting, timber leasing; nothing worked out. He was trying to keep from going back to punching cows. He took a job as a dude wrangler in Yellowstone Park. His natural friendliness, his knowledge of horses and everything, attracted a lot of business. He had several chances to marry rich widows and cowboy-smitten girls. But he never could decide when the time came. He had heard that all was not roses and sweet violets with the rich dames. A man had to go around with his hand out all the time.

At last, though, he chose to take on this woman from St. Louis. She had come right out and told him she would buy and pay for a ranch, stock it in his name, and put some money in the bank in the same manner.

Then he got drunk in Pony, Montana, on bootleg whiskey. It poisoned him, and he was laid up out of his head for sixty days. The doctors almost gave up on him. By the time he came to and acquired strength enough to walk and talk, the widow had disappeared. The wrangler who had taken his job ran off to Mexico with her. If only a man could ever make up his mind at the right time, he would have this world singing *his* songs he figured.

He kept trying and bumming around into one thing and

another. He damned near starved. The years were beginning to show. Finally, he returned to his old country and the only thing he really knew—punching cows. The wages were one hundred and twenty-five dollars a month and board. That was tops, as high as he could go in his profession. It was a job that took guts, natural skill, and understanding of the earth and its animals, both wild and domestic, though the present wages wouldn't buy as much as twenty dollars had in his youth. But there he was now, riding the draws around the water hole looking for sign and finding none.

It was midafternoon and hot. If he turned back now, he could make it in a little after dark, saddle a fresh horse, and go on into headquarters. It was three days till payday. He could take his check, go into town, buy a new pair of jeans, a new rope, maybe a new hat. If he was careful, he might have enough left over to get a little drunk and maybe even play a little poker. He really needed a pair of new boots, but anything worth working in cost between forty and fifty dollars, so he would just have to wait till next payday—or the next.

He decided to go on and check the water hole just in case he had missed something. It would cost him another night in the line camp but, after all, what was one more night alone to him? He saw the usual sign of wildlife and was surprised to find the day-old tracks of a cow. One lonely cow. She must have strayed in here to calve, he thought. He could tell by the way her hoofs splayed out and by the withered cracks around the edges that she was an old cow.

As he followed her tracks up the trail, he noticed that a coyote and four pups had been ahead of him. Probably went right on, he thought, and then an uneasiness came over him. Man, it was hot. He pulled his hat back and wiped the sweat from his forehead and out of his narrow sunwashed eyes. The

cow had turned off across a small ridge, and he saw the tracks of the coyotes do the same. Pretty soon he felt the horse bunch under him. The head came up, and the ears pitched forward. He thought he heard a sound, a cow bawling maybe, but he wasn't sure. He got down and tied the horse to a bush.

He removed the .30-30 from the scabbard and started easing forward. He was slow in his movement, because of the stiffness from the long day in the saddle and many years of breaks and bruises. Then he was on his belly crawling forward, feeling an excitement that he couldn't define. It was more than the hunter's blood surging now.

He raised up carefully from the side of a yucca plant. He saw the old cow first and then, slowly, one at a time, he located the coyotes. They hadn't seen or heard him yet, because of the dryness and lack of wind.

He eased the rifle and sighted down it at the old mother coyote as she moved forward. Just as he started to pull the trigger, she lay down right out in front of the old cow. For some reason strange to him, he held his fire.

In the little hollow where the man, the coyotes, the cow and her calf lay there was concentrated the most life for miles in every direction. Five miles to the north and west in the cedar- and piñon-covered hills, twenty-six buzzards circled and lighted on the remains of a cow downed two days before by a mountain lion that lay now in the coolness of the rocks with a full belly; to the east another pack of coyotes was desperately stalking a herd of swift antelope with no luck at all.

A hawk circled curiously above the draw with the man and the animals, smelling meat. The land itself was covered

sparsely with buffalo and grama grass, and everywhere the yucca plants bayonetted the sky. Now and then in meandering, meaningless lines, the land was cut by wind and water erosion forming a rolling, twisted terrain that on the face of a man would have portrayed deep torment.

The man felt the trigger of the rifle with his finger. The hammer was thumbed back. His cheek lay hot and sweating along the stock. The sights were centered on the thin rib cage of the coyote lying so very still. He could tell by the torn, powdered earth around the old cow, standing, swaying so weakly with far-drooped head, that she had held them at bay a long number of hours now.

His eyes raised again and counted the pups. One shot would do it. He must have killed two or three hundred of these animals, these varmints, these predators. He was a good shot. He would not miss. His eyes were in the second sight that comes briefly to older men. He could see almost as good as he could at twenty-one. His stomach was hollow. And he thought vaguely that it had been many hours since he had eaten or drunk. It came to him then that the creatures before him had been much longer without repast.

A sudden admiration came over him for the old, hungry, thirsty coyote and the old, hungry, thirsty cow eying each other in the golden blazing, dying sun. His duty, his real job, was to kill the old coyote and as many of her young as possible and drive the old cow to water, carrying the calf across the swells of his saddle for her. In a day or two she would have her strength back, then he could drive her on to the main herd. That was his job. But he didn't move, and all of his long life came to him now as he studied what he saw before him.

The old coyote knew what she must do, and she was doing it with every particle of cunning, courage, and instinct in

her emaciated body. Her pups must be fed, and she must, too, if she was to survive and finish their training.

And the old cow had long ago reconciled herself to her fate. She would stand and fight—win or die.

The indecision was not theirs. This trait was his and had always been so.

Time became a vacuum in the floating dust. The bawling of the old cow, just a whisper now, came to him. The coyote lay like dry wood. The pups watched her, their bodies slowly evaporating in the ceaseless sun. It was everything.

His lungs ached from the shallow breathing, but still he could not move the finger that fraction of an inch that would end it. Time. Timeless time.

Then the old coyote attacked as if hurled from the earth. The pups charged down. The man fired, but the bullet struck into the shoulder of one of the pups instead. The momentum carried it forward and down and over. It kicked its life away. He raised the gun and fired again. The hindquarters of another pup dropped. He levered another shell and shot it through the head.

As the old coyote came in, lips peeled back, fangs sharp and anxious, the old cow pulled a tiny ounce of strength from her heart—a little reserve she had saved for her young. She shuffled forward to meet the terrible threat.

The sound of the shot had caused the old coyote to veer just a fraction at the last thrust, and it was just enough. The lightning-splintered horn of the old cow drove between the lean ribs, and she made one upward swing of her head. The horn tore into the lungs and burst the arteries of the chest apart. The coyote hung there. The cow could not raise her head again. She fell forward, crushing at the earth. When she

pulled her head and horns away, the coyote blinked her yellow, dying eyes just once. It was over.

The other two pups ran out through the brush. They were on their own now.

The calf got to its feet and sucked a little milk from the mother's flabby bag. The man went back to his horse, wondering why he had shot the pups instead of the old one. For a moment he had known. But now the knowledge was gone.

In a little while, as the sun buried itself in the great ocean of space behind the earth, the old cow, her calf at her side, stumbled downhill to water.

CANDLES IN THE BOTTOM OF THE POOL

Joshua Stone III moved along the cool adobe corridor listening to the massive walls. They were over three feet thick, the mud and straw solidified hard as granite. He appeared the same.

The sounds came to him faintly at first, then stronger. He leaned against the smooth dirt plaster and heard the clanking of armor, the twanging of bows, the screams of falling men and horses. His chest rose as his lungs pumped the excited blood. His powerful hands were grabbing their own flesh at his sides. It was real. Then the struggles of the olive conquerors and the brown vanquished faded away like a weak wind.

He opened his eyes, relaxing slightly, and stepped back, staring intently at the wall. Where was she? Would she still come to him smiling, waiting, wanting? Maybe. There was

silence now. Even the singing of the desert birds outside could not penetrate the mighty walls.

Then he heard the other song. The words were unintelligible, ancient, from forever back, back, back, but he felt and understood their meaning. She appeared from the unfathomable reaches of the wall, undulating like a black wisp ripped from a tornado cloud. She was whole now. Her black lace dress clung to her body, emphasizing the delicious smoothness of her face and hands. The comb of Spanish silver glistened like a halo in her hair. His blue eyes stared at her dark ones across the centuries. They knew. She smiled with much warmth, and more. One hand beckoned for him to come. He smiled back, whispering, "Soon. Very soon."

"YES, YES, YES," she said, and the words vibrated about, over, through, under, and around everything. He stood, still staring, but there was only the dry mud now.

He turned, as yet entranced, then shook it off and entered through the heavily timbered archway into the main room. The light shafted in from the patio windows, illuminating the big room not unlike a cathedral. In a way it was. *Santos* and *bultos* were all over. The darkly stained furniture was from another time, hand hewn and permanent like the house itself.

He absorbed the room for a moment, his eyes caressing the old Indian pots spotted about, the rich color of the paintings from Spain, the cochineal rugs dyed from kermes bugs. Yes, the house was old; older than America. He truly loved its feeling of history, glory, and power.

Then his gaze stopped on the only discord in the room. It was a wildly colored, exaggerated painting of himself. He didn't like the idea of his portrait hanging there. He didn't need that. He allowed it only because his niece, Aleta, had done it. He was fond of her.

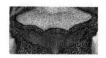

Juanita, the aged servant, entered with a tray. It held guacamole salad, tostados, and the inevitable Bloody Marys. He asked her in perfect Spanish where his wife, Carole, was.

She answered in English, "On the patio, señor. I have your drinks." She moved out ahead of him, bony, stiff, bent, but with an almost girlish quickness about her. She'd been with them for decades. They'd expected her demise for years, then given up.

Carole lounged in the desert sun, dozing the liquor away. He couldn't remember when she started drinking so heavily. He had to admit that she had a tough constitution—almost as much as his own. It was usually around midnight before alcohol dulled her to retire. She removed the oversized sunglasses and sat up as Juanita placed the tray on a small table by her. The wrinkles showed around the eyes, but her figure was still as good as ever. She rubbed at the lotion on her golden legs and then reached for her drink. At her movement, he had a fleeting desire to take her to bed. Was that what had brought them together? Was that what had held them until it was too late? Maybe. She pushed the burnt blonde hair back and placed the edge of the glass against her glistening lips. He thought the red drink was going down her throat like weak blood to give her strength for the day. He gazed out across the green mass of trees, grass, and bushes in the formal garden beyond the patio. He heard the little brook that coursed through it, giving life to the oasis just as the Bloody Marys did his wife.

It was late morning, and already the clouds puffed up beyond the parched mountains, promising much, seldom giving. It was as if the desert of cacti, lizards, scorpions, and coyotes between the mountains and the *hacienda* was too forbidding to pass over. It took many clouds to give the necessary courage to one another. It rarely happened.

He picked up his drink, hypnotized by the rising heat waves of the harsh land.

"I've decided," he said.

"You've decided what?"

"It's time we held the gathering."

She took another sip, set it down, and reached for a cigarette. "You've been talking about that for three years, Joshua."

"I know, but I've made up my mind."

"When?"

"Now."

"Now? Oh God, it'll take days to prepare." She took another swallow of the red drink. "I'm just not up to it. Besides, Lana and Joseph are in Bermuda. Sheila and Ralph are in Honolulu."

"They'll come."

"You can't just order people away from their vacations." She took another swallow, pulled the bra of her bikini up, walked over and sat down on the edge of the pool, and dangled her feet in it. Resentment showed in her back. He still felt a little love for her, which surprised him. There was no question that his money and power had been part of her attraction to him. But at first, it had been good. They'd gone just about everywhere in the world together. The fun, the laughs, the adventure had been there even though some part of his business empire was always intruding. What had happened? Hell, why didn't he admit it? Why didn't she? It had worn out. It was that simple. Just plain worn out from the heaviness of the burdens of empire like an old draft horse or a tired underground coal miner.

She splashed the water over her body, knowing from his silence there was no use. "Well, we might as well get on with it. When do you call?"

He finished the drink, stood up, and moved towards the house, saying, "As I said, now."

Joshua entered the study. His secretary for the past ten years looked up, sensing something in his determined movement.

"All right, Charlotte."

She picked up the pad without questioning. He paced across the Navajo rugs, giving her a long list of names. Occasionally he'd run his hands down a row of books, playing them like an accordion. He really didn't like organization, but when he decided, he could be almost magical at it. There was no hesitation, no lost thought or confusion. He was putting together the "gathering" just as he'd expanded the small fortune his father had left him. It kept growing, moving.

When he finished dictating the names, he said, "We'll have food indigenous to the Southwest. Tons of it. I want for entertainment the Russian dancer from Los Angeles, Alfredo and his guitar from Juárez, the belly dancer what's-her-name from San Francisco, the mariachis from Mexico City, and the brass group from Denver."

His whole huge body was vibrating now. A force exuded from Joshua—the same force that had swayed decisions on many oil field deals, land developments, cattle domains, and, on occasion, even the stock market—but never had Charlotte seen him as he was now. There was something more, something she could not explain. Then he was done. He pushed at his slightly graying mass of hair and walked around the hand-carved desk to her. He pulled her head over to him and held it a moment against his side. They had once been lovers, but

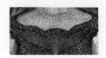

when she came to work for him that was over. There was still a tenderness between them. She was one of those women who just missed being beautiful all the way around, but she had a sensual appeal and a soft strength that was so much more. She had his respect, too, and that was very hard for him to give.

He broke the mood with, "Call Aleta and Rob first."

She took the book of numbers and swiftly dialed, asking, "Are you sure they're in El Paso?"

"Yes. Aleta's painting. She's getting ready for her show in Dallas." He took the phone, "Rob, is Aleta there?"

In El Paso, Rob gave an affirmative answer and put his hand over the phone: "Your Uncle *God* is on the horn."

Aleta wiped the paint from her hands and reached for the receiver. "Don't be so sarcastic, darling; he might leave you out of his will."

The vibrations were instantaneous down the wire between the man and the girl. She would be delighted to come.

When the conversation was over and Aleta informed her husband, he said, "The old bastard! He's a dictator. I'd just love to kill him!"

He finished with Lana and Joseph Helstrom in the Bahamas with, "No kids. Do you understand? This is not for children."

The husband turned to his wife, saying, "We're ordered to attend a gathering at Aqua Dulce."

"A gathering?"

"A party. You know how he is about labeling things."

"Oh Christ, two days on vacation and he orders us to a party."

"I could happily murder the son of a bitch and laugh for years," Joseph said, throwing a beach towel across the room against a bamboo curtain.

Finally, Joshua was finished. Charlotte got up and mixed them a scotch on the rocks from the concealed bar behind the desk. They raised their glasses, and both said at the same time, "To the gathering." They laughed together as they worked together.

Suddenly Charlotte set her glass down and, not having heard the phone conversations, stated almost omnipotently, "Half of them would delight in doing away with you."

Joshua nodded, smiling lightly. "You're wrong, love, a good two-thirds would gladly blow me apart, and all but a few of the others would wish them well."

"Touché."

"They do have a tendency to forget how they arrived at their present positions. However, that's not what concerns me. All are free to leave whenever they wish, but most don't have the guts. They like cinches but never acknowledge that on this earth no such thing exists. Even the sun is slowly burning itself to death."

"Another drink?"

"Of course. This is a moment for great celebration."

She poured the drinks efficiently, enjoying this time with him. Sensing something very special happening. Thrilled to share with him again.

They touched glasses across the desk, and he said, almost jubilantly, "To the Gods, goddamn them!"

Carole instructed Juanita in the cleaning and preparing of the house. She put old Martin, the head caretaker and yard man, and his two younger sons, trimming the garden. This last was unnecessary because old Martin loved the leisure and in-

dependence of his job. He kept everything in shape anyway. It did, however, serve its purpose. Carole felt like she was doing *something*. In fact, an excitement she hadn't felt for a long time came upon her. She remembered the first really important entertaining she'd done for Joshua after their marriage. He was on a crucial Middle East oil deal.

It was in their New York townhouse in the days they were commuting around the world to various homes and apartments. She had really pulled a coup. Carole had worked closely with the sheik's male secretary and found what to her were some surprising facts. At first she'd intended to have food catered native to the guests' own country and utilize local belly dancers of the same origin. But after much consultation she served hamburgers and had three glowing, local-born blondes as dancing girls. The sheiks raved over the Yankee food they'd heard so much about and were obviously taken with the yellow-topped, fair-skinned dancing girls. They were also highly captivated by Carole herself. The whole thing had been a rousing success. Joshua got his oil concessions, and she had felt an enormous sense of accomplishment.

Today, as she moved about the vast *hacienda*, she felt some of that old energy returning. There was something different though. Her excitement was mounting, but it was more like one must feel stalking a man-eating tiger and knowing that at the next parting of the bushes they would look into each other's eyes.

Joshua checked out the wine cellar. He loved the silence and the dank smell. He touched some of the ancient casks as he had the history books in the study. He was drawn to old things now, remembering, recalling, conjuring up the history of his land . . . the great Southwest. He lingered long after he knew the supply of fine wines was more than sufficient. He moved the lantern back and forth, watching the shadows hide

from the moving light. Carole had long wanted him to have electricity installed down here, but he'd refused. Some things need to remain as they are, he felt. Many of the old ways were better. Many worse. He'd wondered uncounted times why men who could build computers and fly to distant planets were too blind, or stupid, to select the best of the old and the best of the new and weld them together. He knew that at least the moderate happiness of mankind was that simple. An idiot could see it if he opened up and looked. It would not happen during Joshua's brief encounter with this planet. He knew it and was disgusted by it.

He set the lantern on a shelf and stood gazing at the wall ending the cellar. It was awhile before the visions would begin coming to him. He didn't mind. Time was both nothing and everything. Then he heard the hoofs of many horses walking methodically forward. It was like the beat of countless drumsticks against the earth. A rhythm, a pattern, a definite purpose in the sound. Closer. Louder. The song came as a sigh at first, then a whisper; finally it was clear and hauntingly lovely. He felt thousands of years old, perhaps millions, perhaps ageless. Colors in circular and elongated patterns danced about in the wall. Slowly they took form as if just being born. Swiftly now, they melded into shape, and he saw Cortés majestically leading his men and horses in clothing of iron. From the left came Montezuma and his followers in dazzling costumes so wildly colored they appeared to be walking rainbows. They knelt and prostrated themselves to the gods with four legs. Beauty had bent to force.

Joshua was witnessing the beginning of the Americas. The vision dissolved like a panoramic movie, and the song seeped away.

Then Oñate appeared, splashing his column across the

Rio Grande at the pueblo of Juárez, and headed north up the river. The cellar suddenly reverberated with the swish of a sword into red flesh, and there was a huge, moving collage of churning, charging horses, and arrows whistling into the cracks of armor, and many things fell to the earth and became still. Oñate sat astride his horse surveying the compound of a conquered pueblo.

The song came again suddenly, shatteringly, crescendoing as Joshua's Spanish princess stood on a hill looking down. She came towards him, appearing to walk just above the earth. As she neared, smiling, with both arms out, he moved to the wall. As they came closer, he reached the wall with his arms outspread, trying to physically feel into it, but she was gone. He stayed thusly for a while, his head turned sideways, pushing his whole body against the dirt. For a moment he sagged and took a breath into his body that released him. He turned, picked up the lantern, and zombied his way up to the other world. The one here.

All was ready. The tables were filled with every delicacy of the land from which Joshua, his father, and grandfathers twice back had sprouted. The *hacienda* shined from repeated dusting and polishing. A *cantina* holding many bottles from many other lands was set up in the main room, and an even greater display was waiting for eager hands, dry throats, and tight emotions in the patio.

Carole moved about, checking over and over that which was already done. Joshua had one chore left.

"Martin, drain the pool."

Martin looked at his master, puzzled. "But sir, the guests will . . ."

"Just drain the pool."

"Well . . . yes sir."

When Carole saw this, she hurried to Martin and asked in agitated confusion what in hell's madness possessed him to do such a thing.

"It was on orders of Mr. Joshua, madam."

"Then he's mad! We cleaned the pool only yesterday!"

She found Joshua in the study and burst in just as Charlotte finished rechecking her own list and was saying, "Everything has been done, Joshua. The doctors are even releasing Grebbs from the hospital so he can make it."

"Of course, I knew you'd take care of . . ."

"Joshua!"

He turned slowly to her.

"Have you lost all your sanity? Why did you have Martin drain the pool?"

"It's simple, my dear. Pools can become hypnotic and distracting. We have far greater forms of entertainment coming up."

She stood there unable to speak momentarily. She pushed at her hair and rubbed her perspiring palms on her hips, walking in a small circle around the room, finally giving utterance, "*I* know you're crazy, but do you want everyone else to know it?"

"It will give them much pleasure to finally find this flaw in my nature they have so desperately been seeking."

She turned and cascaded from the room, hurling back, "Oh, my God!"

Forty-eight hours later they came from all around the world. They arrived in jets, Rolls-Royces, Cadillacs, Mercedes, and pickup trucks. They moved to the *hacienda* magnetized.

The greetings were both formal and friendly, fearful and cheerful. Carole was at her gracious best, only half-drunk, ex-

pertly suppressing their initial dread with her trained talk. But there was a difference in the hands and arms and bodies that floated in the air towards Joshua. These appurtenances involved a massive movement of trepidation, hate, and fatherhood.

Joshua took Aleta in his grand and strong arms and lifted her from the floor in teasing love and respect. Her husband, Rob, died a little bit right there. His impulse of murder to the being of this man was intensified and verified. Rob wanted *in* desperately. He craved to become part of the Stone domain; craved to be part of the prestige and power. Marrying the favorite niece had seemed the proper first step. It hadn't worked. Joshua had never asked him, and Aleta absolutely forbade Rob to even hint at it. His lean, handsome face had a pinched appearance about it from the hatred. He had dwelled on it so long now that it was an obsession—an obsession to destroy that which he felt had ignored and destroyed him. It was unjustified. Joshua simply didn't want to see Rob subservient to him—not the husband of his artist niece. Aleta had never asked Joshua for anything but his best wishes. He felt that Rob must be as independent as she or else they wouldn't be married. He was wrong. Being a junior partner in a local stock brokerage firm didn't do it for Rob. And their being simply ordered here to Aleta's obvious joy had tilted his rage until he could hardly contain it.

Others—who were *in*—felt just as passionately about Joshua, but they all had their separate and different reasons.

Lana and Joseph Helstrom certainly had a different wish for Joshua. Joseph just hadn't moved as high in the organization as swiftly as he felt he should, and Lana had a hidden yen for Joshua. In fact, she often daydreamed of replacing Carole.

And there was the senior vice president, Grebbs, who wanted and believed that Joshua should step up to the position

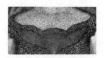

of chairman of the board and allow him his long overdue presidency. He had lately been entering hospitals for checkups, which repeatedly disclosed nothing wrong—but then x-rays do not show hatred or they would have been white with explosions all over his body.

None of these things bothered Joshua now. The gathering grew in momentum of sound, emotion, and color. The drinks were consumed along with the food, and the talk was of many things. People split up into ever-changing groups. Those who had been to the *hacienda* before remarked about this alteration or that. Those who were new to its centuries made many, many comments about all the priceless objects of art and craft. Whether they hated or loved the master of the house, they were somehow awed and honored to be in this museum of the spirit of man and Joshua himself.

Alfredo, the guitarist from Juárez, played. His dark head bent over his instrument, and the long delicate fingers stroked from the wood and steel the tenderness of love, the savagery of death. It seemed that these songs, too, came from the walls. Maybe somehow they did.

The music surged into the total system of Joshua. He felt stronger, truer than ever before. He was ready now to make his first move—the beginning of his final commitment. He looked about the room, observing with penetration his followers. His eyes settled on Charlotte. And then, as if knowing, unable to resist, she came to him. She handed him a new scotch and water, holding her own drink with practiced care. He turned, and she followed at his side. They wandered to the outer confines of the house—to his childhood room. She did not question. He turned on a small lamp that still left many shadows.

"My darling," he said softly, touching the walls with one hand, "this is where it all started."

She looked at him, puzzled, but with patience.

"I think I was five when I first heard the walls. It was gunfire and screams, and I knew it had once happened here. You see, this, in the days of the vast Spanish land grants, was a roadhouse, a *cantina*, an oasis where the dons and their ladies gathered to fight and fornicate. They are in the walls, you know, and I hear them. I even see them. I had just turned thirteen when I first *saw* into the walls."

Joshua's eyes gleamed like a coyote's in lantern light. His breath was growing, and there was an electricity charging through all his being. Charlotte was hypnotized at his voice and what was under it. His hand moved down the walls as he told her of some of the things he'd seen and heard. Then he turned to her and raised his glass for a toast.

"To you, dear loyal, wonderful Charlotte, my love and my thanks."

"It has all been a fine trip with you, Joshua. I could not have asked more from life than to have been a part of you and what you've done. Thank you, thank you."

He took the drink from her hand and set it on a dresser. Taking her gently by the arm, he pulled her to the wall. "Now lean against it and listen and you, too, will hear." She did so, straining with all her worth. "Listen! Listen," he whispered, and his powerful hands went around her neck. She struggled very little, and in a few moments she went limp. He held her a brief second longer, bending to kiss her on the back of the neck he'd just broken. Then with much care he picked her up, carried her to the closet, and placed her out of sight behind some luggage. He quietly closed the door, standing there a while looking at it. He moved, picked up his drink, and returned to his people.

In the patio, Misha, the Russian dancer from Kavkaz on Sunset Boulevard, was leaping wildly about, crouching, kicking. A circle formed around him, and the bulk of Joshua Stone III dominated it all. He was enjoying himself to the fullest, clapping his hands and yelling encouragement. The dance had turned everyone on a few more kilocycles. They started drinking more, talking more and louder, even gaining a little courage.

The gray, fiftyish Grebbs tugged at Joshua, trying to get his true attention. He kept bringing up matters of far-flung business interests. He might remind one in attitude of a presidential campaign manager, just after a victory, wondering if he'd be needed now. He rubbed at his crew-cut hair nervously, trying to figure an approach to Joshua. His gray eyes darted about slightly. His bone-edged nose presented certain signs of strength and character, but weakness around the mouth gave him away. He was clever and did everything that cleverness could give to keep all underlings out of touch with Joshua. He had hoped for a while that this gathering had been called to announce Joshua's chairmanship, and the fulfillment of his own desperate dream.

Joshua motioned to Lotus Flower, the belly dancer, and she moved gracefully out into the patio ahead of the music. Then the music caught up with her. The Oriental lady undulated and performed the moves that have always pleased men.

As Grebbs tugged at Joshua again, he said, without taking his eyes from the dancer, "Grebbs, go talk business to your dictaphone." Just that. Now Grebbs knew. He moved away, hurting.

Lana stood with Carole. They were both watching Joshua with far different emotions.

Lana spoke first, about their mutual interest. "Has Joshua put on some weight?"

"No, it's the same old stomach."

"He's always amazed everyone with his athletic abilities."

"Really?" This last had a flint edge to it.

"Well, for a man who appears so awkward, it is rather surprising to find how swiftly and strongly he can move when he decides to. Carole, you do remember the time he leaped into Spring Lake and swam all the way across it, and then just turned around and swam all the way back. You must remember that, darling. We all had such a good time."

"Oh, I remember many things, *darling*."

Rob was saying to Joseph Helstrom, "There's something wrong here. I feel it. Here it's only September, and he's already drained the pool."

Joseph touched his heavy-rimmed glasses and let the hand slowly slide down his round face, "Yeah, he demanded we all come here on instant notice, and he's not really with us."

"The selfish bastard." Rob exhaled this like ridding himself of morning spittum.

The dancer swirled ever closer to Joshua, her head back, long black hair swishing across her shoulders. He smiled, absorbed in the movement of flesh as little beams of hatred were cast across the patio from Grebbs, Rob, Joseph—and others. Joshua didn't care—didn't even feel it. As the dance finished, Rob walked out into the garden and removed a small automatic pistol from the back of his belt under his jacket. He checked the breech and replaced the gun.

Joshua worked his way through the crowd, spoken to and speaking back in a distracted manner. His people looked puzzled after his broad back. He made his way slowly down

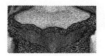

the stairs towards the wine cellar, one hand caressing the wall. He stopped and waited. The song came from eternities away, soft, soothing, amidst the whispers of men planning daring moves.

The whole wall now spun with colors slowly forming into warriors. Then, there before Joshua's eyes was Esteban, the black man, standing amidst the Pueblo Indians. Joshua had always felt that Esteban was one of the most exciting and mysterious—even neglected—figures in the history of America. It has never been settled for sure how or why he arrived in the Southwest. However, his influence would always be there. He had started the legend of the Seven Golden Cities of Cíbola, which Coronado and many others searched for in vain. He was a major factor in the Pueblo Revolt of 1680, afterwards becoming the chief of several of these communities. He became a famous medicine man and was looked on as a god. But, like all earthly gods, he fell. A seven-year drought came upon the land of the Tewas, and when he could not dissipate it, he was blamed for it. They killed him, and the superstitious Zuñis skinned him like a deer to see if he was black all the way through.

Now, at last, Joshua was looking upon this man of dark skin and searing soul, as he spoke in the Indian tongue to his worshippers. He talked to them of survival without the rule of iron. They mumbled low in agreement. Maybe Joshua would learn some of the dark secrets before this apparition dissolved back to dried mud.

Joshua watched as up and down the river the Indians threw rock and wood at steel in savage dedication. Men died screaming in agony, sobbing their way painfully to the silence of death. The river flowed peacefully before him now, covering the entire wall and beyond. Then the feet splashed into his

view, and he saw the remnants of the defeated Spanish straggle across the river back into Mexico.

Joshua's Spanish lady in black lace sat on a smooth, round rock staring across a valley dripping with the gold of autumn. She was in a land he'd never seen. She turned her head toward him and gave a smile that said so much he couldn't stand it. He reached towards the wall, and she nodded her head up and down and faded away with the music. Silence. More silence. Then, "Joshua."

He turned. It was Lana. She moved to him, putting her hands on his chest. "Joshua, what is it? You're acting so strangely."

"Did you see? Did you hear?" he asked, looking out over her head.

"I . . . I . . . don't know what you mean, darling. See what?"

"Nothing. Nothing," he sighed.

"Can I help? Is there *anything* I can do?"

He pulled her against him and kissed her with purpose. She was at first surprised and then gave back to him. He picked her up and shoved her violently against the wooden frame between two wine barrels.

"No, no, not here."

"There is no other time," he said. "No other place." As he reached under her, one elbow struck a spigot on a barrel. He loved her standing there while a thin stream of red wine poured out on the cellar floor, forming an immediate pool not unlike blood.

She uttered only one word, "Joshua," and the wine sound continued.

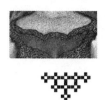

Both he and Lana were back among the people now. Carole came to him.

"Where've you been? Where is Charlotte? The phone is ringing constantly. Where is she?"

"She's on vacation."

"Today? I can't believe you, Joshua. You always bragged about how she was there when you needed her."

"We don't need her now."

"You really are mad. Mad! Today of all days we need her to answer the phone."

"Take the damned phone off the hook. No one ever calls good news on a phone, anyway. If they have anything good to say, they come and see you personally." He walked away and left her standing there looking after him in much confusion.

All afternoon he had been wanting to visit his old friend Chalo Gonzales from the Apache Reservation. They met when they were kids. Chalo's father had worked the nearby orchards and alfalfa fields for Joshua's father. He and Chalo hunted, fished, adventured together off and on for years. He'd gone with him to the reservation many times and learned much of nature and Indian ways. Chalo had given him as much as anyone—things of real value. He found him dressed in a regular business suit and tie, but he wore a band around his coarse, dark hair.

"Ah, amigo, let's walk in the garden away from this . . ." and he made a gesture with his arm to the scattered crowd. "How does it go with you and your people?"

"Slow, Joshua, but better. As always, there's conflict with the old and the young. The old want to stay with their own ways. The young want to rush into the outside world."

"It's the nature of youth to be impatient. It can't be helped."

"Oh, sure, that is the truth. But our young want to take the best of the old and good ways with them. They want both sides now. Now."

"That's good, Chalo. They're right."

"But nothing happens that fast. It has been too many centuries one way. You can't change it in a few years."

"It's a big problem I admit, but you will survive and finally win. You always have, you know."

"You've always given me encouragement. I feel better already."

They talked of hunts, and later adventures when they both came home for the summer from school. Chalo had been one of few to make it from his land to Bacone, the Indian college.

Joshua felt Chalo was his equal. He was comfortable with him. They stood together and talked in a far recess of the secluded garden where they could see the mountains they'd so often explored. Joshua felt a surge of love for his old friend. He knew what he must do. He'd spotted the root a few minutes back. He didn't dare risk it with his hands. Chalo was almost as strong as he was in both will and muscle.

He picked up the root and began drawing designs with it in a spot of loose ground, as men will do who are from the earth. Then, as his friend glanced away, Joshua swung it with much force, striking him just back of the ear. He heard the bone crunch and was greatly relieved to know he wouldn't have to do more. Without any wasted time, he dragged and pushed him into a thick clump of brush. He checked to see if the body was totally hidden, tossed the root in after it, walked to the wall, and looked out across the desert to the mountains

again. He was very still; then he turned, smiling ineluctably, and proceeded to the party.

Dusk came swiftly and hung awhile, giving the party a sudden subdued quality. It was the time of day that Joshua liked best. He finally escaped the clutchers and went to his study, locking the door and grinning at the phone Carole had taken off the hook and deliberately dangled across the lamp.

He drew the shades back and sat there absorbed in the hiding sun, and watched the glowing oranges and reds turn to violet and then a soft blue above the desert to the west. He knew that life started stirring there with the death of the sun. The coyotes and bobcats were already moving, sniffing the ground and the air for other living creatures. Many mice, rabbits, and birds would die this night so they could live. The great owl would soon be swooping above them in direct competition. The next day the sun would be reborn, and the vultures would dine on any remains, keeping the desert clean and in balance.

Someone knocked on the door. It was Carole.

"Joshua, are you in there?" Then louder, "Joshua, I know you're there because the door is locked from the inside. What are you doing with the door locked anyway?" Silence. "At least you could come and mix with your guests. You did *invite* them, you know." She pounded on the door now. "My God, at least speak to me. I am your wife, you know." Silence. She turned in frustration and stamped off down the hall, mumbling about his madness.

Joshua turned his lounge chair away from the window and stared at the wall across the room. There were things he had to see before he made the final move. Pieces of the past

that he must reconstruct properly in his mind before he took the last step.

It did come. As always he heard it first, then saw it form, whirling like pieces of an abstract world—a new world, an old world, being broken and born, falling together again. The Spanish returned. They came now with fresh men, armor, horses, and cannon. They marched and rode up the Rio Grande setting up the artillery, blasting the adobe walls to dust. Then they charged with sabers drawn and whittled the shell-shocked Indians into slavery. They mined the gold from the virgin mountains with the Indians as their tools. And then it all vanished inwardly.

There was quiet and darkness now until he heard his name. "Joshua, Joshua, Joshua." It came floating from afar as if elongated, closer, closer. She was there. He leaned forward in the chair, his body tense, anxious. She stood by a river of emerald green. It was so clear that he could see the separate grains of white sand on its bottom. The trees, trunks thicker than the *hacienda*, rose into the sky. They went up, up past his ability to see. The leaves were as thick as watermelons, and fifty people could stand in the shade of a single leaf. The air danced with the light of four suns shafting great golden beams down through the trees.

She moved towards him through one of the beams and for a moment vanished with its brilliance. Now she was whole again, standing there before him. He ached to touch her. He hurt. An endless string of silver fish swam up the river now. The four suns penetrated the pure water and made them appear to be parts of a metallic lava flow from a far-off volcano. But they were fish, moving relentlessly, with no hesitation whatsoever, knowing their destination and fate without doubt.

Again the word came from her as she turned and walked

down the river, vanishing behind a tree. "Joshua."

For a fleeting moment he heard the song. He closed his eyes. When he opened them, there was just the darkness of the room. He didn't know how long he sat there before returning to the party.

He moved directly to the bar in the patio and ordered a double scotch and water. His people were scattered out now, having dined, and were back into the drinking and talking. The volume was beginning to rise again. It was second wind time. As the bartender served the drink, he felt something touch his hand. It was Maria Windsor.

She smiled like champagne pouring, her red lips pulling back over almost startling white teeth. She smiled with her blue eyes, too.

"It has been such a long time," she said.

"Maria, goddamn, it's good to see you." And he hugged her, picking her off the floor without intending to. She was very small and at first appeared to be delicate. But this was a strong little lady. She was a barmaid in his favorite place in El Paso when he first met her. He'd always deeply admired the polite and friendly smoothness with which she did her job. One never had to wait for a drink, the ashtray was emptied at the proper moment, and she knew when to leave or when to stand and chat. Joshua had introduced her to John Windsor, one of his junior vice presidents, and now they were married.

"I love the portrait Aleta did of you."

"Well, I feel embarrassed hanging it there, but what could I do after she worked so hard on it? How are you and John getting along?" he asked.

"How do you mean? Personally or otherwise?"

"Oh, all around I suppose."

"Good," she said. "Like all wives, I think he works too

hard sometimes, but I suppose that's natural. Here he comes now."

John shook hands and greeted his boss without showing any apparent fear and revealing a genuine liking for him. He once told Maria that he'd love Joshua to his death, just for introducing her to him. He was about five eleven, straight and well-muscled, and had thick brown hair that he wore longer than anyone in the whole international organization. He, too, had a nice, white smile.

Joshua ordered a round for the three of them. He raised his glass: "My friends, you'll be receiving a memo in the next few days that I think you will enjoy. Here's to it." Several days before the party, Joshua had made out a paper giving John Windsor control of the company. It had not been delivered yet.

He left them glowing in anticipation and went to find his favorite kin, Aleta. As he moved, the eyes of hatred moved with him . . . drunker now, braver. He walked into the garden, bowing, speaking here and there, but not stopping. The moon, hung in place by galactic gravity, beamed back the sun in a blue softness. The insects and night birds hummed a song in the caressing desert breeze. The leaves on the trees moved just enough to make love. There was a combination of warmth and coolness that only the desert can give.

Aleta had seen her uncle and somehow knew he was looking for her. She came to him from where she'd been sitting on a tree that was alive but bent to the ground. She'd been studying the light patterns throughout the garden for a painting she had in mind.

"Uncle Joshua, it's time we had a visit."

He took both her hands and stood back looking at her. "Yes, it's time, my dear. You are even more beautiful than the best of your paintings."

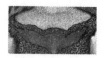

"Well, Uncle, that's not saying much," she said, being pleasingly flattered just the same.

He led her to an archway and opened the iron gate. They walked up a tiny, rutted wagon road into the desert. The sounds of the gathering became subdued. The yucca bushes and Joshua trees—that he'd been named after—speared the sky like frozen battalions of soldiers on guard duty forever.

"Remember when we used to ride up this trail?" she asked.

"Yes, it seems like yesterday."

"It seems like a hundred years ago to me."

He laughed. "Time has a way of telescoping in and out according to your own time. That's the way it should be. You were a tough little shit," he added with fondness. "You were the only one who could ride with me all day."

"That was simple bullheadedness. I knew I was going to be an artist someday, and you have to have a skull made of granite to be an artist."

He was amused by her even now. "But you also had a bottom made of rawhide."

They talked of some of her childhood adventures they'd shared. Then the coyotes howled off in a little draw. The strollers stood like the cacti, listening, absorbing the oldest cry left.

When the howls stopped, he spoke: "I love to hear them. I always have. I even get lonely to hear them. They're the only true survivors."

"That somehow frightens me," she said with a little shudder.

"It shouldn't. You should be encouraged. As long as they howl, people have a chance here on earth. No longer, no less. It is the final cry for freedom. It's hope."

They walked on silently for a spell. "You really are a

romantic, Uncle. When I hear people say how cold you are, I laugh to myself."

"You know, Aleta darling, you're the only person who never asked me for anything."

"I didn't have to. You've always given me love and confidence. What more could you give?"

"I don't know. I wish I did."

"No, Uncle, there's no greater gift than that."

"Aleta, the world is strange. Mankind has forgotten what was always true—that a clean breath is worth more than the most elegant bank building. A new flower opening is more beautiful than a marble palace. All things rot. Michelangelo's sculpture is even now slowly breaking apart. All empires vanish. The largest buildings in the world will turn back to sand. The great paintings are cracking, the negatives of the best films ever made are right now losing their color and becoming brittle. The tallest mountains are coming down a rock at a time. Only thoughts live. You are only what you think."

"That's good," she said, "then I'm a painting, even if I am already beginning to crack."

He liked her words and added some of his own: "You know, honey, the worms favor the rich."

"Why?"

He rubbed his great belly. "Because they're usually fatter and more easily digestible."

"Do you speak of yourself?"

"Of course," he smiled. The coyotes howled again, and he said, "I love you, my dear Aleta."

"And I love you."

He stroked her hair and moved his hand downward. It had to be swift, clean. With all his strength, even more than he'd ever had before. He grabbed her long, graceful neck and

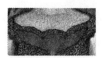

twisted her head. He heard the bones rip apart. She gasped only once, and then a long sigh of her last breath exuded from her. He gathered her carefully in his arms and walked out through the brush to the little draw where the coyotes had so recently hunted. Then he stretched her out on the ground with her hands at her sides and gently brushed her hair back. She slept in the moonlight.

He walked swiftly back to the *hacienda*. As he left the garden for the patio, Rob stepped in front of him.

"Joshua, have you seen Aleta?"

"Of course, my boy, of course."

"Well, where is she?"

"Look, I don't follow your wife around. She's certainly more capable than most of taking care of herself." Joshua moved on. Rob followed him a few steps, looking at his back with glazed eyes.

Grebbs grabbed at him in one last desperate hope that Joshua was saving the announcement to the last.

"Joshua, I have to talk with you. Please."

Joshua stopped and looked at the man. He was drunk, and that was something Grebbs rarely allowed himself to be in public. He looked as if pieces of flesh were about to start dropping down into his clothing. His mouth was open, slack and watery.

Joshua said, with a certainty in his voice that settled Grebbs's question, "Grebbs, you're a bad drinker. I have no respect for bad drinkers." And he moved on.

Grebbs stared at the same back the same way Rob had. He muttered, actually having trouble keeping from openly crying, "The bastard. The dirty bastard. I'll kill you! You son of a bitch!"

The thing some of these people had been uttering about

Joshua now possessed them. A madness hovered about, waiting for the right moment, and then swiftly moved into them. Now all the people of music started playing at once. The Russian was dancing even more wildly, if not so expertly. The belly dancer swished about from man to man, teasing. The mariachis walked about in dominance for a while, then the brass group would break through. It was a cacophony of sound that entered the heads of all there . . . throbbing like blood poison.

Carole started sobbing uncontrollably. Lana began cursing her husband, Joseph, in vile terms—bitterly, with total malice. Joseph just reached out and slapped her down across the chaise lounge, and a little blood oozed from the corner of her mouth. He could only think of a weapon, any weapon to use on the man who he felt was totally responsible for the matrix of doom echoing all around. We always must have something to hate for our own failures and smallness. But this did not occur to Joseph, or Lana, or Carole, or the others. Only Alfredo, the guitarist, sat alone on the same old bent tree that Aleta had cherished, touching his guitar with love.

Maria took John aside and told him they were leaving, that something terrible was happening. She was not—and could not be—a part of it. He hesitated but listened. They did finally drive away, confused, but feeling they were right.

Grebbs dazedly shuffled to the kitchen looking for a knife, but old Juanita and her two sisters were there. He then remembered an East Indian dagger that lay on the mantel in the library as a paperweight. In his few trips to the *hacienda* he'd often studied it, thinking what a pleasure it would be to drive it into the jerking heart of Joshua Stone III.

He picked it up and pulled the arched blade from the jeweled sheath. He touched the sharp unused point with

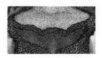

shaking fingers. At that precise instant, Rob felt in the back of his belt and touched the automatic. He removed it and put it in his jacket pocket. Joseph Helstrom looked about the patio for an instrument to satisfy his own destructive instincts.

Joshua entered the door to the cellar, shut it, and shoved the heavy iron bolt into place. He called on all his resources now in another direction. An implosion to the very core of time struck Joshua. Now, right now, he must visualize all the rest of the history of his land that occurred before his first childish awareness. Then, and only then, could he make his last destined move. It began to form. The long lines of Conestoga wagons tape-wormed across the prairies and struggled through the mountain passes, bringing goods and people from all over the world to settle this awesome land. They came in spite of flood, droughts, blizzards, Indian attacks, and disease. They were drawn here by the golden talk of dreamers, and promising facts.

The ruts of the Santa Fe Trail were cut so deep they would last a century. The mountain men took the last of the beaver from the sweet, churning waters of the mountains above Taos and came down to trade, to dance the wild fandangos, to drink and pursue the dark-eyed lovelies of that village of many flags.

A troop of cavalry charged over the horizon into a camp of Indians, and the battle splashed across the adobe valleys in crimson. Thousands of cattle and sheep were driven there and finally settled into their own territories. Cowboys strained to stay aboard bucking horses, and these same men roped and jerked steers, thumping them hard against the earth. They gambled and fought and raised hell in the villages of deserts and mountains, creating written and filmed legends that covered the world more thoroughly than Shakespeare.

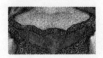

The prospectors walked over the mountains searching for—and some finding—large deposits of gold, silver, and copper. And, as always, men of money took away the rewards of their labors and built themselves great palaces.

And Joshua saw the Italians, Chinese, and many other nationalities driving the spikes into the rail ties. The trains came like the covered wagons before them—faster, more powerful—hauling more people and goods than ever before. The double-bitted axes and two-man saws cut the majestic pines of the high places, taking away the shelter of the deer, lion, and bear.

Now Joshua closed his eyes, for he knew all the rest. When he opened them, he heard the song begin again. It was both older and newer each time he heard it. There was a massive adobe church, and his lady walked right through the walls and into the one he sat staring at. Now, as she spoke his name, he knew his final move was near. For the first time, he turned away from her and headed for the door. She smiled, somehow exactly like the song.

As he opened the door and pulled it shut, he felt a presence come at him. He was so keyed up, so full of his feelings, that he just stepped aside and let it hurtle past. It was Grebbs. He'd driven the dagger so deep into the door that he couldn't pull it out to strike again. Grebbs had missed all the way. Joshua gathered him up around the neck with one hand, jerked the dagger from the door with the other, and smashed him against the wall. He shoved the point of the dagger just barely under the skin of Grebbs's guts. Grebbs's eyes bulged, and he almost died of fright right there, but the hand of his master cut any words off. It was quite a long moment for the corporate vice president.

"What I should do, Grebbs, is cut your filthy entrails out and shove them down your dead throat. But that's far too easy for you."

Joshua dropped him to the floor and drove the knife to the hilt in the door. He then strode up the stairs three at a time, hearing only a low, broken sob below him.

As he entered the world of people again, Carole grabbed at him, visibly drunk and more. She said, "God! God! What are you doing?" He moved on from her as she shrieked, "You don't love me!" He ignored this, too, and when she raked her painted claws into the back of his neck, he ignored that as well. She stood looking at her fingers and the bits of bloody flesh clinging to her nails.

Rob blocked his way, again demanding attention. "I'm asking you for the last time! Do you hear me? Where is Aleta?"

He pushed the young man aside, saying as he went, "I'll tell you in a few minutes." This surprised and stopped Rob right where he stood.

Then Joshua raised his arms and shouted, "Music, you fools! Play and dance!" The drunken musicians all started up again, jerky, horrendously out of synchronization.

Joshua went to the kitchen and very tenderly lifted an exhausted and sleeping Juanita from her chair. He explained to her two sisters that he would take Juanita to her room on the other side of the *hacienda*. They were glad and went on cleaning up. He led her slowly out a side door. On the other side of many walls could be heard the so-called music sailing up, dissipating itself in the peaceful desert air.

As he walked the bent old woman along, he spoke to her softly, "It's time for you to rest, Juanita. You've been faithful all these decades. Your sisters can do the labors. You will have time of your own now. A long, long time that will belong just

to you. You've served many people who did not even deserve your presence."

There was an old well near the working shed where her little house stood. They stopped here.

"Juanita, you are like this—this dried-up well. It gave so much for so long, it now has no water left."

He pulled the plank top off. Juanita was weary and still partially in the world of sleep. Joshua steadied the bony old shoulders with both his hands. He looked at her in the moonlight and said, "Juanita, you are a beautiful woman."

She twitched the tiniest of smiles across her worn face and tilted her head just a little in an almost girlish move.

Then he said, "Juanita, I love you." He slipped a hand-kerchief from his pocket, crammed it into her mouth, jerked her upside down, and hurled her head-first into the well. There was just a crumpled thud. No more.

In the patio, the music was beginning to die. A dullness had come over the area. A deadly dullness. But heads started turning, one, two, three at a time towards the *hacienda* door. Their center of attention, Joshua, strode amongst them. There were only whispers now. Joshua saw a movement and stopped. The heavy earthen vase smashed to bits in front of him. He looked up, and there on a low wall stood Helstrom like a clown without makeup. He, too, had missed.

Joshua grabbed him by both legs and jerked him down against the bricks of the patio floor. He hit, and his head bounced. Joshua gripped him by the neck and the side of one leg and tossed him over and beyond the wall.

He turned slowly around, his eyes covering all the crowd. No one moved. Not at all. He walked back through them to the house and in a few moments returned. He carried a huge silver candelabra, from the first Spanish days, with twenty

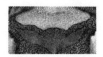

lighted candles. He walked with it held high. None moved, except to get out of his way. Alfredo sat on the edge of the empty pool. His feet dangled down into its empty space. He tilted his head the way only he could do and softly, so very softly, strummed an old Spanish love song—a song older than the *hacienda*. Joshua walked to the steps of the pool and with absolute certainty of purpose stepped carefully down into it. It seemed a long time, but it was not. He placed the candelabra in the deepest part of the pool, stepped back, and looked into the flames. Then he raised his head and stared upwards at all the faces that now circled the pool to stare down at him. He turned in a complete circle so that he looked into the soft reflections in each of their eyes. He was all things in that small turn. None of them knew what *they* were seeing. He walked back up the steps, and there stood Rob.

Joshua said, "Come now, Rob, and I'll tell you what you really want to know."

Alfredo went on singing in Spanish as if he were making quiet love. The circle still looked downwards at the glowing candles.

Near the largest expanse of wall on the whole of the *hacienda*, Joshua said quietly to Rob, "I killed her. I took her into the desert and killed sweet Aleta."

Rob was momentarily paralyzed. Then a terrible cry and sound of murder burst from him as he ripped the edge of his pocket pulling out the gun. He fired right into the chest of Joshua, knocking him against the wall. He pulled at the trigger until there was nothing left. Joshua stayed upright for a moment, full of holes, and then fell forward, rolling over, face up. The crowd from the pool moved towards Rob, hesitantly, fearfully. They made a half-circle around the body.

Rob spoke, not looking away from Joshua's dead, smiling

face as if afraid he'd rise up again, "He killed Aleta."

Grebbs, saying things unintelligible like a slavering idiot, pushed his way through the mass, stopping with his face above Joshua's. Then he vented a little stuttering laugh. It broke forth louder and louder, and haltingly the others were caught up with him. They laughed and cried at the same time, not knowing really which they were doing. None thought to look at the wall above the body. It didn't matter, though, for all those who might have seen were already there. On a thin-edged hill stood Charlotte the dedicated, Aleta the beloved, Chalo the companion, and old Juanita the faithful. They were in a row, smiling with contentment. Just below them, the lady in black lace walked forward to meet Joshua.

As he moved into the wall, there came from his throat another form of laughter that far, far transcended the hysterical cackling in the patio. He glanced back just once, and the song overcame his mirth. He took her into his arms and held her. They had waited so very long. It was over. They walked, holding hands, up the hill to join those he loved, and they all disappeared into a new world.

The wall turned back to dirt.

None could stay at the *hacienda* that night. Just before the sun announced the dawn, the last candle in the bottom of the pool flickered out. The light was gone.

OLD BUM

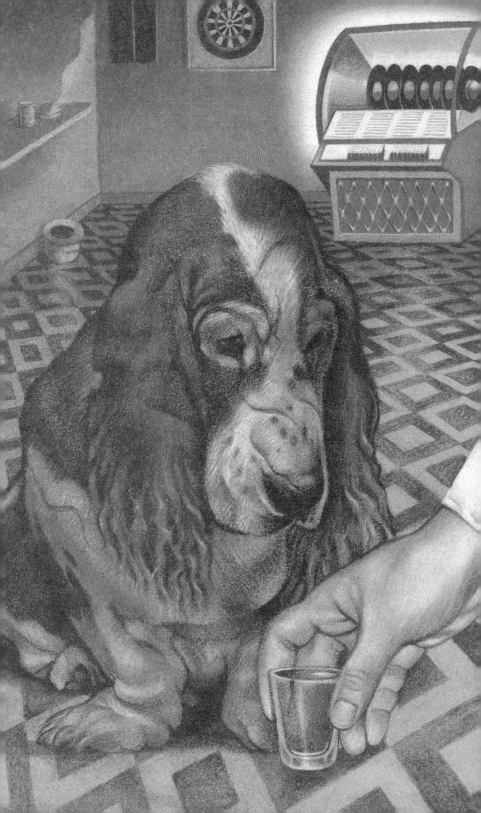

"Hey, Mark, guess what I've got in here," Tom Creswell said, clicking his store-bought teeth and licking his lips as he pointed to the trunk of his old Plymouth. His watery, light blue eyes were almost gleaming.

I figured by all this facial action that he surely must have a forty-pound sack of diamonds in there. It turned out to be almost that rare and priceless to us "great white" hunters—even if I was three-sixteenths Indian.

Tom C. was a sixty-odd-year-old rock mason, and we were partners in the rock building business; and we were friends in fun, drinking, and coyote hunting. He was a "hound-dog man" from all the way back to the first hunting genes.

He opened the trunk and out jumped this black and tan coon dog, and it looked all around the wide-open grasslands of northern New Mexico. That was back in the early fall of 1947,

MAX EVANS ✛ 225

when Tom introduced me to this creature that would alter my entire life.

"What do you think about this old hobo? I reckon he's just what we need for our hunting," Tom C. said with a certain pride.

"Why it's a flop-eared trail hound," I said, surprised. "What in the hell are we going to do with him? He couldn't catch a coyote in a month of hard running."

"Coons, Mark. We'll use him on coons. We can double our hunting and trapping income in no time at all."

I believed him. That's the way it is with mentors. You have to believe everything they say, even if it's wrong. Of course, mentors are so seldom wrong, you are supposed to just let it whiz right on by. Code of the West, you know.

"Where did you get him?" I asked.

"Found him about a quarter of a mile out of Grenville, walking smack down the middle of the Denver–Fort Worth railroad. He looked like he was on the trail of a fast freight. I just whistled, and he came to me."

There is a lot of good hunting in the rolling hills of northeastern New Mexico, and Tom and I hunted with dogs all the time. We hunted for the hides and the bounty. We had never used anything except long-legged, long-jawed running dogs—greyhounds, stags, and Russian wolfhounds. So, this trail hound was something new.

Before I get carried away about this wondrously unpredictable creature, I think it's fair to tell why the ranchers commissioned Tom Creswell and me to hunt coyotes for them.

I have on occasion helped ranchers pull calves from birthing heifers to save the lives of both the first-time mother and the new calf. It can be an agonizing struggle, taking hours to inch the calf out of a heifer with bare hands or a pulley. The

suffering is often great for all concerned. Sometimes it fails, and one or both is lost. After one of those successful deliveries, a rancher will usually ride back the next day to check on the animals that feed, clothe, and give life to his tough world and family. He expects to see a mother-licked-clean, big-eyed calf, bucking and playing around with his little contemporaries; or, sucking white liquid growth from his mother's swelled bag; or, having done that, sleeping off his contented fullness in the green grass of spring. However, if this rancher sees buzzards circling before he gets there and then just finds small bits of his protégé scattered about the land from a coyote's fangs, and sees and hears the heifer walking and bawling, looking for her first-born, her untapped milk painfully filling her udder until it drips out wasted onto the earth, the rancher gets real mad. He has lost part of the family's survival here, and he has lost some-thing he gave his heart and hands to bring into the world.

Once I was sitting, waiting for Tom C. to deliver a load of rocks to a windmill site for building a tank on Jim Ed Love's JL Ranch, when his son Clyde drove up in a pickup checking on things. We were visiting about the lack of rain, the price of cattle, the best bar in Raton, and the best hooker in Juárez when we heard a calf bawl over a hill to the north.

"Something's getting after that calf," Clyde said. "Come on."

So I jumped into the pickup with him, and he gunned it over to a gate. I leapt out, opened it, and he slowed just barely enough for me to get back in. Then we ran smack up against a sheer-drop arroyo. We bailed out and scurried to the top of a rise and saw a sight to make a rancher sick.

Two grown coyotes had hold of an early calf. One held onto the tail that was already chewed down to a nub, while the other had it by the muzzle. They were methodically circling.

The calf would drop soon, and then they would tear it into shreds and feast.

We both yelled as we ran downhill. The coyotes turned loose and ran up on a hill where they stopped to watch us. They always know if you have a gun or not. I could tell by their boldness they had a den of pups nearby. The little white-faced—now all red—calf had its tail torn off to the spine. Its eyes were bitten blind, and its muzzle hung in shreds of bloody meat. The poor little thing sensed we were not the enemy. Seeking some kind of comfort, it kept rubbing up against our legs, smearing us with blood. It was beyond help. Clyde grabbed up a ten-inch sandstone rock and hit it between the eyes as hard as he could strike. It went to its knees, then rolled over, jerked a couple of times, and died. We both understood that was all that could be done.

We numbly wiped the blood from our Levi's the best we could with wads of bunch grass, then slowly, silently walked back to the pickup. I looked up on the hill. I couldn't see the coyotes now, but I knew they could see us. In a little while they would come back, satiate themselves, taking a stomach full back to their den to regurgitate for their pups' sustenance—just as natural to them as moonlight. It was just as natural for the rancher to try to kill the coyotes to protect his own family. That is what the ranchers hired Tom C. and me to do for them. A terrible impasse.

I had to explain this distasteful truth so the monumentality of what happened later to make me quit hunting can be somewhat better understood.

Anyway, this new dog, this stranger in a lonely land of lonely people, would somehow become the cause of my soul-tearing turnaround. We called him Old Bum, instead of Hobo, but we sure never dreamed that he would live up to his name

the way he did and turn into a real out-and-out mooch. We soon found out he had all the vices of his two-legged brothers: heavy drinking, staying up all night at poker games, chasing the opposite sex, and finally even becoming addicted to hillbilly music. And with all this going for him, it turned out that he was also a downright snob. However, in the beginning he was a hunter tried-and-true, even though he was somewhat strange about his methods.

Back when this all happened—in the late forties—my eyesight was perfect, but the totality of my vision was sometimes cloudy. It's hard enough to get a young man to change his mind about a way of life he loves, but to have it altered in one day—with a single mysterious action that lasted less than a couple of minutes—is miraculous.

Now as I look back forty-five—or is it fifty?—years, I marvel at how that old flop-eared hound indirectly led me to such a dazzling enlightenment. And he wasn't even there at the time. Maybe that was part of it.

It was right after I returned from fighting with the combat infantry in Europe, and all that ground-tearing, sky-piercing madness that went on there, that I finally joined up with Tom Creswell. Since he was about thirty-five years older than me, he became my rock-mason mentor. Before the war I had learned the finer points of hunting and trapping from him, and now I was honored for him to teach me how to select, size, smear cement, and lay rocks so that they could form a water tank, a good horse shed, a milk house, or a fence.

I was able to keep my wife, Ortha, and four-year-old daughter Connie well fed and clothed and living in a house that sat on a hundred and ten acres just on the edge of Hi Lo. We had a milk cow and laying hens that were fat and producing. It was good to be young.

· The cattle ranchers around Hi Lo had been making a lot of money for the first time in quite a spell because of the demand for beef during World War II. The price of cattle just kept going up. Even in those boom times, only a very few had running water in the house or indoor plumbing. Some had electricity supplied by wind motors, but mostly they used kerosene or carbide lamps. The only TV in the whole Hi Lo country, that I knew of, was in a bar in Raton, about thirty miles to the west. Some people had battery radios for their only worldly communication. In 1947, ranchers still kept milk cows and laying and eating hens, and they butchered their own pork. This not only made economic sense, but people were still fearful because of the drought and the Great Depression of the thirties, which was still fresh in their minds. Even so, these extra chores made it especially hard on the ranch women, who were always overburdened anyway.

In spite of the somewhat primitive living conditions, the ranchers were busy expanding and improving their landholdings, which meant the big lizard swallowing the little lizard just like always. Tom C. and I prospered by specializing in building rock stock tanks for them, and since the coyote population was increasing at the same time the calf losses were, it wasn't too hard to convince the ranchers over this vast lonely spread of land to contract us to hunt coyotes at ten dollars a pair of ears.

So, there we were, "settin' purty." We were getting paid for laying rocks way out in the boonies and drawing down ten dollars a kill for the predators we pursued anyway, just for the thrill of it. Oh yeah, I almost forgot. On top of the ranchers' bonus, we got between five and fifteen dollars for each coyote hide. These extras made it possible for us to support our hunting habit without taking too much out of our construction income.

Coyote hunting was a pretty expensive sport. We had to feed the running hounds; buy traps and gasoline; replace busted tires, steel springs, and burned-out pistons on our pickups; and also, there were those drinks we had to buy in the bar while bragging about what great dogs we owned and what cunning, courageous hunters we were. We didn't really need drinks to tell these heart-rapping, mind-jouncing tales, but it made everybody more interested in listening. The stories were so wonderful and wild that we had to tone the truth down most of the time. Of course, everybody thought we were stretching things a little—like most other sportsmen have to do. Not us, though. You could bet your sister's drawers on that. This will be better understood after witnessing a few of the incidents that happened after Old Bum came into our lives. To be fair, he entered lots of lives.

Ortha had always been fairly patient with me and Tom C. talking about our adventures until Old Bum came along and we got to making her listen to the endless adventures about him. I really had not noticed it as closely as I should—ain't that a failing in most men? But she had taken to going off in another room and reading *Ready Romance Magazine* when we started up our natural hunting conversation. It wasn't long until she included *Romantic Interludes, Always Love*, and *Hearts the Same* on her subscription list of literary pursuits. Since we didn't have any TV, and the batteries on the radio were dead half the time, I read some myself. I liked Jack London and James M. Cain the best.

Now, looking back on it, I swear it seems impossible that I didn't see the train coming while I was sitting on the crossing. I reckon I misled myself by the fact she still kept the house, the yard, my daughter Connie, and herself neat and clean, the garden watered, the meals cooked, and even took care of the

cow and chickens. At that time she was getting only one or two headaches a week at bedtime, but when those increased to three and four, any idiot should have caught on that aspirins were going to be useless.

Ortha was a hardworking, loving woman built as well as a quarter horse mare. She had green eyes that could have been worn as emeralds on a queen's necklace, lips as luscious as strawberries, teeth so even and white that brushing seemed like a waste of time, and a voice that rolled out soft words to make warblers and jazz musicians bow down in homage; and I didn't appreciate her as much as I did my hounds. I was a master fool and then some, but I didn't get the illumination until the sun had already set.

I told Tom C., "Blessings be, ole partner, I do believe she almost smiled at breakfast this morning."

He just looked at me blankly, his mind on our upcoming hunt: "Sounds promising."

How does the song go? "So far, far away and forever ago." Something like that, I do believe. As I sit here in a comfortable lawn chair looking over the barns and the big house in the middle of four green, landscaped acres that belong to my daughter Connie and her husband, Jack Oldham, I can see as clearly as night lightning back to those days before I quit hunting so suddenly, forever.

Yeah, Ortha did leave me, and she took my precious little Connie with her to stay with her folks in Texas until we could get divorced and she could start a new life. No use going on much more about that, except to say that Ortha married a realtor from Fort Worth. Connie grew up beautiful as all the fresh colors sprouting from the earth after a spring rain, and as

smart and graceful as a circus pony. Ortha turned back to her naturally decent self and let Connie spend a month or so with me every summer way out here in the Hi Lo country. Before I could say "General Patton" or "holy halleluja hell" Connie was in her second year in college at Texas University in El Paso. She wrote and said she would be out in a week to stay a week.

At the time, I was building—Tom C. had finally retired because of arthritis and one short leg—a stock tank for Jack Oldham, a young rancher over south of Raton. I took Connie with me one day. Jack came by to check out the project. I'll never know how it happened, but Connie wound up married to him four months later. Jack was director in a Raton bank, owned some interest in a producing coal mine, and kept this great house just on the edge of the northeast city limits. We got along like coffee and doughnuts.

Since I was so handy with rocks, and not too shabby with wood and nails either, my son-in-law kept me working on the ranch for years. When I started to stumble over little tiny pebbles and lean permanently to the northeast, he let me have the guest house in town, and all I had to do was keep the four acres slicked up some and look after the twin boys, Fred and Ted, whenever Jack and Connie wanted to go off to Acapulco, Las Vegas, Nevada, or Hillsboro, New Mexico, for a little of the so-called "rest and regeneration."

Like I said, this very day I was sitting in one of those outdoor chairs Connie kept all over the yard, letting the early summer sun loosen my old muscles so they didn't bend my bones. I felt good. All the family, and a couple of the twins' high school friends, was all out at the ranch, riding and roping to beat seven hundred, I reckoned.

Anyway, I kept dozing some, and every time I woke up a little my mind's eyes went traveling into the past about thirty

miles east to the lonely village of Hi Lo. For some reason I kept seeing all that malpai, sandstone, wind-ripped country, and everywhere I looked I seemed to see Old Bum, who was the critter that led up to my neck-snapping, nerve-cracking turnaround. Like the song goes, "Long away and far, far ago," or something like that.

Anyway . . . we were mighty restless waiting for nightfall so we could get Old Bum out in the field. Tom C. chose the Cimarron River country below Folsom for our first venture. Cottonwood trees lined the banks of the creek, and enough perch and other small crustaceans inhabited it to entice the coons. When the coon hunted, that's when we hunted him.

We bailed out of a pickup truck carrying a twenty-two rifle, a powerful flashlight, two running hounds, and Old Bum. The moon was just beginning to climb over the hill, casting black, night shadows all about. The crickets and a billion other insects sang their eternal songs.

"What's that?" I asked quietly after hearing a noise.

"Deer, I think," Tom whispered. "They come down at night to graze in the ranchers' alfalfa patches along the river."

I listened to the whomping noise they made as they ran back towards the hills, and then I said, "Well, that's one thing in Old Bum's favor. He doesn't run deer."

"Yeah. Now, let's hope he doesn't take after a porcupine and get his head loaded up with quills."

We shut up then and began to hunt. Old Bum was moving ahead in erratic circles, his nose to the ground and his tail sticking straight up in the air. He acted like a real "cooner." The running dogs just walked along taking a sniff of the air now and then, mostly watching the new, short-legged member

of the pack, insultingly, as if they wondered what a snail was doing trying to run with the racers.

Then we heard him bawl. Just once, that's all. The running hounds took off with their long legs eating the ground. I snapped on the flashlight. Tom and I tore through the brush, falling now and then but following the course of the river just the same. Then we heard the hoglike squeal of the coon.

"Here, Tom!" I yelled, flashing the light on the frenzied battle.

It was a hugh boar coon. The running dogs had never been on a coon hunt before. They were having trouble deciding on the proper method of attack. The coon was up and down, rolling over and over, slashing with his razor-sharp teeth at the hounds. Finally, Brownie, half stag, half grey, and the heavier of the two, got the throat. Then Pug, the Russian wolfhound, moved in to the brisket, crushing down with powerful jaws. The coon was finished. And where do you suppose Old Bum had taken hold? The tail, that's where, and almost halfheartedly at that. I reckon he figured this end didn't have any teeth.

We caught two more coons that night. Old Bum would work out ahead and jump one. The running dogs would listen for his single squawk, then they would move out fast and down the coon before he had a chance to climb a tree. It was a new and exciting hunting combination—the trail hound to track, the running dogs to catch and kill. As far as Old Bum was concerned, that was just the way it was from the first coon on. He refused to get in close enough to be bitten by the wildly fighting coons. He acted a little stuck-up about it, as if he figured the smelling part of the job was the most important. He wouldn't lower himself to the actual bloody business of fighting.

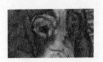

Overnight, the big dogs had developed a reserved admiration for one whose special talents they couldn't match. The combination improved as the dogs learned to get into the neck quicker by throwing the coon on his back. Old Bum would voice his single bawl. That was like a trigger to the other hounds.

All that fall we hunted up and down the Cimarron with Old Bum, taking about forty coons. We hunted at Weatherly Lake and caught eighteen nice ones. Just three coons made their escape to the scattered cottonwoods that entire season. The eighteen skins brought only about three dollars and fifty cents each, but that was better than a bee in the ear. Hey! Whiskey was thirty-five cents a drink, the jukebox was a nickel a song—six for a quarter—and a loaf of bread cost the same as a shot of the brown whiskey. Two coon hides would finance a small meal, a small drunk, and a big hangover. Those were the good old days and nights—or so it seemed for a while.

Naturally, we began to brag a little about our coon hunting prowess. Then in the natural process of things, we got to wondering how Old Bum would do on a coyote hunt. I wish we had never thought of that.

We turned the hounds out about a mile and a half from Cow Mountain. It was good rolling country. The coyote had about a hundred yard start. The running dogs leaped out of the back of the pickup. They sailed smoothly across the grasslands after the coyote, who was now racing madly. If a person had never run coyotes, there is no way to explain how your entire body and probably your boots, hat, and underwear are flooded with adrenalin to the point of feeling as if you were swimming in it. Your heart knocks ribs apart and causes lungs to swell like helium balloons. We once ran right through a rock wall, actually speeding up before the pile of rubble settled behind us.

Crazed. Nuts. A person is instantly hurled back into the time before the wheel was invented and fire was something that only flashed down from the sky in a storm or boiled up from volcanos. Ancient emotions. Raw.

Well, anyway, Old Bum hit the ground on his short legs, rolled over about three times in a cloud of dust, then got up and headed in the wrong direction. He had been knocked silly from the fall, causing his inner-head compass to spin erratically.

We could see the running dogs pull up closer and closer on their coyote in long, graceful, ground-eating strides. Then one hound was alongside the coyote. He reached over, took hold of the coyote's neck, and down they went! The other dogs piled on. But where was Old Bum? Well, he had accidentally jumped the running mate to the other coyote and was running as fast as his legs would carry him in pursuit. The coyote just loped along, easily outdistancing him. Teasing.

We drove on to where the other running hounds were scattering the coyote's insides across the prairie. We pulled the dogs off and loaded them into the pickup. Then we started looking for Old Bum.

Way off to the west, we could see two tiny clouds of dust heading into the hills. Old Bum didn't show up again for twenty-four hours, and when he did he was chewed all over, his ears ripped, and his nose was covered with cuts. It looked like the coyote had led him into an ambush, where several of the varmints had given him a real working over. We felt mighty lucky to have him back alive. He seemed to appreciate breathing, however painfully, himself. We never took Old Bum coyote hunting again. It wasn't the thing to do. I don't think he wanted to go anyway.

We did use him that winter to trail animals that had escaped with our steel traps. He proved invaluable on the trap

line, paying for his upkeep many times above and beyond.

I didn't know then, as I've already explained, what was slowly separating me from my family. I started spending quite a number of evenings up on the main street of Hi Lo—which consisted of four blocks split by Highway 87. There was just too much going on up town, and I didn't want to miss any of it. Well, this move, as it turned out later, didn't do me much good, but what it did for Old Bum was something to sit down with my head in my hands and ponder about.

The first step in his changeover from a damned good coon dog to a hard-drinking hound—if not a downright drunkard—came about one Saturday afternoon in the Wild Cat Bar where the sidewalk curb was smack up against the aforementioned highway.

Hi Lo is a little cow town—population of about one hundred and fifty—on a long piece of pavement from way down somewhere in Texas into, and across, northern New Mexico. To the south of town is Sierra Grande Mountain. Some claim it to be the largest lone mountain in the world. It is forty-five miles around the base and about nine thousand feet high. It takes a full day to hunt around its edges. To the north, east, and west is rolling grama-covered rangeland broken now and then by a steep, jagged, malpai-studded canyon—the Carrummpah. There were two grocery stores, Chick Johnson's small hotel, two cafés, an all-night service station, and two bars. The bars are the busiest places in town. The ranchers, cowboys, and odd-job boys—like me and Tom C.—all hang out there when they come to town. They do a little drinking—sometimes a lot of drinking—and catch up on the gossip, find out who won the latest street fights, and other such sporting activities.

The bars are directly across the street from each other;

the Wild Cat to the south, the Double Duty to the north. It was very convenient for all concerned. If a fight started in front of one, the customers of both places had what you might call ringside seats. If a feller was a little wobbly on his feet and wished to change company, he could just aim himself right straight across the highway and he would be pretty sure to hit a bull's-eye as far as bars are concerned. There wasn't enough traffic in those days to worry about the odds of getting run over.

The wind blows in Hi Lo at least two-thirds of the time. It comes howling around the Sierra Grande Mountain in a grass-bending fury. I think the reason so many fistfights break out is because the people are all on edge from bucking this infernal wind. In fact, after all these decades I've had to think about it, I know that's the main reason.

That Saturday, I left Old Bum in the pickup and walked into the Wild Cat to do a little visiting. It just happened that a friendly pitch game was going on in a booth, and several wind-bent, sun-cured cowboys were standing at the bar giving Lollypop, the bartender, a lot of business. It was a cold day, but the Wild Cat was warm, and the only wind blowing inside was some cowboy bragging about what a bronc rider and calf roper he was. And then, I just couldn't help myself, I began to brag a little about Old Bum.

As the talk got mellower, somebody suggested that it was a dirty, stinking shame to leave such a remarkable dog out in the pickup where he might catch cold or get snakebit or something. We invited Old Bum inside. He stopped just past the door and looked the place over like General Montgomery surveying a battlefield. For a minute we were afraid he wasn't going to like the place. All of a sudden he trotted over to the bar, wagged his tail just a tad, and stared right straight up at the

bartender. That was too much. The thirst pains showed up so strong on Old Bum's face that we kindhearted cowboys, railroaders, and rock masons just broke down and bought Old Bum a double shot.

The bartender set it on the floor in front of him. He looked at it. He looked at me. Then he ran his tongue out and took a lick. Something happened right then and there to Old Bum. Sort of a quiver came over him, and after the booze he went. In his hurry, he turned the glass over, and about half of it poured out on the floor. But it didn't evaporate or get stale, or go to waste or anything like that. He licked it right up, almost taking up what was left of the design from the linoleum-covered floor.

A lot of cheers went up. Over and over the glasses were set up for the greatest of all coon dogs; this aristocratic reveler; this friend of man and his vices, as well; this cool cucumber of a canine; this . . . aww hell, there were no words to describe him that first night of his debauchery. As the song says, "Away so far, so long ago."

The pitch players couldn't hear their bids, so they got up and joined the party. After a while somebody punched the jukebox full of nickels, and Old Bum sort of waltzed over and cocked his head to one side. Whenever a hillbilly tune came on, Old Bum would throw that proud, flop-eared head up and join the singing. We all agreed that he sounded better than some of the records. When anything played other than hillbilly, the head came down, the tail stopped wagging, and a sad, sour expression came over his face.

After a time Old Bum wobbled over to the door and scratched to get out. I figured maybe he was sick or something, but it turned out that he, unlike most of us, knew when he had had enough and wanted to get some sleep. This animal seemed

to have had experiences we would, or could, only guess at. I helped him into the front of the pickup, not wanting him to suffer from the wind.

About four hours later, I decided it was time to go home. Every time I tried to open the pickup door to get in, Old Bum would snarl and leap at me. It came to me then that he understood himself a lot better than we did. This wasn't the first time for him. Far from it. He probably knew he got mean when he reached a certain stage and wanted to bed down before he got unfriendly and hurt somebody.

I waited down at the all-night station until about daylight. I stumbled back up to my pickup feeling worn out and sleepy. Old Bum didn't make a move. He was lying there passed out, snorting and jerking once in a while as he dreamed his private dreams of the past. And what a past he must have enjoyed. I was certain of it.

I crawled in real slow and careful, and then drove the half-mile home just as the sun came up. Since I lived right on the edge of town at that time, I don't know why I didn't just walk on home and turn the pickup over to that dog. But, of course, that would be letting him take advantage of me. Just because Old Bum pulled this one big drunk was no sign he was going straight to hell as fast as he did, but it was a slight indication. Just like it was with my own family, I didn't move soon enough with Old Bum to prevent the sure deterioration. Anyway, I carried his sleeping body into the house with me.

We both woke up lying side by side on the living room floor. For just a minute I felt like running outside with Old Bum and going till we fell off in a deep, dark, secret canyon. It was too late. Ortha was already making extra-loud banging noises cooking breakfast. She saw us both struggling to sur-

vive, and she didn't say "Good morning." In fact, she didn't speak at all.

My little Connie made an effort to be her true, sweet self, but soon leapt away from the breakfast table, running outside for an early playtime, shouting, "That dog stinks." I didn't know which one of us she really meant.

When I saw Ortha wash the butcher knife for the seventh time, I got out of there and headed for town. I suppose, for a spell anyway, me and Old Bum sort of got lost in the wicked wilderness. It's hard, all these years later, to realize how thoughtless I could be with the exuberance of youth driving me on and on.

I quit working rocks with my mentor. The reason being, I decided to become a painter—not a house painter, but the other kind who paints pictures. Tom C. never said much about it, but I could tell he was deeply hurt by the foolish actions of his protégé. I still hunted with him, though. He had to give me credit there.

Levi Gomez, a part-Spanish, part-Apache, part-French, part . . . I don't know what . . . artist friend, was showing me some *bultos* (standing figures of saints) he had carved from cedar. He told me that some people knocked down as much as twenty bucks apiece for such like. I was somewhat amazed at this. A few days later I read in the *Saturday Evening Post* about a cowboy artist called Charlie Russell receiving thousands of dollars for just one painting. This seemed like a good idea to me. Why shouldn't a rock mason/coyote/coon hunter have just as good a chance at getting rich and famous as a dumb-ass cowboy? I know it sounds stupid now, but during those old times at Hi Lo I believed almost everything was possible.

So Levi and I discussed things over a quart of good brown whiskey and decided we would set up a studio and get rich. We

sure did the first, but we missed the last by a country music mile.

Next door to the Double Duty bar (that's the one across the street) was an ugly old building held together by a bunch of brown rusted tin. We rented one end of this for fifteen dollars a month.

I bought a lot of paint in little metal tubes, some brushes made out of camel hair, a sketch pad and a few canvas boards, and started painting horses and cowboys. You talk about going crazy. For a while it was hard to tell which was the horse and which was the cowboy. Whenever I finished a picture, I would tack it up on the wall at a fancy price. I had gone that silly. No one else in that country did any serious painting. We soon found out that the citizens of Hi Lo didn't have much interest in art of any kind, so we went it all alone.

We got an idea then that we might attract a little tourist trade if we had a sign. So Levi painted us a fancy one, and we nailed it up on the front of the building. We called our place "Ye Olde Masters Art Gallery." Nobody ever stopped by. It took awhile for us to catch on to the dearth of cultural interest along Highway 87 at that time.

Our only company was Old Bum. He hung around the gallery with us most of the time. Well, no wonder. We fed him there, it was out of the wind, and it was really handy to both bars. It was also a great place for him to sober up and recover from his hangovers. At these times he didn't tolerate any talk or bother. More than one person in town was snapped at for trying to pet him when he was under the influence. He was a pretty severe art critic, too. Every time I asked him how he liked one of my paintings, he'd scratch on the door wanting out.

In small country towns, cats and dogs roam free. There are no restrictions on a pet's freedom except whatever the

owner wants to impose. So, it didn't surprise me one day when I drove into town to do some painting, to see about nine dogs all in a fighting pile. I caught glimpses of what I knew were parts of Old Bum. I jumped out of the pickup and tried to knock them off of him with a long-handled shovel I always carried in the back. When they all left, there lay Old Bum bloody and chewed all over. His tongue was hanging out, and it looked like it had already turned blue. I was sure he was dead.

I laid him in the back of the pickup and started to drive the short distance downtown to tell Levi the bad news. I glanced into the rearview mirror to check for traffic before I pulled onto the highway, and durned if I didn't see Old Bum get up and jump out. He ran across the pavement in pursuit of the same little black-and-white female that had started all the trouble. How Old Bum succeeded in this love affair, against such great and resentful odds, no one could guess, but there was no denying the five little flop-eared, half-breeds born a few months later.

One afternoon I was standing out in front of our "unvisited" gallery, leaning against a telephone pole just soaking up some sun. Old Bum was squatted on his hunkers beside me trying to recover from a little overindulgence of the night before. I studied the condition of our old friend. He was a mess. His eyes were red and watery from his heavy drinking, and there were scars over his whole body. His ears were in little threads and knots out at the ends where they had been bitten so much. But he was tough, and a real mixture of contradiction. A lot of big dogs chewed him up, but none of them ever made him run. He was too high-classed to pitch in and fight an over-matched coon, but when it came to privileges with the female, he would fight any dog in town right to the death.

As much as he admired the women folks of his own kind, he couldn't stand the human breed of female at all. He was strictly a man's dog. I imagine that came about somewhere in his past when a strong, wise woman must have told him to straighten up and do right or he was going to be shunned. Ortha was telling me the same thing in her own way, but like I said, I'd gone over—way over—the dark crack in the earth and couldn't see any daylight.

Old Bum had been around town long enough now to have a regular circuit worked out for himself. He stayed at the gallery until we began to run out of money and couldn't feed him what he liked. After that, he just dropped by to give the critic's cold eye to our artwork or whenever he was too drunk to make it to his more distant hangouts. Everyone on his appointed route was a bachelor.

Pal England—one of the more sporting lads in town—lived with his retired, widowed, old father. Pal had a short leg from parachuting into a bad landing after his bomber was shot down over the Third Reich, and had spent a spell in one of their POW camps, so the government gave him a small pension for his short leg and long memories.

Pal said, "By all odds, I should be recognized as the town drunk since Vince Moore's unintentional retirement, but Old Bum has more experience, so I'm giving him the title for now."

Vince Moore had held the undisputed title a long time before Pal. He was a part-time bootlegger who had moved his large family into town after being *nudged* out of his single section of land. He proudly claimed the title of official town drunk. He once told me, "I've been drunk for forty years because I'm afraid of falling dead with a hangover." His worrying all that time was wasted. As he was hurrying to his outhouse,

one of those Hi Lo wind gusts blew the roof off and knocked him as dead as last year's Christmas tree. If any creature had a chance to match these great accomplishments of the past, it was Old Bum.

Knowel Denny, a foreman on the railroad, lived across the tracks about three hundred yards from Pal. They were close friends, and Old Bum liked them both. They made quiet talk and always had something good cooking on the stove, like venison stew, or biscuits and gravy, and other tasty handouts that appealed to his taster.

Another place the old hound visited was down to the east about a quarter of a mile at Rube Fields'. Rube was an old-time well driller and widower. Rube's specialty was chile and beans. Old Bum kept pretty well fed by making his circuit.

Besides the food stations, he checked on the bars three times a day. The first inspection was around ten in the morning to see if any holdover party from the night before was still going on; then again about three in the afternoon when the pitch and poker games were on the way; and, of course, around nine or ten at night when the more serious drinking was beginning. He would stand up close to the bar and look sad, and somebody was bound to take pity and give him a refreshment.

Old Bum's obvious enjoyment of hillbilly music (his favorite singer was Eddy Arnold) would cause somebody else to buy him a drink, so he could relax and more fully enjoy this place of country culture. A couple of drinks and he was well on his way to becoming part of the musical entertainment.

He had a knack for hearing, smelling, or in some way sensing a really jam-up, bottle-throwing, fist-fighting party. Whiskey, female dogs, and fistfights were the things that excited him most. When a fight would break out, Old Bum

would jump around, all alert, not missing a punch. But he never took sides.

The only time I remembered him showing any pity on a loser was when I made a feeble effort to save him from the fun and drinking that was making the both of us wobble and shake like a gravel separator. I told this big cowboy, who worked for the JL Ranch, that I didn't want him or anyone else giving any more drinks to my hunting dog.

He turned away from the bar, looking at me as if I was that sneaky bronc that kicked him in the belly last week, and said quietly, "He's just a dawg."

Talk about foolish, I replied, "No, he ain't just a dawg. He is a first-class coon hound, and you're going to ruin his smeller."

The cowboy grabbed my collar and the seat of my Levi's and hustled me outside faster than thought. That's as fast as it gets.

He said, just as he hit me in the nose, "You got it wrong, partner. It's your smeller I'm gonna ruin."

He did. It always turned to the southwest after that. I went face down in the gutter of the sidewalk with his two hundred and more pounds on top of me flailing away from my kidneys to my ears with fists as hard as horseshoes. While the old boy had me down where the sidewalk joins the highway, trying to push my face into the dirt, I kept turning my head to the side to avoid permanent gravel implants. Every time I turned, Old Bum would lick me with a long, wet tongue right across my eyes.

I gasped, "Why don't you get the S.O.B. on top of me by the throat, if you love me so much."

After a while, Levi came and picked me up and led me over to Ye Ole Masters Art Gallery and helped me wash the

road tar and gravel from my face. He picked up one of the cedar *bultos*—Saint George, slayer of dragons, I think—and said he was going over to beat that cowboy's head into pudding with it. I said, "Naw, Levi, let it go. Killing a cowboy with a saint is not going to be good for our artistic image." He reluctantly saw the wisdom, and soon all became calm.

As time passed, Old Bum's personality changed along with his appearance. He was becoming jaded, stuck-up, and more than half cranky. During this period, somebody shot Old Bum in the shoulder with a twenty-two rifle. An amateur horse doctor said to leave it alone and it would heal around the bullet. Which it did, but it gave him a kind of stiff-legged limp in his left front leg. It made him appear to walk in an even more stuck-up manner. By this time, he had also acquired a big rip over one eye, leaving a scar that added to his aristocratic appearance, looking more like a monocle than anything else. He also became very possessive about his territorial rights as well. Not only did the sidewalks belong to him, but so did four blocks of Highway 87. Sometimes when he was crossing from one bar to the other, he would stop right in the middle of the highway and just stand there with his head up looking mighty important through his drink-blurred eyes. Many times we would hear tires screeching against the asphalt and know someone was trying to miss killing the current town drunk. He would not move, nor bat an eye, with a ten-ton truck bearing down on him at top speed. It was the greatest wonder in the world that Old Bum didn't get a lot of sober people killed.

Finally to my great relief, after I had made about a thousand sly hints, people began to worry about him, and sort of by mutual consent we decided to cut him off the bottle for a while and try to straighten him out. Trying to be an inspiration

to him, I quit drinking myself. Tom C. was thrilled when I said I was ready for another hunt now.

Old Bum had been sober for over a week when we decided it would do him good to take him coon hunting and get him interested again in what he was born and bred to do. We didn't have any trouble finding him, but we were about three hours too late. Some tourist had stopped for a drink on his way up to Colorado, and Old Bum had slipped in, looking kind of lost and pitiful. Before long he had beggared himself a load-on.

Tom C. had spent his long life hunting and handling hound dogs, but this presented a brand-new problem.

I said, "We might throw him in the river. It could sober him up."

"It might work at that," Tom C. agreed.

Old Bum loaded into the back of the pickup with the other dogs without any trouble. He was at this happy stage now, but if we had waited another hour to rescue him from the saloon and demon drink, it would have been too bad. The big running dogs gave Old Bum some strange looks, wondering what in the world had happened to their faithful, helpful hunting partner.

When we unloaded, down on the Cimarron, it was dark and cloudy. My flashlight beam knocked a bright round hole in the night. We eased up beside Old Bum and pushed him off into the river with a big, wet splash. He crawled up out of there, shaking the water from his hide and struck out for the brush without giving us a glance.

Suddenly, we heard him bawl. And bawl again, then again. He had never bawled over once before. Tom C. and I looked at each other. The running dogs were already racing after Old Bum ready for the easy kill.

"What in the world do you think he's got treed?" I asked.

"Well, I sure don't know, but it's bound to be something different. I ain't never heard him bawl twice before."

"Yeah," I said. "I guess he finally had the 'one too many' drinks we all talk about but never believe."

We headed out as fast as we could. The other dogs—always silent hunters before—were barking and growling in sounds of dismay and puzzlement. All of a sudden the light beam found them. A bull! Old Bum had treed a big, white-faced bull. The bull lowered his head and charged Old Bum at full speed. The dog sort of stumbled out of the way, still making that loud bawling noise. The bull whirled, pawed the ground, snorted, and charged again. He didn't miss Old Bum three inches. The other hounds had become so excited, they had forgotten their training and were running in circles around the uneven contest like amateur cheerleaders when the baton is dropped.

"A hell of a big coon!" Tom C. yelled.

"Yeah," I answered. "We've got to do something quick, Tom, or that bull's going to kill Old Bum."

The bull charged. We scattered and ran for the pickup. I tried to lead him away from the much slower Tom C. I was successful. He hooked me under one leg with a horn and tossed me like a wet dishrag up on the hood of the pickup. While at the apex of this unwanted fight, I threw the flashlight at a clump of bunch grass. The bull took in after the light until he decided he was in the wrong pasture. We were saved. I rolled over on the ground, my breath knocked loose, wondering if I was dead. I knew I was alive when I heard the bull tearing up brush heading for the hills.

Then Tom C. shined the lifesaving flashlight in my face and asked, "You all right?"

I sat up. I moved. I felt of my legs and all. I couldn't feel any rips in my skin, and everything seemed to be in its rightful place. Before I could determine an answer, Old Bum was in my lap licking my face like it was smeared with wild honey. You can say, or think, whatever you want about this animal that had created all the fun and excitement, but he and that slobbering tongue of his always came to the aid of the down and out.

I stumbled to my feet, saying, "I'm the luckiest man alive."

"I reckon we all are," Tom C. said with profound truth.

We just breathed in the moonlight awhile, not talking. There was a little numbness in my leg where the horn had hooked under, and it was beginning to swell a little. I was thanking God and all his kinfolks that that was the extent of the damage. I could have been standing there with my entrails or my privates in my hands. It was at least an hour before we gathered the dogs up and headed for town.

On the drive back home that night, my mentor told me something special. He lifted the wrinkled little tan hat from his head and ran a large, perpetually chapped hand through his thin gray hair. As he tried to push his false teeth solid with his tongue so he could speak clearly, he said, "You know something, Mark? To be conceived is dangerous to life, but being born is even more so."

Later—after my semiretirement in Raton—I would remember what he said, because now all these medical scientists were telling us that just about everything, including ice cream, eggs, beef, and even dreaming, would kill us. The old man's wisdom became even more special by the day. Like I said before, that's what mentors are for, but I didn't understand all he meant back then.

The next day when the boys asked how we did on our hunt last night, we said, "Not much good. Too dark." Old Bum didn't show the least sign of shame.

A few weeks later, Levi and I were working at the gallery while my sore body loosened up. Old Bum had not had a drink since the night of the coon hunt. His eyes looked a lot better. All evening, though, we noticed how restless he was. Ever so often he would get up and walk to the door. He didn't scratch to get out, so we didn't pay much attention. Then he started whining.

Levi said, "I believe he needs to hunt a post."

I let him out. I didn't know we would never see him again and it would be decades before I would know all that happened.

Tom C. and I had finished putting some new rigging on the pickup with two compartments in the bed. We had rope pulleys attached to sliding gates on the bottom half of the back end. Each pulley was clamped by opposite windows on the truck cab. When we spotted a coyote, we could jerk the back gate open with the rope and let out one team of dogs at a time. This way we would always have a fresh team ready. We figured we could double our production of coyote ears for the ranchers' bounty. We could hardly wait to try it out. For some unexplained reason, I was determined to take Old Bum along. Tom C. thought I was crazy. Just the same I had the urge for his company; but we couldn't find him anywhere, and nobody in town would admit to having seen him. Later, of course, the story would leak out. It always does in these little one- and two-bar towns.

It was one of those days that the poets talk about happening just once in a lifetime. Everything changed forever that day for me. Everything.

I felt a little vacancy for Old Bum as we drove by Weatherly Dam on out to Pete Jones's outfit for our first testing of the fancy-rigged coyote truck. Pete's ranch rolled downhill north to Carrummpah Canyon and creek. We drove on down about a half-mile this side of the canyon's rim, knowing from many years of past hunts that most flushed coyotes would head straight towards their protective wildness.

The dogs moved about restlessly in the back, knowing we were hunting, but not yet used to the new setup. In spite of my prior emptiness, because of the missing flop-eared hound, my heart was jump-starting as I stared across the yucca-dotted grassland. I was gripping the steering wheel so hard my hands were almost numb. I could smell coyotes. I couldn't see them yet, but the scent-notifiers in my brain already were stirring little squirts of adrenalin all through my body.

The wind was whipping the grama grass in golden rhythms. The electricity that generates somewhere in the brain and the heart was sparking fiery impulses through the flesh of my entire being. Old Tom C. was leaning stiffly forward with both of his huge, knobby hands gripping the dashboard with desperate force. They looked as strong and hard as the thousands of rocks they had shaped into beauty and usefulness. His eternally weakening, blue-gray eyes seemed to project tiny rays of light ahead, trying to call back the sight of his younger days. I nearly always spotted our prey first, but when the ancient hunter's blood started pulsing and pumping, Tom C. never quit trying. In these few moments out of eternity, it seemed that we were separated from the usual progression of earth, moon, sun, and stars. It was as if our limited chunk of this

hard, wind-agitated land had been removed to another time and galaxy for our own special events of life and death to occur.

I spotted the mother coyote's ears. They were shaped wider, different from the swordlike blades of the large yucca clump she watched us through. I drove on silently, trying to keep all the tearing turmoil in my body from exuding out so the dogs would not pick up the silent message and start raising hell too soon.

Tom C. had already felt it, but our blood communication was so perfect the only sign he showed was the rising of his chest trying to keep his lungs in place. That's the way it is with longtime hunting partners.

The coyote had four pups, three-quarter-grown, lying low in the tall grass, but I spotted their outlines because their bodies created a motionless little void in the ocean of wind-dancing stems. She was sure we were going to drive on by and miss her, I knew. We were very close to that point you can never return to or from. That immeasurable portion of space where everything will happen.

I kept my foot easing up and down delicately on the accelerator, trying to keep the mother coyote from noticing any untoward movement. I wanted to get exactly between her and the canyon, hoping we could catch her and maybe one of the pups before she could head for the canyon's safety.

Just a few more yards now. The world was a blur of red. There was no breath. The wind had no air for that moment. Then it all exploded at the same precise instant.

I hit the brakes. The mother coyote knew we had spotted them. She whirled, racing east, followed by her scattering pups, who looked back at us in a quick hesitation as they tried to follow their mother's lead and at the same time satisfy their

curiosity of our movement. It was a fatal half-second of hesitation. Tom C. jerked the cage rope, and one team of the hounds leapt upon the ground. I jerked the other rope, and now two teams were stretching full out. Their long legs were just graceful, ground-swallowing blurs.

Our timing had been exact as a dagger tip. The first team downed a pup—one by the neck, the other at the brisket. The wind had whipped the battle-dust away by the time Old Pug and Brownie had caught the mother. Just as hundreds of times before, Brownie raced right up parallel, reaching his mighty jaws out, clamping down on the neck of the coyote. They rolled completely over twice before Brownie would stand up still crushing the neck. Before the coyote had a chance to rise, Pug was there to secure the prone position and demise of the coyote by crushing the ribs right into the heart and lungs.

Tom C. and I were so caught up in this moment of intense action and sudden death, and the unspoken success of our first hunt with double teams, that we forgot all about the pickup.

I raced afoot across the rolling world towards the kill, driven on by things so old, so deeply rooted, that I would have dived off a twenty-foot bluff without hesitation to be there at the moment of the ultimate. The kill!

Tom C. stumbled along behind, his old heart unable to supply enough air to fuel his movements any faster. Then it happened. My eyes, trained so long to seek out the tiniest form and movement, flashed uncontrollably to the three pups racing for safety over the crest of a hill perhaps an eighth of a mile distant. Two of them disappeared, and thereby lived as their many millions of years of genes instructed them. But one stopped. The universe stopped. Then, as always, it exploded again. The pup, without any hesitation charged back down the

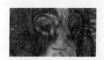

hill, gathering speed in its descent, heading straight for the trio of Pug, Brownie, and its dying mother. It charged with all the speed of its body, with all its ancient fury, into the two hounds whose combined weight and bulk was at least eight times that of the pup. Its momentum knocked both dogs loose from the mother. It bounced over the dogs in a complete flip, rolling over several times, stumbling up stunned.

The hounds were also momentarily numbed. The pup's action had no place in their world of directed instincts. For an unmeasured space of time, they hesitated. Then all their millions of years of trained genes took control, and they downed the addled pup and killed it almost instantly.

All this had happened before our eyes in just under two minutes. But somehow in that tiny space of clock time, a millennium had whizzed by.

I was still standing motionless, except for the wind pushing me. The act of the coyote pup was beyond any scientific knowledge in existence. I knew I had witnessed a true sacrificial event against all human knowing. I was numbed and humbled beyond speech.

Old Tom C. finally stumbled up beside me, gasping. He, too, had extended his heart's strength as far as it could be crowded without its own final explosion. He hesitantly reached one of his great old hands out to my shoulder for support. It was trembling so that it shook my body, and myself, back to awareness of this present world. His painful, breathing body struggled to keep him upright one more time, through one more hunt. Finally, he was composed enough to stand without using my body as a brace.

Then he said, quietly, "I never saw anything like that in my whole life. Have you, Mark?"

"No," I answered, and the single word was taken away by the wind.

We loaded our dogs and the three dead coyotes—when there should have been, by all the laws, only two. I drove back to town. Neither one of us talked for a spell. We just stared straight and far down the road. I knew I could never hunt coyotes again. Not ever. I didn't.

That same fateful day, Ortha had left for Texas with my sweet little Connie, but I've already told about that. My wife didn't leave me for chasing women. She left me for running coyotes.

As I sit now in this comfortable lawn chair thinking back, reliving those days decades ago, I realize how lucky I was to wind up here comfortable and being able to help my loved ones now and then. It had been luck when Tom C. had introduced me to Old Bum. It had been luck when I found out a couple of years back where, and how, that flop-eared wonder had disappeared from Hi Lo. Well, I'm using that word luck a lot, but I know it plays a big part in everybody's life one way or another, but then maybe it isn't just luck. Maybe it's more. I don't know for sure, but I have a feeling it is.

Anyway, back to how I finally got a tracer on Old Bum's disappearance. My son-in-law is sure enough enterprising in a lot of different ways. As a good example, he was the first one around here to make his cowboys use two-way radios as they rode in pickups or on horseback across his hundred and eighty thousand acres of land. The working cowboys checked into headquarters with the ranch manager every scheduled hour of each working day. It wouldn't be long before they would be

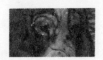

riding with two-way videos and a little compact camcorder as well. Then the ranch manager could just set there on his butt watching wall-sized pictures of the ranch and all its operations, giving orders while he had his iced tea or hot chocolate—according to the time of year.

The open range cowboy was gone before 1900, then the barbed-wire cowboy gave way to the pickup cowboy, and now they were going to be forced to move over for the electronic, hi-tech cowboy. Oh, dear Jesus, help us all. So much for the individualism that used to mark the American cowboy.

When the government agency poisoned the coyotes, and trapped all the mountain lions, the deer became so thick they were dying of starvation; so, my go-getter of a son-in-law just set up a hunting outfit. Every fall Jack and the entire family, and half of the cowboys, guided, fed, and entertained, charging hunters from Oklahoma and Texas lots of money for each deer bagged. The smart son of a gun was profiting from everything being forced out of balance. It would no doubt teeter and tilt again before long, but right now he was doing a hell of a balancing job with all the misunderstanding going on between the ranchers, the world-savers, and most of the Washington, D.C., ding-a-lings. One thing for sure, when the newest technological medium comes on the market, my son-in-law will be there the next day to haul it to the ranch. If politics has become the newest religion, appealing as far left as atheism, and as far right as the most rabid fundamentalist, then television is its pope. Jack knew how the media used these infinitely advancing sciences for ever-growing power. He would always make their knowledge his own.

Mind you, I'm not trying to shovel any of my personal notions off on anybody else. However, revealing the so-called "progressive attitude" of my son-in-law shows what a vast

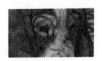

change has occurred in the world—and in me—between the time I first met Old Bum and the four-odd decades later when I finally learned what happened to him.

A while back—before Jack got everything organized to perfection on the hunt, two-way radios and all—everyone used to gather here at the Raton house before going on down to the ranch. So now, as much as I enjoy keeping the stock tanks and house all in top shape, about all I contribute to the actual hunts are a few hound dog stories.

I don't hold it against anyone who hunts the right way, don't you know. It's just that I personally never can, nor ever will, hunt again, after that single portentous day when I knew for sure Old Bum was gone, my wife and child were gone, and I had witnessed that coyote pup die over there east of Hi Lo.

It was only two, or maybe three, years back that I was visiting with some of the excited men as they checked guns, bedrolls, and all that stuff before the big event on the oak-brushed mesas and in the canyons of the ranch. I was telling this hunter, Jim from Oklahoma, about some of our adventures with Old Bum when he interrupted with a look on his face like he had just shook hands with God and been assured he had a first-class reservation to heaven waiting with his name on it.

"That dog wasn't a black and tan was he?" Jim asked.

"Yeah. Yeah he was," I said.

"That dog wasn't the one whose floppy ears looked like they'd been run through a CIA shredder, was he?" Jim asked and inched forward on his chair.

"That's his ears, all right," I agreed, getting pretty interested in the questions.

"That dog didn't limp from a bullet wound in his left front shoulder when he got tired, did he?"

Now that long-unused hunter's adrenalin and electricity was stirring up in my body. "He did that exactly and for sure." I almost yelled.

Leaning forward with his eyes stretched open, Jim whispered, "And he only bawled once when he treed a coon, didn't he?"

"That's him. That's Old Bum!" I yelled this time loud enough to make the ears spin on a stone statue.

"Old Bum, huh? Well, we called him Old Traveler," Jim said.

"Same thing," I said.

Then we both began to babble, trying to talk at the same time like folks do on those TV talk shows, or when they've been drinking too much. Just the same, I found out Jim's grandfather, and some friends, had stopped in Hi Lo for a beer, and they wound up buying Old Bum from Rube Fields, the well driller. That old scoundrel.

It seems that somehow a party got going, and Rube had started feeling so good he thought everything in the world belonged to him, including Old Bum. After listening to Rube brag, for a total of two hours, about what a hunter the dog was, these guys from Oklahoma just bought him—for an undisclosed price—to shut Rube up. It didn't matter if it was fifty dollars or fifty million, they still got the bargain of their lives, when I think about what's truly valuable on this circle of fire, air, water, and rock called earth.

With his still-keen ears, Old Bum had heard this party in the making. Then someone invited him into the Wild Cat. They all broke down and let him join the party, but he fooled everybody—just like he always had. He would not take a single drink no matter how he was enticed. As impossible as it seems—even now—Old Bum had quit cold turkey when he

found out that stuff made him pick fights with thousand-pound bulls.

Jim's grandfather had hauled Old Bum back to Laverne, Oklahoma, near the west edge of the Panhandle, and gave him to Jim for an early Christmas present; then he took them on a coon hunt.

"Traveler didn't stay home a lot," Jim continued, "but he always came back. Seemed like he knew when a man was getting a bad case of hunter's itch." The young man was smiling all the time he talked now. So was I. "I was afraid something would happen to him," Jim continued, "and tried to keep him penned up, but that didn't work at all. He wouldn't take a lick of water or a bite of food until I turned him out of the dog pen. I mean to tell you he would have starved himself plumb to death before he would give up his freedom. I just gave in and let him go his own way. Sometimes when he'd come home, he'd be full of new scars from fighting and chasing the gals."

"Wonder how old he was when he died?" I asked.

"Oh, I don't know Mr. McClure, but we had him seven years. My dad said he was durn sure over a hundred years old in human time. You know, I rode the school bus to and from school, because in those days we lived four miles from Laverne on a farm. Whenever Old Traveler was home, he'd wait for me halfway across the front yard. That's as far as he would come to meet me. He'd wag his tail about one and a half times and give me a glancing lick on the leg. You had to know him to understand that this was as joyful a greeting as he was gonna give anyone."

"Yeah, I remember."

"Then one day he wasn't there. It was nothing unusual, but somehow I knew in my gut he was gone for good. I looked

everywhere for him, but found nothing. I guess he just traveled on." Jim paused, and became quieter. Then he added, "One thing for sure, though, I'll forget a lot of people before I do that old dog."

"Yeah, son, I savvy that clear as morning dew." I didn't want to talk about Old Bum the traveler anymore right then myself.

Now I sit here enjoying recollecting.

Tom C. went back to his childhood home in Missouri to die and was buried by the side of his young wife. I still miss him very much. Knowel Denny, Pal England, Rube Fields, and a lot of other sporting boys and girls are up on Graveyard Hill north of town.

I remember Levi Gomez telling me one day, "You know what, Mark? Original thinking and doing are deadly. I'm leaving this burg." He moved west over the Rocky Mountains to Taos and became a truly distinguished "*santero*." His saints carved from cedar wood were blessed by the pope, and his work was collected by rich and famous people from faraway places. He's gone, too.

And me, old Mark McClure? Well, I really wasn't much of an artist anyway, so right after Levi left Hi Lo, I quit painting, and started back laying rocks and doing odd-job carpenter work. I kept seeing these people's houses all over whose poor walls were covered with bad paintings forced on them as gifts from friends. Seems suddenly half of America started doing these westerns and scenery paintings—as the locals called them. This world needed a lot of fixing, but one more bad painter sure wasn't going to help it.

I don't know hardly anyone at Hi Lo anymore. One of

the two saloons is gone, and the other will surely follow. Now it would be impossible to get up a poker game in a month of Saturday nights. When Old Bum left, he took part of a spirited era with him. Hell, that wise old dog saw it coming and allowed himself to be sold so he could ride, instead of walk, out of a country soon to turn more boring with each hour. In these little towns, on far-scattered ranches, people were now getting their secondhand thrills from the perversely soul-diminishing, possessive little box called TV; and being told every single second—on one channel or another—how to vote, how to love, how to die, how to everything.

There ain't even any more hillbilly music. It's called country, country western, rock-a-billy, country rock, country this, and rock that. One thing, though, there are still hundreds of thousands of acres of grasslands out there broken by lonely malpai and sandstone mesas. Maybe it's even lonelier between the far spread ranch houses than it was in my time.

There are more raccoons, antelopes, and deer out there now, in spite of all the programs of poison, airplane hunters, and all that stuff; and the coyotes are still howling when they damn well feel like it, and the Hi Lo wind blows their messages across a deaf world.

Boy howdy, and gobblin geese, this late spring sun feels good to my old ex-hunter's bones. It is also a grand and comforting feeling to know that dogs and coyotes are equally as important as kings, queens, or cockroaches. Of course, it's probably not, but the sun seems like it is shining just special for me today. I keep looking down the graveled driveway for Old Bum to come limping in from some kind of chase, bringing along his great zeal for life as the most precious of gifts. I don't worry about him because if he doesn't show up today, he will tomorrow, or in a day or so after that, for sure. Like the song says, "Long ago and far away . . ."

SHADOW OF
THUNDER

She saw the wagon coming along the road followed by a man on horseback. Two matching bays pulled it, and the man who trailed behind was mounted on a pinto. As the vehicle rolled nearer, she could see the figure on the wagon seat was dressed in dark purple from his wide felt hat to the long-tailed coat on down to his high-topped boots. The mounted man was an Indian. Apache.

She smoothed her hands down her dress front and over her high pitched breasts, then straightened her long hair—hair as shiny blue-black as the mane of the pinto.

The man pulled back on the reins, saying quietly, "Whoa." He dismounted and tied the reins to the wagon wheel. Then he strode towards the porch. He was not as big as he had seemed sitting up on the wagon. Actually he was of medium height, but his arms hung long and the hands at their ends

were outsized. His walk was one of certainty and purpose, as if every step he took must count.

Marta Ames stared curiously out her very dark, shining eyes. An unknown feeling stroked across her body ever so lightly. A few goose bumps pimpled on the white, fair skin of her rounded forearms. Her lavender-red lips parted slightly. Visitors were few out here, and mostly they came to talk cows with her husband.

This one was different. She stepped back from the front door as he raised a heavy hand to knock. She waited a moment then opened it. The eyes she looked into were darker than her own, and the skin was almost as white. It was evident that this man didn't spend too much time under the sunburned sky. His lips were thin but moist. His face was also thin, and his firm set jaw showed small, permanent muscle knots.

"How do you do, fair lady? I fear I've lost my way. I look for the road to the city of Two Mesas."

She started to answer and give directions, but he went on in a voice deep but smooth, like the flowing of pure water over fine silk.

"Perchance the gods have cast favorable glances at my humble wagon, for where else would one meet such lovely and charming female flesh? Where else indeed?"

The blood pushed the redness under Marta's white skin. "Well, I . . . ," she started, but again the honeyed words flowed out.

"Do not be taken aback by my words. I do not mean to be forward, but I was greatly surprised to meet one of such extreme beauty here in the wilderness. Is the man of the house about?"

"Why yes, he and Marcus are doctoring cattle out in the corral," she said.

"Sickness?" he asked.

"Only a few head," she answered.

"My card," he said, reaching long fingers into his inner coat while with the other hand sweeping his hat from his thick-haired head.

Marta took it and read: DUVALL—DOCTOR OF THE MIND AND BODY. GIFTED WITH A MULTITUDE OF DIVINE ABILITIES.

"I am Duvall," he said, holding a hand out to her.

For a moment she hesitated, then boldly took it. The soft hugeness of it enveloped hers in a warm, almost but not quite, damp embrace. The bumps came again. This time she felt them over all her body.

"If I might be so bold, could I ask for a cup of water? The road has been long, and my thirst is great."

"Surely. Come in," she said, flashing a look at the Indian now dismounted and squatting by the wagon.

In answer to her look he said, "Never mind him, he's like a camel of the desert. One Lion is an Apache. He's trained in the ways of the desert."

She handed him the tin dipper from the wooden bucket. He took the cool water to himself in long, smooth swallows.

"Now," he said, wiping the drippings from the corner of his mouth with a blue silk handkerchief, "I shall repay this golden kindness by assisting your husband in the corrals."

Rick Ames spurred the Appaloosa gelding after the white-faced yearling. When the distance was just right, he whirled the catch-rope and let the loop fly. It sailed out and around the yearling's head. Rick jerked the slack out of the loop and

turned, spurring the gelding in the opposite direction. The rope tightened and spun the yearling around, his four feet planted stiff, bawling at the top of his voice.

Marcus, the Mexican cowhand, reined in and dropped a slow loop under the calf's belly and up against its hind legs. The legs moved into the loop. He, too, jerked the slack and rode in the opposite direction from Rick. The calf was flopped hard upon the ground, stretched out flat.

Quickly the Appaloosa turned his head down the rope, holding it tight, as Rick dismounted. He moved to the side of the corral and picked up a flat smooth stick, a small bottle of chloroform, and a can of pine tar. With practiced motion he poured the chloroform into the cavity where the calf had recently been dehorned. At the touch of the liquid, the worms wiggled and twisted up out of the rotting wound. He scooped them all out with the wooden spatula, then coated the sore with the pine tar.

They turned the yearling loose. It got up shaking its head in the corral dust and ambled off addled but in much better health.

Rick liked things on his ranch to be in shape. He kept his fences tight and well cared for, his cows doctored and fat. His horses were the best in the country. Appaloosas. Indians long before bred these spotted-rumped animals for their toughness and endurance over the long haul.

He pushed his hat back over his forehead, which was paste white in comparison to the bronze skin on the rest of his face. A shock of light brown hair showed beneath the brim.

"It's going to get hot early this year, huh, Marcus?"

"Looks like," answered Marcus in a heavy Mexican accent. "Maybe, so we got the cows moved to the forest lease just in time, no?"

"Yeah, looks like they'll get an early start. Should be licking themselves and piling on the fat right now."

He straightened his six-foot-one frame and stared out of light brown, steady eyes at the yearling steer standing in the corner with the wide, swelled belly and the watery, red eyes. Marcus stood leaning against the corral pulling smoke deep into his lungs. His eyes followed those of his boss.

"What we do about that water-belly steer?" he asked.

"I don't know, Marcus. I've never saved one yet. Looks like this one's goin' to be a goner in another couple of days. Cain't figure it out. It only happens once ever two or three years. Last time we lost six head. Something about the water makes a rock form in their bladder. Then they pass it down into their pecker, and that's that. The water all backs up, and pretty soon there's no room for grass or fresh water either. Then it's just a matter of a few days until they're done."

"What cause this . . . this pecker stopping?" asked Marcus, frowning in the bright sun. "You think maybe he got a dose of clap? Huh?"

"I don't know," Rick grinned. "Old man Randall said it was calcium in the water that caused it to form. I just cain't understand it. Oh well, no matter what, a feller can always count on a 10 percent stock loss. Hell, you could raise 'em in the kitchen and you'd lose the same percentage."

He saw the wagon pull up in front and wondered where old Ring, the dog, was. He usually barked when company came. *Guess he's off hunting*, he thought to himself. The wagon pulled out of sight, hidden by the house. Well, whoever it was Marta'd send them on out to the corral.

Marta. At the thought of her he had that funny, mellow feeling. He'd never get over it. He knew that, now. They'd been married seven years, and he still got it every time he

thought of her. There was just one thing he was more proud of than his spotted-rumped horses and that was Marta.

By damn, he was lucky—a good little ranch, several hundred head of well-bred cattle to go on it; it was fenced and cross-fenced so he could rotate his cattle and not eat any one pasture down too close to the ground—and the most beautiful woman in the world to fix his meals, take care of the chickens, the garden, sew, and take him to bed. All paid for, too. In fact, that's how he'd gotten Marta.

It was a regular business deal, like trading for a bunch of good springing heifers. He'd showed what he owned, what he made every year, and pointed out to her, and her family, all the advantages of marrying up with Rick Ames. She'd taken him up on it. As if she could refuse a deal like that.

There was just one thing missing though. No kids. He wanted that very much. He reckoned it was Marta's fault. She must have been born barren. Well, too bad. One of these days if she didn't do her duty in that line why they'd just adopt one. Some nester gal over on Salt River was always getting in a family way and would be mighty glad to have a place to put a young 'un like that. He'd give her one more year though. Maybe she'd come through.

"I hear Tony Archuleta lost four two year olds last week," Rick said to Marcus.

"Whooooeee," Marcus said, "four head. Sone of a beetch. Tony ees always loosin' them young heifers. What cause it, Reeck? Huh? What cause it? Tony hees take very good care of his stock. I know this for chure. Huh?"

"I've told him and told him not to feed too much grain to springing heifers. They get too fat around the hips, and they can't force the calf out. Why, old Tony spends three-fourths of his time pullin' calves in the spring. I bet he loses 50 percent of

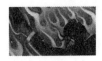

his two-year-old calves every year. There ain't no use in tryin' to explain to him, Marcus. He thinks that the fatter anything is, the healthier."

"Whooooeee, I say he chure does. Look at Rosita. She's always fat and always having the bambinos. No?"

"Yeah, women are different. Looks like the fatter they get the easier it is to shell out."

"Say, Reeck, when you goin' to start making the young ones? Huh?"

Rick swallowed and looked away as he said, "It's about time ain't it? At least I got me a woman to start on. That's more'n you can say."

"You right, Reeck, I'm goin' to get me a big, skinny bones so she won't be sloughing no bambinos. Huh? I tell you, Reeck, I tell you something fonny. I already got me two leetle ones." Marcus looked around, then whispered so quietly that the saints probably had to strain to hear. "You know Maria Sanchez at Two Mesas?"

"Yeah."

"Thass her. Thass the one. Both little bulls handsome like the papa, no?"

Rick saw them coming. The figures in a triangle. Marta and the dark-clad stranger walking abreast and the huge Apache following behind. It was strange, he thought, Marta never came to the corrals unless he asked her to. As they neared, he noticed how much smaller the man was than he'd first thought.

Marta said, "Rick, this is Mr. Duvall. Mr. Duvall, my husband, Rick Ames."

He took the huge hand and even his rope- and saddle-stretched hand was swallowed.

"Your wife has been so kind to proffer my parched and dust-raw throat a cup of the most gratifying liquid. In return I

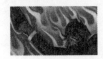

thought I might contribute some of my small, but heaven-sent, gift of healing to your sick cattle."

"Thanks," said Rick, feeling somehow resentful. "I reckon we've done about all that can be done."

"What about the one standing there so evidently afflicted with what the layman calls the waterbelly?"

"Aw, that one's already gone. Besides even the vet cain't do nothin' about that."

"My dear Mr. Ames, I am not a veterinarian," and with a great sweep of his arm he offered his card to Rick.

"Well . . . what do you think you could do for *that* yearlin'?" He said it as a question, but he meant it as a challenge.

Duvall turned to the Apache and spoke in Indian. The Apache stared ahead. He didn't seem to focus his eyes on anything in particular. It was almost as if he were dead except for some lonely living cell that moved only when Duvall spoke.

The Indian was dressed in the way of the Apache, almost knee-high moccasins with a drawstring around the ankles. The long square-bottomed shirt hung down over britches split up each leg and partially laced with buckskin string. He wore a wide belt around his middle and a red rag tied around his head to keep the heavy, shoulder-length hair pulled out of his face. Expressionless, the Apache turned and walked swiftly back to the wagon.

"The Apaches," Duvall said, in answer to the look on Rick's face, "are fine people. I have a large debt to them in much of my knowledge of healing. Now," he said, pulling off the long dark coat and folding it neatly atop the corral, "I presume you have chloroform, seeing as you have been doctoring for worms."

"Yeah," said Rick walking over and picking up the bottle.

"Now, if you don't mind, I'd like you to throw the steer and hold him in any manner you deem suitable."

"What're you goin' to do?" asked Rick, humping up just a little.

"You want to save this poor creature, do you not?"

"Well . . ."

"You have nothing to lose, is that not correct?"

"Yeah, I reckon . . ."

"Then let's begin."

Marcus joined Rick, and they threw the steer into the ground-up dust and manure of the corral. Rick pulled a foreleg up with his knee on the steer's shoulder. Marcus took the tail and stretched it back between the widespread hind legs. The sick animal put up very little struggle. Its swollen belly stuck up high, and the pressure of its weight made the breath come hard. Little furrows were plowed in the corral dust by the breathing, and some of it collected around the wet nostrils.

Smoothly, Duvall took a pure white handkerchief from inside a black silk one and poured a small amount of chloroform on it. Then he held it over the steer's nostrils, counting as he did so.

The Apache returned and without a word handed Duvall the square-bottomed, leather bag. Duvall nodded at a place by his side and continued counting. Then he finished. He opened the bag. He took out a long-handled, steel knife with a very short and very sharp blade. He poured something out of a bottle on the protruding penis of the steer, rubbing it all over the stomach and up between its legs.

"What's that?" asked Rick.

"Its main ingredient is the oil of sagebrush," answered Duvall. "It has other things in it. Sage oil is a wonderful healing agent and disinfectant."

"I knew the Indians drank it for colds," said Rick, "but I didn't know it was good for anything else."

"Few do, Mr. Ames. Most of us are blind to all the wonderful healing agents nature has laid at our very doorsteps." He set three other bottles out of the bag, and he arranged them in proper order. Then he took a needle and heavy thread and laid them out on a piece of soft leather.

The steer breathed now without struggling. Duvall picked a spot behind the penis and deftly split through the skin and flesh all the way to the inner penis in three swift strokes. The blood poured out on the hide and trickled down through the red and white hairs to the dirt. He opened a wide cut, mopping the blood up now and then with an absorbent cloth. He cut the penis. His hands, covered with red now, worked magically, large and flexible with certain knowledge of what his mind told them to do.

Marta stood still, pale. Her eyes were fixed to the gaping insides of the steer.

Duvall cut the penis out, took the bladder, and sewed it to another smaller split farther back between the steer's legs. The stitching took longer than all the rest. He tied a knot in the end of the string and cut it. Then he poured a portion of bitter-smelling, greenish-colored liquid into the wound and sewed the first cut up. He inserted a small piece of hollow bone in the second hole.

"That's it," he said.

Rick felt the sweat rolling from under his hat, and he wiped at the saltiness of it where it was getting in his eyes.

Marcus got up stiffly and backed to the corral, leaning weakly, staring hard at Duvall.

Duvall said calmly as he split the long, narrow, red penis apart, "We should find the culprit here." With the end of the

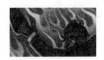

blood-gummed knife he picked the hard pebble-like forma-
tion out and held it for all to see. Then he spoke, "The swelling will hold that piece of bone in place for a few days. When
the swelling is gone enough for the bone to drop out, the
animal will be healed sufficiently to do without it. You no
longer have a steer, Mr. Ames. You now, for all practical purposes, except breeding, have a heifer. But a live heifer is much
more to your advantage than a dead steer."

Rick Ames had watched the unheard-of skill of Duvall's
hands perform a miraculous operation. He was stunned. He
spoke, "I don't know what to say."

"Never mind," said Duvall, raising a wide-spread, red-
stained hand. "Never mind. It is enough reward to have the
ability."

Marta looked at the mighty hand. Her nostrils flared a
little more than before, and a deep gleaming light seemed to
crowd its way to the misty surface of her eyes. Her breathing
raised her breasts in and out, up and down.

"Now if you will be so kind to show me to a wash basin,
we will be soon on our way."

He washed his hands several times, then applied a gray,
cool-looking lotion, almost tenderly. He spoke once more as
he donned his coat, "My friends, if you would honor me a
week from today with your presence at our little musical to be
held somewhere in the vicinity of Two Mesas, I will leave with
happiness in my heart and a glow of appreciation over all my
being."

"We're the ones to appreciate," said Rick.

"We'll come," said Marta softly.

"Then I leave you with this in mind, good people. If
perchance you should need help with your mind or body,
please call upon Duvall." He strode out to his wagon, untied

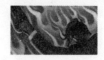

the reins, mounted easily, and drove the wagon away. The Apache followed close behind.

Marta stood as yet in one spot, and Rick looked out the back porch and saw that indeed the old dog had been there all the time. He stood motionless, soundless, and sniffed the air.

Rick stretched and stapled a fence line tight and returned the tools to a saddle pouch.

He untracked Brother Bill, his Appaloosa, mounted, and rode down off the hill towards the water gap in the sandy draw. He was sure the heavy rains day before yesterday had washed it out. Brother Bill walked along, fox-trotting and chewing at the bits. He was full of life and wanted to work.

"Okay, Brother Bill, in about three weeks, me and Marcus will take some of this spunk outa you when we go up on the forest land to brand."

Marcus was up there now taking a count of the mother cows and calves, locating their watering places so they could be gathered in a hurry when they were ready for the branding. They still had about thirty or forty more head to brand, counting the late calves yet to be born.

The day was clear, and the sunlight sparkled in the air from the lush dampness all about. The grass was deep green and growing with a swift tenderness.

The water gap *had* pulled loose on one side, and the three wires were strung along the draw with dirt, sticks, and dead grass all entangled in it. He pulled the wires free, dragged them across the draw, and tied them back after resetting the heavy cedar post. Then he retied the rock weights out in the middle so it would pull the wires down to the ground. His pastures were back in shape again.

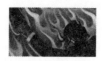

With a feeling of satisfaction he mounted up and rode towards the low-lying ranch house, thinking of Marta and the good meal she would have ready.

Then he saw a horse-backer riding down the road that led into the ranch proper. He could tell, even from that distance, by the way he sat his horse, that it was his neighbor to the north, old man George Randall. George was stiff as a cedar post and just as tough. He had merry, watery-blue eyes that had gazed into a lot of hot and cold winds; many dry years had wrinkled his skin like the bark of a pine tree. He always timed his rides in this direction to catch a meal of Marta's, claiming her to be the best cook around.

They came together riding in a V at the ranch gate.

"Howdy, George," Rick said, smiling, glad to see his weathered old friend.

"Watcha say, Rick? Looks like I timed it just right. Marta oughta have the chuck on the table 'bout now."

"You sure did, George. Tie your horse and come on in."

George tied the roan he was riding, while Rick turned his horse loose in the corral. Together they walked to the back porch and into the kitchen. The smell of fresh, fried beef was evident, and Marta was just taking the biscuits out of the oven.

"Hello, George. How's Frieda?"

"Aw, she's just like any other old woman, always bellyachin' and makin' it miserable for me," he laughed good-naturedly.

"I bet you wouldn't take for her though," said Marta.

"Well, I reckon she does come in handy around the place."

"That's how all you ranchers feel about your women," said Marta, only half teasing.

"Sit down, George, and help yourself to the chow," Rick

said. "How're your cows doin'?"

"Sure comin' along good this year. I believe my calves will pass four hundred pounds apiece come shipping time. Sure hope the price holds up till fall. Dang, I wish we could get the rail-spur on into Two Mesas. It takes lots of beef off makin' that drive to Stanton."

"Well, old man Ords got a petition signed by every cowman in the country. If the goddamned nesters would sign, we could probably get it through," said Rick.

"Yeah, but they won't. They ain't got over the war yet."

The war referred to by Randall had been over for several years now, but neither side forgot. The nesters had moved in all over the West, homesteading farms along river bottoms and around water holes, settling one-hundred-and-sixty-acre plots. The nesters were within the law, but the ranchers felt that morally they themselves were in the right. The ranchers resented the land being broken up into little pieces; it undercut their entire system of ranching. Range wars and killings spread across the land. Finally, nature took care of the nesters who had fought the dry-land farms. They were simply starved out, and the ranchers took over the land again. But along Salt River it was different. Here they got a little irrigation water and farmed small patches of vegetables and kept milk cows, chickens, and hogs. They made an existence; that was all they could boast. Such was also the relationship now between the ranchers and the nesters; it was an existence, an impasse; few could boast of friendship.

"They don't ship enough cattle to count—or care," Rick said bitterly. "All they keep is a bunch of hogs and a milk cow around them sodbustin' flats over on Salt River. Too damn bad. Oh well," he added, "I look for all them nesters to starve out anyway in another five years."

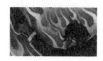

"I hope so," said Randall.

Marta pushed the curl from her forehead and finished setting the meal of pinto beans, fried beef, home-canned peaches, hot biscuits, and country butter. They set to and drank deep swallows of hot coffee from the large tin cups.

Marta wished Rick could see his way clear to let her order some china cups. But he kept putting all his money in cows. "Spreading out," as he said. "A man's got to spread out while he's goin' good."

The talk went on, cows, cows, cows, horses, and more cows. She liked cows. She liked ranch life, but an unknown craving for some spice to go with it gnawed at her breast. Maybe that get-together of Duvall's would give them something else to think about for a change. Duvall, what a strange and fascinating man. Where did he come from? What was he really? Marta wondered.

"Marta, when you and old Rick goin' to get some young'ns around here?"

Rick felt the red creep into his face. *My god, why did everybody have to bring that up lately?*

George went on jokingly, "If I wasn't so cockeyed old, I'd do you a good neighborly turn and help you out, Rick." George bellowed across a fork full of beef.

Rick grinned, "I'll let you know if I need any help," he said lamely.

After the filling meal, they rolled smokes and talked on as Marta cleared the table and prepared to wash the dishes. A big pan of water was heating on the iron range, its steam wiggling up into the kitchen.

George spent a couple of hours rolling smokes and talking more cows, then he got up, thanked Marta for the fine feed, and rode on west, where he, too, had a lease from the

forest for grazing purposes.

Rick sat and finished his last smoke. "Well, I reckon I'll go out and patch the corrals. I noticed a few loose posts the other day when that Duvall feller was working on the yearlin'."

Marta put down the dish she was drying. She said, "Have you forgotten what day it is?"

Rick thought hard—*anniversary? birthday?* "I . . . I . . . don't know, honey. What day is it?"

"You mean you don't know after what he did for us?"

"Oh, you mean Duvall? That's right, this is the night for the big meeting. I'd plumb forgot."

"We'll have to get started soon, because I have some things to get in town," she said.

"All right, I'll go out and warm up the truck. I don't need to shave, seeing as how I just did this morning."

In a little while, Rick returned to the house. He was stunned at the sight of his wife. He had never seen her done up so pretty. The heavy black hair was all tied high in a bundle on top of her head. She wore a lavender dress and a black half-coat. And a big silver comb was stuck in her hair. Her lips were coated with lavender paint to match the dress. Her eyes glowed bright and excited out at him as she waited for his comment.

"You're as pretty as a peach tree in new bloom, Marta."

She smiled slightly. "You like the dress?" She asked.

"Like it? It's the prettiest thing I ever saw in my life—except maybe the woman in it." He smiled. "That Duvall ought to be mighty proud to have the likes of you attending his meetin'. Say, by the way, I saw that yearlin' this morning. Most of the swelling's gone, and he's eatin' good. You know, Marta, I just cain't figure it out. I've never heard of anything like what he did to that steer. It just ain't natural. There's something plumb spooky about the way he operated on that animal."

"There's probably lots of things we haven't heard about in this world, Rick."

They bounded along in the creaking truck; every now and then Marta straightened her hair from the jostling it took as they struck innumerable holes and ruts in the dirt road.

"Rick, don't you think it's about time we bought a car? This old truck is for hauling fence posts and baled hay."

"It's a lot faster than a buggy."

"The day of the buggy is over."

"If a buggy was good enough for my dad and his pa, a truck is fine for us. When they pioneered the first cow ranch in this country, there were no roads at all. This road we're travelin' right now was first a cow trail, then a wagon trail, then a buggy trail, and here we are sailin' along over it at twenty miles an hour."

"I really don't call this sailing," said Marta. She was racked against the door by an especially deep hole.

"Nobody's ever satisfied in this world," Rick said.

Marta said, "It's not that we can't afford it. We got through the Depression and the drought better than anybody around."

"Well, that's because I hadn't gone in debt for a bunch of things we didn't need and had all that hay stored in case of an emergency."

"I know," she said, "but it's different now. We have money in the bank. The grass is good this year."

"Yeah, but you never know about next year."

"You can't just go on thinking about next year. We're alive now. Right now in nineteen hundred and thirty seven, in

the beautiful month of June."

"Look, a wagon and team is still good enough for this Duvall."

"That's for effect," she said. "I want a car for comfort and because I get tired and embarrassed driving this truck like a hayhand to social gatherings."

"A woman as good lookin' as you could go to a social on a hundred-year-old mule, and they'd all be glad to have her."

"You just don't understand," she said resignedly, "you never will."

They drove into the farming and ranching town of Two Mesas. It was half adobe structures and half crude, boxlike, frame houses—some with no paint, others with a little, clinging to the weathered boards. A reminder of someone's attempt at beauty in a land hot and dry in the summer, and so cold and wind-cursed in the winter that paint was only a wasted gesture.

Old cars and trucks stood about. A few wagons and teams were tied here and there. And once in a great while a new car stood out saying for the owner to all, "the drought is over, I've made a crop. I believe in the land again."

Rick pulled up in front of the Allen Hardware to get some ranch supplies. Marta got the few essential grocery purchases made in the mercantile then walked across the street to Berg's Dry Goods.

Berg welcomed her with, "Ah, Mrs. Ames, you look like all the flowers in the world today. Is there a reason for such beauty? No, no," he went on, "just let it be. Let us accept this bounty without question. How is Mr. Ames?"

"Just fine. Working hard as usual."

"Did you come in for the camp meeting or whatever it is?"

"Yes, and to do some shopping."

"Good, good," Mr. Berg said, and he rubbed his little potbelly, took off his glasses, and pointed to a hanging of new dresses.

"That yellow one was just made for you. You alone."

Marta fingered the soft, frilly dress as yellow as a new ray of sun beaming through a deep, green forest. She wanted it. For a frivolous moment she craved it, then she said, "I'd like to look at some material." She knew Rick would be irritated for days if she bought the dress when she could easily make one of her own. She did pick out a yellow cloth as near that of the ready-made as possible. She chose a pattern and bought the thread and everything she'd need to make the dress. Suddenly she was determined to design one that would cause the other to look secondhand.

"If you made the dress you're wearing, it is easy to understand why a factory dress, even one as fine as that," he pointed again at the yellow dress, "would seem awkward and ugly to you."

Marta blushed a little at this flattery and said, "Yes, I did. I made it, thank you."

Mr. Berg put all the purchases in a sack. Marta paid by check. She made it out to the exact cent and wrote on it each item purchased. This, too, would please Rick. Even though the actual expense of the material had been almost as much as the new ready-to-wear dress would have cost.

"How's the family, Mr. Berg?"

"Oh, fine, fine, except Mama's got the gout again. Always gets it right after the first summer rains. Makes her hungry. She eats far too much you know. Mama's big, big!" He made a proud measurement with his little arms.

"And the children?"

"Well, they work in the store evenings. We stay open till

nine now you know. Abie doesn't like it. He only likes the violin. He has a mail-order course. Miss Bridge, the music teacher at school, says he's 'gifted.'"

"I'd like to hear him play sometime. There are very few gifted people around Two Mesas."

"Oh, fine, fine, I'll tell him. He'll be pleased."

Marta told him goodbye as Berg followed her out on the wooden porch, thanking her effusively for her trade.

Rick was loading some wire and other ranch goods in the back of the truck.

"Come on," he said, "let's go over to Lil's and have some coffee."

They walked together, and she told him about the dress material she'd bought and that she intended to make it up right away so she could wear it to the next camp meeting.

"The next one?" he said. "How do you know you'll like this one?"

"Well, it's something different to do. A change."

He looked at her, starting to speak, but held it back as they entered Lil's Cafe.

Lil was right there. "It's about time you kids came into town near sundown. I ain't seen you in this late for months."

"Goin' to the meetin' or whatever it is," Rick said.

"That's twice today I've heard 'whatever it is,'" said Marta.

"What?" said Rick.

"Nothing."

Lil folded her heavy arms under her heavier breasts and said, smiling from a round pleasant face, "Now don't tell me you're goin' to just have coffee. It's not too long till supper time, and I've got some roast beef that'd make a well-fed prisoner break slap out of jail just to get one teeny little bite."

"Anything that good is worth waitin' for. Coffee first, Lil,

and then the roast beef. All right, honey?" Rick asked.

Marta nodded, amazed that he'd buy a meal. He always worked it so they got into town in the afternoon, shopped fast, and drove home for supper. Maybe there was hope yet.

When Lil served the meal, Marta learned the reason for his new generosity.

"Say, Lil, been any cow buyers in town yet?"

"There's two here now. They'll be gettin' around to you after old man Moss, I reckon."

"What're they buyin'?"

"Calves for fall delivery. Makin' a guaranteed offer on 'em now."

After Lil left, Rick cut at his beef, smiling, "You know what that means, honey?"

"What?" she said dryly.

"That means cattle are goin' to go up this fall, in the eyes of the experts at least. I ain't contractin' a single head."

Marta sipped her coffee a moment before eating, and watched Rick devour his beef in great bites. *Just like he wants to devour me*, she suddenly thought. *I'm only good to give him strength to run his damned ranch and make it grow, grow, grow.*

Lil spoke from behind the counter where she served several cowhands, "The meeting's down by Salt River. Guess this Duvall didn't figure any of you ranchers would come, so he's playing up to the nesters and garden farmers."

"They need preachin' to worse than we do anyhow," Rick said.

"It seems that poor folks always need preaching to worse than the well off," Marta said quietly.

"Aw, come on, you're getting on edge for no reason."

Rick got up to join several of the hands who were talking, here and there, about grass and all that goes with ranching.

Marta sat alone, staring out the window at more and more people coming into Two Mesas for the meeting. Even so, she thought the town was still lonely and dead. She was relieved when Rick came over and said, "It's about time for the great meetin'. Let's go."

The old truck rattled out of town towards Salt River about a mile from the city limits. Rick drove along the winding road where dust hung in the air from the vehicles ahead of them.

"I never saw such a crowd at an opening before," he said. "Later on, yes, but never before the word got out."

People were coming in old, worn-out cars that wheezed and jerked. Some were horseback, and others came by wagon and team, blocking the road so the cars had to stop or pull around. Some were ranchers; most were nesters.

The Salt River nesters turned out for the meeting almost 100 percent. They came afoot and in wagons. Very few owned cars. The men were dressed mostly in old blue overalls, and the women wore faded, but clean, cotton dresses for the "show" as they called it. The kids hung around in noisy, excited, little groups on the fringe, playing games, flirting, and challenging each other with insults, strength, and laughter.

Most of the grownups moved towards the wooden platform against the wagon. The nesters gathered into the largest group, while the ranchers clung together visiting and making nervous jokes.

Watching Duvall and the Apache place a heavy copper kettle on a fire in an iron grill, Rick said, "Well, the carnival's

about to start. Wonder when the bearded lady and the two-headed calf'll be introduced."

Marta looked at him a moment to see if he really was joking, but she saw it was derision.

"It's not a carnival," she said, "it's a display of the power of medicine, just as you witnessed on the waterbelly steer."

"Here, here," Rick said, "I was only jokin'."

Marta turned from him, studying the movements of Duvall. The Apache started slowly beating a large Indian drum, almost in rhythm with Duvall's taking herbs and powder from some leather bags. He sprinkled some of each in the tub, moving his massive hands in a delicate rhythm to the slowly increasing throb of the drums. The crowd quieted and moved forward now. The children crowded close around the platform in front of the grownups or climbed on wagons to see better.

Now a young Apache woman came out of the wagon and started beating one of the drums in exact time with the male. The music picked up in tempo, and the heads of the onlookers swayed in motion with Duvall's hands. Their eyes locked hypnotically on those powerful hands. He poured a bag of peyote into the steaming kettle, and, rising with hands held above his head and the palms towards the crowd, he said: "The last powder completes the brew, my friends. It is an ancient one used for centuries by the Apaches and only now, here today, made available for all. Its powers to heal and soothe are from the body of Christ himself. It elates and quiets the tormented in a single swallow. It lifts you from the devil's depths to the glorious soaring heights of the gods of the rainbowed heavens. It takes you through doors of gold with windows of diamonds into a castle miles high. There, you'll hear," his voice increased measurably now, as did the drums, "the sweet voices of ten million angels lifted in eternal song. The fruits of all the

many worlds will be stacked fresh, crisp, and delicious for your hungry tongues."

The hands of Duvall moved in slow circles now, and the breathing of all the audience was getting heavier.

"And there," he continued, "in silken cloth you'll lounge with velvet flesh, and feast and drink and love in a vast, limitless, golden sun, warm with seductiveness!"

The drums were at their peak now—speaking to, shifting, jerking the nerves of all.

Marta stood staring, swaying, trembling. Her flesh seemed loosened from her bones with an enormous vibration of warmth. She heard Duvall pleading above the drums for the first to taste his nectar. Slowly she moved towards him, not feeling the tug of her husband's hand, seeing only the eyes and hands of Duvall.

She took the large gourd dipper and drank deeply of its hot fluid, never taking her eyes from Duvall. She could feel it slither down her throat and into her stomach and spread through her blood to the surface of her skin and behind her eyes and into the depths of her skull. And now she was sure she stood above the ground, floating in air so warm and softly caressing that her body flowed with all the juices of love.

Several of the large gourds were passed about, and the drums pounded into the night and into the being of everyone, just as the liquid did. And there was a sweating in the cool night as the fluid moved to the skin and the bodies began to jerk harder with the drums.

There was a murmur rising now, a slow, soft, communal voice of mass love. It rose slowly like the howl of a steady wind, and then it broke into pieces as the nesters began to pair off and move about dancing to the drums. Then some lay rolling on the ground as Duvall shouted into the night.

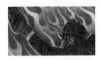

"Love, love, you heathens. Love and be complete! Heal all your aches and sorrows with the ecstasy of perfect, purified love."

Some of the ranchers left. Others stood, torn by it all.

Marta moved to Rick, slowly enveloping him in her arms. For a moment he took her almost desperately, and then he pushed her away, grabbed her by one arm, and dragged her past the couples rolling on the ground and embracing against trees. A moaning came from them now, and Duvall screamed, "Now, brothers, now. Talk to and embrace the gods!"

The gourds went the rounds among those still standing, and moans and a loud shout of unintelligible words broke into the night. Shrieks of every kind rent the air like flashing swords as Duvall shouted over and over, "Now, now, now!" His words were like the drums, like the shrieks; and all the air and all the earth and all the flesh became one, filled hot with rhythm and with lust.

Rick pulled Marta away from the sound, even though she looked and struggled back towards it mutely, and with surprising strength. He finally got her to the truck. He could feel the drink still searing at his own inner body. He felt like a fool for partaking of it.

Marta crawled across the cab to him, and he could not fend her off. He drove with difficulty. Finally, he pulled from the road and took her to the ground and moved savagely into her quivering flesh. The sounds were soft in the distance now, like wolves howling in a far canyon.

"You don't mean to tell me you're goin' back again?" Rick asked.

"Of course. It's a fine thing the Reverend Duvall is doing."

"A fine thing! God uh mighty, woman!"

"It's all free. It's the only relief those poor nesters have had in years."

"That's the whole damn problem, Marta. There's a catch to it somewhere. It just ain't natural for that Duvall to be givin' things away free. There's goin' to be a mighty big catch come to light. A mighty big one."

"All you ranchers are alike. You want all the land and power. When someone comes among you who doesn't care, and has something to give mankind, you just go blank and start cursing it."

"Well, the way he had those folks rollin' about on the ground, I ain't settled in my mind yet just what it is he has to give."

"Don't try to make something vulgar out of it. He's given those poor creatures love. They've found love again for the first time since you ranchers ran them off their land."

Rick pushed at his hair, scratched his head, got up, and walked over to the stove to pour himself another cup of coffee.

"How long is Duvall intending to stay here in the Two Mesas country?"

"Just this summer," Marta said, looking at Rick with eyes that spoke only inwardly.

"Since he's been here, five weeks ain't it, you haven't tended to your chores worth a damn. Everything is just half-done. That ain't no way for a rancher's wife to carry on. It just ain't done, that's all. It don't pay. All these years we've been gainin', and all of a sudden we come to a standstill, all over some crazy preacher."

"No, Rick, that's not all. We've talked this over a *thousand*

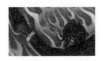

times, but you've never heard *once*. There's things a woman needs. Especially since she's helped earn them and there's money in the bank to buy them."

"Now, let's not go into that again."

"See, you close up every time. You can't face it. You can't face up to what's happening."

"All right, all right, if that's all that'll do you, just go on to the preachin' as long as the summer's a third over anyway. But this fall, early, it's goin' to be different. We're goin' back to actin' like we always have. You hear?"

"Oh yes, I hear you all right, Rick. How could I help it?" Marta turned to do the morning dishes.

Marcus had long since gone out to work on the haystack fence. Rick got up, swallowed the last of the coffee, put the cup down hard, got his hat from the deer horns on the wall, jerked it down over his head, and clomped out. He walked down to see how Marcus was doing at the feed lot.

"Have eet finish by night, Reeck. We can start cutting hay *mañana*."

"Good." Rick looked down south to the subirrigated vega grass meadows. "Looks like we'll have a big first cuttin'."

"*Sí*, the summer is a good wan for the grass."

"Well, we're due another hard winter. Comes every nine years for sure. Real bad ones, I mean. If a man's ready, lots can happen in his favor."

Marcus stopped a moment and looked at his boss, then silently went back to work stapling the wire on the newly set posts.

Rick said, still staring at the lush meadows, "I got to go work Brother Bill. He's getting a little soft."

But he went by the garden first, and, taking a hoe where it leaned up against the fence, he dug the furrows so that all

would water. He noticed that the beans were doing well as usual because of the early rains, but the rest of the garden—the tomatoes, carrots, and corn—all looked just a little wilted.

He took a piece of bent tin and put it sideways under the windmill spout. The water moved out into the garden soil. He could feel Marta's eyes on him from the kitchen window. This was her job, and she knew it. It gave Rick a satisfaction that he couldn't define to do this chore in front of her.

Then he walked to the corral, and caught and saddled the Appaloosa. He reined him out across the lengthening grama grass and rode down to his meadows. He had many stacks of old feed left, and he would add a lot of new to the reserve. The next time a blizzard struck, he'd buy up a lot more of the cattle and the land. Feed would do it. Plenty of feed was money in more than one bank. A man had to see ahead and figure to make it out here in this weather-controlled land. Yes sir.

He felt a warm glow as he rode back out towards the foothills to the north. Might as well check out the bull pasture while he worked his horse. He kept a few high-blooded bulls here in a good, protected pasture. That was another way he was ahead of most of the ranchers, even those much bigger than he—he kept improving the blood of his stock.

He was just leaning over to step down from Brother Bill and open the gate into the bull pasture when he sensed riders coming.

He turned and looked to the east and recognized three of his neighbors: George Randall, Scott Allen, and Moreno Cruz.

They rode up, all cattlemen, except Moreno, who ran cows and sheep both. They got through the "howdys" fairly quickly. Rick could tell they had something else on their minds.

George came right out with it first, "Rick, we was headin' over to see you."

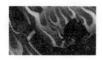

"Yeah, what can I do for you, George?"

"It's like this, Rick. That Duvall is messin' up our country."

"How's that?" Rick asked, feeling cold in his spine and thinking of Marta, who was probably driving the old truck into town right now for a meeting.

"Well, he's stirrin' up the nesters somethin' terrible. He's got 'em half drunk all the time on that free whiskey or whatever the hell it is."

Moreno Cruz pushed his black hat back from his kinky, gray hair and said, "It ain't really free. All during the week, the nesters have been bringin' gifts."

"Yeah, they're called love gifts," Scott Allen said, rolling a smoke of Prince Albert and pushing his hat back from his sad horseface.

"The way it looks to us," Randall interrupted, "is the gifts are all for the love of Duvall. These nesters are bringin' him their canned goods, and some are even droppin' money on him. Others bring grain and early garden stuff. Duvall's been peddling this stuff in town at half wholesale. The merchants can't afford to turn it down, cuz he'd just haul it on over to Flagstaff."

"Well, watcha want me to do about it?" Rick asked.

"Rick, at the risk of makin' you mad, I'm goin' to say this. All the ranchers have flat forbidden any of their kin to attend. They've all quit but Marta. Now the nesters kind of look up to her there. You know how it is. If she'd drop out of those meetin's and sort of pass the word around, we feel the nesters would get the message. They're goin' to wind up on the dole this winter if that Duvall keeps after 'em."

Moreno Cruz added, "Guess who's going to have to keep them from starving?"

"Well, I'll talk to Marta," Rick said stiffly, "but what she does is her business." He got down, opened the gate, and rode into his bull pasture without another word.

His old friend Randall yelled after him, something he'd never done before in Rick's whole life, "Your old daddy would've recognized the fact he ain't no reverend, Rick. He's some kind of a demon."

Rick rode on feeling an embarrassment, and a slow, infinitesimal wrath building deep down in his craw.

He rode slowly this day as he checked out and made a count of the bulls. Many things were on his mind. Many new emotions crossed the heavy, dedicated frame. He finally admitted to himself that he knew what to do about a cow or horse under any conditions, but this preacher business his wife was mixed up in was something else. He sure didn't want to lose her. He'd been a long time training her and preparing her for the big, acquisitive years ahead. It would be a hell of a loss. No, he couldn't just flatly forbid her to go. He'd already made his promise that she could attend until the end of the summer. There'd just have to be some other way. Maybe she'd tire of the hullabaloo, or maybe he could discreetly point out the drawback and the consequent damage it was doing him among the other ranchers.

With all these thoughts twisting and undulating through his mind another message penetrated: one of the old bulls was missing.

He rode the fence awhile, then he came to the place where the wires were down. There the fresh, big tracks, much rounder than a cow's, had passed through. By the time he'd tracked the bull, driven him back to the pasture, and repaired the fence, it was after dark.

The coyotes howled and sang at a three-quarter moon

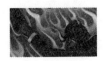

hanging in perpetual gravity, reflecting a soft blue light a quarter of a million miles through space to give voice to the coyote, light to lovers' eyes, and an easier path home for a rancher's tired horse.

As he rode, Rick's thoughts left the cattle, and he wondered if Marta would be home when he got there. Then way below, near the ranch, he saw the lights of a vehicle moving to his house. No doubt that was Marta.

It took him another hour to wind around and enter the home pasture. Why didn't the old dog bark? He wondered about this as he unsaddled and fed his horse. Then he walked slowly towards the house. Out of the shadows of the henhouse stepped the old dog. He moved up behind Rick, his bristles up, totally silent. There were no lights on in the house. No night birds voiced their approval of this mellow evening. Then he saw her. Marta stood on the porch in the moon rays. She was naked, and the blue lights caught at her breasts, caressed her round belly, and outlined her dark head. She stood, arms upraised, stretching, swaying slightly like a grass stem in a small breeze. A noise came from her, not words, not moans, just a soft noise, almost like a cat purring, but smoother.

Rick was struck by the beauty, the symmetry, of the luscious, blue-cast body, and he could not think logically. This was something he had no knowledge of, no answer for. He didn't even have a question.

He whispered softly, "Marta."

Her head came down from the sky and turned slowly to him. Her eyes were brighter in the moonlight than he'd ever seen them in the noon sun. She swayed from the porch towards him, and he caught her smooth, naked body and stood shaking violently as she slowly, expertly took his shirt from him. She dropped it, and he awkwardly and in desperation

took the rest of his clothing off. Holding her feet just off the porch, her naked body tight against his own, he carried her into the house and dropped her on the rug in the living room, where a shaft of moonlight stole through a window and drew a place on the floor for their lust.

She was wild and soft, mean and kind. She was a bitch mate to the coyote that howled again in the draw just in front of the house. She was mistress to the bobcat that prowled on the mesa a mile to the west. She lusted and whored for the brown bear in the mountains miles to the north, and she was all of these and more for the man who moved, grasping above her in abandon. Then everything became motionless, wet, and soft except the lungs. They, too, finally subsided, and the woman slept.

Her husband carried her to bed and lay beside her where they both slept deep, deep down in rest and darkness. And the coyotes hunted on as the moon arced over until its light was destroyed by the orange heat of the rising sun.

Marcus, usually talkative and good-humored no matter what the labor in the pastures had taken in physical effort, ate breakfast in silence. Rick gulped his food and sat drinking coffee, looking out at the pastures without seeing them. Marta seemed almost normal, like she was before the coming of Duvall.

Finally, Rick broke the silence, "Get the workhorses harnessed and ready, Marcus. We might as well start cutting hay today."

Marcus gulped down the hot coffee, got up, and left. The two sat again. Marta waited. Rick cleared his throat. He

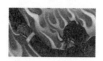

got up and poured another cup of coffee. Suddenly he had to talk. It hurt to think of it. He told her of the conversation with the neighbors. She didn't speak, only looked at him with huge eyes that spoke not.

He said tensely, "I've promised you can go if he stays the summer, and I'll keep it, but don't you see or care about the position you're puttin' me in?"

Marta seemed to shrug off an invisible shroud. Her eyes had expression now, her nerves came alive, her whole body warmed and seemed to be quivering inside. She got up, went to the cupboard, and brought out an empty bottle. She set it in front of Rick. He stared at it.

"What's that for? It's empty."

"It wasn't empty last night on Salt River. I've invited the maker of its contents here tonight."

Rick felt that little tiny wrath swell in his belly and cord up into his chest and face. He leaped to his feet.

"You've invited that devil here, here to my house?"

"*Our* house, dear. Yes, he's coming this afternoon."

Rick leaped at her and jerked her head sideways, violently, and there he held her off balance. "It's not enough that you go and make a fool of me with those goddamn nesters, is it? Well, he's not coming here. I'll kill the son of a bitch. Do you hear me? I'll kill the son of a bitch!"

"Let me go," she said, straining her whole body in an awkward position.

He flung her across the table. Things jarred and broke from the impact, and Marta fell among them on the floor. He stood heaving, wanting to strike her and hurt her.

Calmly, she got up and straightened herself. Then she opened her robe, and he stared at her nakedness. She rubbed her hand across the smooth, oval belly and said softly, "You

curse him and you curse his medicine, but now you have a son in here because of it." She patted the belly tenderly, and an enigmatic smile formed on all her face.

A whole world of dark blue and charging, jumping, little pieces of lightning shot all around and through Rick's body. The knees ran together and helped each other to stand.

"You mean it? You mean it? You mean it?"

She moved to him, took his face, and kissed the repetition out of his mouth. Then she stepped back and said, "Go to your work. You'll soon have many extra responsibilities. Many you don't dream of now."

The big man walked out to the team, and in a little while he was following Marcus, doing what he knew how to do best. Marcus's team pulled the mower, and the click, click of the blade made the world real again for Rick. He drove his team, pulling the rake and dragging the cut hay into little windrows so it would be easy to load and stack later.

Now he'd have an heir and a helper, and the ranchers could no longer taunt him. Oh, it was a great day! He smelled the new-fallen hay, and it smelled just as Marta had the night before. He wanted to yell at Marcus the news and wonder of the day, but somehow held it back. He failed to see the purple-clad figure on a horse ride to his house and stay awhile and then ride away.

After they finished the day's work and were turning the horses to feed, Rick felt he must tell Marcus. Marcus had shared in the labor for many steady years; he would rejoice just as Rick had rejoiced about the son to come. But before he could say anything, Marcus himself spoke.

"Boss, I donn won to tell you thees, bot Terrasina the witch tells me last Saturday in town for you to watch. Much

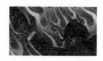

evil is to come unless you watch. Eet ees not my beezness, Boss, bot watch."

"Watch what, Marcus?"

"She donn say what, Boss. She just say."

Rick walked towards the house. He could see the old dog standing, stiff, motionless, sniffing down the road towards town.

Marcus lifted the last fork of grass hay from the wide bed wagon up on the stack. Rick finished rounding out and tamping right the top of the stack. This would keep the moisture out. He slid down one end, and the two of them pulled a strand of barbed wire across the top of the stack and tied a heavy rock to each end. This constant weight would hold the stack solid and preserve it for several years if necessary.

Rick wiped the sweat from his head, taking his hat off to cool a moment. The haying for the summer was finished. He looked over row after row of stacks. He had more hay up now than any three ranchers in the country. He was ready. It had to come. Either a bad drought or a blizzard. They always did. In fact, it was very dry now. Although the grama grass was up long, it had turned brown and matured early. In the fall, the cows would tromp down as much as they'd eat. Then if the blizzards came, Rick would sell the hay high and buy the cattle cheap. It was nothing new. You just had to save the dollars during the good times and get ready. Disaster had always struck the land, and Rick knew it always would.

He was also pleased that Marta had gone ahead with the garden and finished most of her canning. They would save lots of money on groceries this winter besides eating well.

It was midafternoon and a little hotter than usual for this time of late summer, and in midafternoon there was always more work to be done. But the thoughts of all the accomplishments made Rick suddenly generous with a little time.

"Marcus, you might as well take a nap, or plait on that rawhide bridle you been makin' for the youngun'."

"Boss, maybe now you got the windmill turned on, you have much fruit. Huh?" Marcus grinned big. "That's the same way with me, Boss. I donn stop. Not ol' Marcus. I got another one comin' out of the same pot. Maria Sanchez. I donn open my eyes ever agin when we make the love."

"What's that got to do with it?"

"That's what makes the bambinos. I tell you, Boss, three times I open my eyes. Three times now the leetle ones. A man should not see so much in the world. No?"

Rick felt warm with the sun and thoughts of the new haystacks and the child in the lovely belly of his wife. He went to the house. She looked at him puzzled and said, "Something wrong?" He never quit this early. Never.

"No, just thought I'd come visit a spell. The hayin's all done. We had a big crop. This last cuttin' was almost as good as the first. We're ready for 'em."

"That's good," she said flatly, and went on with her sewing. She was making new curtains for the living room.

"Rick, do you think we could have a new rug to match the curtains. This one's awfully old, and Allen's Hardware has a new assortment priced plenty reasonable."

"Well, let's wait and see how the calf crop weighs out. It's goin' to be a hard winter, and you never can tell when a man might get in a tight."

Marta went on sewing silently. How could she penetrate through to this man? How in holy hell could she make him

see something besides his fat cattle, his stacks of premeditated hay? She had helped make it all, including the bank account in town. She'd sewed, canned, dug in the garden, helped at brandings, cooked, skimped, done without, until now they were safe. What was it all for? She wanted what was normal—a car, a few new things for herself and the house. Not a lot, but some. And a little time in town to be sociable, to meet and talk and dream a little with other women. All this she ached to tell Rick. But her voice stopped and choked in her throat, holding the emotions back with it.

Rick uneasily got up and poured himself a drink of bourbon.

"Care for one?" he asked Marta.

She shook her head and continued sewing.

He sipped a moment at the brown liquid and then belted it all down. He drank little. It was a luxury. He stared at the woman, thinking about the child in her hardening belly. He had her now. She hadn't insisted on the rug and caused a scene as she usually would. It was the kid. It had mellowed her. He wanted to make her feel how he felt. How it had been in the early days. How it was when his grandfather had come to Two Mesas with the first herd of cattle.

There had been a big gold-mining boom. The town had grown and pulled—with the magic word *gold*—the miners, the merchants, the whores from all over the West. The mines had paid off for everyone for a while. The town had been wild and mean and greedy. The boom crowded the mines, took the best ore out, ruined the tunnels, and then it died swiftly. The ghosts of people stayed and others moved on hunting the same elusive fortune, and their ghosts clung to the rotting buildings and to the wind whistling along the streets and through the windowless buildings.

Other cattlemen came. They settled right here. Lived on this land. Rick's grandfather spread out until he ran over two thousand head of cattle and it was a two-day ride across the land. The old man died and was buried on the little hill behind the house. Rick's father had taken over and spread out even bigger. Two Mesas grew and became a solid little cow town, serving its people well, supplying the extras—the salt and pepper of life.

But then, when Rick was a very small boy, he remembered the great blizzard and how the cattle vanished breathing the searing cold into their lungs and freezing their red hearts, and how finally the few left were moved to the stack lots, and they tailed them up by the hour trying to save some for seed. His mother had stood there in the terrible cold, working like a man. Then pneumonia had killed her just like the cattle. The tiny haystack had vanished and the cattle, too. They'd sold part of the land, and then some more, to hold together and restock. Finally, things began to look good again, and Rick rode with his father; he had become a hand. Shortly thereafter the drought came, and the wind lifted little bits of the earth from around the dying grass, and everything became earth and dust—the sky, the insides of a man's head, his thoughts; even his dreams turned to dust. Once again he'd seen the hay dwindle and the cattle get down and breathe the dust like they had the iced air and die just the same. This last had killed his father. He just fell over dead one day.

Well, Rick took over the ranch as a very young man. How could he tell this feeling to Marta. He'd tried. She seemed to listen, but she'd never once said, "I understand."

He had learned a long and hard lesson, and when the drought hit in thirty-four he'd been ready. All the good years before he'd put up hay. True he'd had to sell the ranch down to

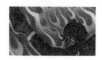

its present modest size, but it was solid and it would grow again. *He'd* be buying up the land next time. It was his turn. Nothing could stop him. Nothing.

Marta sat looking at Rick now, as he stared out the window. She wondered what emotion made his jaw muscles knot and his breath come hard. Maybe he'd been thinking things over. Maybe she *should* approach him again about her desires.

"Rick," she said timidly. He turned to her. "Rick, I was just thinking about the new rug. We'll wait and see if the calves weigh out, but we both know they will. But, in the meantime, maybe I could have Mr. Allen put the rug back while I still have a good choice. There's a brown and red patterned one I want so bad."

Rick felt the flow of blood to his face. He leaped up. *"Want, want,* that's all you do is want. Can't you see what we're building for. If it's not a new car, it's a new rug. Why don't you have the Reverend Duvall buy you one. He's robbed the nesters until they'll all be on the dole this winter. It'll be the taxes we working people pay that'll be takin' care of 'em!"

Marta laid the sewing down in her lap and pushed her hair back. A color came into her cheeks as if they'd been freshly rouged. Her eyes and her nostrils widened measurably.

"Well, you can rest assured the Reverend knows when the old ways are done. He's selling his wagon and buying a new limousine in just two weeks. He knows the days of the horse-drawn show are over, but you don't, Rick. You'll die horseback on the way to the bank."

"Speakin' of the reverend," Rick snapped short each word, "when is he going to finish up sacking out our country?"

"He'll finish two weeks from this Saturday, and we're all going to miss him terribly."

"Well, I know a lot of people that won't."

At that instant the old dog barked for the first time in three months. Rick put on his hat and walked out to see what could have stirred the old critter up. Then he saw it! Down to the southwest a great line of blue and black smoke.

"Prairie fire!" he yelled, "Marta, it's movin' this way! The brooms!" he said, "get me all the brooms!" He raced to the corrals and got Brother Bill, then he rode to the house. Marta handed him the brooms from the kitchen door. He didn't tell her goodbye. He spurred to the bunkhouse where Marcus napped.

"Marcus! Marcus! Get up! There's a prairie fire! Get the plow, get the team, plow around the haystacks!"

He rode swiftly now, across the prairie towards the coming fire. Marta stood in the yard watching, breathing heavily, and the old dog just barked and barked as if he'd never bark again.

About a mile and a half from the front point of the fire, Rick saw his first bunch of deer. Several coyotes ran right among them. They were scattered, wildly leaping and running from the line of smoke and flame. Then he saw cattle rumbling ahead, slower, but just as frantic.

As he neared, he began to see the small things. Quail burst in frenzied rhythms across the sky. Rats dodged back and forth, some turning madly into the fire. Jackrabbits and cottontails seemed to lose direction, and many of them leaped right into the flames, running, burning, then falling in a kicking, smoking wad. A badger waddled ahead, side by side with a skunk, and there were all sorts of things moving, too small to

see, lizards, scorpions, ants, grasshoppers, spiders, all roasted and turned black like the grass.

The wind was getting up from the southwest now as the sun set. All over the land people poured towards the battle line, in trucks, cars, wagons, and on horseback they came. Up and down the line they fought with brooms, shovels, raincoats, whatever they could throw at the fire.

Brother Bill was wild and scared of the fire, but Rick fought him under control. He got down with the brooms and moved in between several blackened, smoky men who were swinging various implements to smother the fire. They swung and fought and moved on. Finally, Rick could see they weren't gaining any. The fire would be put out for a short distance then leap ahead to another point.

Darkness came, and all up and down the line for two miles the black night figures flailed and struggled, and little pincers kept moving ahead with the wind.

If something desperate wasn't done, it would move on towards Rick's place, destroy it, and then take in Two Mesas itself. No doubt Salt River would be hit before it stopped.

Rick went back to get Brother Bill where he'd tied him to a tree. It took twenty minutes to walk back. He was amazed at how far the fire had run. He rode swiftly down the line. He could see where someone had attempted to plow in front of it, but the fire had simply run around. He saw Moreno Cruz and a group of ranchers trying to get a tractor ahead of the fire. Then two cowboys came racing down the line dragging a freshly butchered cowhide tied between two ropes. This checked the fire until the tractor could be moved out in front. But it didn't do any good. It was only a temporary relief. The cowhide dried swiftly; the rope burned in two.

Rick yelled at Moreno, "The only chance we got is to backfire it."

"Can't as long as the wind is straight out of the southwest. It's changing a little, but not enough yet."

All over the land, women and small children stood in the yards of the ranches and looked at the red, mad glow flickering into the sky. Some had already seen their houses, barns, and fences go, cattle burn, and run away in flames. The rest just stood waiting, praying, and hurting with their men. The nesters' homes were safe because of the river, but they came and fought till they dropped or until some little dent was made in the line of destructive flame. All worked, hoped, and fought together now.

The man on the tractor kept trying, moving ahead, ripping at the untouched grass, and it did finally help. In his elation he forgot to watch, and the fire crept up on the tractor. There was a loud explosion, and another flame shot higher into the sky than any of the prairie fire. The tractor had caught fire and blown up. The flames were so hot that nothing could be done. The people of the land just fought on wearily around it.

The fire moved on. The main point now reached out within a mile and a quarter of Rick's southernmost pasture. He was sick all over. He called a conference with the ranchers.

"We've got to backfire now!" he screamed into the night. "The wind is coming from the side now. There's a chance we can blunt the point. Moreno, you, Scott, Darby, Holzein, scatter to the west and backfire. I'll get a group and fight the main point."

But just as he gathered the men to him and rode, ran, and stumbled for the blazing, searing front point, the wind increased and shot the flames higher and faster ahead. They

fought hard and many were burned, but the anxious wind would not listen as it hurried, crowded, and shoved the fire forward where it licked and devoured all life ahead of it.

Then there was a loud rumble, and Rick looked to see the white canvas of a wagon hurtling along the fire line towards them. It came to a halt so suddenly that the wagon almost overturned and the horses were nearly jerked from the harness. It was Duvall's Apache at the reins, and beside him, on horseback, rode Duvall himself.

He alighted like a calf roper from the horse, handed the reins to the Indian, and yelled. "Here, help!"

Rick ran to him and helped drop a barrel from the back of the wagon into the burnt earth.

"Get your horse," Duvall yelled, and with huge hands he jerked an iron loop from the barrel and ripped a canvas cover from its top.

Rick ran back for Brother Bill not knowing why he obeyed. He spurred back, and Duvall dragged a huge buffalo hide out of the barrel of dark liquid.

"Here," he shouted, "dip your rope in here."

Rick pitched the rope to him and dipped it in. Duvall had already dipped his. Swiftly the mighty hands tied the ropes on opposite sides of the hide. Rick didn't have to be told what to do. He and Duvall mounted and dallied their ropes around the horns of their saddles. He could tell by the expert and practiced way Duvall did this that he'd worked with the California *vaqueros* at one time. They split now on each side of the fire and rode. Oh, how they rode!

Brother Bill sensed a job to do now. This was what Rick had trained him for—to be ready for any job and to handle it. They rode and dragged the hide. As it hit the flame, great phosphorescent lights ricocheted out from it like little concen-

trated bits of moonlight, and the fire died. They spurred back to the barrel, dipped the hide, and rode wildly again into the night.

The horses were heaving and sweating, and their hair became singed. The lungs of the men filled with smoke, and the whites of their eyes turned red and profane like the prairie fire itself. But all held together. They broke the point of the fire, and then dulled it more, and there was a great gap where it was dead. Then the backfire met the main line, and the two points fought themselves out of flame and into smoke and died together.

Now the people of the land sensed victory, and they struck at the tiny little outbreaks. Soon the line was only black and smoking.

As the sun came up, the people stayed. Back behind, things still smoked, carcasses, dry cow dung, and lumps of things, but on the front line itself all had been pounded out.

Duvall was gone. He'd taken the hide with him. The people left one by one.

Rick, a half-mile from his land now, could see the gate standing up. It stood erect, steady, and unburned. And the dry, rich grass still waved in the now-soft wind across his land. His haystacks were still there to serve his purposes. And in the house, his wife with the beautiful belly surrounding a child from his loins would be there waiting.

He rode the tired horse across the black, weaving fire line that caressed the brown, waving grassy one, towards his world. He hadn't even had a chance to thank Duvall. Everyone had been too busy. Well, he'd do that, and he'd tell Marta how wrong he'd been. But by the time he rode past the haystacks to the house, a part of this vow had slipped his mind.

Marcus stood waiting where he'd plowed all night long

around the stacks. And the old dog stood with bristles up, and he was silent again.

With the saving of the land from the devouring fire, a new fear came over Rick. He could not say what this fear was exactly. He *felt* like the old dog *looked*; that was as close as he could come to it.

It was the last night of Reverend Duvall's meetings. He didn't want Marta to go. Still, he knew she would. Everyone in the country knew that it was a healing and marrying night. He was afraid of this night.

Suddenly he said to Marta, "I'm going with you."

The hand holding the brush that caressed her hair stopped its motion for an instant only, "All right. It's about time," she said, in that voice that spoke only words.

He tried to watch her as the old truck bumped along. But the huge eyes had a film over them that he could not penetrate. His uneasiness increased as they neared town.

"Do we need anything from Allen's?" he asked, and then wished he hadn't as he remembered the rug she wanted.

"No, we don't need anything."

"Would you like a cup of coffee?" he asked.

"I guess so."

They walked to Lil's place just as several cowboys they knew were getting up to leave.

"Howdy, Rick," they all said. None of them spoke to Marta. Rick noticed this but couldn't define it. Lil came over, saying, "I hear you just missed burning out, Rick."

"Yeah, it was close."

"They're telling around that Reverend what's-his-name saved the day."

"He helped," Rick said. "Coffee, Lil, and I'll take some of that peach cobbler of yours."

Lil looked at Marta, waiting.

Marta said, "Just for the fun of it I'll take the same as Rick." She looked up at Lil and smiled. Lil looked away, then went to get the order.

They were silent until it was delivered. Lil went straight back to the kitchen, saying over her shoulder, "If you need anything just holler. I've got some chores to do in the kitchen."

Rick could feel a certain coldness all around them. It was like seeing a warm pond turn to ice on a sweating hot day. It made no sense to him. He felt alone.

Marta studied Rick now. She thought, he just doesn't get it. He's forgotten that I gave up a fine life in California for him. If nothing else I could be living with my parents who are well-to-do merchants. I could have had the pick of the men in Fresno. How did I go wrong? Where did I misjudge this man? Then she recalled it was his dedicated talk of power and wealth regained that had sold her in the first place. But, God, what was it all for? Just to have it was nothing. It was only the use it was put to that counted. She'd done her part, of that she was certain.

Rick looked at her and saw nothing but a beautiful statue with her arms folded across the growing and fertile belly. He strained. He tried to open himself to her feelings, but nothing came through. It was like a broadcast station with no receivers. He was like a hunting hound with nothing to scent. The air became static and a vacuum of opposites. They sat, these two persons, feeling much, knowing much, but her emotions bounced from the south wall and his from the north.

The nesters came to the wagon in little groups and couples. They came to the magnetic core of something that gave a fleeting time of escape to them. It was different. It was a release and a relief from the grinding poverty and indignity of their surroundings. For a time now they had felt big, even as big as the ranchers and the vast land that destroyed them.

For the children it had been a dream. Never before had their parents been as free with them. Never before had they been as generous with the pitiful supplies of food. And instead of the constant petty bickering before Duvall came, there was now a semblance of loving and being loved.

And the word had spread, the story told and retold—of his stopping the prairie fire with another magical brew. This, the last night, saw the people of the little river come almost in awe. They were not rowdy as before, but restrained, anticipating a last great event, yet fearful of its outcome.

Rick and Marta stood watching the "love offerings" placed in a large pile. They could see the steam already coming out of the pot, but Duvall and the Indians were still in the wagon.

One old man, obviously hooked on either Duvall's medicine or a concoction of his own, slithered up to Rick and smiled a toothless smile, twisting his hands in his overall pockets.

"Well, it's good to see you here, Mr. Ames. The missus has kept us real good company. Real good." And he laughed in a screaming, choking laugh that made Rick want to smash the old man in the face.

He controlled himself, not wanting these nesters to get the best of him in any way. He realized a rancher would lose

face for years that way. What was the matter with him? He was not under his usual rocklike control.

Suddenly the Apache and his sister leaped up on the platform and moved to the drums. The crowd closed around now like gamblers at a cockfight. Slowly the drums started. The Indians played, looking out above the crowd. They only participated with the primitive beat. Their faces appeared made of red clay, fired, and set forever in the vacant look of *nothing*, or maybe *all*. . . .

Then there was Duvall, his hands up, seeming to hide his husky body with their spread.

"Friends," he said softly, glancing slowly all through the crowd, lingering a moment on Rick and Marta. "Friends," and the black eyes seemed to have little electric bulbs in them, and a smile pulled one side of his face. "This will be our last glorious night together."

"No, no," came a couple of protesting voices from the crowd, and then a chant rose, "No, no."

The hands moved slightly, and the chant died. "Thank you, but other lands call us. We have done extraordinarily well here. We have given rise to old, long-dead emotions, and we have created an atmosphere of pure love. Love," the voice raised imperceptibly, "love, and now tonight we'll consummate those loves among the young of marrying temperament, and we'll heal all the lame and halt. All! Do you hear, my brothers?"

"Yes," came the loud chorus back.

"Good. Ah excellent. I feel this is going to be one of our greatest nights. I've traveled all the world gathering the knowledge of the ancients. It must not be wasted. That would be an unredeemable sin. Right brothers?"

"Yes, yes," they yelled. "Yes!"

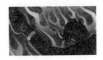

Now the drums picked up gradually but definitely. The hands moved in tiny little circles.

"I ask you, my brothers, to come forward and bring your ill, and weak, and worried. Come to me." The hands moved out above the crowd, and he drew all he mentioned with a motion of the hands.

They came now, the arthritic, the rheumatic, those with sinus and heart diseases, and those who were just old. There was one idiot who had been born an idiot and was now a fifty-seven-year-old baby. They led him like a mule, and everyone now stood waiting in a single line, looking around the ones in front of them, waiting for Duvall.

Suddenly he leaped from the platform with a large gourd. He passed it down the line of sick.

"Drink, my brothers, drink and feel the blood purified, and the soul soothed like a baby at a sweet teat."

They drank the hot liquid, swallowed it down until tears swamped their eyes.

First in line was an old man on homemade crutches who couldn't stand alone. His wife helped him forward. The wife looked aglow with a fervor that Rick had seen only here, now, and the night he'd loved Marta in the moonlight. She held the old man as if Duvall would turn him into a golden, everlasting statue.

Duvall swept his hands swiftly back and forth through the air above the old man and said, "Now, brother, what's your trouble?"

The woman said, "Arthritis, sir. He's had it nigh onto twenty years now. He ain't able to sleep er nothin' fer hit."

"Well, dear lady, hold this old crippled man. Hold him tight because he might just run off with a young widow in just one minute." The crowd laughed nervously but with a build-

ing excitement. "Old man, you want to be well?" The old man nodded *yes,* grinning like a fool. "Well, you are," Duvall screamed, leaping off the ground and waving his hands in powerful, swift arcs. "You are healed! You are cured! You are FREE!" and he jerked the crutches from the old man and threw them out of sight into the night brush. "Dance," he screamed at him, and the old man, fearful at first, took a tender step. A strange, unreal expression came over his face, and he did dance. His fat wife cried and screamed, and now all the crowd picked it up.

The voice of Duvall shafted through the mighty fingers, and the words *heal* and *cure* and *free* rent the skulls of all in line. All there. People moaned and prayed and thanked God and Duvall. They cried and fell and danced and vibrated to the tune of his voice, and the wild Indian drums were like balloons above a powerful fan. No one was ill anymore. They brought out their bottles like beggars, holding them forward to Duvall. The Indian woman quit the drum and helped fill them.

Rick stood, laying his hand on the quivering arm of Marta. He could feel vibrations running through her as if a mighty wind full of ice had blown her naked. He could feel some of this chill in his own blood, and he fought at it and was ashamed. Yet he stood transfixed. It was the last night, and he'd promised.

Then Marta took a bottle out of her purse and held it to Duvall, who bowed slightly and filled it for her. She brought it back and handed it to Rick. He shook his head *no,* and she shrugged, pulling deeply at the fiery liquid.

Now the bottles were filled, and Duvall leaped on the platform again, raising the hands. All heads and eyes moved up with them and stayed there moving to the side or down only as the hands did.

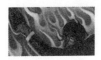

"Now, my brothers, the healing is done. You have been cleansed of the devil's curse, and the gods are smiling on your blood. Ah, red, red blood, pure as high-country snow, warm as love, young love. All is blood, my brothers. All is blood. Come drink now and warm that blood and let it know life is there circulating, crying to break out of the prison of your ribs. Pour your life out to each other. You have an abundance of life tonight, my brothers. Pour it and revive! Now, now is the moment! All the young, the marrying young come here. Come, come." And again the hands made the wide, powerful gathering motion, and the young came and stood in heat, the heat of the drink, of the voice, and the natural heat of stimulated youth, and he married them.

"Now, you are man and wife. Act! Act! Love! Be what you were born to be! You were born out of love. Now live from it. Give love. Receive!"

The vibration of the drums and the voice filled everything. There was not a single atom of the air that was not propelled by it. It came out of the earth, and the bodies that breathed the air and stood on that earth absorbed it and emanated it, and the young fell into each others' arms, and they moved in the grass. All the unknown tongues of lost civilizations returned and entered these bodies as they talked, grunted, and fell about writhing. Some lost their new mates and found others, and all were one single mind to Duvall's hands.

Rick looked in wonder at first; then the cannibalistic, hoglike noises nauseated him, and he felt the slow anger that burned like a coal stove flame, stoked slightly. He saw Duvall's hands reaching toward them in the sky. He shook his head and almost fell. He wanted to sleep, but refused it. He willed it not to be. Then he saw Marta's face upturned, filled with the look of every captive woman who ever lived, every woman who was

sold, conned, and deceived since the beginning.

Marta moved towards Duvall, looking up at the hands, and now he looked down at her and spoke softly, "Come. Come."

The Apaches no longer played. The noise of the earth was not of the drums, now, but of mating tigers and hyenas.

Rick leaped at Marta, grabbed her around the waist, and started with her to the truck, and then it was all gone. There was one stab of pencil-straight lightning that shot like a comet into his universe and disappeared, leaving nothing but the darkness.

It was still dark when Rick awakened. The bed was hard to ride. It whirled about, and his head pained. He reached to feel the knot and the gash on the back side of his head. It still throbbed. It must have been the Apache. Duvall could never have reached him that quickly. He lay awhile, and then he heard Marcus in the kitchen.

Daylight came, cool and gray through the bedroom window. Marta lay now with a peaceful look on her face. She always awoke when he did and fixed breakfast for the three of them. This morning she slept sounder than she'd ever done before.

He decided to leave her be. He put on his pants and bent to pull on his boots. The blood pounded in his head, and he almost fell. By the time he'd dressed and walked to the kitchen, he could feel the rage churning about through his being. He looked at the .30-30 above the door. Then he flexed his hands and thought of Duvall's throat.

Marcus sat drinking coffee. "Mornin', Boss. I kept the team up und they ready."

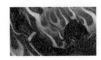

"What for?"

"To help feenesh Randall's tank. Donn you remember? We promise lass week."

"Oh hell, that's right. Well, we'll just have to go."

Rick poured himself a cup of coffee. Then took a side of bacon and sliced some. He fried them two eggs apiece. The sourdough bread baked quickly in the hot oven. They ate in silence.

Rick decided he had to give Duvall a whipping. There was no other way, but he couldn't go back on his word to help a neighbor. No telling when he'd need that help himself. Randall had broken a leg last week when a horse fell on him. The tank would dam up a long draw near Randall's headquarters. It was government-financed, so Randall would draw wages for all his work. According to the government, it was a way of helping the ranchers to overcome the drought and recent Depression, and at the same time improve the land.

Well maybe Duvall would stay a few days longer, to cash in his love offerings. If he did, they had to have it out, that was all. Duvall had it coming, but, even more, Rick needed to give it to him.

They cleaned their plates with home-canned strawberry jam and hot, buttered sourdough biscuits. After a final cup of coffee, Marcus walked out and Rick looked for his hat. He always threw it on the deer horns in the kitchen, but it wasn't there. He found it by the bed. He could see the dent where he'd been hit with a hard object. He pulled it over his sore head and started out.

Then Marta's voice stopped him at the door. "When will you be back?" She spoke in the flat tones she'd used lately.

"Two and a half or three days, I reckon. Why?"

There was no answer. He left.

Marcus had the horses all harnessed and leaped up on one bareback. Rick rode Red Spot, a three-year-old gelding Appaloosa that would someday be as good a horse as Brother Bill. The horse moved out under him with the good running walk he liked. It helped his feelings. He rode beside Marcus, wondering why he was silent. Everything seemed against nature lately. Then he noticed the old dog following lamely. He reined up and yelled, "Go home you old fool. What's the matter with you?" The old dog stood and watched him until he moved ahead, then he followed again. The third time, Rick took his rope from the saddle and shook it at the old dog. "Now, get on back." To Marcus he said, "That old dog ain't tried to follow me in two years. Hell, he cain't hardly walk." The old dog refused to be cowed, but stopped and stood immobile, watching as they rode away.

Rick thought, *Why in hell doesn't Marcus comment?* The world he had regulated, cornered, and so efficiently controlled was suddenly deserting him. It was the helplessness he felt that brought on the rage. He had to do something just as soon as he finished Randall's tank. A move to stop all this must be made. He would damn well do it.

Now the sun came up over the two mesas that gave the town its name. It radiated out in oranges and yellows, and the beams topped the grass in golden waves, warming the earth like hindquarters against a fast-burning fireplace. The blue jays whipped about, swishing a little of the vast sky color among the deep green of the scrub-cedars. The coyotes and bobcats had gone to bed now, and the deer were hiding in little sunlit parks. The air was pure and quiet with a hint of the coming fall as it passed into the lungs.

Rick's feelings improved again as he saw a bunch of his cattle lying fat and full. The calves stood about, some jumping

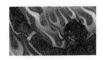

and running, full of the life and fat that meant money and power. He still wondered why Marcus was so silent. He was sure a good hand. He'd groomed him a long time now in every phase of ranch life from the doctoring of cattle to the cutting and stacking of hay. He had dug post holes, built fence, topped off a bronc, pulled calves from dying mothers, tailed up old cows in blizzards, broken ice for stock water in the winter, and hauled feed when the snow was two feet deep on the level. Marcus was an all-around hand. Soon, now, the ranch would grow and demand more help. Marcus was to be the foreman. Hell yes. The years had not been wasted, not if he held things together as before. But . . . but . . .

Marcus sensed his boss, knew there was turmoil in his soul. He feared to approach him about it, having always been gentleman enough not to infringe on the other man's privacy. And yet, he felt a great urge to comfort him. Maybe the boss suffered some of the confusion that he felt within himself. Things were not the same anymore. He had heard his boss called a tight-fisted, greedy, grasping rancher many times. He knew better. Rick had always worked him hard, paid and fed him well—and he even allowed for his weekend drunks with understanding. He could not imagine being treated better. And Marta, too, had given him respect and a place at their table. He could not conceive living without the two of them. But now something threatened his home, his life, his dedication. Something that Terrasina the witch had consistently warned him about. But he could not approach his boss from that angle. It was too delicate, and the results too fearful. Still he *had* to cheer him up. He would think of something to make him feel better.

"Boss, when you get your leetle one, I goin' to borrow him and take him to see all three of mine. Donn you think

they'd like that? Who knows, Boss, maybe someday your son marry with my gurrl. Huh?"

Rick said, "Might be. A feller never knows what's goin' to happen these days."

"Boss, I aver tells you about thees time I wins seven hondred dollar in a game of the dice?"

"No."

"Well, the dice talk altogether for ol' Marcus. They says over und over seven, seven, seven. Booms, booms, booms. All the time I take the money an' put een my pockets. Pretty soon I ron out uv pockets and so I queets the game. I go across the streets to another bar. There is poker game. I get in the poker game and thees man he give me all thees cards, and all thees whiskey I'm buying for ourselves. Preety soons I donn know if I got aces or deuces. Then I bat it all. All in wan pot. I know wat you goin' to theenks, Boss, bot you theenks wrong. I ween'! I tell you I weens eet all! I donn have enough pockets so I poot eet in my hat. Then I hire me one cowboy to drive me to Flagstaff, and there I meet a girl een thees place. She say she ees married bot her hosbond donn be in town. Well, I buy wheesky, jeen, beers, und the wines. I go to spend time with thees pretty woman." Marcus looked hard at Rick and thought he sensed a slightly different feeling coming from his boss now. "Und, Boss, I stay, I donn know, maybe wan hour, maybe wan day. Then this man breaks up the door with muscles. He ees yelling noises at me. I jomp op and ron like hell. I geet plomb away that ees for chure. Bot, I donn got no pants. And that ees how I got broke on the dice games. Boss, donn never poot no money in your pants. Huh? Spend it on the bar, and you donn lose nothin'. Huh?"

Rick grinned and said, "I'll try to remember that the next time I'm in Flag. By the way when's the last time you were in Flagstaff, Marcus?"

"Never no mores, Boss. The welcome she ees gone, gone."

Now they came to the tank. There was the slip, or steel fresno as it was sometimes called. Marcus hitched the team to it, and Rick tied his horse and took the reins. They went to work. The sun seared down, and the dust came and choked them, filled their eyes, got under their collars, and mixed with the sweat trickling from under their hats.

Randall was soon there, driving up in his old pickup to bring them lunch. Randall got out of the pickup, holding back with the leg that was in a cast.

He yelled, "You fellers like somethin' to eat?" and added, "I didn't really expect you to be here."

Rick said, "Did Sybil break that leg so she could keep you home awhile?"

"Hell, I ain't been anywhere but your place and mine in a month. I ain't goin' around Two Mesas till that Duvall is gone."

There was a silence now. Rick felt the anger come back, twisting around hot and bitter, wanting out, craving release.

They all sat down in the shade of the pickup. Rick took the bacon sandwich from the box and said, "Well, get it off your chest, George. You ain't let me alone since that bastard's been in the country."

"Well, I might as well get it over with like you say. Seeing as how your daddy and me was the closest friends in the country, it sorta hurt me to see you lettin' Marta go to them damn meetin's. You know I don't give a damn about gossip, but everyone in the country is talking about it. It could hurt you later on, Rick."

Marcus chewed nervously at his sandwich, not tasting it now.

"I know you're right, George, but there's things you don't know."

"Well, out with it, boy. Since I'm goin' to nose in my neighbor's business I might as well know it all."

"Well, it's like this. Marta's pregnant, and I thought since it'd been so long comin' about I'd just humor her."

"Pregnant! Good Lord, boy, how come you didn't jist up and tell me? Hells Bells!" Randall leaped up, forgetting about his broken leg and crawled across the pickup seat to the glove compartment. "Here, by God, we got to have a little toast to that."

Rick said, smiling, feeling another form of warmness and pride now, "Here's to the future governor of the state."

Marcus took a slug, feeling silly and happy again for the first time in a long spell. "Here's to the son of the boss. We hopes he makes half as good as the papa and mama."

Randall took two swallows before he let the bottle down. He wiped his mouth and the tears from his eyes, and said, "If he turns into a first-class bank robber, we'll toast him again, but if he's a petty thief, we'll all help hang him."

They all yelled.

Sometime later, after the sandwiches and the bottle were finished, Randall took a nap, and his two neighbors worked like four mules. The tank was almost done when sundown came. They woke up Randall, who was embarrassed at his being caught asleep at that time of day. He said, "Hell of a note ain't it? Got my neighbors over here doin' my government work for me, then I drink most of the whiskey to celebrate the new son. Don't look like to me you boys 'er getting a fair deal out of this."

"I wouldn't trade places with you for a new set of harness," Rick said. "Besides, Sybil will have some of that tongue-

melting peach cobbler for supper. That'll even us up for a whole month."

After the horses were watered and fed, the men retired to the ranch house. Sybil and George ran it all now, except during haying season. Their two sons were off in California somewhere, bumming around as George said, just wasting time till they came back to the ranch. Sybil was one of those women, tough and tender, strong-armed and flexible-backed—tight jaws below smiling eyes. You knew that if she'd been raised in society, she'd have been its queen. And since it was a cow ranch instead, she was the queen of the ranch. There was no other word that fit her.

"How's Marta?" were her first words to Rick, and there was none of the questing and accusation he had heard in others' voices when they asked him that. She really meant it, and paid no mind to others' thoughts, figuring she was capable of having plenty of her own.

"Oh, she's just fine, Sybil. Finished her cannin'. Had lots of strawberries this year."

"Now wait a minute, Rick," said Randall, "tell her how she *really* is."

Rick hung his head and felt he was blushing through the seat of his Levi's.

"They're goin' to colt this winter," Randall said, watching the joy spread over Sybil's face.

"Well, my goodness," she said, "That calls for somethin' special." She went to a cupboard and pulled out a gallon jar of homemade chokecherry wine.

Since this was Marcus's favorite drink in the whole world, he just stood there in the middle of the floor like he was going to fly out over the windmill and tried to rub the kinky hair out of his head while he waited for his glass.

They all toasted the new one again and again. The kitchen warmed up from the stove, the wine, the friendship, and joy of a newcomer to an old, old world. Then Sybil cooked the venison steak and hot biscuits and gravy that steamed and scented up the whole place. They all sat down and ate four bellies' full. Then, the now slightly cooled peach cobbler was dipped out with an extra portion for Rick.

"The new papa'll need a lot of extra strength from here on in," Sybil said.

They all slept that night, full and happy. Yes, even Marcus and Rick felt that things were right again.

Rick and Marcus were up, breakfasted, and at the tank right after sunrise. By ten o'clock that morning the wind was getting up, but all the fresnoing was done. Rick took a shovel and helped Marcus tamp the tank awhile. Then they were done.

Rick smiled, "We did it, Marcus. She's finished. Ol' George can collect his money from the government and sweat out the spring rains from now on. Listen, you head on in home with the team; Marta isn't expectin' us back till tomorrow night, so tell her I'm helping George move some cattle. I want to go by the ranch and visit awhile with George and then drift on by Two Mesas and get a little surprise for Marta."

The wind blasted the dust from the freshly moved earth around them.

"Hell, let's get out of here," he said. They left.

Rick stopped and tied Red Spot and got in out of the wind. Sybil poured a cup of hot coffee for Rick and George, who sat with his busted leg propped up on a chair.

"It's done, George."

"You fellers worked like you owned the place. I wasn't expectin' this for two or three more days."

"It was that chokecherry wine of Sybil's."

"If I thought it'd make you men work like that all the time, I'd keep a batch brewin' day and night," she said.

"Say, Sybil," Rick asked, "what's Marta's favorite color?"

"You mean you don't know?"

"Naw."

"You're just like George. Everything that I bought in this house is blue, and the last time he bought me a dress it was red. You men."

"That's the reason I'm askin'. I thought I'd ride over by town and get her a new dress at Berg's."

"In that case, I'll tell you. She likes yellow best of all."

"I'll be damned. I'd have bought your color—blue."

"See, you men ought to pay more attention."

George said, "I still like red on Sybil."

The men had two more cups of coffee and talked of the coming child, the Randalls' sons, and cows.

Rick said, "I better get goin'. I just hate to make that ride in this damned wind. I reckon I'm gettin' old."

He rode across the rolling prairie, feeling the relentless force pull at his hat and watched the horse's mane and tail flip out and back in ceaseless motion.

In the Absolute Saloon in Two Mesas at just the time Rick and Marcus finished the tank, two cowboys who had been on an all-night drunk were trying to cure their hangovers and were getting the job done. They worked for Scott Allen,

but had taken a little time off just before fall roundup and shipping came along.

One, Ellis Carter, a big, heavy-bellied but lean-faced cowboy said, "Now, I'm tellin' you, Tiny," his pardner was huge all over, "we never had much fun last night. Here, bartender, give us another. As I was sayin' we never had much fun 'cause we never got in jail, a poker game, or no fistfights."

Tiny Sands answered, pushing his hat back from his red, corrugated face. "By god, you're right. We didn't even try to find any of the town whores."

Ellis added, "That's right, we just got drunk. Just plain ol' drunk and told a bunch of lies. I remember one thing you said. That if that Duvall stepped foot in town you was goin' to whup hell out of him."

Tiny blinked and finished the straight shot of bourbon, "I said that?"

"Yeah."

"What else did I say?"

"You said that he was tryin' to make a run at Rick's wife and that he'd messed up the whole country by breaking the nesters so all us cow people'd have to winter 'em or they'd starve."

"I said all that, out loud?"

"Yeah."

"Give us another'n, bartender. Now, Ellis, don't you go puttin' me on. Now, sure 'nough did I make all them comments . . .'bout . . ." The two cowhands emptied another shot glass, wiping their mouths. ". . .'bout that Duvall?"

"Yeah."

"I sure 'nough said I was goin' to whup him?"

"Yeah."

"Well then, I reckon I better get after it. There the son of a bitch goes to his new car."

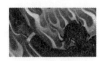

Duvall strolled across the street to the new Dodge. He'd decided the horse and wagon days were over for healers. From now on he intended to work out of school auditoriums, local theaters, and such. The Dodge and trailer would get him there. It would speed things up and pay much faster. He'd done well here though. He stuck the big roll of money from the "love offerings" in his pocket when he heard the voice of Tiny Sands.

"Duvall!"

He stopped and waited silently, as the large cowboy loomed towards him followed by another. He could see Mr. Allen looking out the window of his hardware store, and he took a quick look at the general mercantile. Nobody else seemed to be on the street. He'd been in this same spot before in other lands.

Tiny could see that they had him cut off from his car. He moved on to him and said softly, "Mr. Duvall, you ain't leavin' town?"

"Yes, tonight."

"How about right now."

"I'm not through packing."

"Well, pack this off with you," Tiny said, and swung a heavy, vicious blow through the wind at Duvall's face. The face wasn't there. Tiny felt himself leaving the ground as Duvall caught his momentum and hurled him sideways and down. Tiny was almost up but still off balance when Duvall's hand came slapping into his Adam's apple. All the wind vanished from Tiny's body. He grabbed at his throat, and the world turned as purple as Duvall's preaching clothes. Duvall jerked him up and let go with the other hand, the right and most powerful one, to the side of Tiny's jaw. It snapped and broke like a dead pine twig, and Tiny collapsed in a large pile of helplessness.

Ellis had fished quickly for a knife, and he snapped the three-inch blade open. Now a crowd came upon the sidewalks, a small crowd, but mysteriously, suddenly there—but no one moved into the street.

Ellis stalked forward toward the waiting, crouching Duvall. "I'm goin' to skin you alive for doin' that to my friend." He slashed at Duvall's chest, and missed a foot as Duvall slipped swiftly aside. Ellis looked at the two hands up in front of him now. It seemed they completely covered the body of Duvall. He could see the dark eyes peering straight at him through the widespread fingers.

He moved forward. Duvall was saying something in a low humming voice, but he didn't hear the words. *Hell, he'd just cut those hands off.* He slashed and missed and saw the hands move and circle and heard the humming again, and suddenly all he could see were the beaming eyes, and he cut at them and cut again as they danced away.

Then Duvall came at him swiftly, but Ellis didn't move until far too late. Duvall took his elbow in one hand, and in the other he took the hand with the knife in it and drove it into the inverted V of Ellis's front ribs and upwards. It expertly split the main artery and plunged into the heart, and Duvall hurled him away and down dead, before the spewing redness could splatter a drop on him.

It was useless for the people of Two Mesas to call the sheriff. He was already there at the tail end of the fight. It was self-defense. But an enormous feeling of loathing and hate had risen up in the town and was soon spread by phone and some other unknown manner across the lonely land. But Rick had already mounted to ride towards this tragedy without knowing or feeling it. He was thinking of Marta and a new dress for her sweet body. She would be too big to wear it in another six

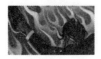

weeks, but she would have it to look at and to touch.

He felt a strange warmth surge around in him where there had been hot anger the day before. From now on he was going to do more for her. And he made a firm promise to himself that if the calves weighed out at four hundred pounds this fall, he'd get the new car for her. He couldn't wait to tell her.

At this moment Ellis Carter was turning cold, and Duvall was driving the new car towards the Ames's ranch.

Several hours later, Rick tied Red Spot in front of Berg's Dry Goods. He didn't feel the town, but they all knew he'd just ridden in.

Mr. Berg said, "Hello Rick, it was terrible wasn't it?"

"What's that?"

"The killing."

"The killin'?"

"Yes, didn't you hear? Duvall killed Ellis Carter."

"Ellis? God uh mighty, Ellis is a good friend of mine. How'd it happen?"

"With a knife. With Ellis's own knife."

"Have they got the bastard in jail?"

"No," and then Mr. Berg described the whole thing to Rick.

A sick, painful feeling hit Rick, as if he had a belly full of stinging ants. He shook his head numbly. "That's too bad, just too damn bad." The urge struck him to get Duvall and tear him in little shreds and feed them to the magpies and coyotes. This same feeling was on most of the land. But there was also this one of helplessness, and it, too, came over Rick. "Well, I

came after a new dress for Marta, Berg, and I aim to get it for her."

Berg showed him the yellow one she'd admired, "I know that's her favorite color."

"Yeah."

"And she liked this dress. It's rather expensive. That's the reason we still have it."

"To hell with the expense, wrap it up."

Rick rode out of town with the dress tied in a flat box on the back of the saddle. He soon forgot it. Wanting now to tell Marta about Ellis. Wanting to shove the knife of words into her about Duvall. He almost broke the horse into a lope— something he never did when heading home. It was the wrong thing with a horse. It would get so that's all they thought about was getting to the feed barn. But Rick also wanted time. Time to sort out in his mind all the things that had happened in the past hours, days. He cut across country, slowly, away from the winding road—or he might have noticed the tracks of a car in the road. His eyes had many other visions dancing along before them today.

He was home. He stepped down, tied the horse to the garden fence—then he saw it. The old dog in the yard. Dead. There was no question about it. He lay with the wind stirring the hair on his back just as some unspoken fear had all summer.

Rick ran into the house. There on the floor sat Marcus leaning back against the wall. He knelt by him. At first he thought he, too, was dead. But it was just his breathing. It was very shallow. He slapped him hard and yelled. It did no good. He grabbed up a bucket of water and threw it at him. Marcus remained out. He was off somewhere. Far, far off.

Then he saw the note on the table. It was in Marta's hand-

writing but stiff, very stiff. It said: *Rick it's all over. I must go. Marta.*

He ran outside. So many feelings racked through him now that he couldn't possibly categorize them, but his whole life's training came back to him in one thought straight and true.

He mounted and rode hard for town. About a mile from the edge of Two Mesas he reined off, taking a shortcut on high ground through thick brush for Salt River. He reined up about two-thirds of a mile above Duvall's camp. He could see Duvall, Marta, and the Indian woman moving around below. He strained his eyes but couldn't spot the male Apache. He'd known Marta'd be here. There had been no question about that.

He clamped his jaws down and ground his teeth audibly as Red Spot picked his way down through the brush towards the camp. He wanted a surprise now, but he was worried about the Indian, One Lion. He had to win this. Losing Marta was only a part of it. His heir was going away in her lovely belly. A friend of his lay dead in the morgue, another was in Flag having a screw twisted into his shattered jawbones, and old dog was dead. All this was enough, but there was one other reason he rode forward and down. There was something that had to be removed from the earth. Something that had to be ripped and torn and turned back to dust.

It was the bunching of Red Spot's muscles that saved him. He caught the glimpse of One Lion moving in front of him through the brush before the Indian could level the gun to shoot. At the second he stepped between the two large bushes, Rick jammed the spurs deep into the Appaloosa's sides and laid forward on his neck. The horse lunged powerfully forward, striking the Indian in the chest with eleven hundred pounds of hard-muscled force.

The gun fired in the air, and it flew into the brush. Rick turned and rode the horse back and forth across the Indian, and the meat peeled from his scalp and the bones crunched in his chest and shoved into his lungs. He was a part of Duvall and must be destroyed!

Then he rode on down the hill again, holding the excited horse in check. He caught a glimpse of Duvall coming up the hill in the blowing dust carrying a gun. *Damn, he was a fool. He should have known the Indian would be spotted there, waiting, guarding.* Rick hadn't even brought his gun, and now he'd lost the Indian's in the brush. Rage brings on foolish acts.

He could see Duvall's dark clothes coming closer now. He reined around behind a big cedar and waited. He took his rope down and tied it hard to his saddle horn and formed a calf-sized loop. Well, this is all he had. Hell, he wasn't much of a shot anyway. But he could fit this rope around a steer's neck in a small opening in thick brush at full horse speed. Why not this man's neck that he wanted now more than all the steers in the world.

The wind moaned and talked of life and death and love, and for a moment it was touched with mocking laughter. He'd heard this wind all his life. It drove killing snow and ice. It shoved dust that mutilated the grass and vegetation. It also brought the spring rains and the summer storms and then always blew back to destruction. It was the same wind that had turned the windmills the day he was born, and he was sure it was the one sound that would penetrate his final grave. He couldn't hear Duvall's steps for it now, but on the other hand it was a great equalizer—Duvall couldn't hear him.

He pulled back slightly on the reins and gripped Red Spot with his knees, trying to tell him not to move—that all life depended on his not moving. The horse stood like a per-

fectly trained roping horse in a roping box. And then he saw the little blur of Duvall's darkness on the other side of the tree. The horse's ears tossed forward hearing, smelling, and sensing Duvall's essence. Rick felt him tremble, but the great-grandson of the Nez Percé's war horses held his place.

Duvall stepped into the tiny clearing, crouched, the gun forward and cocked. It was too late! The rope shot out sure and clean around the neck. Rick jerked the slack tight and turned, reining and spurring hard downhill. He spurred the horse through trees and bushes in wild descent. He could feel the weight come and go as it hung and broke loose behind him. Suddenly the hill steepened, and a thick growth of cedar rose right up before them. Their momentum was such that they splintered straight through them. Rick was almost knocked from the saddle but righted himself and held onto the rope. The wide shoulders of Duvall stuck in the forks of one of the cedars, and for a fleeting second the horse and rider were checked. Then the rope pulled loose and free in his hand as they plunged downward to the camp. Something rolled past them and came to rest against the gleaming hubcap of the shining, new car. And there its eyes stared up into the dust and sun-scorched sky. But they were filled with gravel and saw nothing, hypnotized nothing.

The two women stood staring at the head. Staring. Rick stepped down from Red Spot, who breathed heavily from more than just the work.

Rick walked over to Marta. "Marta," he said.

She still looked at the head. She had no expression of horror, just nothing—like Duvall's face. Rick spoke her name again and again. Slowly she raised her head. Then her eyes widened. She leaped past Rick, grabbed a rock from the ground, and hurled it into the face of the Apache woman. The

woman fell and rolled over and sat up, her nose broken and bleeding. Rick saw the knife she'd dropped on the ground, gleaming, clean, and unused. It had been meant for his back.

Marta knelt by the woman, took the edge of her dress, and wiped the blood tenderly from her face.

"I'm sorry," she said. Then she stood up, looked at Rick, and said, "The Indian was *his* woman."

"Go on home. Drive Duvall's car," Rick said, "and take care of Marcus. I've got to go to town and tell the sheriff."

"Are you coming on home soon?" she asked.

"Yes, I'll be home soon," he said.

She walked towards the car. Well, it was over. She was Rick's forever. Nothing else could tear them apart now. No matter how he treated her, she was his. She started the car and drove down the road. Rick mounted, gathered up his rope, and rode towards town while the Indian woman sat staring, still, like old dog used to do. The horse shied a bit as the yellow dress that had been ripped from the saddle blew across the ground. But Rick didn't see it.

ABOUT THE AUTHOR

Max Evans has lived six decades of his life in New Mexico among the varied cultures of this special land. He has deeply involved himself in many pursuits as an artist in oils, a working cowboy, a prospector and mining speculator, a dealer in antiques and art, a documentary filmmaker, and a writer.

Starting out as a professional writer at age thirty-four, Evans has been a consistent producer of memorable fiction and nonfiction. His stories and novellas have appeared in prestigious literary publications and popular magazines, his work has been adapted to feature and documentary films, and he has won awards from Western Writers of America and the National Cowboy Hall of Fame. The New Mexico Rounders' Award is presented annually in Max Evans's honor, by the Department of Agriculture and the Governor, to an outstanding New Mexican who has shown a lifetime of promoting the western way of life.

THE RED CRANE LITERATURE SERIES

Dancing to Pay the Light Bill:
Essays on New Mexico and the Southwest
by Jim Sagel

Death in the Rain
a novel by Ruth Almog

The Death of Bernadette Lefthand
a novel by Ron Querry

New Mexico Poetry Renaissance
edited by Sharon Niederman and Miriam Sagan

Stay Awhile: A New Mexico Sojourn
essays by Toby Smith

This Dancing Ground of Sky:
The Selected Poetry of Peggy Pond Church
by Peggy Pond Church

Winter of the Holy Iron
a novel by Joseph Marshall III

Working in the Dark: Reflections of a Poet of the Barrio
writings by Jimmy Santiago Baca